PRAISE FOR JERRY IZENBERG

"*After the Fire* is a tour de force on love in a place and time that made love all but impossible. Jerry Izenberg takes us onto the mean streets of riot-scarred Newark. We meet heroes and fools, scheming politicians, Sinatra, Mafia bosses, and a beautiful Juliet with her All-American Romeo. More than once, Izenberg's story will leave you breathless."

— DAVE KINDRED, AUTHOR OF *SOUND AND FURY*, A DUAL BIOGRAPHY OF MUHAMMAD ALI AND HOWARD COSELL

"Jerry Izenberg over many years has maintained a position as one of America's finest sports columnists. It comes as a welcome surprise, indeed, that, in *After the Fire*, he establishes himself as a very fine novelist. The taut drama of a bi-racial love affair and the machinations of ward politics and mob influence in Newark in the turbulent '60s is riveting from beginning to end or, in another context, from the first pitch to the final out."

— IRA BERKOW, PULITZER PRIZE WINNER

"I became Champ because I looked out for sneaky punches. This novel by Jerry Izenberg both KOd and fascinated me because I didn't see such beauty and intrigue coming straight at me. Hold on to your seat and read."

— GEORGE FOREMAN, TWO-TIME HEAVYWEIGHT
CHAMPION OF THE WORLD

"I am a native of northern New Jersey and vividly recall the year 1967 when Newark was burning and multiple factions of both good and bad people were pitted against one another. . . . The fear was real. Jerry Izenberg, a Newark native himself, does a great job recounting these troubled times."

— BILL PARCELLS, JERSEY BRED AND TWICE A
SUPER BOWL CHAMPION

AFTER THE FIRE

LOVE AND HATE IN THE ASHES OF 1967

JERRY IZENBERG

ACKNOWLEDGMENTS

I would like to acknowledge the professionalism, guidance, and new friendship of my editor Lara Bernhardt and the vision of Admission Press for taking a chance on an 90-year-old sportswriter's first novel, Drs. Eddie Mandeville and Barry Nahin. my medical advisors on gunshot wounds, Buddy Fortunato and the Italian Tribune for their help on the Feast of San Gennaro's unique character and added help on the festival and Newark's North Ward, also Loretta Del Grosso, for more help on the festival, Essex County Sheriff Armando Fontura, who as a rookie Newark cop was on the streets during the riot, the man known in the book as Uncle Pete but for obvious reasons is not, Mrs. Felicia Alagia, whose memories and experiences helped me re-create the old Westinghouse Factory, Bob Izenberg, who as always, served as my computer "maven," Tom Walsh, whose contribution went beyond the dotting of i's and the crossing of t's, and Fred Sternburg who did more for me than his counterpart in this book.

Finally, the streets, buildings and psyche of Newark, N.J., itself. treasure trove of the memories that shaped me. It is 2,227 miles away from my current home in Henderson, NV as the 737 flies. But, for me, it will always be home.

For Aileen:
The real Mickey who taught me the power of two.

AUTHOR'S NOTE

This is a work of a fiction. Other than the occasional use of actual names and places, the incidents and other characters portrayed in this book are wholly fictional. I have also transposed some dates and events and embellished the historical record for dramatic purposes.

"How doth the city sit solitary, that was full of people. How has she become as a widow. She weepeth sore in the night, and her tears are on her cheeks. Among all her lovers she hath none to comfort her."

—*The Lamentations of Jeremiah*

PROLOGUE
A TALE OF TWO CITIES

Once, in a world long gone, they had risked everything to escape the poverty of places like Palermo and Milan and Naples. They crossed an ocean to chase their dreams to a place where the language was foreign, the mores were polar opposites from the places they left behind, and, contrary to what they had been told, the streets were not paved with gold.

In Newark, New Jersey, like all newcomers to a foreign land, they huddled together for comfort and sharing and their mutual dignity. It was at this time they built a street all their own, a shimmering artery of hope and community. In the shadow of the concrete banks of Bloomfield Avenue they built their churches, their markets, and their bakeries. Emotionally and ethnically, it was their street.

The street generated its own theme song, marching through each workday to a tarantella beat punctuated by the ubiquitous rumble of the Bloomfield Avenue trolley. The street was the artery that connected them to the outside world. Each morning they rode the trolley downtown and connected with the buses that took them to jobs in the local industrial complex and on to construction sites where cheap Italian labor was in demand, or

1

across the river into Harrison and Kearny and more factories and the Kearny shipyard beyond.

But Bloomfield Avenue, which bisected what would eventually become Newark's North Ward, belonged to them. It would remain so well into the 1950s and '60s. The butchers, the bakers, the factory workers, the construction laborers (who one day would own the construction companies and leave Newark for new lives further west along the Avenue), all of them, the skilled and the unskilled, clung to a common bond.

Everything their parents and grandparents dreamed of was here for them within easy reach, within a few blocks either way —the grocer, the pharmacy, the bakery, restaurants, and even a ballroom.

Here, nobody was a wop, nobody was a guinea, nobody was a dago.

This was home.

It was the model for a city rushing toward social change. Shaped by the rising tide of the great immigration from Europe to America, the city morphed into a series of self-contained ethnic neighborhoods—the Jews, the Irish, the Germans, the Poles, and the Portuguese, separate just as the Italians were. The lines between them were rarely crossed.

As for the moneyed WASPs, their roles were defined by the chain of magnificent mansions in which they lived along Belmont Avenue. They owned the factories and the department stores. They were the captains of industry, the decision-makers at the top in Bell Telephone and Prudential Insurance. They would never dirty their hands in City Hall. They simply chose the ones who would be elected.

Up on the Avenue, Italian Americans remained rooted in common ritual. St. Lucy's and Good Council were their grammar schools. By 1907, Newark High School was moved to the North Ward, within a block of the Avenue, with a new name: Barringer. For multiple decades, most of its student body and its football heroes carried last names that ended in vowels.

But triggered by World War II, a social change brought a new group to the city with a growth rate that would demand a piece of the power structure. They were African Americans. In 1940, they were only 2.7 percent of Newark's population.

The start of the war generated an economic boom in dozens of Northern cities with their factories and shipyards. In the Deep South, black families in search of a better life headed North toward those jobs. Newark, New Jersey, was a prime destination. Ten years after the end of World War II, its black population ballooned to nearly twenty percent and continued growing. By the 1960s, combined with a similar migration from Puerto Rico, people of color were reaching toward a new majority status.

But when the war ended, something nobody had even considered shook the accepted order of life. The wartime jobs dried up—slowly at first, while industries converted to peacetime products and then at a speed that totally impacted the newest migrants. Once again, African Americans heard that old refrain "Last hired, first fired." Twenty thousand manufacturing jobs disappeared between 1950 and 1967. As a result, what had become the Central Ward was crowded with poor housing and poor African Americans. Roughly 60,000 African Americans were crammed into a neighborhood's 460 acres.

White flight was both complicated and hastened by blockbusting real-estate vultures who were not above moving a black family (sometimes at the relocator's expense) into an all-white neighborhood and then ringing doorbells to warn nervous homeowners, "You better sell fast or your house will be worthless."

As jobs melted away, more and more Central Ward properties fell into the hands of slumlords who refused to make improvements. Meanwhile, the advent of federally funded public housing had a mixed impact. The high-rise "cement coffins" and the scattered garden apartments were clearly and without apology or explanation segregated.

To compound the already-strained housing problem, the state

unveiled a master plan to clear housing from a huge slice of the Central Ward to build the University of Medicine and Dentistry Hospital. Thousands of the lowest-income African American residents would be displaced.

And simmering beneath all that tension, African Americans had long had reason to resent the police. The chief was a North Ward Italian American. The mayor, who had become a symbol of corruption, was also an Italian American. Civilian complaints against various police officers for civil-rights violations went nowhere because it was left to the police to do their own investigating.

At the same time, the tense relations between the black community and the Newark Police Department worsened. By 1965, after a Newark cop shot and killed a black man under suspicious circumstances, a group of African American citizens petitioned the mayor to take his police review board in such cases out of police hands and create an all-civilian board. The effort failed.

More than ever, Newark had become a tale of two cities.

Nowhere in the city was the growing tension greater than along the Avenue, where the Italian Americans viewed the shifting demographics as a threat to their neighborhood, their families, and their way of life.

With open anger in both the Central Ward and the North Ward, the divided city was moving toward a perfect storm.

Somebody should have listened.

Maybe the city council should have listened to the confidential informants who told their police handlers, "If this shit don't stop, we gonna have a fuckin' riot on our hands." Instead, they did nothing when the state of New Jersey chose to confiscate 150 acres of Central Ward land for a medical school that would have displaced an army of African Americans with no place to go.

Maybe the mayor should have ignored the self-serving reassuring rhetoric of certain black preachers and listened to Timothy Still, a Newark activist, who warned of the danger while negotiating with City Hall without losing his identity as a community activist.

The inevitable autopsy could be traced directly to what always happens when dialogues are shouted down by monologues and both groups of protagonists see themselves as perennial victims.

According to multiple witnesses, it began like this:

On July 12th, 1967, in the teeth of a broiling summer, the neglect and sins of the past morphed into the most violent confrontation Newark had ever seen. A black taxi driver named John Smith, who had worked for the Safety Cab Co. for five years, drove his taxi around a police car and double-parked on 15th Avenue. According to a police report, Smith was charged with "tailgating," driving in the wrong direction on a one-way street, using offensive language, and physical assault.

The report was later challenged.

Smith's account suggested that the cops, not him, were double-parked and that he had flashed his lights to warn them that he was going to pass them. Following the arrest, as they transported him to the Fourth Precinct House, the two policemen took turns reaching over the seat and beating him ferociously with a billy club.

Not surprisingly, the police department denied the complaint.

Tipped off by a witness, officers of CORE and the United Community Project were allowed to see Smith in his cell. They were appalled by the visible signs of the beating, and the police agreed to transport him to Beth Israel Hospital.

Around 8:00 p.m., black cab drivers began to circulate the report of Smith's arrest on their radios. Word spread down 17th Avenue, west of the precinct station where Smith had been held. Shortly after midnight, two Molotov cocktails were thrown at the precinct. Then, a group of twenty-five people on 17th Avenue started to loot stores. The looting drew larger crowds.

Despite the violence, the mayor announced that Wednesday

night's activities were isolated incidents and were not of riot proportions. The next night, a large group of young kids gathered along 17th Avenue in front of a huge public housing project called Hayes Homes directly across from the precinct house. Police demanded they disperse. They refused. They wanted answers and got none. Two Molotov cocktails were heaved at the precinct house. Newark exploded into a riot.

Police were issued rifles. Gov. Richard Hughes sent in the National Guard armed with live ammunition. Most of the Guardsmen, who had no training in riot control and had never even set foot in Newark before, were young and consequently extremely nervous.

The lighting of a cigarette in a public housing high-rise was mistaken for the flash of a gun—and four deaths were attributed to the response to that. Nobody was ever prosecuted.

Despite the presence of National Guardsmen and state troopers, rioting continued for three more days.

Newark erupted with the acrid smell of burning buildings, the sound of acres of broken storefront windows, and the sight of National Guard tanks rumbling through its streets.

The blacks called it "the Rebellion." The whites called it "the Riot." Within five days, officials had counted 26 bodies, more than 700 injured, the deployment of 7,917 National Guardsmen and city and state law-enforcement officials, and 1,465 arrests.

In the aftermath, the heart and soul of Springfield Avenue (the African Americans' counterpart to Bloomfield Avenue) was a burned-out shell. For the city's old-guard Italian Americans and the exploding black population, hate, anger, and anxiety became primary emotions.

Everyone waited uneasily as the city seemed to tilt off what had been its solid and predictable axis. Fueled by block-busting real-estate sharks and violent memories of what the residents felt had been the start of a mini civil war, white flight followed quickly. The Jews fled. The Irish fled. The Germans and most of the Polish fled.

But the Italians and the blacks were locked into the city—the blacks by lack of opportunity and the North Ward Italians by homes they couldn't sell. The struggle to control the city's shifting political power structure grew more vocal and uglier on both sides. Restraint and logic were dead.

A White Citizens Council was born and flourished along the Avenue, where it was provided with a fertile recruiting ground. Blacks in turn rallied behind newborn African American cultural and political organizations. New babies were given African names, and more than a few adults changed theirs as well. Youths on both sides of the city's divide rushed to brand-new karate dojos in the wake of an epidemic of unfounded fear and rumors.

One year after the Newark riot/rebellion, this was the culture that pervaded the city. The Board of Education eased a long-standing "home school district" policy, allowing more black youths to matriculate at Barringer High School. With the increasing tensions, an African American girl named Michaeletta Washington could pass an Italian American boy named Gerard Friscella Jr. in the halls at Barringer when changing classes or stand in the same line in the cafeteria without ever exchanging a single word or even bothering to learn the other's name.

It was as though the two races had created two separate schools within the school. Neither Michaeletta nor Gerard Jr. even considered the answer to an as-yet-unasked question that would forever change their lives.

Were they ready for what 1968 would bring them?

More important: Was 1968 ready for what they would bring in return?

1

A RESTLESS WIND

Gerard Friscella Jr., Junior to those who knew him, had exciting news and couldn't wait to get home to tell his dad. His coach at Montclair State had called to tell him the school had received acknowledgments from four of the NFL teams to which he had sent a highlight film of Junior's previous season—and each planned to scout his last game in November.

Junior craned his neck, watching for his friend Chooch's Studebaker. Chooch had offered to pick him up and give him a ride home. Junior suspected he really wanted an excuse to scout out the campus coeds, a suspicion that proved true when the Studebaker pulled up to the curb. Chooch wore a T-shirt bearing the legend "Kiss Me, I'm Italian." Music blared from the radio at an ear-piercing volume. Chooch's right hand grasped the steering wheel and his left crooked out of the open window, tapping out the beat to "Mrs. Robinson" against the roof as he sang along.

"Turn that down! I'm beggin' you," Junior shouted into the noise. "Jeez, have a heart. You make it sound like an insult to Joe D."

Chooch lowered the volume.

"Thank you," Junior said. "I'm surprised you haven't gone deaf."

Chooch laughed and said of Mrs. Robinson, the character in the movie "The Graduate" who had an affair with her daughter's boyfriend, "What I want to know, Mr. Smart College Guy, is do you really think the kid would bang an old broad like Mrs. R.?"

"Get serious," Junior said.

"I am serious. Do you think the old lady got into his pants?"

"What I think," Junior replied as he climbed in, "is that what you need to do is stop thinking about life with your little head and start thinking with the big one—if there's anything in it. You got to stop pumping gas and start fixing cars. You got this old gas-eater still running, didn't you? My dad agrees. He thinks you're a pretty good mechanic."

"Hey, speaking of that," Chooch said, leaning out the window and pointing at a large girl in yellow pants two sizes too tight waiting at a bus stop on the Avenue, "I could mechanic that rear end pretty good. How does she get into them pants? Does she butter her thighs?"

And then, with no right-turn signal, without so much as easing his foot off the gas pedal, and with absolutely no thought, he veered across two lanes of traffic, barely missing a red pickup truck, and breezed into Branch Brook Park.

Junior grabbed the door handle to brace himself and held on for dear life. "Hey, man, what are you doing? Don't fool around. My old man will kill me if I'm late for supper. He knows there's no football practice in June."

"Just hang on a minute," Chooch said. "I want to swing past Barringer and check something out. Paulie says he's gonna speak."

Paulie Tedesco. Junior frowned. He had no interest in the guy.

Chooch swung through a corner of the park and exited in front of their old high school, Barringer. Four squad cars with flashing lights were parked on the sidewalk. Patrolmen in crash helmets flanked the front of the building.

Chooch hit the brakes and jolted to a stop. "Holy shit. What the hell is all this?"

Junior rose up on high alert, knowing his younger sister, Angie, would be leaving that building soon.

A crowd of kids had already begun to form in front of the school. Junior searched for Angie.

Paulie Tedesco, a short, florid, barrel-chested man with a voice that sounded as though he had just swallowed a truckload of broken glass, stood atop a black pickup truck. He faced a crowd of white students.

Below him, at ground level with their arms folded stiffly across their chests, his two aides-de-camp struck a kind of military pose. Tedesco wore a white dress shirt with the sleeves rolled halfway up, revealing the tattooed arms of a weightlifter. His collar gaped open. A floral tie hung loosely against the shirt and dangled down below a waist that was fighting a losing battle with his belt.

The kids had come for a show, and Tedesco didn't disappoint: "We di'nt start this shit. The *Star-Ledger* says we are very bad people on this side of town. But I di'nt see none of youse carryin' a television set out of no store last year. They talk about law, but we believe in law. We don't burn no buildings. We don't throw no bottles at the cops." He pointed to the helmeted police. "But young people like you guys ain't gonna lay down and play dead because some politician in the 'burbs craps in his pants. This is the Avenue, and we ain't gonna let people who don't live here play sociology with us. Take a look at them. They may be white, but the only time they come to the Avenue is to eat in our restaurants. They sure as hell ain't Italian."

The kids interrupted his tirade with cheers that Paulie acknowledged before continuing.

"You gotta stand up for what's right. You got sisters in this school. You gotta take a stand—"

Junior, standing near the cops, saw Paulie's gaze land on him.

"Hey, don't take my word. Look at Junior over there. You all know Junior. He was All-State at Barringer. He bleeds Barringer blue—or should I say white. You remember him getting us a state champeenship down the Avenue at Schools Stadium. Come on up here, Junior. Ax him what he thinks. G'wan, ax him. He knows what's at stake. Come on up, Junior. You tell 'em."

Junior gave a half smile and a half wave and turned away. No way would he support this garbage. Retreating toward Chooch's car, he saw a police captain walk over and get in Paulie's face.

"Enough, Paulie," the captain said. "I don't want to see a single living ass blocking this street when the rest of those kids come out of that school."

"Hey, come on, Anthony, give us a break. We're not here to make trouble. We're just here to see that our kids get their rights too. Look at me. Look up my sleeves." Paulie rolled them up higher. "Look, Anthony, ain't no Molotov cocktail up there." He threw both arms up in the air in mock surrender, and the kids broke into loud cheering again.

"Paulie, get the fuck outta here right now. Right now! And take your two goons with you."

Junior saw Chooch spin in a circle, presumably looking for him, then walk back to his car. As Chooch slid back into the driver's seat, he frowned a little. "Man, why di'nt you go up there when Paulie called you? He was just bragging you up. Maybe he can be a little too strong sometimes, but he says a lot of things for true and you know it."

Junior didn't answer. Chooch shook his head and started the car in silence. As they rode away, they stayed quiet. Junior noticed Chooch's grease-stained fingers on the steering wheel, the residue from pumping gas and tinkering with the Studebaker. For the first time, he also noticed the grease spots on his trousers.

"Why don't you ever clean yourself up?" Junior asked.

"Because I fucking work for a living!"

"And why do you always wear those stupid hats?" Junior persisted.

"Because it's me. I'm shorter than you, I'm uglier than you, but it's *me*." Chooch went quiet for a minute, eyes ahead. "Paulie, maybe he ain't so smart. But you gotta admit he got a set of cast-iron balls. Di'nt he keep the niggers from crossing into the Avenue last time? Hey, wasn't he right there with a Louis- ville Slugger and his guys right next to the National Guard roadblock?"

"Yeah," Junior said. "He was there, and except for the National Guard nobody else was—nobody. Every black guy in Newark was three miles away on Springfield Avenue. He was guarding nothing except his ego."

"Sometimes I don't understand you, Junior. Just five minutes ago the man treats you like a hero, and all you can say is he's an asshole."

The Studebaker moved around the block across the Avenue and into a side street lined with carbon-copy multifamily dwellings. Chooch pulled to a stop in front of Junior's house. Junior had been silent the rest of the way. He opened the door, stepped out, and started to walk away, but turned back to the car and rested his elbows on the open window.

"Chooch, don't you ever get tired of it? Jesus Christ—the niggers this, the niggers that." Chooch tried to interrupt but Junior waved him off. "I mean, man, there's just no peace. I know there's times you have to fight, but this ain't one of them. Paulie talks about how many blacks are gonna go to Barringer. It ain't his business. It ain't mine. Far as I can tell, if it's anybody's business, it's theirs. I'm just tired of all this shit." He remem- bered the first year that blacks had started attending Barringer. He hadn't known any of them well, but they hadn't bothered him, or anyone else, either. What did it matter where they went to school?

"My old man is worried that some black guy, who might not even exist, is gonna take his job down at the plant. You're worried about an invasion. Paulie is worried about his ego. Everybody we know is worried about what could happen in this city, and I'm sure the blacks are just as worried as us. There's enough fuckin' guns on either side of the Avenue to start World War III. And nobody really knows why. Look what's happening to us . . . to you and me. Why can't we talk about broads or about the Yankees? I just wanna go to class and play football and live my life. Paulie is full of shit. He's a politician, and white, black, or Italian, what's the damn difference?"

He saw doubt in Chooch's eyes, but then Chooch laughed and said, "Wait a minute. Italian is different." They both laughed.

"You win that one," Junior said. "Bowling tonight?"

"Yeah, pick you up at seven thirty, and tell your mom I won't blow the horn and embarrass her in front of her neighbors." The Studebaker roared down the block.

~

Junior sat in the family room, listening to the clock tick, waiting for his father to get home from work. He couldn't stop thinking about the rift he felt developing between him and Chooch. Pictures of him decorated the walls—Junior in the lead of his school play, Junior after scoring the winning touchdown, Junior receiving an academic award for highest marks. Relatives who saw the same pictures often told him, "You are the image of your dad when he was your age." At six feet three, Junior was taller by three inches, but he had the same broad shoulders, the same dark hair, and the same stereotypically dark Italian American complexion.

He wanted to eat, but supper always waited on his father. No one would eat until his father got home from work and sat at the table. Tonight, they would have supper, not dinner. Dinner was only Sunday afternoon, after the family attended Mass. Dinner was a time for visitors and family. Dinner was a salad and pasta of several varieties along with a traditional meat dish.

Dinner was the sons and daughters and grandchildren coming home. It was "please pass the bread" and "how about the Giants" and a doting aunt laughing and saying, "Junior, I remember you as a baby with the fattest cheeks I ever saw and look at you now."

But this was Thursday and supper. Supper in all those North Ward homes belonged to the fathers. It was a time for eating, but the mood would be totally dictated by Gerard Friscella Sr.

Finally, at 5:30, a key turned in the lock, and Junior's dad walked in the door. The family sprang into action, greeting him, taking his coat, and shifting to the dining room. By 5:40, like every day, their father took his seat and Junior's mother served the food. As always, she was the last to sit.

"So tell me, Angie," Senior asked, once they'd all started eating. "What happened in school today?"

"Paulie Tedesco was there. He made a speech about the niggers."

So she had been outside and witnessed that. Junior cringed. Why did she have to bring that up, of all things? His dad wouldn't like it, and she should know better.

Their father dropped his fork. "Beautiful, just beautiful. That's just what this family needs. I got a daughter spends more time with her mirror than her algebra book, puts Kleenex in her bra, and deliberately shrinks her sweaters, and I'm praying that maybe, just maybe, she can spare fifteen minutes in school to learn something more than how to put on lipstick. And all she can tell me about her school day is the biggest, dumbest fat *gavone* in the North Ward who can't even spell 'nigger' makes a speech about how ten thousand of them are on their way to conquer the Avenue."

Angie dropped her eyes, staring into her plate. "Paulie tried to get Junior to make a speech too, but Junior wouldn't do it."

Gerard Senior turned to Junior. "That right? What were you doing there?"

Junior shrugged. "Chooch wanted to go by to hear Paulie."

"So what happened?"

"Nothing much. He talked about my state championship, but I wouldn't go up with him."

"Good. You both stay away from him. You know I never wanted to pick your friends, son, but that Chooch is nothing but trouble. And you have to admit that if Dominick Pizzoli's IQ was ten points higher, he could qualify as a rutabaga. At least a person could hold an intelligent conversation with that Allie kid you hang with. Of course, I'm just sayin'."

"Yes, sir," Junior answered. His dad knew his friends well. They'd grown up together and been best pals since they were kids. Lately, he'd been feeling the same way about Chooch and Dominick, and he didn't know what to do about it. How do you tell your best friends they're making bad choices?

"And remember this, Angie." Her eyes stayed focused downward on her plate as their dad sharply rebuked her. "Look at me and don't forget what I'm about to say. When your grandfather and our neighbors' grandfathers came here, they were wops— which means 'without papers'—and guineas and dagos. We worked two generations to have people look at us as people, and if you and your friends start listening to Paulie, within a year we'll all be wops and guineas and dagos all over again."

"Gerry," their mother said, her eyes urging peace at the supper table, "don't—"

"I know, I know. It's just that there is enough real trouble out there without having to let an idiot make more. He's playing field marshal, and I'm just trying to keep my job."

"Gerry," Maria said, obviously shaken. "You got trouble down at the plant?"

"Later," he said, dismissing the question with a wave of his hand, making it clear that this was not a subject for the children's ears.

Then, he smiled at Angie and said, "I know you did something in school today before that jerk showed up, so tell me what you learned."

"I got a C on my English test today," she said.

"All right. That's better. Considering that it's the language of our country, then maybe there's some hope." He smiled broadly, looking a little guilty over what he had told her earlier.

Through all this, Junior ate quietly, preoccupied by his thoughts of the sudden and abrupt tension between him and Chooch.

"I got news, Dad," Junior said, eager to change the conversation. "Coach says four NFL teams are sending scouts in the fall to watch me play."

His dad slammed a palm on the table. "You hear that, Maria? You hear that? Four scouts coming to watch him play this fall! That's my boy."

His mom smiled, clearly pleased about the news as well as the switch in topic.

"Hey, All-State pass-catcher," his father said, looking at him fondly. "What about this summer? You're off until football practice the end of August. What do you plan to do? You got a job yet?"

"I think so. Allie knows this guy at the post office downtown. We went down today and filled out applications for summer jobs. He says I got a good chance. They hire a lot of college kids as summer-vacation fill-ins."

Senior's face lit up and he turned to Angie. "You see what a college education can do for you?" He grinned again. "Hey, Maria, what's for dessert?"

Angie smiled, Junior smiled, and their mom smiled, all relieved that the thunder created by the mere mention of Paulie Tedesco's name had left the supper table.

2

JUNE 1968

Junior watched his best friends in the world take turns throwing bowling balls at pins. Chooch, Dominick, Allie, and Junior were the last remaining members of the Newark Bombers—a name they'd acquired in grammar school and now clung to fiercely, even as the changing world pulled them apart.

The Newark Bombers were not friends. They were family.

Back in Good Counsel Grammar School, they were a team in the summer twilight softball league over at Branch Brook Park, which abutted the Avenue. In high school at Barringer, they remained the Newark Bombers on the blacktop basketball court behind First Avenue School.

They drank their first alcohol in that schoolyard when Chooch Castano copped a bottle of wine his grandfather had made in the basement of his Ridge Street home. They played cards on Tuesday nights. On the weekends they took the #29 bus to the Royal Theater in Bloomfield to watch *Thunderball* with James Bond and *Major Dundee* with Charlton Heston.

But these young men were growing up. A year earlier, the Selective Service Act had been extended, and now half the group was scattered throughout the world in the military. Tony Cano, a decent running back at Barringer, could not run fast enough when it counted, and was serving an armed-robbery sentence in Trenton State Prison. A few of the others had simply moved away. Their storefront clubhouse on Bloomfield Avenue near the Chinese restaurant became a bodega.

The remaining four Bombers had less and less in common, Junior realized. All that remained was their traditional bowling night up at Valley. They didn't particularly like the sport—except for Dominick, who liked the sound of the ball slamming into pins and always followed it with the cry, "I ax you, di'nt you see me cream them?"

They bowled because it was their last shot at competition and because of their relationship with the owner, Scoots DeLorenzo, heavy of paunch now but remembered in the neighborhood as a Barringer football hero twenty years earlier and who still revered the memory of the three touchdown passes he saw Junior catch on Thanksgiving Day his senior year against archrival East Orange. Consequently, Scoots never complained about the inordinate amount of time his waitress, Mary Theresa Gianetti—the Duchess, as the Bombers called her—spent trying to flirt with Junior.

On bowling night, they still wore their blue and white jackets with "Newark Bombers" emblazoned across the back, but little by little their mutual interests were shrinking.

Chooch pumped gas at the Hess station on Park Avenue and spent too much time each day working on his car. His real name was Gino, but Chooch was what the Bombers always called him —not because he was a moron or a jackass, the traditional definitions, but rather because he had absolutely no common sense and always acted before he thought.

Dominick Pizzoli, a Barringer graduate through the gift of automatic promotion, rode the Newark Sanitation trucks as an assistant because his uncle, the ward heeler, had placed him there, much to the relief of his widowed mother. Even his fellow Bombers conceded that he got through life with only forty-one cards in his deck.

Allie (not even his mother dared to call him Alphonse) Costa was a sophomore at Montclair State with Junior, who as the all-league wide receiver on a winning high school football team now played for Montclair State and had become a campus hero.

Chooch provided the wheels: his lavender '54 Studebaker, which he had customized. Dominick provided the muscle—even when none was needed. His verbal contribution to "outsiders" was generally, "OK, I axed you. You wanna piece of me?"

Allie, who had recently applied to Rutgers Law School, had a talent that was a source of unanimous admiration to the group. He could pick up girls in a wide range of strange venues, ranging from the steps of St. Lucy's Church to a plethora of fast-food joints and diners along State Highway 3. His oft-stated goal was to finish college and get a teaching job anywhere in America except New Jersey.

And Junior was their unchallenged field marshal, father figure, and perennial link to the real world. Ever since their days at Good Counsel Grammar, it had always been Junior who got the lead in the school play, who always earned the best report cards, caught the winning touchdown passes, got the prettiest prom dates and had, by their own estimation, the brightest future of them all.

At age twenty, the Bombers (except for Junior) won no more games. They were held together by bowling nights and by habit —not in that order.

Dominick leaned over and picked up his ball off the return trolley. He stared down at the pins like a surgeon analyzing the first cut. He grunted, stepped forward, and uttered what sounded like a primal shriek, unleashing the ball, which headed straight for the pocket that all good bowlers make their target. The ball hit, pins flew and scattered—all of them. Dominick turned and strutted back to the Bombers' scoring tables with a disco move more stumble than dance step.

"Here we go," Allie said, sotto voce.

"Tell me about it," Junior whispered back.

"Now I ax you guys," Dominick said after beating his chest Tarzan-style. "Is that the way to do it? You bet your ass. I said, I ax you, is that the way to do it or not?" He spotted the Duchess picking up a tray of beers from the circular serving bar just behind the row of scoring tables occupied by the bowlers.

"Hey," he yelled over to her. "Hey, Mary T! Ya see that? Ya see it? That's the kind of wood I'd love to put to you, sweetie."

Mary T, who clearly thought he was an idiot and only had eyes for Junior, smiled and shouted back, "What, and disappoint your mother, who's waiting for you in bed?"

The Bombers broke up with laughter.

"Better quit while you can," Allie said. "You mess with her, you're in the big leagues for real."

"Yeah," Dominick growled back. "She wasn't in the big leagues back when we all put it to her for two bucks a shot in the First Avenue schoolyard. Worst fuck I ever had," he added bitterly.

"Wrong," Chooch said. "*Only* fuck you ever had."

Dominick started toward Chooch, and like a shot Junior jumped off the bench where he had been keeping score and pushed his way between them. "Hey, man, take it easy," he said, pulling Dominick away. "You gonna lose your cool over some broad like that? Chooch was just joking. Come on." He hit Dominick on the arm and grinned. "You're blocking the alley, and I gotta bowl."

He selected a ball. Over by the bar, a television played the Yankee game. The Yanks had a rally going and all the bowling stopped. In the North Ward, the spiritual forces that used to draw comfort from the great DiMaggio made sure that every kid grew up a fan of number five on the scorecard and number one in your heart: Joe D.

They had loaded the bases against the Tigers. Bob Wilson, a black pitcher, was on the mound for Detroit.

"Who's up?" Allie asked.

"Roy White!" somebody shouted.

"A buck he gets a hit," Allie said.

"Covered, man. You are covered," Chooch replied.

Dominick, totally uninterested in the game, sidled over to the service bar, where he cornered Mary T, who immediately offered to kick him in the crotch so hard he would spend the rest of his life speaking like a boy soprano.

"All right, here we go," said the game announcer. "White stepping in against Wilson. White is zero for three tonight, struck out twice and popped to short. Bases loaded, bottom of the ninth. Yanks trail, four to two. Wilson looks in, gets the sign. Here's the pitch." The voice was suddenly swallowed by cheers so loud they rocked the bowling alley. White had hit a grand-slam homer to win the game.

"Pay me," Allie said to Chooch.

"Awright," Chooch mumbled, fishing in his pocket for a dollar. "But the damn bougie was wrong. He should have curved him."

"No, you got it all wrong. Didn't you see my colored boy hit one off your nigger?"

Junior cringed. Maybe he didn't want to come to bowling night anymore. He watched his best friends clowning around, wondering when things would change.

3

ROMEO MEETS JULIET IN THE
INNER CITY

Junior stared up at the main post office of Newark, New Jersey. The massive building covered three city blocks. His instructions were that employees enter through a side door. Once he found it, he emerged into a world of noise and cavernous space under an incredibly high ceiling. The volume of machinery (including the clang-bangs of the canceling machines) made the dimensions of the enormous floor deceptive, as though it were a maze of several rooms. But it wasn't. High above the entire scene, postal inspectors kept a lonely vigil on a narrow catwalk, focused mainly on the sorters below, making sure none of them stole mail.

Junior searched for his supervisor, once again thinking how lucky he was to land this summer job. He passed row after row of individual braces of pigeonholes elevated over small individual counters.

He saw sorters sitting on high stools as they worked. Others appeared to prefer to stand or lean against the stools. Every few minutes, deliverymen carried metal trays of outgoing mail to their proper venues. The sorters reached down, plucked an envelope, and slid it into the correct pigeonhole.

Junior continued to take in the wonderful chaos of his new

workplace until his supervisor pointed to an empty pigeonhole. "This is your station. Get busy."

An attractive girl sat in the station beside him. He stole glances at her as he began sorting mail, but she seemed not to even realize he had joined her.

He had to talk to her. "My name is Gerard Friscella. I went to Barringer. Graduated in 1966."

"Me, too," the girl answered with very little enthusiasm. She sorted mail at a much faster pace and didn't even look at him as she responded.

"What's your name?"

"Michaeletta."

He waited for her to ask his, but she didn't. He tried conversation again. "You look familiar, but I can't place the face. You don't seem to remember me either. I was captain of the football team. We won the state championship. Us going to the same school and all, it seems to me like you would remember me."

"Why?"

"Well, we went to the same school, and I just—"

"Oh, sure," she said, suddenly pivoting to look at him for the first time. There was a subtext of anger on her face and in her voice that shocked Junior. "I mean, a black beacon like me in that big sea of white faces two years ago. Sure, you'd take the time to know me just like all the other white boys and white girls wanted to make friends with all the black boys and black girls. Right."

She turned away and went back to work.

"Hey, I'm not like that, and you got no right to talk that way. You don't know anything about me. You got your feelings hurt by somebody back then, so it's my fault? What am I supposed to do? Apologize for everything that ever happened to blacks in this country? Am I supposed to ask for forgiveness from everybody who got a raw deal?"

She turned and stood up, hands on hips. "Not everybody. Just me. You want to do something for me? Shut up. Please, just shut up. The next thing out of your mouth will be that some of your best friends are black."

They both faced their stations and sorted mail at a furious pace. He snuck glances at her from the corner of his eye because he wouldn't look directly at her. She ignored him completely.

They worked in silence until an older white employee hurried by, carrying a tray of incoming mail down the aisle toward another station. The man stopped and banged the tray against the corner of Michaeletta's shoulder. The force of the blow indicated that it may not have been accidental.

She jumped back and shouted, "Hey, watch where you're going."

He stopped, leering at her, and draped an arm around her shoulder, letting his free hand slide across her breasts. "Sorry, sweet thing. Here, let me rub it and make it better."

"Get your hands off me right now before I—"

"Hey, sweet thing," he repeated, still pawing her. "I said I was sorry. Don't get your panties in a bunch. Be nice." He leaned in closer. "Play your cards right and you can make an easy twenty bucks. Just meet me on the loading dock later."

She shoved him. "Get your filthy hands off me. You're a pig. You're disgusting."

Junior saw the whole thing. For as long as he could remember, his father had told him, "You see a guy molesting a girl, you make it your business. If it's your sister, you break his neck." He didn't stop to think as he jumped from his stool and leaned over to face the man. He deliberately brought his right foot down as hard as he could on the man's left foot in a move only the three of them could see.

"Get the fuck off my foot, motherfucker," the guy whined.

Junior wrapped an arm around the man's neck and pulled his head close. "If I do, it will be because I'm going to ram it halfway up your ass." He spun the guy around and unleashed a violent left hook that caught him in the solar plexus and doubled him over.

Both Junior and Michaeletta jumped back as the man bent forward and dry-heaved. Then he limped away, shouting over his shoulder, "This ain't over, punk."

They returned to their stools without looking at each other. Michaeletta pretended to sort mail. She stopped and turned toward him. "I . . . I guess I ought to thank you. About before, I'm sorry that I—"

"Do me a favor," he said. "Shut up. Please, just shut up. The next thing out of your mouth will be that some of your best friends are white."

They stared at each other for a frozen moment, and then both of them broke into laughter.

~

Each sorter got two ten-minute breaks per shift and an hour off for lunch. Because of the post office's isolated location (there were no stores within easy walking distance), there was nowhere to go except the employees' lounge, an antiseptic-looking room of tables and assorted chairs. Vending machines flanked the rear wall, but most sorters brown-bagged their lunches.

Michaeletta sat alone at a corner table, a Coke and a half-eaten ham-and-cheese sandwich in front of her. As Junior approached, she quickly turned her head away. He noticed and made a big production out of spotting the empty chair next to her. "Sorry, but it's the only empty seat in the room. Do you mind if I sit down?"

Michaeletta nodded and pointed at the chair. He could see her silently studying him out of the corner of her eye.

He studied her in return. A tall, willowy girl with high cheek-bones, she had her hair pulled back in a ponytail. Her skin was caramel-colored. She wore dark slacks and a short-sleeved pink blouse. Her eyes met his, and she smiled. "Truce?" she asked.

"Truce," he said. "Let's start over again. My name is Gerard

26

Friscella, and my friends call me Junior. I'm twenty years old. I live in Newark just off Bloomfield Avenue. I go to Montclair State. I study hard, and I'm a wide receiver on the football team. I'm here as summer help. So who are you?"

"I'm summer help, too. I live in Newark. I'm twenty, and I just got my associate's degree at Essex County College. And, lucky you"—she smiled—"I'll be going to your school this fall. My name is Michaeletta Washington."

"You're kidding." Junior laughed.

"What's so funny?"

"Michaeletta? Michael? That's a boy's name. I don't know a single girl named Michael." He stopped laughing. "But you know something, Michaeletta Washington?"

"What's that, Junior Friscella?"

"You sure as hell don't look like any boy I ever met."

They both laughed, and then he thought, *Black, white, yellow, or brown, she is sure one beautiful lady.*

4

JOY AND ANGER IN ANNIE MAE'S HOUSE

M ichaeletta Washington's bedroom was testimony to the gap between her everyday world and that of Junior Friscella. Full-color photos, clipped from *Ebony* magazine, of Harry Belafonte and Sidney Poitier, were Scotch-taped to the wall above her desk. On the opposite wall were a series of photos of the Supremes and their lead singer, Diana Ross. The Supremes were accorded that honor as much for the gowns they wore as for their hit records.

The room was painted a light pink with a matching inexpensive pink chenille bedspread. Tucked into the mirror over her dresser were candid photos of her best friends—all female African Americans. Back in high school, the volume of black young men was very limited. She didn't even attend her senior prom.

Her record collection was housed in a wire holder on the floor, and the album covers included the Supremes, James Brown, Aretha Franklin, Stevie Wonder.

Michaeletta sat on the bed, wearing a blue babydoll nightie with matching bloomers, a single braid pinned to the top of her head. Phone pressed to her ear, she gossiped with her best friend, Lois, while painting her toenails, the nail-polish bottle balanced precariously on the bed.

"So how's the post office thing going?" Lois asked.

"Well, mostly it's just plain boring, reaching up and throwing all those letters into those little boxes. *Hon-ey*," she said, dragging the word into two distinct syllables, "the first two weeks, my right arm liked to kill me from all that stretching. Of course, there's this guy who sits next to me and—"

Lois squealed. "Well, why didn't you say so in the first place instead of telling me how the U.S. mail works? Tell me the good stuff right now. What's his name? How tall is he? Did he try to hit on you? Is he dark- or light-complected? I want details, girl, details!"

"Well, I wouldn't say he's light-skinned. I wouldn't say he's dark, either. I'd say it depends on who's doing the looking."

"Mickey, don't you tease me. I don't want to hear what he's not. Tell me what he is."

"He's tall. Must be over six feet. Athletically built with short-cropped hair. Cute. Definitely cute."

"He sounds perfect! What's the catch?"

"I guess I have to tell you. But don't you go ballistic on me. The truth is, well, he's white."

"He's *what*? Girl, have you lost your mind? What's your mother gonna say? What's your dashiki-wearing brother gonna say when he finds out you're dating a white guy?"

"Listen, it's nothing like that. It isn't like we ever see each other outside of the post office."

"But you will, won't you?" Lois shot back, like she was afraid she wouldn't be the confidante in her best friend's drama. "I've known you since kindergarten, Mickey. You've always been a drama queen. You'll do it."

"Hold on a minute. I don't know. I mean, I have to admit he's not like anyone either of us ever dated." She told Lois about the way he came to her defense at the post office. "I don't know anyone else who would have even thought of doing that for me, or maybe even you. What makes it so crazy is that we actually had a really nasty argument just before it happened. I kinda think I even might have started it."

"But you'll go out with him, won't you? I know you will," Lois said again.

"Hey, girl, slow down. He hasn't even asked me out yet." She paused, smiled, and then said with absolute certainty, "But he will."

"What makes you so sure? Did he hint at it? Did you?"

"No, nothing like that. It's just something in the way he looked at me after I told him my name and the way we wound up laughing together. I know, girl. I just know. He'll ask me."

"You better think it over, Mickey. If that crazy brother of yours finds out, he'll kill the both of you—if your mother doesn't do it first."

"Hold on a second."' Mickey cut her off and placed the receiver on the bed, making sure she didn't knock over the nail-polish bottle. She moved quickly to the door and opened it a crack. She saw her mother sitting in the living room with T.C., watching television. She quietly closed the door and ran back to the bed. "Lois, to tell you the truth, I'm scared to death. I don't know what to do. I mean, he's nice. He's really nice. He never even tried to touch me. And, girl, you ought to see that smile of his."

"Well, it's no wonder he didn't know your name. Back in high school, whites didn't mix much with us, and we didn't exactly reach out to any of them. I wouldn't even know how to talk to a white boy. What could you possibly talk about with him? The Temptations? They like the Beatles. Collard greens? They don't eat 'em. The Philly Dog? They do the Lindy Hop. Who are you kiddin'? Girl, you better realize that there's more to something like this than just good looks no matter how fine he seems to you. Although I admit that's a pretty good place to start. Both of you better make sure this isn't one of those forbidden-fruit things."

"Right now, this isn't what you call 'a thing,' forbidden or otherwise. He's just a nice guy."

"A nice, good-looking guy. I'm just sayin' be careful. Don't let your body rule your mind."

"It never has, so don't be a smartass, Lois. We haven't talked all that much yet. But you're right about his looks. He's tall, and he's got great hair, and I guess I'd have to say he's got bedroom eyes." She laughed. "Damn, girl, you tricked me into that. But like I said, I want to know more about him."

"What's his name?"

"Gerard Friscella."

"Friscella? Marvelous. Just what you need. Now I know you're crazy. Half this city hates the other half, and you're sitting smack in the middle trying to hit on some Italian. Who do you think you are, Lena Horne? God help you. If he don't know better, then God help him. In fact, God help the both of you."

"I told you. I'm not hitting on him. Well, not exactly. I mean, he spoke first and, oh, it's nothing like you think it is. It's just that I . . . I . . . really like him and I . . . I . . . really like him a lot. Listen, Lois, I can't talk no more. My mom's coming. Listen to me. Don't you dare say anything about this to anybody. I mean anybody."

"You know me better than that, but only if you call me tomorrow. Lord have mercy! I need to know how this turns out."

"So do I, Lois. So do I."

Her mother called her for dinner. "I gotta go!"

She joined her mother and two brothers at the dinner table.

"So how was your day, Mickey?" her mother, Annie Mae, asked.

Mickey, still giddy from her talk with Lois, beamed. "It was good, Mama. You won't have to buy a thing for me for school this fall, absolutely not one stitch of clothes. I'm making my own money now."

"You a mailman now, Mickey?" her younger brother, T.C., asked, his mouth full of food.

"No, baby." Michaeletta laughed, reaching over to rub the top of his head. "I just sort the mail. Maybe Charles will get out of the bathroom before noon from now on. I was almost late this morning." She hoped to bring Charles into the conversation, but all he did was glare back at her.

"I've been thinking," her mom said, not looking at Charles. "I forgot to mention to you, I'm going on vacation in a few days. With your new job it's a little complicated, but you obviously can't go down to Virginia to see Aunt Dee with us."

"Well, I ain't going anywhere," Charles interrupted, "and damn sure not back to visit your sister and the old homestead down in Dixie."

"Thanks for your opinion, Charles," her mother said. "We see you so seldom I forgot you're a member of this family. I mean, you bein' in the struggle with so many important things to do. I mean, now that you're not wasting your time in school and you're doing all those *constructive* things like learning to break boards with your feet in karate and learning to count to three in Swahili."

Michaeletta knew how badly Charles vexed their mother, who worked hard all their lives to support them while their absent, drunken father contributed nothing but heartache. And sometimes worse.

Her mom turned back to face Michaeletta. "Like I said, Mickey, T.C. and I will be gone about three weeks. I'm sure you can manage, particularly with Charles here to help."

"Damn! Damn!" Charles shouted, banging both fists alongside his plate.

"What?" Annie Mae shouted back.

T.C. and Michaeletta sat frozen, waiting for the inevitable, impending explosion. She covered one of T.C.'s hands, hoping to comfort him.

"Leave me alone!" Charles shot back. "What you want me to do? Find some chump job like yours and sit there all day, every day, for a chump-change paycheck and smile at the honky supervisor? The New Jersey Bell Telephone Company service ought to be free to poor people, and someday it will. Believe me on that. There's only so much a man can take."

"A man, Charles? But you are not a man. You are a boy. But time is even running out for you on that. T.C., go watch television. Mickey, please leave the room."

Mickey left the table and the room, but she watched from around the corner, unable to tear herself away from the scene— and concerned for her mother.

Charles started to rise in anger.

"You!" she hollered, pointing a finger at Charles. "You sit down and don't so much as move your eyelids. I'm tired of this foolishness. I'm tired of your playacting, and even though you are my child I am getting very tired of you. Times are hard, boy, and you better grow up. You either go back to school or you get yourself a job. Ain't no heroes where you been hangin' out. They fill your head with poison down there, and that Kiongosi isn't doing you any favors. Only hero in my lifetime I can recall is Martin Luther King, and he's dead."

"That faggot?"

Annie Mae, despite her girth, moved around the table quickly and slapped him across the face. Mickey sucked in a breath but didn't make a sound.

"I don't know what you're thinking!" her mom said. "I don't even know if you do any thinking these days! But you are a part of this family, and whether you know it or not you will always be my son. I will always love you. But I will not sacrifice the futures of T.C. and Mickey because you want to play revolutionary. So hear what I'm saying. You got to help guide your little brother when he needs help. You got to respect Mickey as both a woman and your sister. And you got to respect me for putting the food on this table, the clothes on your back, and because my love for you won't let me turn my back on you. Charles, you have to be a part of us, starting now, or you have to leave this house. If you do, you take a piece of my heart with you, but there are limits. I'd like to believe you are not like your father. Don't look away. Listen to me."

Charles clenched his fists. His low voice worried Mickey. "I hear you, all right. I hear you just the way my father did. I hear you the way every other black man in America has been hearing every other black woman in America. It's what kept us stuck where we are. You don't know half what you think you know. If you did, my father would still be here at the head of the table and you wouldn't be just another lonely old single mother. The next time this city explodes, *you* think about *that*."

He brushed her arm aside and stormed out of the room, the sound of awful silence broken by the ferocious slam of his bedroom door.

Later that night, Michaeletta's attempt at sleep was once again interrupted by the familiar sound of her mother crying behind her closed bedroom door. She slipped quietly out of her room and tapped softly on Annie Mae's door. No answer. Twice. Slowly she opened the door and saw her mother sitting on an edge of the bed, head in hands, softly sobbing. Michaeletta went to her and put her arms around her, holding her close.

Her mother looked up, used her thumb to wipe her tears away, and took a deep breath, her body trembling. "Mickey," she said, leaning back so that she could look into her eyes, "I don't know what to do. I always thought I did. But now, I just don't know. When I looked at our lives in the Projects, I knew we had to go, so I did it. When your father became a nighttime runner in the bars, I knew what I had to do for this family. Maybe I waited too long to act, but I knew, and in the end I did it. But now I think, well, a boy needs a father, maybe there was some other way to handle your dad. Maybe Charles would be a little different if Talmadge were here. T.C. is at the age when he needs a father just as much. For the first time in my life, I feel helpless. I don't expect you to understand that. I mean, I don't want you to think of anything except school and growing into full womanhood. I don't want to burden you with this, but I just don't know what to do."

"It's not a burden, Mommy. It's like you said—we are family, and we have to fight to keep that together. Maybe in some way I can reach him." She began to cry too. This time her mother consoled her. Mama held her and rocked her back and forth gently, swaying together in a kind of metronome of love.

Then Annie Mae held her at arm's length. "Lord, child, what am I thinking? Look at your eyes, red and puffy, and you needing to be at that brand-new job tomorrow. You got to look your best. First impressions mean a lot. I'm sure they'll be watching you close the first week."

"I'm fine, Mom," Mickey said, thinking again about Junior and how he'd protected her from that creep. "I'll be just fine tomorrow." Then she laughed. "How does that old post-office saying go? 'Neither snow nor rain nor heat nor gloom of night stays these couriers from the swift completion of their appointed rounds.' Look out, world, Mickey is on the appointed round."

They laughed, and Annie Mae hugged her again. "Mickey, I love you. Now get your little flat rear end back into bed."

Over her shoulder Mickey shouted, "It's not so little and definitely not flat, Mom. Ask the boys!" And then she ran out of the room, avoiding her mother's playful slap.

5

A PROMISE OF LOVE

Junior saw Mickey before she spotted him. She wore a green T-shirt with gold lettering across her chest that spelled out "Essex County College." She stood on the corner of Franklin Street near the employee entrance. To his surprise she held two cups of coffee. When Junior saw her, his face broke into an aurora borealis of a grin because he realized they were both deliberately early.

She turned, caught sight of him, smiled back, and handed him a Styrofoam container. "Coffee, cream, no sugar, as ordered, sir." She bent into an exaggerated curtsy, almost spilling both cups.

"Hey, careful there." He grabbed her arm to steady her. Then he laughed and grunted in a deep voice, "Coffee. Coffee. Gotta have coffee!" He led her to a bench in the nearby park.

"If that's your Tarzan imitation, I suggest you stick to football."

They looked at each other for a moment and then he said, "Coffee, milk, no sugar. You've been watching me, haven't you? Thanks. I'm surprised you were still outside. I wasn't sure you would come."

"I had no choice. After all, we do have to go to work."

They laughed again.

"Speaking of which," he said, "we got about five minutes to talk, and then if we don't get inside, both of us will be fired, in which case we'd never see each other again." The look he gave her asked for an answer to his unspoken question: *How would she feel about that?*

She glanced away and didn't answer. Instead, she said, "Yes, sir, we'd better get inside. And let's keep Newark green." She stood up, reached out for his empty container, and dropped them both in a receptacle. When they reached the entrance, she paused and said, "You go first."

He started to ask why they couldn't go inside together but wasn't sure how she'd react. He simply nodded and went ahead of her to punch in.

They were at work perhaps ten minutes when they saw the postmaster walking toward them. "I need to talk to both of you," he said. "I heard what happened the other day." He put a hand on each of their shoulders, leaned in, and said softly so others wouldn't hear, "He won't bother either of you or anyone else again. He's been written up before. He's done here. Okay. See ya around." He turned and strolled away.

Mickey immediately blurted to Junior, "That's the nicest thing anyone has done for me here since you . . ."

"Since I what?"

"Since . . . you know. But don't think I want you to go around punching people for me."

"Maybe I would—if you asked me."

"Well, I won't ask you to."

They returned to work in silence until Mickey said, "Tell me about your family. Are you an only child?"

"I've got a younger sister. A good kid but a little goofy. She's more interested in boys than school. My dad is a good guy, works at Westinghouse, never missed one of my games. My mom worries I won't meet a nice girl."

"So you have a girlfriend."

He thought he detected a note of concern in her voice. "Well, there's one girl I'm interested in, but she's playing hard to get."

"Oh? Do I know her?"

"You know her better than anyone else in the world does."

"Maybe I can ask her for you."

"You're the only one who can." He noticed the tiny smile she tried to hide. "Anyway, you didn't tell me anything about *your* family."

"My mom is a single mother, and she's an angel. She has to deal with more problems than Job. She's worked at the telephone company for as long as I can remember, raised the three of us by herself, and I never heard her complain. Ever. My baby brother is in elementary school. He's really a great kid."

"Didn't you say the three of us?"

"Well, yeah. My brother Charles is the middle child. I guess you could say he's my mom's big problem." She paused as though she wasn't sure she should continue. She took a breath. "I don't think it's his fault. He always needed a full-time dad. He never had one. I don't know how much sense that makes to you, but I know it's a real problem in a lot of black families. My dad is what a lot of black women call a runner. Monogamy is not in his vocabulary. Since I was a little girl, I can remember he would come home when he needed money or a place to sleep. He has always been full of promises that broke my mother's heart. I don't know how it is with single Italian mothers, but it's that way in my family."

"That sounds really rough."

"The thing is, he still sees Charles on occasion and he always gives him the same old jive about how black women do the black men and how they want to control them. Charles is hurt and confused and antagonistic toward my mom. He needs a role model, and the one he chose is somebody you might have heard about: Kiongosi. Charles hangs out at his headquarters. He dropped out of high school. He is troubled, and I guess you might say isolated. But if there is any way to help him, any way at all, I will. So . . . now you know just about everything there is to know about me."

She turned her head away, dabbed at her eyes with a tissue. Then she suddenly turned back and said in a soft, barely audible voice, "Sorry, but I have to go on break now." And she was gone, leaving Junior alone with his thoughts.

For most of the rest of the day, she said very little. Near quitting time, they shared a bit of small talk, and then she added, "My mom took T.C. with her to Virginia to see my aunt for a couple of weeks, so it's just Charles and me at home, and he's not there very much. So it's usually me and my TV set and my best friend, Lois, on the phone. Sometimes that gets just a little bit lonely."

He jumped at the opening. "I could fix that."

"Please don't. There's just too much to think about. Look at us. I mean, really look. I'm sure you never dated a black girl, and I never . . . I . . . I . . . well, I don't know what to do. It's getting so complicated. I like you. I like you a lot. And I guess you can sense that. But we are who we are, and you know what I mean. If you don't, then look in the mirror. I still have a lot of thinking to do, and so do you."

But she reached into her purse and pulled out a pen. "Hold out your hand."

"What?"

"Do what I tell you. Hold out your hand, palm up." She took it gently and wrote on his hand. "If you ever feel like it, here's my phone number. Call me."

They walked out of the building and melted into the crowd, going their separate ways. Junior stared down at his hand as he walked home and shivered slightly. It was the first time she'd touched him, and when she did, he felt like a jolt of electricity had shot through him.

~

Mickey stopped at a pizzeria near her home and ordered two slices and a soda, paid, and started back out when she realized that Charles might be home, so she went back and got a whole pie. But when she got home, Charles wasn't there.

There was no note on the table. She put the pie in the fridge, scribbled a note to Charles in case he came home later, kicked off her shoes, picked up the two slices and the soda, and went to her bedroom.

She put the meal on her bedside table, but just as she took a bite, the phone rang. She was in such a hurry to pick it up that she dropped the receiver.

She was devastated when she heard Lois' voice.

"Oh, it's you," she said.

"Sorry to disappoint you. Who did you expect? Your White Knight?"

"Come on, Lois. I had a tough day and I'm just worn out."

"Did you see him?"

"Of course I saw him. Our stations are next to each other. Remember? As a matter of fact, we were both early and I bought him coffee and then I got so clumsy when he reached for it, I almost dropped it in his lap. I was so embarrassed I had to apologize."

"Well, that's not cool, girl. I mean, now he knows he's got you. I hope you didn't giggle."

"He doesn't know any such thing. In fact, our supervisor stopped by—you remember that guy that tried to feel me up the first day? Well, he told us he fired the guy. But then, when he walked away, I told Junior that it was the nicest thing anyone had done for me there since he . . . well, you know what he did. And then I got a little stupid and cut myself off and said I didn't expect him to go around punching people out for me and then . . . well, I started feeling dumber and dumber. I don't know what was wrong with me."

"No mystery there, girl. You been bitten by the *luvvv* bug. For your sake, I hope he is as cute as you're afraid to admit he is. This is Lois, child. I know you. And it sounds to me like there's no turnin' around left for you now. So where's he taking you on this first date?"

"Listen to me, Lois. There's no date. If there was, I'd tell you. So get serious. You're right. I do like him—a lot. But you said it yourself. You said black and white—particularly white Italian—don't mix in this town. But when he looks at me—you know he's got great eyes—I just melt."

"So you going out when he asks you?"

"I wish I knew. I wish. I gotta go, girl! I'm waiting for a call. Let it be him."

"You gave him your phone number?"

"Lois, I got to go! I don't want to miss his call."

She hung up. Within seconds, the phone rang again. She snatched the receiver.

"Hey, coffee lady, is that you?"

"Well, who did you expect?"

"I don't know. Today was kind of crazy and I thought you gave me the number for dial-a-prayer or something like that."

"Junior! Junior, I swear—"

"No, stay cool. I'm only kidding. It's great to hear your voice."

"Well, you heard it all day long. I'm the girl who almost spilled coffee down your pants, remember?"

"Listen, I really appreciate you telling me about your family, especially your mom. She really does sound like an angel."

Baby, you sure do know the right things to say and when to say them. Her heart melted a little. "You know when you said that thing about how you could fix me bein' lonely and I kinda snapped at you? Well, I didn't mean it to come out like that. You have to understand, and I'm not sure you do. I know you like me, and I guess you know how I feel about you. But, baby, we are in uncharted territory in a city that's gone crazy, and I have to be afraid for both of us. If I did go out with you, where could

41

we go? For dinner, where in Newark? The same for a movie. In the North Ward, you'd worry about me. I know. You proved it that first day at the job. And in the Central Ward, I'd worry about your lily-white skin. You know, you're pitiful. You don't even look dark enough to be Italian."

"We'll go to New York. I don't care where we go as long as it's us. Listen, you got to make a decision. Otherwise neither one of us will ever find out. And I don't want to spend forever wondering 'what if.' Look, we both have lots of time. We both know the first thing is we need to graduate. We aren't going to be stupid. We both know what we need to do. But I don't want anyone telling us what we can't do."

"What if it does turn out to be love? I'm not saying it will, but would you introduce me to your mom and dad?"

"Yes. Would you introduce me to your mom and your brothers?"

"Yes. But not yet. Give me a little more time and understand how I feel about you and what still holds me back. In the meantime, relax. I'll bring your coffee tomorrow, cream, no sugar. And Junior?"

"Yes."

"If it turns out to be love . . . if I'm sure . . . if we're sure . . . I'll jump straight off the Jackson Street Bridge with you right into the Passaic River. After all, I know if that happens, you'll be my life preserver. But honestly, for all the hormones and all the feelings, I still don't know what love is, and neither do you."

"Agreed," he said. "But we won't know unless we try."

She nodded as she listened but then added, "Just give us a little more time. We're in a city that lost its ability to love. There's so much hate. It would take all we have to face that—even together. So don't push me. Not now. I'll tell you when. In the meantime, enjoy the coffee tomorrow and—"

A furious banging on the bedroom door, which she had locked, cut her off and made her heart pound.

"Mickey! Who you talking to on the phone? You been on for an hour. Who you been talking to?"

"None of your business, Charles! You're not my mother and you're not my father."

"When Mom ain't here, I'm in charge. I'm the man. Now open the damn door before I kick it in. I want answers."

"Sorry. Got to go, Junior."

She hung up before he could say goodbye.

6

AN ACT OF HATE

J unior stared at the phone in his hand, now blaring a dial
tone. He knew from this conversation that the relationship
had passed beyond the bounds of a workplace flirtation.
He sat there somewhat confused by how she'd abruptly hung
up but almost euphoric over the warmth he detected in her
voice when she said, "See you tomorrow. I'll bring your
coffee."

The blast of a car horn jolted him out of his reverie. It was
bowling night. He raced to get downstairs before his father
reacted to the noise, which he knew would anger him. But he
was too late.

"You tell that *gavone* of a gas jockey this ain't the Central
Ward," Senior said. "This is a nice, quiet Italian neighborhood
where people respect each other. If he does that one more time,
I'm going outside—I'll blow his horn for him, and he won't
forget it."

Junior made it to the door and hollered over his shoulder.
"Sorry, Dad! I'll tell him. I'll be home around eleven."

Chooch sat behind the wheel, with Allie in the front seat.
Junior threw his bowling gear into the back and jumped in
beside it. "Man, when are you going to grow up? My dad is hot

as hell about your damn horn. He thinks you're disrespecting the neighborhood."

"All right, all right. Tell him I'm sorry I disturbed his serenity." Chooch wheeled away from the curb with a tremendous roar of the engine, but as he turned toward the Avenue he saw a parked cop car and slowed down. They passed the Howard Savings Bank, where a group of longhaired kids were across the street. A growing pile of empty beer cans bore testimony to the direction of their lives. So did the joints two of them smoked. Junior noticed several girls in the group.

"Hey, what we got over there?" Chooch said. "What do the broads look like?"

"Bad news," Allie said. "Burnouts, man, total burnouts. I wouldn't screw them with *your* dick. Although you might. So take a good look, because you just might be seeing the future. Can you imagine my old man if I ever did anything like that at their age?"

"Hey, we just passed a cop car a while back—how come the cops don't hassle these kids?" Junior asked.

"Paulie made a deal for them," Allie said. "He told the cops if the kids give them any trouble, he'd set them straight. Figures it makes him a big man, says they're his army of the future."

"Hey, don't knock Paulie," Chooch said. "It's about time somebody stood up to the cops for some of our own. Cops on the other side of town never make *those* kids move."

"Yeah, it gives me a kinda warm feeling all over," Junior said, "knowing that we got our own mob of separate-but-equal creeps."

"Aw, you just got this big thing about Paulie because your old man don't like him," Chooch replied. "But I notice your old man went out and bought a gun like most everyone else here did. You gotta admit there's a lot of people who sleep better nights on our side of the Avenue knowing Paulie is out there for us."

"Yeah," Junior said, noticing the genuine hostility in his

voice. "Guys who carry bicycle chains and brass knuckles and—"

"Speaking of those kinds of guys," Allie said, clearly trying to change the subject and ease the tension, "where is Dominick tonight?"

"I dunno," Chooch responded. "I went by his house first and blew the horn, and when he didn't come out I rang the bell, and his old lady said she hadn't seen him since he left for the sanitation department garage this morning."

"I wouldn't get too alarmed," Allie said. "He's either out there with the Citizens Council making Bloomfield Avenue safe for America, or there's a hot wrestling match on TV."

Junior knew Dominick had joined Paulie's White Citizens Council and didn't like it one bit.

Chooch parked the car and they went inside the bowling alley. At the desk, Scoots DeLorenzo, the owner, was all smiles. He made a big show of greeting them but it was really all for Junior, who, like him, was an All-State football player at Barringer.

"Hey, All-Stater, is that really a football team you amateurs have up at Montclair State?" he shouted over the twin sounds of falling bowling pins and the bar's television set. "I mean, di'nt I read where you guys are gonna play the nuns from Good Counsel in your opener?"

"Well, hello, Junior," Mary T purred from the service bar, where she was picking up a tray of drinks. She blew him a kiss.

"Darling," Allie shouted back, pretending that her performance was meant for him and rushing toward her with open arms. "What do you say to a little screw?"

"I say 'goodbye, little screw,'" she said. She walked off, deliberately exaggerating the wiggle of her rear end.

"Alley twenty-two," Scoots said, handing a scorecard to Junior. "And it don't make me cry to see that you guys left Dominick home. No broad in her right mind would come in the joint if she knew that gorilla was here."

They walked down to their alley and settled in. As they changed into bowling shoes, they looked up to follow the Yankee game on the big TV screen behind them.

Then they heard Scoots on the PA system. "Telephone call for Allie Costa. Allie, you got a phone call at the front desk."

"Hey, Allie," Chooch hollered after him, "see if she got a friend for me."

A minute later he was back, looking shaken. Junior was busy selecting a ball from the rack and Chooch was tying his shoes. Junior looked up. Allie's face clearly indicated he was pissed off.

"Dominick. That fuckin' Dominick," Allie said.

"Where the hell is he?" Chooch asked.

"In jail, where he belongs," Allie said. "The dumb son of a bitch hit a black kid with a lead pipe this afternoon on Bloomfield Avenue."

"He did *what*?" Junior shouted. "That stupid fuck. He's even dumber than I thought. Can you imagine going to war to make the North Ward safe for that asshole? How could this happen? I know it couldn't have been self-defense."

"I don't know," Allie said. "Half the time you can't understand him and the other half you can't believe a word he says. Some black kid was waiting for a bus, and Dominick told him to start walking because he couldn't wait there. He said he was a deputized officer of the White Citizens Council and he was on official patrol and the kid had to go. Then the kid said he wouldn't, that it was America and he had rights. Beyond that, all I know is the kid is in Presbyterian Hospital and Dominick is in Newark Street jail."

"A lead pipe," Chooch interjected. "That's some serious shit. Shouldn't we get him a lawyer?"

"Beautiful," Junior said, "just fuckin' beautiful. Why couldn't he do us all a favor and get himself sucked up into his own garbage truck?"

"So what do we do?" Allie asked.

"I know what I'd like to do," Junior said, "but we got no

choice. We got to get back in the car and get the *stunad* out of the can before he challenges all the black prisoners to a duel. I tell you, I've almost had it with—"

His words were lost in noise from the PA system. It was Scoots again—this time it was, "Junior Friscella, you have a telephone call at the front desk. Call for Junior Friscella."

"Damn," Allie said. "It sounds like we're too late."

Junior walked to the front desk. As he reached for the phone, he saw Mary T smiling at him from the service bar. She leaned on it as far down as she could, revealing most of each breast. She smiled again and then stuck out her tongue and wiggled it. Disgusted, he waved her off, turned his back, and picked up the phone.

By the time he hung up, Allie and Chooch had joined him. "No rush now," Junior said. "He's out."

"He's out?" Allie said. "How the hell did he get out? What did he do? Hang a sheet and slide all the way down or just jump out the window?"

"Paulie sprung him. He went into the jail one minute and came out with Dominick the next. I don't know how Paulie did it, but he's out. That's the bad news. Now for the worse news. He's with Paulie now. They're on patrol together and Dominick is driving."

"Mother of God. He's doing what?" Allie said. "He's driving and his license has been suspended, what, maybe four hundred times?"

"Wait, there's even more. He wants the three of us to ride with them."

"Where we gonna meet them?" Chooch asked, displaying genuine interest.

"'Where,' your ass—we're gonna go back and bowl," Junior said.

But they didn't. Chooch insisted they leave so he could go meet Dominick, whether Junior and Allie came or not. Junior told Chooch to take him home.

When Chooch dropped him back home on Clifton Avenue, the street was silent. He walked slowly up the front steps, turned, and looked up at the night sky. He stood lost in thought, and then he took a long, deep breath. For the first time since the city had been torn apart by fear and hate, he was beginning to realize that all four of them had been drawn into the eye of the same tensions that had changed their city forever.

"Four lifetimes of friendship and suddenly we're all different since the riot. What have we become?" Then he lowered his voice, almost as though he were afraid of being overheard or afraid to acknowledge a truth that was slowly growing inside him—something he had never questioned before. *The Newark Bombers—we're not in the schoolyard anymore. We're not kids anymore. It just might be leaving time.*

7

ANNIE MAE FACES TWIN PROBLEMS

Gerard Friscella Sr. stepped out of his front door at 7:00 a.m. and into the glare of early-morning sunshine. In his left hand he carried the usual brown-bag lunch that his wife had packed the night before. He walked down the four stone steps that led to his home, leaned down to pick up his morning paper, and was jolted by what he saw: a new mayoral candidate had joined the race.

A huge portrait accompanied by two smaller ones and a lengthy article shared the space above the fold. He'd never seen this new candidate before. He scanned the article. Jackson Anderson was a Jersey guy—but not the kind that grew up in the North or Central Wards. As far as the newspaper knew, he had never even been to Newark. But he'd just announced he would take up residence there and run for mayor.

And he was a black man.

Not a Newark black man, but out of the North Jersey affluent suburb of Mountain Lakes, who did his undergraduate work at Rutgers University and earned his law degree at Princeton. Gerard Sr. studied the picture for a minute. Alongside his photo were smaller pictures of Paulie Tedesco and Kiongosi.

The headline stretching above all three photos read, "Now It's a Horse Race."

Senior turned the corner and picked up his pace. He saw the #29 bus coming and ran to catch it. As he settled into his seat, he thought about the continuing ethnic and racial tension in his city and the fear among many that a second riot—triggered by either side—was a distinct possibility. The catalyst could well be this battle for City Hall. He had no idea whether Jackson Anderson was good news or bad news. He was still wondering when he hit the buzzer and got off the bus at Westinghouse.

The building was more than a century old. The original orange-and-blue sign over the loading dock still hung in place. The red bricks stood firm around arched windows and doorways, as did the yellow shift siren and the black smokestack. Once, the plant had employed more than three thousand workers. But now its future was clearly eroding, like the plant itself.

It seemed symptomatic of everything physical in a once-great city.

The machine shop where Senior worked was probably the most active spot in the plant. The walls were decorated with cartoons about worker safety and notices about workmen's compensation. The talk among his co-workers was more banter than conversation, because lack of concentration could cost any one of them a finger—or worse.

When the siren signaled lunch, Senior and a few others settled down on the long concrete riser that fronted the side of the building. They talked as they unwrapped their lunches.

"You see that black guy in the suit?" one of them said, referring to a tall man whom Senior had seen earlier, holding a clipboard as he spoke to the shift foreman.

"Yeah, what's up with that?" a second guy asked.

"He's here to count black faces. Well, he's seen Harry, so he can stop counting, because Harry is all there is."

"Why's he doing this?" Senior asked.

"He's working on a report for the governor's riot commission."

"Shit," the first guy said, "why don't he go over to Hayes Homes and count all the television sets?"

"It's something to do with economic opportunity for their kind. I talked to him for a while this morning. He don't seem like a bad guy. He asked me a lot of questions about how many colored we got workin' here . . . how many used to work here . . . stuff like that. Asked a lot of questions about the union, too, like, how does a colored guy get in and what keeps 'em out. Whaddya think, Gerard?"

Senior sat quietly for a moment, disturbed by all of this. "I don't think anybody can go messing with seniority. The union ain't gonna stand for that. But something is gonna happen."

"Yeah," a third guy said. "What's gonna happen is that some of us ain't gonna be workin' here this time next year. Shit, the governor got his thumb up his ass and he can't get it out. All that bullshit about police brutality. That's just what it is: bullshit. They burned the stores. Those things they were carryin' were television sets. I di'nt hear about nobody going into no super-market and demanding, 'Gimme a loaf of bread and a quart of milk.'"

"Well, it's like Paulie said," the first man chimed in. "We gotta take a stand here. I worked for this job and I worked for my home, and no black son of a bitch is gonna get a piece of what I earned. If we have to fight this time, we will. If Paulie gets elected mayor—"

"Hold on a second," Senior said. "Let me tell you about Paulie and that Kiongosi, too. Without each other, they're nothing. They feed on each other. Somebody has got to be mayor, and I'm wondering about that black guy on the front page of today's *Star-Ledger*. I don't know what the answer is, but it ain't either one of them. We got a hell of a problem here. I'm scared for my family. I'm scared for my job. Just like everyone else, I bought a gun, but you know something? I don't care if he's black, white, yellow, or purple. I wanna know more about this guy Jackson Anderson."

"Well, I don't," one guy said.

"And neither do I," said another.

Senior shook his head. "Both you guys don't know nothing about him. Neither do I. But I'm damn sure gonna find out."

~

Charles fumed as he headed across town. He was ready to fight someone and didn't know where to direct his fury. His fight the night before with Michaeletta, who had refused to tell him who was on the other end of that hour-long telephone call, still weighed heavily on him. He'd broken the lock on the door and grabbed her hard by each shoulder. Then he repeated, louder, what he'd yelled from the other side. "I want an answer! You better learn now that when Mom isn't here, I am in charge. I am the man."

Her response had been more devastating than if she'd slapped his face. "Mom called it right. You ain't no man. You failed in school and you're failing in life. Don't you dare put your hands on me. You ain't nothin' more than my baby brother. Get out of my room."

For a moment, he'd balled up his fists and thought about hitting her. But he managed to control his anger. He slept very little. When he awakened that morning, she was gone. He left an unfinished bowl of corn flakes on the table and slammed the door behind him.

He rode the bus downtown to Halsey and Branford Place and walked the short block to Kiongosi's political headquarters. He was early. The private office behind campaign headquarters was empty. Somebody had placed that morning's *Star-Ledger* on the desk.

Charles saw the three pictures looking up at him from above the fold. From the moment Charles had met Kiongosi, the man had preached a single theme: *We are one.* It was what he believed and convincingly transmitted throughout the black community —that since Newark was headed toward becoming a black majority, it was inevitable that he be elected mayor.

But now there was another black man in the game.

"Motherfuckin' Uncle Tom," Charles shouted at the newspaper. "Don't know nothin' about the city. Don't know nothin' about the struggle. Don't know nothin'—period. He'll split the vote. He might as well be on the honkies' payroll. He damn sure dresses the part with his fancy suit."

He was so absorbed in his rant that he didn't hear Kiongosi enter the office. "I think you better learn to keep yourself under control," the man quietly told Charles. "He ain't goin' away. But, yeah, he presents a hell of a problem."

Kiongosi's tone, when it was calm, such as now, belied his dramatic physical appearance: short but powerfully built, still looking like the football lineman he was; his unique pigmentation was an almost lemon-like shade; his piercing green eyes, framed by black horn-rimmed glasses, gazed out from beneath his precisely styled Afro.

"We got a crisis here and we need a new strategy to consider," he continued, "particularly since he says he's actually setting up residence in the North Ward. What the hell does that mean? We got to find out in a hurry."

"The man is crazy."

"No, the man is dangerous. What we got to do is set up a meet with him, and I mean soon. If we don't find out who he really is, then we can't fight. When he opens his campaign headquarters, I want you to be there. I want you to be respectful. Call him brother. Tell him we are all brothers. You be tactful. You will be my ambassador. I want to meet with him, and I want that meeting held here in this office."

Charles stood taller, swelling with pride at being tasked with this important job. "I won't let you down."

"I don't think you will. You are an important lieutenant. The sooner we know this devil, the quicker we can find a solution. Get out there with the people and find out what they know about him and what they think."

～

W hen Mickey turned the key in the lock, she expected Charles would still be there and steeled herself for yet another argument. She was relieved he wasn't but astonished at who was. Annie Mae Washington had cut short her vacation. She was at the stove preparing supper.

"I left T.C. there with Aunt Dee," her mom explained. "I didn't like the way you sounded when you called me today on your lunch break. I'm your mother—I know you better than anybody else. I get the strong feeling that something is really wrong. What has happened?"

She moved to the living room and the couch, motioning Mickey to sit next to her. Mickey took a deep breath and told her about her fight with Charles. Before she finished, she put her head on her mother's shoulder and sobbed. "I want to help him, but he's so hung up on his race. And now after last night, the way he broke down the door and grabbed me, he scares me."

Before either of them could say another word, they heard another key turn in the lock. Charles entered the living room.

Mickey jumped up from the couch, faced him, and said with surprising force, "You know, Charles, I figured out your problem. You are ignorant."

"Mickey!" Annie Mae shouted.

"My daddy was right about both of you," Charles said. "Man, I understand why he couldn't put up with either of you."

Annie Mae had had enough. "If you did see your father— which I doubt—then challenge your dropout self with a little arithmetic and ask him why in all these years that you have walked this earth—in shoes for which I paid, I might add, as well as the clothes on your back and the food that you eat—why has it been so difficult for him to pay the thirty dollars a month the judge ordered?"

"You don't understand Daddy. If you did, he'd still be here."

Mickey went after him again. "Charles, you have a big mouth, and as usual you don't know what you're talking about. Have you got enough mouth to say 'dropout' in Swahili?"

"I'll bust your damn—"

Annie Mae jumped between them and pushed Charles away.

"You may be my mama, but there's some things a man—"

"Hold it right there. You don't know nothin' about being a man, and you don't know nothin' about the pain a woman with a husband like your father has to suffer. That's probably my fault. I always felt that what was between him and me should stay between him and me. But I was wrong. I hoped if he couldn't be a faithful husband, he at least could be a father. But I was wrong about that, too. Now understand this. Don't you ever again dare to use his name to start trouble in this house."

As he usually did, Charles backed off. Then he raced out the front door, slamming it behind him.

Annie Mae returned to the kitchen to check on supper and then motioned Mickey to sit across from her at the kitchen table.

"Honey, we need to talk. We should have had this talk before. I need to make sure you understand something. What happened between me and your father . . . well, that was a long time ago. I know what he was, and I know what he will always be. I can accept that and even the loneliness that comes with it, and, child, it can be very lonely when you are a woman. You're the oldest and you heard us fight. And you remember it more than the boys. You have seen and heard some ugly things, but, believe me, baby, I was just unlucky. It doesn't have to be that way at all."

She got up, moved behind Mickey, and began to stroke her hair. Mickey remembered how much she'd loved the feel of her mama's soothing hands when she was little.

"What I'm trying to tell you is that you are a beautiful

woman." She bent down and kissed her forehead. "Not just on the outside but on the inside as well. I know because I was once beautiful on the outside myself. And, baby, somewhere out there is a man who doesn't know it yet, but he carries your name in his heart in big capital letters. And when it comes time to judge him . . . if he's tender . . . if he looks at you as if the sun ain't never gonna shine no more if you go away . . . if he's gentle, then, baby, that's something you never saw in this house. But it's out there. And you deserve it. If you find a man like that"—she crushed Mickey in a fierce hug—"then you don't listen to nobody with their he-said/she-said. If you find a man like that, then you gotta love him as hard as you can love. You gotta love him until you can't love no more, and then you got to go back and love him all over again."

They remained in a silent embrace, broken only when Mickey let go, leaned back, and told her, "Mama, you are still beautiful, and I love you."

~

Mickey sat beside Junior in the park just beyond the postal building, sipping their coffee in what had become a Monday-through-Friday ritual. The telephone calls had brought them closer together—almost close enough to say what they really felt. Her mom's lecture about good men was on Mickey's mind all night long and remained burned into her psyche since she awoke that morning. As Junior talked, she listened, smiled, and secretly measured him against her mother's check list.

Gentle . . . tender . . . and the way he looks at me.

"What are you smiling at?" he asked. It was apparent that she had really stopped listening. "I didn't say anything that clever."

"Not *at* you . . . with you. It must be rubbing off on me and into that Italian brain of yours. You are in serious danger of learning the meaning of cool."

"You think so? I told you all along where I got it. You need to listen to Sinatra every day."

She punched him on the arm, and they walked into the building—this time side by side.

The work passed easier that morning. Neither of them felt the need to make small talk. Both were delighted with the happy residue of their earlier conversation. Both were lost in the silence of their private monologues.

Mickey replayed last night's intimate talk with her mother. It was as though Annie Mae knew everything about Junior—except, of course, that he was white. And the silent check list she measured him by in the park added up to a perfect score.

She will welcome him and love him if it goes that far. I think she will. I hope she will, but I don't honestly know. She doesn't know he exists, and we haven't even been on a date yet.

He gently tapped her right foot with his left. She turned and smiled at him. He mouthed words with exaggerated pantomime. Though he was silent, she understood without trouble.

"Take a break. Meet me in the lunchroom."

She nodded and left first. When they arrived, the lounge was empty but for them. Junior went to the Coke machine to buy two sodas. Mickey got the feeling he was stalling. She watched him closely, smiling when he missed the slot in his nervousness and dropped a quarter on the floor.

She bent to pick it up at the same time he did. Crouched down, they looked up, faces just inches apart.

"Well, Junior Friscella, do you come here often?" she asked.

"Mickey, let's give it a try. Let's go out Friday night."

She stood slowly. He slowly followed, still talking. "Listen, I'm not a bad guy. I clean up pretty good. I'm tall enough so you can wear heels if you want. There's no dirt under my fingernails. And I won't get fresh." He said this last with a grin. "So there it is."

She glanced away from the intense look in his eyes. "You know how I feel. Please, Junior, try to understand. It's not you. It could never be you. It's not me. The trouble is them. The trouble is that the memory of the riot never will die until they stop talking about it. The trouble is everything in this damn city is about color."

"I know what you're thinking. But don't talk about it now. It's summer. The sun is out until eight at night. I always tan well in the summer, if that will help."

They both laughed. She reached out and gently touched his cheek. "Logic says I shouldn't, but a great woman last night all but told me I should. So just let me think about it a little longer. Okay? Call me tonight."

Junior smiled broadly and squeezed her hand. Then he frowned and scratched his head. "Okay, Mike. You still don't look like any boy I ever knew."

~

M ickey stared at her bedroom telephone. Eight thirty, and he still hadn't called. Where was he? She jumped when she heard the doorbell. Oh, he didn't . . . surely he wouldn't have . . .

But it wasn't. She sighed in relief when she heard her mother greet Lois.

"She's in her room. Go on in."

Lois closed the bedroom door behind her and cocked her head, listening to the Parliaments on Mickey's record player singing "I Wanna Testify." She laughed. "I bet that's exactly what you want to do, but you can't. But I know you didn't tell your mom, did you? I thought she was the one who got you to reconsider the White Knight."

"No, I didn't tell her. But, Lois, a strange thing happened the other night after Charles acted out. She sat me down in the kitchen, and we had the most beautiful talk we've ever had. She told me not to judge all men by my dad. She talked about loneliness and love and tenderness, and this morning I looked at

Junior when we were having coffee in the park, and, girl, it was like, without even knowing him, my mom had guided me. He fits everything she said."

"So are you going out with him or not?"

"I might have a date Friday. He's supposed to call tonight—and if you say one word he can overhear, I swear I'll kill you."

"But then I'll miss the wedding. And I was so hoping you and I could go to the movies on Friday. Sidney is playing at the Royal in *Guess Who's Coming to Dinner?* I think that's kinda appropriate."

Mickey grabbed the pillow off the bed and whacked Lois over the head with it. "That's just a sample, girl. I'll kill you if you talk during his phone call. And if he doesn't call, I'll kill the two of you. And yes, he asked me out."

"What did you tell him? Details, girl, details! Don't hold back. I want it all. Did you say, 'Yes, darling, of course,' and then jump into his big, strong, Italian arms? Now that would have been romantic!"

Her urgency revealed her own inner struggles about her best friend. As a classmate of hers since kindergarten, Lois had always felt protective about Mickey. On the other hand, slightly overweight with a limited history of dating, Lois longed to be a kind of Cyrano in their relationship.

"All I said was I'd think about it."

"*Mmm-mmm-mmm.*" Three quick grunts from Lois conveyed her disgust and disappointment loud and clear. "Friday night, cuddling with a white boy. If Charles knew, his Afro would grow six inches higher. But you better make sure he doesn't know."

"Right and right again. He still thinks we're in the middle of another riot and Kiongosi is some kind of Marcus Garvey."

"So what are you gonna do? You know that boy ain't gonna keep coming back hitting on you. He doesn't need to if he's as cute as your love-struck mind keeps telling you. Do something—even if it's wrong."

"I'm gonna do exactly what my mama told me to do."

"But you said you didn't tell her."

"No, I didn't. I wanted to, but I didn't. And no, she doesn't know he's white. Actually, she doesn't even know he exists. But the things she told me last night helped me make up my mind. I still don't know what love is, but she sure gave me one serious clue."

And then the phone rang. They froze. "Make him wait," Lois said.

One more ring, and Mickey dived across the bed and grabbed the phone. She put an index finger to her lips and Lois nodded assent.

"Coffee to go," she said in what she hoped was a sexy voice. "Mickey the manager speaking. May I help you?"

"Well, I guess that's some sort of progress. How are you?"

"A lot better now that you called."

Lois made a gagging gesture. Mickey shook a fist at her.

"Well, that's one thing out of the way. I haven't washed my hand since you wrote your phone number on it, and it's starting to smell a little. You know, I still owe you a soda because neither one of us picked up that quarter."

Lois doubled up on the bed, laughing and mouthing the words "Tell him yes, dummy! Tell him now!"

Mickey scowled and put a cautionary finger to her lips. "Did you see the story in the *Star-Ledger* about the new black man who says he's going to run for mayor?"

"Mickey, I don't give a damn whether Pete Rose, Frank Sinatra, or the Pope is running. Well, Frank Sinatra, maybe. But if you decide against going out with me, I will put a huge sign up in the post office over your pigeonholes tomorrow saying 'Michaeletta Washington is afraid of Italians.'"

"That's not funny. It's also not true. Because I think we have a date on Friday."

Lois pumped both fists in the air from her seat on the bed. Then, before she could stifle it, she let out a clearly audible, "Hurray!"

"What was that?" Junior said. "You got a dog?"

"No, but sometimes she acts like it. That was Lois. My friend since kindergarten and the only one anywhere in the city of Newark who knows about us."

"Put her on."

"Are you serious? Junior, if you pick on her I'll spill coffee on your pants tomorrow."

"I said put her on. There's something I need to tell her."

She covered the receiver with one hand. "All right, tough girl. You asked for it. Now come and take your medicine."

Lois took the telephone, eyes wide, looking a bit unsure. "Hello?" Her voice was barely audible. "You want to speak to me?"

Mickey pulled the receiver away and smashed her head alongside Lois' so she could hear what Junior said to her best friend.

"Yeah, you bet I do. I want to speak to you, but only if you helped persuade her about this date. If not for you, she wouldn't know what she's missing. Is she always so stubborn?"

"Definitely," Lois said, knowing she'd pay for her honesty later. Mickey jabbed her in the side, but she stifled a squeal. "That's her ever since we were little kids. Are you as cool and as cute as she says you—"

Mickey yanked the phone out of her hand. "That's enough."

"I like her," Junior said. "I was about to ask her if she'd meet me in case you backed out."

"Right. I'd kill you both. Once I commit, I commit. See you in the morning, Sinatra. This time you bring the coffee."

8

ALONE AT LAST

J unior jogged with Allie on the circular track at the edge of Branch Brook Park, the new sports complex. They both wore shorts and T-shirts.

Allie was obviously laboring to keep up with Junior, his breath coming in short bursts. "You're killing me. We already been around once. Take a break, superhero. I'm a lover, not an athlete." He stopped suddenly and heaved his body onto the grass.

Junior squatted beside him. "You run like an old man. No, that's wrong. You run like a very old man."

"Why are you so frenetic? Don't you ever just play it cool?"

"Funny you should say that. A very pretty girl told me earlier this week that she thought I was pretty cool."

"Get her to an optometrist. And by the way, what girl do you know who would tell you a lie like that? In fact, what girl do you know, period, Mr. I Can't Take a Drink Because I'm Getting Ready for Football Season? I hope it wasn't Mary T. She could give you the clap just by breathing on you."

"No, give me a little more credit than that. It wasn't Mary T."

"So who was it?"

"It's not important. Do me a favor. I left a couple of footballs in that duffel bag over there. Get 'em out and you can throw to me."

"I know I shouldn't do this," Allie said when he returned. "Post pattern on three. Hut one . . . hut two . . . hut three." He took five awkward steps back and saw Junior going into his break. The pass sailed ten yards over his head.

"My bad," Allie said. "I should have brought it down."

"Yeah. Next time find a bad spot, like my hands. You're bad? No. You're terrible."

"Hey, unlike you, I gave up kids' games for girls."

"All right, so throw me another. This time buttonhook."

They worked out for another half hour and then Junior squatted in a half crouch and ran straight at Allie.

Allie, still holding a ball, looked up just in time to see Junior barreling down on him. "Come on, Junior, give me a break."

Junior slowed his charge to not hurt him. But with the impact, the ball squirted loose. They both lay on the ground laughing.

"Two hours in the hot sun and now you're trying to kill me," Allie said. "You wanna wrestle, go find Mary T."

"Not even with yours," Junior said as he retrieved the ball.

"Need a favor, Junior. I'm a little short. Loan me twenty for the week, huh?"

"Can't do it. I got a date tomorrow."

"With who?"

"Just a girl. You don't know her." He nervously twisted the ball between his hands.

"Whaddya mean, I don't know her? Hey, man, don't forget who you are talking to. This is Allie, King of the Jungle. If she's in the North Ward, I know her."

"Hey, look. It's just not that important."

"Not important? Whaddya mean? Am I or am I not your sex adviser? Who was it got Mary T for the Bombers that night in the schoolyard? Boy, what a sight you guys were. I wish I had a camera—fourteen years old, all of you cherry and scared to death."

Junior remembered all too well the night all four of them had lost their virginity to Mary T. And wished he could forget. She'd been after him ever since, but he did not reciprocate her interest in another go. "Yeah," he shot back, "and who put up your two bucks?"

"Hey, that's like sayin' 'who buys Picasso's paints?' I'm an artist, man. I can't be worried about money. Besides, you . . . you wanted it so badly you would have put up a hundred if you had it. You almost pissed in your pants."

"No, man. That was Dominick—and he did."

They laughed.

"Dominick." Allie shook his head. "You got any idea how many fights I got into because of that asshole? He was always puttin' me in the middle of something. Thank God for you and Chooch. Even Muhammad Ali couldn't have made it out of the neighborhood by himself."

"You? How about the night before we played Eastside my junior year and he called up that big linebacker—you know, that Italian kid that got the scholarship to Duke—and he says he's gonna catch his sister and do her on the way home from school. And the kid really loses it and he says, 'Who is this?' And Dominick says, 'This is Junior Friscella, and we're going to kick the shit out of you tomorrow,' and then he hangs up."

When they stopped laughing, Junior added, "And the whole game I'm wondering why that big son of a bitch is trying to kick me in the balls after every play. Christ!"

"Yeah, but you played some game that day. Seemed like you caught fifty passes. And that block you threw during that punt return! You could have knocked down a wall. You don't know shit about pickin' up chicks, but you got a straight-A average without crackin' a single book. How come you didn't take the scholarship to Northwestern?"

Junior tossed the ball from hand to hand. "I'll tell you something I never told anybody—not even my old man. Shit, Allie. The Big Ten against Barringer, against Central. I guess I was a little scared, you know, and then they don't give scholarships but they play pretty good football at Montclair State, and, yeah, well . . ." He paused, knowing he was about to make a lame excuse. "And they're on up the road so my folks could be at every home game. But Allie, and I wouldn't say this to anyone else, I was scared. Ever since Pop Warner League, my dad treated me like a hero. I wasn't sure I wouldn't let him down."

"Well, I can understand that, but I can't forgive what that done to me. My mother says"—he switched to a falsetto voice —"'Junior Friscella can go to Montclair State. It's good enough for him, so that's where you're headed, and I've already told your father, so you better get ready to go there.' So I go, and I'm taking business administration, and I don't even know what that means. And my grades are okay, so my old man says, 'We think you should try Rutgers Law School.' And I apply, and you're the only one I can tell, but, Junior, I'm scared shitless. I know I'll never make it. Even if they take me, I'll still bust out and then it's me and my old man's power mowers and all those lawns up in Short Hills that he used to say would be mine one day."

Junior was moved by the two secrets they'd pulled out of the dark sides of their minds. He grabbed Allie's arm and looked him in the face. "You'll make it. You ain't Dominick or Chooch. Don't sell yourself short."

"Neither are you. And I know you'll make it. You'll get your degree and you're a football hero. You got smarts and you know how to talk to people. You could do anything you want. You ever think about the future?"

"I guess that's why I chose Montclair State. They got a good phys-ed department. They got good connections. They might get me into the Newark school system. I could teach. I could coach. Someday, who knows, that could be my football team coming out of the Barringer locker room."

"Yeah, and if the school runs out of money, you could use

Dominick and Chooch as tackling dummies." Allie shook his head. "Jeez, I don't know why I even said that. The four of us, we been through a lot. We're the last of the Newark Bombers."

"Allie, I wonder about that. Lately, I wonder a lot. We're not Chooch and Dominick. And we sure as hell are not fourteen years old anymore."

"Lately I been thinking the same thing," Allie said. They awkwardly reached out and embraced. Embarrassed, they pulled away. In that instant, Junior knew that this was one bond that wouldn't be broken.

"And, Junior," Allie said, "about that girl that I don't know and you say isn't important. Forget about it. That's one secret that stays with me."

"You mean that?"

"Hey, I ain't Chooch and I ain't Dominick. Is she that special?"

"Allie, she's coming to Montclair State this fall. Is she special? She's beautiful inside and outside. She's someone I can talk to and laugh with. I never knew a girl like her before."

"Damn. I never heard you talk that way about any girl. She must really be something. When do I meet her?"

"Very soon. For now, this is between you and me and nobody else till she and I figure this out. But I got to tell you something else. You're my best friend and I trust you, but I don't know how you'll take this." He paused.

"Her name is Mickey Washington. She's black, and I think I'm falling in love."

Allie looked him directly in the eyes. "Like I told you, I ain't Dominick and I ain't Chooch—and if she's like you say, then you guys deserve each other." He stood quietly a moment as if deep in thought, then laughed and slapped Junior on the back. "See if she has a sister."

∾

Junior cruised down Bloomfield Avenue behind the wheel of Chooch's lavender Studebaker with Tom Jones' "She's a Lady" blaring out of the radio. He wore a long-sleeved, multicolored shirt and tan slacks. As he drove, Bloomfield Avenue melted first into Broadway and then into Broad Street.

He moved past the Bronze Hotel, where the hookers gathered to offer curb-service pickup. At the southern end of Washington Park, he turned right, then right again at Washington Street. At the end of the block, he pulled into a spot facing the public library. Michaeletta, who had been sitting on the library steps waiting for him, ran down them and to the car. She climbed in.

She wore a white scoop-necked blouse with ruffles on the neckline, a powder-blue straight skirt, and white sandals. She'd accessorized the outfit with a multicolored necklace and matching powder-blue and white earrings.

Junior caught his breath at the sight of her. "Pardon me, Miss, but you clean up exceptionally well."

"Boy," she said as he pulled away from the curb, "this is without a doubt the ugliest automobile I have ever seen. Here I am expecting Prince Charming to be driving a big, long Cadillac, and what do I get? Dopey in the Ugh-mobile. And that shirt? What am I gonna do with you?"

"You say one more word and I'll drive you straight up Bloomfield Avenue, park at Paulie's house, and blow the horn."

"You wouldn't!"

"You bet your life I wouldn't."

"That's exactly what I would be betting."

They laughed.

"Hey. Is this really your car?"

"No, it belongs to a friend of mine named Chooch."

"What's Chooch stand for?"

"I don't know. It's just Chooch."

"Well, it has to be short for something."

"I grew up with him. When we were little, he was fascinated

by trains. He wanted to grow up to be a railroad engineer on a big freight train, and he—"

"Really?"

"No, but that's the only way I could shut you up."

They laughed again.

"Where are we going?" Mickey asked.

"Relax, you're safe. You're with the White Knight, remember?"

"Who in this town is ever gonna let me forget?"

Avoiding both Bloomfield Avenue and a black section of town, he swung out of Broad to McCarter Highway and out to State Highways 1 and 9 heading east. He had the windows down. A breeze floated in through the open windows. It was a beautiful night.

As they drove, she scooted closer to him. "Tell me something," she said.

"Sure."

"Back at Barringer . . . I mean, when we were both there . . . what would have happened if you paid attention to me?"

"I don't know. I guess . . . I might . . . look, Mickey, I'm not the person I was then and neither are you. I'm just happy . . . really happy it's now and we're here. And even happier that you broke down and decided to date me."

"I didn't break down," Michaeletta said and laughed. "I just had to make you earn it."

They moved on through the Holland Tunnel and emerged at Canal Street in Chinatown. Junior found a parking spot on the street. He got out, opened her door, and hand in hand they walked toward Mott Street. Along the way they peered into storefront windows. In front of a little curio shop, he stopped and pulled her through the doorway and into a section of Chinese carvings. She was intrigued by the attention to detail.

"That's it—stay right here," he told her. He beckoned the saleslady and moved further into the shop. When he returned, he held a small brown bag.

"So what did you buy?" she asked.

"Later," he answered. They left, turned onto Mott Street, and stepped into another world. It had everything the North and Central wards of Newark had: teeny-boppers, young women in tight capri pants, guys wearing Giants and Jets jackets, older men in fedoras, and elderly folks with canes and walkers.

Just like home.

Except for one thing.

They paused before a basement restaurant sign, started down the three steps, poised to enter.

Mickey smiled. "I know something you might not."

"Is this a test?"

"No, because you know the answer. It's why we're here," she said. "Everyone has yellow skin. Is anyone staring? Does anyone care? Nobody here even wants to talk to the famous White Knight."

Junior shook his head. "Lady, you amaze me. I didn't think it was possible, but you just might be even smarter than you are beautiful."

"You said the right thing, but you are not off the hook. I'm starving."

The hostess smiled at them and asked, *"Ne how mah?"* At their blank stares, she laughed and said, "How are you? Welcome."

She led them to a table. As she reached for the back of Mickey's chair, Junior waved her off and told Mickey, "Sit down. I'm proving I'm a gentleman."

They ordered. Then she picked up the china teapot and poured for him.

"No espresso on the table," he deadpanned.

"Behave yourself or I'll tell you what's wrong with that rainbow disguised as a shirt you are wearing."

Dinner presented them their first opportunity to focus solely on each other. They could have been eating in a phone booth for all the attention they paid to those around them—and for all the attention the other diners paid them.

At meal's end, Junior paid the check and looked at his watch. "Eight thirty, and we have one more stop to make. Come on, Cinderella, before the Choochmobile turns into a pumpkin." They walked out the door holding hands.

"All right, what's in the bag?" she asked.

"What bag?"

She punched his arm. "That bag."

"Oh, that bag. Just like you told me all these weeks, be patient with me."

Once they were back in the car, he headed for Eleventh Avenue a few blocks away, turned left, and made a straight run down to the water.

"Where are we?"

He nosed into a small line of cars. "Look up there." He pointed to an overhead sign that read STATEN ISLAND FERRY.

"This is a real adventure for me," she said. "I've never been here."

"I came once with my mom and dad when I was about ten. They took me to Canal Street to save money on my school clothes. You can imagine how I felt when my dad showed me the Statue of Liberty. I want to see it again. But this time with you."

An attendant motioned them to a parking space at the boat's bottom. They walked to the rear on the starboard side of the ferry and made their way upstairs to the outdoor deck. Ahead of them lay the Hudson River.

"I never saw anything like this," Mickey said, locking an arm inside his. "It's like we're floating in a giant inkwell."

"Wait till you see the lights."

"We don't need them. Look at those stars." They could have actually been on a movie set. She tightened the link of her arm in his. He pulled her closer. The horn sounded, and with a gentle jerk the ferry moved out toward Staten Island.

From their vantage point, the skyscrapers and bridges of

Lower Manhattan began to recede as they slowly pulled away. And then the magic seemed to explode—with the lights of Manhattan glowing from the background, the Statue of Liberty suddenly appeared.

The black water picked up the reflection of the skyline lights, forming a giant liquid necklace. The other couples on the boat did not exist. For them, this was the first moment they felt truly alone.

Junior leaned forward, their kiss long and intense. They were so close their bodies seemed to melt and fuse together. She placed the palms of both hands gently on his cheeks. He pulled her even closer.

When she stepped back, she sighed, still holding his face between her hands. "Wow."

"Wow."

"Well, now we know."

She dropped her hands and laid her cheek on his shoulder. He stroked her hair. Then she broke the silence.

"What's out there?" she asked, staring at the horizon. "I mean, really out there."

"I don't know. It depends on how far you want to go. Europe. I guess China if you want to keep going."

She looked at him. "I wonder if it could ever be far enough."

"Hey, come on. Look at us. It will get better."

"I know it will get better. My mother told me so."

"Your mother what?"

"Something. It's just something I thought." She looked at him tenderly.

"Oh, yeah, I almost forgot." He reached into his back pocket, pulled out the little brown bag, and handed it to her.

She poured the contents into her hand and looked down at two tiny carved images of the revered Chinese symbol Ho Tai, the Laughing Buddha—one black and one white.

"The lady told me he is the god of people in love."

"Really?"

"No, but I thought that's what you'd want to hear. Anyway, I got the right color scheme. So I have one more question." He pointed to the refreshment stand. "What would you say about a hot dog?"

"At last, El Cheapo. I thought you'd never ask."

"Not my idea. Ho Tai made me do it."

9

A NEW FACE, A NEW PROBLEM

The lunch whistle blew, and Senior settled down with his usual group on the long concrete riser on the side of the Westinghouse building. Though the Yankees had lost to the Red Sox, three to two, the previous night, the men uncharacteristically had something more pressing to discuss and talk quickly turned to the new mayoral candidate.

One of the guys asked the question everyone wanted answered. "Who the hell is Jackson Anderson, anyway?"

"Yeah," another joined in. "He shows up by limo on Monday with some high-powered New York press agent and a high-rolling Wall Street investor in tow, meets behind closed doors with the CEO of a powerful insurance company and the state's top banker. Two days later billboards suddenly sprout up all over the place saying 'One City. One People.' What the hell does he know about our city?"

"He's a hustler," another said as he unwrapped his lunch. "He comes to town in a limo with a PR flack and New York money. You watch. In a week he'll be throwing that money around to buy votes. Well, he won't buy mine. I ain't turnin' my back on Paulie Tedesco. He will always be one of us. He was the only guy to stand up for us when all the other pols ran like scared rabbits. A lot of people laugh at his citizen patrols, but we ain't had one incident on the Avenue since they started."

"Yeah," another said, "he's one of us. This new guy might as well be from Mars. The first thing this guy says is that he's moving into our ward. Our ward! Nobody wants him here. That tells me all I need to know about him. He ain't nothin' but a fuckin' nigger carpetbagger."

The back-and-forth continued among them until the first guy turned to Senior and said, "You're awful quiet about this, Gerry. What do you really think about this *mulignan*?"

Gerard Sr. put down his sandwich, stood, and addressed all of them.

"I don't know yet. I don't like this guy. I don't hate this guy. I don't *know* this guy. None of us do. All I'm gonna say is that you guys know me—born and bred right here in this city, a product of this ward. We vote. We pay taxes. We fight the wars and some of the guys we grew up with, friends and neighbors, fathers and brothers, didn't come back. We never had to face an election like this one. Maybe we're all afraid of that. You guys know I never made a secret of the fact that I don't like Tedesco. I don't like Kiongosi, and nobody who works here does—not even Harry, and he's a black guy. But the way I see it, I ain't gonna write this new guy off until I know who he is."

One of the guys squinted up at him. "You got a daughter. You don't worry about her with the blacks movin' in? You don't worry about the number of Italian kids leaving Barringer and goin' to that new all-boys Catholic school? Where does that leave her or any of our daughters? You don't worry about that?"

Gerard shook his head. "No. What I worry about is her report card. I worry about teaching her right from wrong and hoping she gets it. I worry about teaching her respect. I worry, like all of us do, about the guy who dates her not coming to the house first so I can size him up. I worry about everything close to my home and my family no matter who wins the damn election. But when I worry about something outside of my home or my job, it's about when we can get back to our business and stop worrying about *their* business. Now, I don't know why this guy is here. I don't know what he's after. We're not hicks. We grew up in this city. We got enough time and smarts to study him. We won't get fooled. But I'll tell you one thing for sure. If it turns out that this guy can actually cool everybody down—and I hope he can—he'll get my vote. If he can't do that, then he's just another hustler taking advantage of us. We've seen too many of them not to figure it out."

Lunch was over, but the conversation continued as they gathered their things and headed back inside. And Senior heard, loud and clear, the guy just behind him, a guy he had known as a friend for more than twenty years, say, "Let's see how you feel if your kid brings home a nigger baby."

Senior flinched and gritted his teeth. He didn't want to fight. He let the comment go. For the moment.

～

K iongosi sat behind his desk in the private office of his Branford Place campaign headquarters, put down his paper, and waited. Moments later an aide tapped on the door.

"Come in. You're twenty minutes late. So tell me something about this guy I don't know."

"The locals never heard of him," the aide said. "Not the Nation of Islam, not the Baptists, not even the Sunday storefront tambourine-shakin' holy-ghost sanctifiers. I got a friend who went to Rutgers when he was there, and he says all he remembers about the guy is that he was Ivy League-dressed, a 110 percent sadiddy, 24-karat black bougie."

Kiongosi nodded in recognition of the two ghetto terms, the first signifying a wanna-be-above-the-lower-class-blacks, the second an imitator of the perceived style of the white upper class.

"That figures, or those CEOs wouldn't give him the time of

day. What do we know about his lifestyle? Where does his money come from? Did he have any contacts in the city? Who's on his staff? Are they local? Where does he go to church? Does he date white women? Does he date white men?"

"Far as we can tell, he don't date nobody. At Rutgers, he played some football and he pledged an integrated fraternity. Money was no problem in his family even then. At Princeton, from what I'm told, he was first in his class."

"Law?"

"No, something called public administration. I don't even know what that is, but the family lives in Mountain Lakes, so he didn't exactly starve as a kid. The old man is on the board of this huge investment firm on Wall Street. So he took the kid into the business after he graduated. And that's where Mr. Jackson Anderson made his new money and his contacts."

"You hear any reaction from the Tedesco people?"

"None, but they got to be scared."

Kiongosi smiled. "So am I. We got to study on this and do some heavy planning. Two black men in one race for votes in a city we know will eventually be turning black, or at least colored, because we both know the Puerto Ricans are coming. Say he splits the vote? That could beat both me and him. Say he makes a deal with Paulie. That could be just as bad. We got to figure what he's after—and then we got to do something drastic."

"I could send Charles down there at night to trash his head-quarters. Maybe we could pin it on Paulie."

"Right, and get the North Ward to hate us even more? No, we need to know more before we do anything. Maybe we got to find a way to play this guy, or even play Tedesco. Maybe we'll discover that we don't need to act at all. Be alert. Find out how he plans to win and, most of all, why he plans to move, and where." He leaned back in his chair. "Find out. Find out. Find out everything about him you can. Knowledge is power."

~

Annie Mae was on the fourth floor of the New Jersey Bell Telephone Company, a red-brick building at the corner of Branford Place and Williams Street. Like the other operators in the cord room, she perched on a high stool. An enormous switchboard stretched before them, each operator responsible for perhaps twelve circuits.

As an operator at the telephone company, she earned $140 a week with occasional overtime. At forty-two years old, and with the exception of two maternity leaves, she had been with the company for eighteen years. As a young girl, she had been beautiful, but the years spent with Talmadge had taken their toll. She was prematurely gray, and her face was marked by worry lines.

Her job offered stability and enabled her to raise her three children, since their deadbeat of a father failed so miserably to support them in any way.

At seventeen, naive and gullible, she had met and succumbed to the false promises of a tall, muscular, light-skinned classmate at Central High School named Talmadge Washington. He promised first not to impregnate her and second to love her forever. When the first vow went by the wayside, he immediately dropped out of school and disappeared for a week.

It was then that her uncle, a big man who worked in the moving business, had promised to rearrange the molecules in Talmadge's skull with a lead pipe unless he showed up at the Shining Star of the Resurrection Church and Tabernacle of Christ on South Orange Avenue the following Saturday with a wedding ring, a marriage license, and honorable intentions. This Talmadge did with a reluctance dwarfed by his fear of the uncle. She should have known better, but she truly believed she had no other options.

As for the second pledge, he believed that he had honored it in his fashion. In hard times or after each breakup in a series of assorted nightlife romances, he would return for a brief period of time to Annie Mae. In such a fashion were born Michaeletta (the original fruit of the union) and later the two brothers, Charles and T.C. Sometimes she berated herself for ever letting that philandering son of a bitch back into her house. But then again, if she hadn't, she wouldn't have Charles and T.C., and she would never wish them away. Her kids were her life.

Talmadge had been court-ordered to pay thirty dollars a week for the support of his children, but he had delivered only five such money orders on occasions when he had so angered Annie Mae that a visit to the probation department was needed. Money never arrived, and his failure to show up for promised visits resulted in moody, surly sons. Eventually she realized they were all better off without him.

A supervisor walking back and forth behind her, enforcing the strict no-talking rule, jarred Annie Mae out of her wandering thoughts and back to the switchboard in front of her.

Annie Mae was working the same shift as her closest friend, Elizabeth, who sat to her right. On her left was a young black woman, wearing a multicolored African dress and a matching turban. The young woman leaned forward to make a connection for an incoming call.

"Operator," a panic-stricken voice said to her, "my son was just stabbed! Get me an ambulance! Get me the police! We're on Ferry Street just behind the parking lot across from Penn Station. It's dark here. Hurry! Please hurry!"

"Is your son black or white?"

Annie Mae turned abruptly, staring at the younger woman. *What kind of question was that?*

After a pause, the woman on the phone responded, "What's that got to do with it? I can't stop the bleeding and his face is so pale . . . Please just help us. If it matters, he's white!"

"Then let him bleed to death as far as I'm concerned." The younger operator cut the connection.

Annie Mae couldn't hold her tongue. "Child, are you insane?

That boy will die. He's got parents. You want that on your conscience the rest of your life?" Her voice trembled with rage.

"Fuck him," the young woman hissed back.

"What seems to be the trouble over there?" the supervisor shouted from behind them. "Do you have a problem?"

"No trouble over here, ma'am. Yes, ma'am, no problem at all," the young operator sang out. Then she whispered to Annie Mae, low and furious, "What you lookin' at? You open your mouth and say one word and I will kill your old ass."

∼

K iongosi dropped the *Star-Ledger* onto his desk beside the *Newark Evening News*. Both papers carried announcements from Anderson that he had rented the 3,600-seat Mosque Theater for two campaign rallies that would feature celebrities from the worlds of film, music, and business. The guest list featured both a bevy of revered black superstars and the single greatest Italian American entertainment star in the country.

The venue was not without symbolism of its own for the entire city. The Mosque Theater, opened in 1924, was an architectural masterpiece. The interior featured a Greek and Egyptian motif, marble columns, a crystal chandelier, gold-leaf fretwork, and two-columned side promenades. For decades, it was the glue that held many of the city's ethnic populations together.

A blend of the greatest classical concert artists, jazz musicians, and pop performers graced its stage. But with the current tensions, it became geared more to specific ethnicities and racial groups for each performance. Basically, blacks watched black performers, and the North Ward turned out for the biggest Italian names in show business.

"Motherfucker!" Kiongosi thundered at his staff. "Don't the boy ever look in the mirror? Does he think he can play himself off as Italian and black at the same time? Look at his damn rally lineup. Who the fuck does he think he is? Mahatma Gandhi? He ain't just splittin' the black vote. He's carving up the whole damn city."

"We gotta do somethin' quick," one of Kiongosi's aides shot back. "Next thing you know he'll make the whole city color-blind."

Kiongosi's people kept him updated on Jackson Anderson's actions. The man had moved into an apartment house on Mount Pleasant Avenue, in the heart of Paulie Tedesco Country, the same block where Yogi Berra lived before a better Yankee income enabled him to move to suburban Montclair. Then Anderson had opened his official headquarters by breaking through the adjoining walls and combining two large vacant stores on Broad Street, the city's main thoroughfare, just a short walk from that of Kiongosi's base. Neighborhood fliers seeking volunteers had resulted in a full staff of election-ready foot soldiers. The response also indicated that there was an untapped pool of residents who were fed up with the antics of Kiongosi and Tedesco.

"You're right—he's trying to take away our edge, and he's gonna use the Italians to help him," Kiongosi said. "I don't know what he's planning, but you can bet that dumbass Tedesco is gonna fall for it hook, line, and sinker. And on top of that, the fuckin' business community is greedy enough to fall in line for him. Maybe we got to think about talking to Paulie. Hard to say if it will help, but that son of a bitch is so dumb it might. Mean-time we got to figure something out. We got to find a way to expose this guy. I know he is a hypocrite. There's something there. He hides it well, but we got to find something that proves it."

"I'll keep lookin', boss."

~

But Paulie Tedesco wasn't waiting for something to happen. Instead, he initiated it. Even as Kiongosi pleaded with his staff halfway across town for new ammunition about the new opponent, Paulie Tedesco walked out his front door, past the white Chevy with its "Citizen on Patrol" legend painted on the side, went to the car's trunk, and popped it open. He looked around, satisfied that the street was empty of potential prying eyes, and retrieved his shotgun.

Twenty minutes later, the quiet of the neighborhood was shattered by the sound of a shotgun blowing out the picture window of his living room. The call hit 911 at 8:35 p.m.

"Tedesco, White Citizens Council. I need cops and I need them fast. Three niggers in a blue Pontiac pulled up in front of my house and fired at me and my family. I think I got part of the license-plate number."

The operator did her civic duty and immediately alerted the police dispatcher. Then she did her personal duty, as she often did in breaking-news situations. She dialed the newsroom at WOR Radio, as per her money-for-heads-up-tips agreement.

Within five minutes, the news was on the air.

~

The residue of the original Newark Bombers, with the exception of Junior, were getting ready to bowl when the panic-stricken voice of Scoots DeLorenzo babbled over the PA system. "Holy shit, they just shot Paulie! He could be dead!"

Everybody ran to the front desk, but Dominick was the first of the confused crowd to get there. He grabbed Scoots by the neck. "What happened? Who did it? Where is he?"

"If you'd shut the fuck up, we'll find out." Scoots turned the radio up full blast.

The reporter continued the story. ". . . Newark police report that three men in a blue Pontiac fired shots through the living room window of Paulie Tedesco, a prominent politician and founder of the city's White Citizens Council and director of Citizens on Patrol, a controversial paramilitary group. Nobody was injured. Tedesco told the police that the car containing three

Negros turned east on Bloomfield Avenue. People with any knowledge of the incident are asked to call the Newark Police Tip Line at . . ."

The bowling alley erupted in total confusion. People ran for their cars.

Chooch stood near the front door screaming, "Them black bastards will wish they never heard of us. They want our avenue, they got it. We'll bury their asses six feet underneath it."

When he heard this, Scoots reached under the desk and pulled out a lead pipe, a baseball bat, and a shotgun. "Whatta we waitin' for?" he shouted.

"We got to get to Paulie," Dominick shouted back as he and Chooch ran for the door.

Allie stood back, hesitating, watching chaos erupt around him.

Dominick turned and looked back at Allie, hollering, "Let's go. Let's go! Whatta ya waitin' for?"

Allie shouted back, "What I'm thinking is that Tedesco lives six blocks from Bloomfield Avenue. What I'm thinking is that you could give him Superman's X-ray vision, he couldn't even see Bloomfield Avenue, much less know which way that car turned—if there was a car."

Dominick pulled up short, looking dumbfounded. "You sayin' he shot out his own living room window?"

"I'm thinkin' that *stunad* might just start the damned riots all over again if we don't watch our asses. I ain't going down there. You and Chooch go if you wanna play National Guard."

Allie couldn't hear what Dominick muttered under his breath as he and Chooch turned and took off out the door. He hoped the idiots didn't get themselves killed.

~

D own at Tedesco's home, two police cars had parked on the lawn, their red lights flashing a beacon to the neighborhood. More than a hundred people had gathered to see if Paulie was all right. They filled part of the lawn, with the overflow spilling onto the sidewalk. Paulie stood on the top step of the red-brick stairs that fronted the two-family house, Dominick beside him. Chooch was in the crowd below.

"Them *mulignans* think they can scare me. Well, they got another think coming—if they can think at all. They can't scare me. They can't scare you. That would be the biggest mistake of their lives."

The crowd nodded and cheered in agreement.

"Tell you what I think. I think those niggers work for Jackson Anderson with Kiongosi's blessing. I think we still have one opponent in this election, but he's got two heads—and both of them are black. But it don't matter. They are nothing when we stand up to them as real Americans . . . as white Americans. We can match them fist against fist or gun against gun if it comes to that. If it does, so be it. You see that shattered window behind me. They got no guts. They sneaked up out of the darkness and shot at me and my family. They delivered their message, and now we're gonna deliver ours. We di'nt ask for this, but we ain't backin' up. In two weeks, we got our July Fourth fireworks in Schools Stadium. That's our stadium . . . in our ward . . . where our people come because we love our flag and our country. It's still America, so they can come if they want. So we don't start nothing. That's up to them. But if they do . . . well, don't worry. The neighborhood and the stadium will be filled with our people on patrol. No old ladies are gonna get mugged. Nobody is gonna be molested. Nobody is gonna get hurt. If you older people need an escort home, just call the Citizens on Patrol. I know some of youse who are good people think we ought to meet with them and negotiate. Wake up. They had a chance for that and they didn't. The time for that has passed. If they start it, we will finish it—and them."

~

J ackson Anderson sat behind his huge desk at the Broad Street headquarters, facing key members of his staff. A stack of telegrams had piled up on the desk. He held one in his hand as he exulted, "You know, we struck a nerve with that redneck. Does anybody think three black guys in a mystery car shot out his living room window? I'm sure all the glass shards are on the floor of his living room. But let's not waste time on that charade. Look at what I got here. Lena Horne will be there for the rally. So will Ruby Dee and Ossie Davis and, specially in honor of the Central Ward, I give you"—he paused for effect —"James 'Shout It Loud, I'm Black and I'm Proud'. . . Mr. James Brown himself.' That's bound to make every paper in the country."

"With all due respect, boss, without somebody to bring the Italians out, you don't have a chance," his hotshot New York City press agent, Fast Freddy Sternburg, cautioned.

"How about this?" Anderson said, deliberately drawing the drama out. "How about as our free gift to the Italians of the city's North Ward, we proudly present, with respect, Mr. Francis . . . Albert . . . Sinatra—bearing the hope of every Italian American who is tired of this garbage."

Sternburg jumped out of his seat and pumped both fists in the air, yelling, "Home run. Game over. Four black superstars and the great Italian Chairman of the Board. Boss, you just won the war."

"Not yet, but let me explain how we'll do this. You need to understand how this works," he told the staff, "because, yes, we are going to win this election, and as mayor I will need all of you to stick with me, because what comes after that will be the United States Senate. We are in Newark, New Jersey. You got to understand the rules of the game. Here's how we can get Sinatra if we make the right contact. As you know, the current mayor, who happens to be Italian, is on the verge of indictment. He, however, is connected with a major Mafia capo named Richie 'The Boot' Boiardo, who, as a member of the Genovese family, is a major North Jersey player."

"What are you getting at, boss?" Sternburg asked.

"Sinatra's roots go back to Hoboken, New Jersey. His New Jersey Mafia relationships extended beyond Boiardo. They included Genovese underboss Willie Moretti, his first wife's godfather and the man that forced Tommy Dorsey to release him from their contract. Remember, we are presenting Sinatra as our gift for all the Italians in the North Ward. You're all in this room because you are smart. So I hope I don't have to explain any further."

He paused to look each of them in the eye, emphasizing the importance of this.

"One last thing. I meet with the bankers again tomorrow. They will help us pack the house. Our job that night is to produce the biggest epidermal rainbow this city and this state have ever seen. I mean to fill all 3,500 seats with it. Now get going. Give the volunteers what I gave you. Sell it to them. Tell them this is urgent. Remember, we got these people in all shapes and colors, college kids and retirees, men and women. They are the living, walking proof to this city that we are not carpetbaggers, that this isn't racial. It's the triumph of honest government over hustlers and poverty pimps and the kind of people we will make sure will never run this city again. So let's go."

His staff turned to leave, but he had one more thing to handle. "Freddy, please stick around a few minutes. I know you got a lot to do, but we gotta talk. I believe I may have one more surprise that could win us the North Ward before the first ballot is cast."

10

THE OUTSIDERS

Junior held Mickey's hand as they strolled along Coney Island, surrounded by the midway and within easy walking distance to the beach. Mickey wore a white bikini under her navy-blue-and-white-striped coverup. Junior had on dark boxer-type trunks and a red Montclair State T-shirt.

Their dates had fallen into a comfortable pattern. They talked openly of love. They laughed together. They teased each other. They embraced and kissed at the slightest opportunity. Sometimes, they almost forgot themselves at work. They went to drive-in movies in Morris County. They sat in the car at night up at the Eagle Rock Reservation in West Orange like countless lovers before them had always done, marveling at the beauty of the lights from the New York skyline a river away, and lost themselves in each other.

But as always, it never left their minds that they were the outsiders. As precious as all this was to them, reality brought them back to that fact. Every shared moment they stole outside the post office was always somewhere else. Newark was off-limits for their kind of love.

But for now, they enjoyed being lost in the midway crowd.

Junior noticed Mickey's eyes drift to a basketball booth—three shots for a dollar—and stopped.

"You want that stuffed fox terrier? You got it. You think Willis Reed is the only guy who can shoot a jump shot? Watch this."

"Go ahead, Willis. Show me what you got."

His first shot hit the front of the rim. His second hit the backboard and bounced free. The third one spun around the rim and failed to drop.

Neither of them knew that the rims were deliberately made a touch too small to dupe the tourists.

"Hey, Joe Willie Namath," she said, laughing as hard as she could. "Stick to football."

"How do you know about him?"

"Best-looking white football player I ever saw."

They laughed. They wandered down the midway and to the beach. She put down two bath towels she'd brought, and they kicked back, gazing at the ocean.

Junior broke the silence. "Remember when we were on the ferry and looked out at the water and you asked if it could ever carry us far enough away from this?"

She nodded.

"Well, what do you think now?"

"I think"—she stared out at the ocean—"it's time to tell my mother. I'm scared because I don't know what she's going to say. I want to make it through college for her. She gives so much. I want to make it for my little brother, who has so few people to look up to. I'm hoping one day you could be the one to teach him about real life and goals. But in the meantime, I'm gonna make it for her so she doesn't have to be afraid that my father is going to show up and bully her anymore. I'm gonna make it for her and help her and find a place where I'm not afraid to be my own person. I dream, Junior. I used to dream about not being lonely. Now I'm not lonely anymore." She looked directly at him. "Not since the first day I went to work at the post office and met you and began to start falling in love with you." She broke into laughter again. "If you could have seen your face the day we met. *'Excuuuuse* me. I forgot I'm supposed to apologize for the past four hundred years.'"

"Baby, you were so cute."

"Cute? Puppies are cute. I was pissed off."

"I know, I know. Come on, you were trying to hit on me, and you know it. Big football star . . . big class president." He knew those things hadn't impressed her in high school, but he couldn't resist teasing.

She laughed again, but she looked at him with tenderness. "Well, you are, you know. Or at least you were at Barringer. I don't know what you are at Montclair State. I don't even know why you are there. I know more about you and football than you think. My cousin told me all about you."

"Your cousin?"

"Yeah, he played football with you at Barringer. Chuck Washington."

"Oh, sure! Left guard. Man, we ran this wide-receiver reverse —he had the broadest, safest ass a ball carrier could hide behind. A good player and a good guy. How's he doing?"

"Fine. He's at Grambling playing football. He's home for the summer. He told me all about you."

"And you told him all about me?"

"Of course. Ever since we were twelve, he's been my ace boon coon."

"Your what?"

"Sorry. Language difference. In my neighborhood it means your closest friend. When I was scared of what my father was doing to my mother, I would sneak over to his house and his mom would feed me. I'd trust him with anything, and he would trust me the same way."

"Well, does that make me your new ace boon coon?"

"Oh, no. Not even close. I have much better and more passionate plans for you. There's something you don't know about Chuck. Things being what they were at Barringer, he's probably the black kid who admired you the most, but he was afraid to show it. He really likes you. He told me everything he knew about you except for one thing. Why didn't you take the scholarship to Northwestern? He still doesn't understand why you didn't go."

"I don't know. Maybe I was afraid I would get homesick or maybe fall on my ass against all those Big Ten hotshots. It was hard for me. You wanna know something? I'm twenty years old and I never been away from home. Not even Boy Scout camp. What did I need the Boy Scouts for? I was a Bomber."

"You were a what?" she asked in alarm.

"No, it's not like it sounds." He laughed at the shock on her face. "It was a club—the Newark Bombers. We were kids. We played softball in the park, and that's what we called ourselves. But we all lived in the same neighborhood. We did just about everything together from then on. Allie, he was a Bomber and he was at Barringer. He goes to Montclair State with me now. He's my best friend."

"Best friend? You never mentioned him."

"Yeah, well, come to think of it, he's my own ace boon coon, the only one I told about us. I trust him the way you trust Chuck Washington. When we got to high school, we all got blue jackets with white letters on the back saying Newark Bombers. Most of the Bombers are gone. Some went to Vietnam and never came back. Some just moved away. One guy your cousin and I played football with is in state prison. Only four of us are left in the neighborhood. But people change. Really, Allie and I don't have much in common with the other two. I guess after fourteen years the Bombers are dead."

"Well, you bullied me into putting Lois on the phone, so I want some payback. I want to meet your best friend, and soon."

"You will, and you'll really like him. But getting back to the Bombers, we weren't ever a gang or anything like one. Jesus, a gang? My old man would have ganged me, all right."

"What's he like, your father? You never talk about him."

"I should. My father, he's like nobody else in the world. He's good. He's tough. Boy, can he be. You know why I don't smoke?"

"Football, I guess."

"No, this was long before football. I was about twelve years old, and one day he caught me in the bathroom. I locked the door, you know, which was against his rules. I guess he and my mom thought I was doing something else in there." They both laughed and Junior continued.

"He bangs on the door and he hollers, 'Junior, you come out of there right now!' And when my old man yells like that, you jump. So I unlock the door after I duck the cigarette in the toilet bowl, but I didn't have time to flush. He sees it and says, 'Well, if you're that big, you need to try a real man's smoke,' and he sits me down in the kitchen and puts an Italian DiNobili stogie in my mouth and lights it. 'Take a big draw,' he says. 'Inhale and hold it.' So now I think I'm really big stuff. I keep inhaling and he keeps smiling, and after four more puffs I get dizzy and start to vomit."

Mickey laughed so hard, tears leaked from her eyes.

"You think that's funny? You'll love this. I'm about to fall on the floor and my father says, 'Enough. You will remember. But in case you don't . . .' *Whammo!* He slaps me. I never forgot that. And I don't smoke."

"I wish my brothers had a dad like that."

"My old man, he saw every game I ever played from Pop Warner PeeWees on up and he never missed a report card, although there were times I wish he had. I don't know how he knew. He just knew. It was like he was getting vibrations from my homeroom. My old man thinks this is the greatest country in the world. He thinks that my mother is the most beautiful woman God ever created. When I graduated from Barringer, he cried like a baby when I walked across the stage to get my diploma. He keeps a scrapbook with every newspaper clipping ever written about me. But you know something, he never told me. I found it by accident."

"What did he say when you told him?"

"I didn't. I felt it was his private thing. I figured it was very personal to him."

"He must love you very much."

"I never thought about him that way. You don't think of love with my father. You just think of him as, well, you think of his being there when you need him."

"It's the same thing as love, only needed even more. I know. I never had a father. Did he ever say anything to you about Northwestern?"

"Hey, enough about Northwestern. You're the second person this week who got on me about that. You sure you never met Allie? He's all over me about how I blew my big chance. What's so different about what I'm doing now? The textbooks they use at Montclair are the same ones they use at Northwestern. The football fields are exactly the same length—one hundred yards."

"Baby, it's not important that you didn't go to Northwestern. What is important is that you know why you didn't go to Northwestern."

"Hey, look, I like what I'm doing. I'm gonna play the best football I can and then I'm gonna graduate. I'm gonna teach and coach. If one day I could get any job I want, then I'd want to coach Barringer and be a vice principal. But none of this . . . I mean absolutely none of this . . . would matter to me if we weren't there together."

She took his face in her hands and kissed him—long and hard, their bodies melting into each other. When they pulled way he said softly, "Miss Washington, you are a very intelligent woman, even though at times you make it awfully hard to follow what you mean. Although with a body like yours I would follow you anywhere. Now, speaking of expectations, what do you expect of me?"

"Right now I expect you to take on a mission of mercy for me."

"And that is . . ."

"Why don't you put some suntan lotion on my back so I don't catch fire in this sun?" She rolled over on her stomach.

Junior frowned. "Come on. Don't make me into an idiot in front of all these people."

"Why?"

"Well, suntan oil? I mean, you are black, and you don't—"

"Come here, dummy." She propped herself up on one elbow and laughed.

"What's so funny?"

"You. What do you think I'm made of? Chocolate ice cream? You told me yourself that half your family is darker than I am. Junior, touch me." She spilled some of the oil on his hands, then placed them on her shoulders. "See, I'm made out of skin. Now hold me and tell me something."

He left his hands resting on her shoulders. They looked at each other for a very long time and then he said, "I think I love you."

"Come on, boy, let's go eat. I think you've had too much sun for one day. So have I. Because I'm starting to feel I love you too."

THE NIGHT THE STARS FELL

J unior and his family sat at the supper table. His mom stood directly behind his dad, laughing and waving frantically to her children, who got the hint and waited in anticipation. She walked around to her husband's side, put a hand on his shoulder, and said, "You know, Gerry, I stopped by the rectory at St. Lucy's today for a rosary-society meeting." She turned her head so that only the children could see her wink at them. "And I bumped into Father Giuseppe."

"Imagine that. So you ran into a parish priest at church. Wow, Maria, you sure can tell a story."

Junior and his sister laughed openly at their parents' teasing.

"Well, I know this. Father said that with the Fourth of July pageant coming up right after the holiday and the festival committee still in the planning stage, he said maybe you ought to think about showing up at church now and then."

"So let me get this straight. This priest who has been here fifteen years and whose English vocabulary doesn't go much beyond 'Atsa very nice,' he told you all those thoughts in one understandable sentence?"

All of them laughed again. Then she said, "Gerard Friscella, just you wait! God will punish you. If you weren't so good-looking I would do it myself."

After the laughter finally subsided, Angie took advantage of the moment. "Daddy, can I go to the fireworks tomorrow night at the stadium?"

"With who?"

"Just some kids."

"They have names, I would think."

"Sure. You know, Rose and Geneva and, well, you know."

"So tell me. Who is this Mr. You Know?"

"Well. Uh, Tony."

"And who is Mr. Uh Tony?"

"Come on, Daddy. He's just a guy in my algebra class."

"Considering your grades, it's nice to know you drop into algebra class now and then." Then he smiled, clearly enjoying her discomfort, and added, "You know, I think it would be very nice if your brother went along and spent some time with you."

Junior sat up straight. He had been working on a different plan and had just been thinking how perfect it would be if Angie went her own way. Watching her screw around with her friends was not his idea of a great night. "I sorta have something else to do."

Maria jumped in. "Gerry, let her go. It's just a couple of blocks and she'll come straight home. Won't you, Angie? Leave Junior alone. He works hard. He's entitled to more private time."

"Okay. But Tony comes upstairs to pick you up like a human being and I see what he's like first."

Angie squealed with delight, jumped up, and ran to kiss her father, who made a show out of wiping her kisses away but couldn't completely hide the smile they brought. He turned to Junior to clarify what he had just agreed on.

"Junior, it will be the Fourth of July and we have a lot of family coming here. All I ask of you is to just stay for the cookout. After that, well, I'll be the one stuck with your mother's aunts, uncles, sisters, brothers, cousins, and Lord only knows who else. Take the car if you need it." He winked. "I won't be able to use it anyway."

"Thanks, Dad. I really need it."

Pleased everything had turned out perfectly for his plans, he turned to Angie. "Come on, squirt. Let's take a walk. I owe you one because he let me off the hook. You just earned an Italian lemon ice at Ting-a-Ling's."

Ting-a-Ling's stood guard near the entrance to Branch Brook Park, and along with Dickie Dee's and Jimmy Buff's formed a North Ward institutional troika that dominated the heavily Italian North Ward. The other two places offered better hot dogs, but Ting-a-Ling's stood as the unchallenged king of lemon Italian ice, a kind of North Ward national dish.

As they waited for a break in traffic to cross the Avenue, they heard the ferocious roar of a siren. Barreling down the street came a red, white, and blue Citizens on Patrol car. Dominick Pizzoli hit the brakes so hard, the car shuddered as it jolted to a stop right in front of them.

"Hey, Junior, what's happening, man?"

Junior was not happy to see him. "Nothing much."

"I stopped by your house, but your old man wasn't too happy to see me. He said you and the kid went for dessert." Dominick's gaze took notice of Angie, who appeared very impressed with both the car and the C.O.P. armband he wore on the arm he leaned against the open window. "Hey, Angie, did I say 'kid'? What happened? Who is this beautiful mystery woman who has suddenly appeared at my old buddy's side?"

When Angie giggled and seemed ready to swoon, Junior looked daggers at Dominick. "Dominick, that's my sister you're talking about, remember. My *fifteen-year-old* . . . kid . . . sister."

"Hey, Junior. Come on. It's me. Dominick. What do you think I am?"

"I might just be beginning to find out. You catch any gunmen tonight?"

"Hey, look, you can say what you want about Paulie and the

C.O. Patrol, but you don't see any trouble on the Avenue these days. Paulie has got this street snowy-white, and we're gonna keep it that way."

"Yeah, well, if that makes you happy, that's swell. But we gotta go now. See you later." Junior steered his sister away.

Dominick hollered after them, "You gonna bowl Friday night? You don't come over to the alley much these days. What's keeping you so busy?"

"Life, Dominick, life. I gotta go."

"Oh, I almost forgot to ax you. You know Chooch just joined the Citizen Council. Paulie says in a war like this you're either on our side or against us. I told him you would never be against us. We really need leaders like you. Whaddya say, man?"

"I said I gotta go, Dominick. I'll see you around."

∿

Junior kept looking at his watch. He had relieved his father at the grill, tended the hot charcoal, and joked with the bunch of excited children about how they wanted their burgers or their hot dogs cooked, telling the youngest among them that they had to pay for their food with a hug. The Fourth of July cookout—and the invasion of those "uncle, aunts, and cousins by the dozens" that Gerard Sr. had forecast—was well underway.

Junior worked hard at presenting a busy and involved facade, but all the time he was thinking about Mickey. After he and Angie returned from Ting-a-Ling's, he had put the Yankee game on the living room TV and hung around a respectful amount of time before he hollered in to the kitchen to tell his mom and dad he was going to put gas in the car for his evening plans.

Once on the Avenue he turned near the stadium, nosed the car next to the curb, hustled into the telephone booth that fronted the building, and dialed her number. "Yeah?" a belligerent voice answered the line.

"May I speak with Miss . . . Michaeletta. Uh, yes, I believe that's the name. Michaeletta Washington?"

"Who is this?'

"Uh, this is Mr. Wisnewski. I'm her supervisor at the post office, and it's important I talk to her about a sudden schedule change."

"She ain't your slave. Why didn't you tell her at work yesterday? I'll see if she wants to speak to you."

Junior heard what had to be deliberate banging of the receiver. Twice. In the background, a radio played Aretha Franklin's "Chain of Love," and then he heard Mickey say, "My boss?" To which Charles replied, "You the only one here in this house at this moment who work for a honky. Yeah, you. What the hell he callin' you at home for?" There was an unintelligible exchange of voices, and then Mickey was on the phone.

"It's me," Junior said.

"Yes, I know that." Clearly, Charles was standing next to her trying to listen in, and she was trying to maintain as much professional cool as possible.

"I got a surprise for you. Tomorrow night, we are going to watch the fireworks together from Schools Stadium."

"Well, I'm afraid that would be impossible," she said, staying as detached as she could for Charles' benefit.

The fireworks each Fourth of July at Schools Stadium were the highlight of the North Ward summer—one of the rare events that attracted people from all wards to watch. Traditionally the event crowd was roughly ninety percent white. The tension in the city had everyone on edge. Nobody knew what to expect.

"I didn't say *in* Schools Stadium. I said *from* Schools Stadium. You'll see. It will be great."

"Well, I don't know."

"Mickey, trust me. We will be fine, and I can't wait. The post office lobby at seven o'clock."

After a moment he heard her reluctantly respond. "I guess I don't have any choice." She sighed. "The night shift and over-time. Thanks for being considerate. If it's that kind of emergency, I'll have to fill in for her. Thank you for calling and tell her I hope things work out for her. She's in my prayers."

~

The cookout at the Friscella house was a Fourth of July tradition. For Gerard Sr., despite all his feigned annoy-ance, there was genuine relief that this annual party returned them all to less-tense times. Forgotten for this one night would be the worry about job security in the aftermath of the riot/re-bellion. Forgotten was the spectacle of Paulie's histrionics and the repeated sound of the pointless sirens on the Citizen Patrol cars. Forgotten was the constant war of rhetoric between the North and Central wards. Even forgotten was the simmering tensions in the post-riot/rebellion world that seemed to be gaining momentum.

But here, surrounded by Maria's aunts, uncles, and cousins by the dozens, he was again part of something that would remain the very oxygen and heartbeat of the Avenue until decades later, when the ward population turned heavily Puerto Rican. The ritual had its roots in the patriotism and gratitude of those early arrivals, starting back in the late 1800s.

There was a time when the wine was a genuine homegrown product straight from Grandpa's cellar or bathtub, the venue depending on whether it was pre- or post-Prohibition years. But little else had changed. At his dad's request, Junior had draped the family's American flag over the front porch railing. Earlier that morning, some of the older guests had marched in the local July 4th parade. Some of the teenage kids had marched with them as members of the local American Legion drum-and-bugle corps.

Over at the grill, where Senior had relieved his son, the elder

99

Friscella was involved in an intense conversation with a rising young local politician named Les Scarcella, a former school-teacher and union organizer, who had founded a service organization named the St. Gerard Self-Help and Improvement Association.

"Les, I can't seem to come to a logical viewpoint on this us-versus-them war between the wards. I don't like Paulie, and from what you've publicly said I know you don't either. And it isn't that Kiongosi is black as much as it seems to me he is exactly like Paulie. Either one wins, and me or my family loses."

"And what about Jackson Anderson?"

"Who the hell knows him?"

"Gerry, I didn't come here to your party to convert people to my way of thinking. I'm here because we are friends since high school who know why we celebrate Independence Day and haven't forgotten that we also know how to have one hell of a good time. But I'll tell you this. Ask yourself why everyone around here is so out of joint about the Avenue and this big black invasion that nobody has ever even seen. I'm not an advocate of finger-pointing, but I am an advocate of self-discovery. Ask yourself why Paulie even exists. Ask yourself what the hell makes everyone over here so damn afraid. For me, it's not a hard thing to figure. We have to be honest with ourselves. What we are afraid of is the fact that for so many years we treated these people just like total shit. And we know if positions were reversed, we would be guilty of what we're now afraid they will be. I think this is less about race than guilt and trust. I think a good part of this ward might just vote for the right black man out of relief if he's the one who proves he is capable of ending all this bullshit."

"I ain't arguing," Senior said. "I'm just trying to look for a solution. It's something all of us should be doing. I'm glad we had this talk. Now answer the most important question of all for me. How do you want your burger?"

"Like a real man, Gerry. Like a real man. Just stab it a few times until the legs stop moving."

~

By twilight, crowds had gathered and were walking up and down Bloomfield Avenue headed for Schools Stadium and the fireworks. Schools Stadium, a huge, ornate ballpark, mimicked the original plans for both Harvard Stadium and Chicago's Soldier Field. Ornate carved gargoyles sat atop its walls. If they could speak, they would trumpet to the world that this place was built for history.

It was erected in 1925, Newark had an NFL team there, and the New York Giants once came to town because the Newark Tornados could provide a bigger crowd than their scheduled game at the Polo Grounds. This was where the National Women's Olympic trials were held, where a local hero named Eulace Peacock stunned the track-and-field world by beating the great Olympic champion Jesse Owen, and where on hot summer nights the prestigious New Jersey Symphony Orchestra filled the air with music from a bandshell at the south end of the horseshoe. It was here where perhaps as many as 20,000 people often sat on the grass and heard their first opera.

And this was where, for decades, color, ethnicity, and economics played no role on the Fourth of July. Every group came to the North Ward to watch the best fireworks show in the state.

They came, heavily Italian but still a diverse crowd. It was a brutally hot Jersey night, when only the seekers of fireworks spectaculars and king-size bloodthirsty Jersey mosquitos ventured out after dark. Families heading for the stadium choked the Avenue.

Junior drove his father's car past the pedestrian traffic. It was slow going because the walkers crowded the crossings, often ignoring the traffic lights. Occasionally someone recognized Junior, and they exchanged waves.

He wore a red-and-white Montclair State Football T-shirt. The radio played, but instead of the Beatles it was Stevie Wonder singing "Uptight (Everything's Alright)." Junior relaxed. By the time he pulled up to the post office and she ran toward him, he felt absolutely euphoric.

When she climbed in the car, they exchanged a look, long, intense, and meaningful. "Crazy White Knight, you gonna get us killed."

"Yeah, but what a great way to go."

"Junior, what got into you calling me like that? You know my brother is crazy. Don't you ever stop to think before you act? How could you do something like that?"

"I couldn't help it, Mickey. I just had to hear your voice. We have so many plans to make. Maybe we could start by both of us living on campus at Montclair State this fall and—"

"Junior, let's not get ahead of ourselves." She held up a hand, palm raised. "One step at a time. What's all this stuff about fireworks? You plan to rent a helicopter?"

"No, but we'll see them."

"You planning our funerals, too?"

"You'll see. Right now just be cool and sit there. You are so beautiful. The hell with the fireworks. All I want to do is look at you."

"Boy, you are crazy. Do you hear me? You are insane. But keep the compliments coming."

The sun had set. Junior drove cautiously up Bloomfield Avenue and turned left on Lake Street, perhaps six blocks before the stadium, floodlit by its overhead lights in the distance. The darkness, punctuated only by the lights of occasional passing cars, was almost surreal, the night beautiful. He parked under a tree, and they meandered toward the lake, holding hands.

This part of the park was as deserted as Junior knew it would be. They stared at the view. The night lights from the boathouse reflected tiny ripples on the water. Both were reminded of their Staten Island Ferry moment.

"Looks like the same water," Mickey said, "but somebody went and stole our moon." He put his arm around her, pulling her close. Then she looked up at him and said what they both knew was coming. "Junior, we can't just drift along anymore. I need to tell my mother and you need to tell your parents. Maybe we need to tell them together. I don't know. But I do know the real truth, which is that we love each other and if necessary the rest of the world can go to hell if they don't like it. But not our parents, Junior. Not our parents. We deserve each other, but they don't deserve to be deceived. Your parents and my mother, they struggled for us all their lives. They deserve the right to always be a part of us together if they decide that's what they want. So what do we do? I refuse to even think about losing you. This is our life, and it belongs to us and nobody is going to take that from us. But we don't have the right to shut them out. It will be hard for them, but they still love us. We have to give them that chance."

Junior took both her hands and turned her slightly so they were facing each other. "I always knew you were smarter than I am. It's one of the reasons I love you so much. Of course it doesn't hurt that you are beautiful, caring, understanding, and all the things I need so much. So before I kiss you for about two hours and start our own fireworks, let me tell you that what you just said is what we have to do. What we absolutely will do." He gathered her in his arms, clutching her fiercely, and kissed her harder and more passionately than ever before.

On the horizon, the first cherry bomb burst into streaks of soaring fire. She broke away from him, but tenderly, and reached for his hand. Puzzled, he took it and followed where she led him, away from the lake.

"We can see better from up there," she whispered. He heard a kind of loving defiance in her voice. She gestured to a small rise in the landscape further away. As they climbed the hill together, he wondered where this was leading.

The tempo of the fireworks increased. She led him to a small thicket of little trees and bushes, and gently pulled him inside the narrow, protective space. They sat at first and then lay side by side.

She rolled toward him and snaked an arm around his neck, pulling him toward her, and placed his hands on her breasts. They remained like that, pressed close together.

His heart thumped wildly. He knew what she was offering. "Are you sure?"

"I'm sure."

He reached for the buttons on the front of her blue sleeveless blouse, opened the first two, and paused to look at her.

She put her index finger to his lips and said softly, "Not a word. Not one syllable. I'm sure."

The fire in her eyes kindled the embers that had been simmering for her all summer. He removed her blouse and her bra and lowered his head to her now-naked breasts. She shifted her weight beneath him, raised her butt from the ground, and frantically yanked her skirt and then her panties down her legs and off. She sighed and pulled him closer.

"Junior, it's our time. We have all the time in the world. Our place, here and now, and wherever we go. From now on. So love me. Please love me."

Junior slid his tongue from her nipple, down the length of her body, to her belly. The humid night added to the sweat slicking his body. The taste of her, both sweet and salty at once, sent shivers down his spine, heightening every sense at once. He wasn't a virgin, and she'd confided she wasn't either, but suddenly he felt as though they were. Every emotion, every sensation seemed brand-new and ripped him apart in ways he'd never experienced before.

His tongue found a home just below her navel. She pulled his head down as though she wanted to meld with him completely, to absorb every molecule of him deep inside her. He moved lower, found her damp, dark pubic hair, and teased her mercilessly before searching for her trigger button. He tasted a new essence of her, ripe and distinct yet different than anything he had tasted before, and moaned. She writhed beneath him, setting a furious pace when his tongue hit the right spot. Unintelligible sounds erupted from her, guttural, but with a meaning that rocked the both of them to their very core. At the end, their murmured pleasure merged into a sensual duet.

They lay still. She nuzzled his neck and said, "Your turn."

He rolled onto her, eager to join fully, to bring them together as one. She tried but failed to stifle a primal scream when he sunk inside her. He gave one fleeting thought of thanks that the park was completely deserted and that the sound, the moment belonged to them alone.

They settled into a rhythm. Their syncopated breathing morphed into the beat of a passionate metronome, and right in time with it, as their sensual fire reached its climax, she cried out a declaration for both of them. "Yes. Yes! Now!"

Up the Avenue, the fireworks burst into the stunning finale. The sound of "The Stars and Stripes Forever" mingled with the last and loudest of explosions.

The night sky above the empty park ablaze in color, she buttoned her blouse and straightened her skirt while he fastened his pants. He hooked an arm around her and pulled her close, gazing at the multicolored sky of red, white, and blue.

"For us," she said.

"For us," he echoed.

Holding her hand, he walked her down the hill and to the car.

12

A MARRIAGE OF CONVENIENCE

Les Scarcella had a knack for reading people. As a union organizer he was always a jump ahead of the pack. He instinctively knew who he needed, who he had to con, who he had to threaten, and who he had to cajole. As the founder of the St. Gerard Self-Help and Improvement Association, he studied all three candidates in the upcoming election. Pundits and politicians alike had conceded the North Ward vote as in the bag for homegrown Paulie Tedesco.

To Scarcella, a born skeptic, it wasn't necessarily so. Ever since the July 4th cookout at the Friscella home, he had been thinking hard about the elder Friscella's reactions when discussing the election that day. What got him thinking most was Friscella's statement that, yes, he could vote for anyone— black or white—if that candidate could act as the adult in the room and end the racial tension that was tearing the city apart.

A single question had haunted Scarcella ever since: How many Gerard Friscella Seniors are there in the North Ward?

Les Scarcella dreamed that his center could provide desperately needed services for the people in the North Ward. He believed the pathway to that rested not in charity or religion but in acquiring political power. He told a friend, "People don't believe that people with political power can do the right thing. But what if they could?" The current mayor was in deep trouble and probably headed for prison. If Scarcella could be instrumental in electing the new mayor, the new mayor would hardly forget it.

For Scarcella, that thought walked a slippery tightrope between desire and obsession. He found himself constantly pondering how best to substitute the deed for the wish. He finally reached a conclusion. Given the ethnic makeup of the North Ward, there was only one group that could make it happen. How much would he have to give up to make a deal with them? And what was his best approach?

Scarcella and his staff were assembled for their morning meeting at the St. Gerard Self-Help and Improvement Association. He rose from his commanding seat behind his desk and began to pace the floor.

The staff waited. They were used to the fact that whatever major decision he made, no matter what the subject, would be preceded by a lengthy monologue. Today the subject was the upcoming election. Over the past few months, he had yet to make clear what position they would take. Their political-action duties were frozen until they got the word.

"What do you hear on the street, Tony?" he asked his associate director and right-hand man.

"Hard to say. The ward seems to be behind Paulie, but you never know how many blacks from other wards will vote. I was in the Silhouette the other night, and I had a strange feeling just listening to the he-said-/she-said gossip. They hated Kiongosi. They seemed committed to vote for Paulie. But there was a kind of undercurrent that they wanted to know if this guy Anderson could relieve the tension and not interfere with our people while doing it."

Scarcella nodded and turned toward his PR director. "Do you have a feel for how the editorial board at the *Star-Ledger* might react? Who do they favor? Will they take a side, or issue no endorsement at all? Do they speculate, or are they even interested in where we stand?" He pointed a finger and raised his voice. "Don't guess. If you don't know, say so."

"Too soon to tell. I'm having lunch with their politics guy. He's not on the editorial board, but he always has a feel for what it will do."

"Good. Bring him here to our cafeteria for lunch. I want to talk to him." He moved back behind his desk and sat down. His gaze swept the room and the waiting faces. Then he spoke. "'When neither their property nor their honor is threatened, the majority of men live content.'"

The staff exchanged glances, as if they had no idea whether he was talking to them or to some spirit guide, or just babbling.

He repeated the statement. "'When neither their property nor their honor is threatened, the majority of men live content.' You don't get it? Shame on you. A fellow named Niccolo Machiavelli said that about 450 years ago. But it's as good as gold today. Look at the election. Status quo and Paulie wins. What does that mean to us? Not good, because we are fighting for the same constituency. Kiongosi wins, even worse. Jackson Anderson we don't know. But think about Machiavelli and when he says, 'Men live content.' But what if they are led to believe their property and their honor *are* threatened? That's our job. Without Paulie or Kiongosi and with Jackson Anderson, I think our path to that constituency and thus to political power is clear. I'll find a way. You back it."

Heads nodded.

He turned to his PR guy. "J.R., start by writing up a list of talking points for anybody we send out."

"Yes, sir!"

He addressed his chief of staff. "Dante, I want you to spend more time in the Italian clubs, see what the old guys talk about at the bocce courts. Spend some time and a little money—I'll voucher it—and do a lot of listening. When the time comes, we'll make sure that they do feel their property and their honor is threatened. We'll just change their idea about where the threat comes from. All of you look at me and don't forget this. This could be the biggest and most important battle we will ever fight. Now, go do it."

His staff murmured in agreement and headed out the door.

And I'll figure out how to reach someone who can really help us in this endeavor.

~

J ackson Anderson's team rented a speaker truck and repeatedly circled the Kiongosi campaign headquarters, intent on installing concern, if not outright panic. The message blared loud and clear, and the music used to precede each pronouncement was Aretha Franklin's "Respect" with its signature addition of the "R-E-S-P-E-C-T" chorus and the backup singers' refrain of "Sock it to me, sock it to me, sock it to me, sock it to me!"

Anderson's recorded voice declared to everyone in hearing range, "For too long that's what we didn't get. But that's over now. We can make a statement for all the country to see. My name is Jackson Anderson, and I'm running for mayor of the city of Newark. My platform is simple. Just R-E-S-P-E-C-T. Just as we have it for ourselves and our people, we will give it to others and get it back in return. Come to the Mosque Theater on August twenty-first and hear it straight from Aretha and Lena Horne and James Brown. Let's sock it to the doubters. R-E-S-P-E-C-T."

Then Aretha's voice took over again, and the volume increased to the point where it resounded up and down Broad Street, loud enough to penetrate the staff meeting Kiongosi was holding in the back room of his headquarters.

"Goddamn it," he hollered. His fists pounded the wooden desk until they hurt. "What the fuck is he up to? Aretha, my ass. I'll Aretha him. He's a fraud. He's in Paulie's pocket. He's trying to split the black vote so that Paulie wins the damn thing. Well, that's not gonna happen. *You!*" he thundered at his top aide. "You get someone down to City Hall and find out if he has a permit to do this. If he doesn't, stop him. If he does, stop him! I don't care who you bribe or who our muscle has to silence, I want him finished here and now. We let him split the black vote, we don't deserve to win. I want the word on the street that this Uncle Tom is selling us out. Give the *Star-Ledger* that story. Quote me. Check the budget. I want this message to reach every black radio station in the New Jersey and New York area."

He picked up a coffee cup from the desk and hurled it at the wall. It shattered and sent shards flying everywhere. The silence that followed was so deep he could still hear the echo of Aretha's voice bouncing off his own Broad Street facade.

~

C hooch double-parked the lavender Studebaker on Bloomfield Avenue, leaped out, and raced into Paulie's headquarters. He was yelling before he cleared the front door. "That overeducated nigger has gone crazy. He's got a sound truck and he's harassing Kiongosi. People are standing two or three deep in front of Kiongosi's headquarters and they are laughing at him. What the hell is happening here?"

Paulie leaned against the back wall and laughed and laughed. "You know what this educated nigger is doing without even knowing it? He's splitting the black vote into sections. He might have those degrees, but the dumbass is winning this election for us. He'll fill the Mosque, all right. He'll fill it with jungle bunnies and not a single white face. We'll ring every doorbell in the North Ward and expose him as a carpetbagger. We'll push hard. Ask 'em if they want either this uppity Princeton snob or this Afrocentric jerk to be their next mayor. Ask them if they are willing to surrender a piece of the Avenue to appease these guys. Push it hard. Hit the social clubs. Spread the word at the Silhouette and the Cabaret. Buy 'em drinks, tell 'em we should cheer the niggers on and let them bust each other's balls because we . . . I said *we* . . . have all the votes we need if they can't and don't unite." Paulie rubbed his hands together. "I think we just won the election three months early. It's never too soon to work on my acceptance speech."

~

O ver at the Jackson Anderson headquarters, Fast Freddy Sternburg had been deputized to set phase two of the master plan in motion. He was writing a press release for the New Jersey and New York radio stations and for the *Star-Ledger.* He quoted his boss as attacking what he called the betrayal of the black community by Kiongosi.

"I don't get the sound-truck deal," he had told his boss earlier in the day. "Seems like you may be splitting the black vote. And we can't afford to do that."

Anderson had smiled, looked at him for a second, and said, "Psychology 101. The madder he gets, the quicker he will do something spectacularly stupid, and all those black votes will fall right in our lap. And I mean *all* the black votes. Make sure we hit him hard in your press release. Let's ask the question. Who is the real Uncle Tom?"

"Yeah. That'll drive him bonkers. And you might check out that karate school of his. Find something wrong or illegal going on there. If you can't find it, then infer it. Find out where he was during the riot. Yeah, that could lead to something. Let's find out how brave he really was. I want to see that plastered all over the front page of the *Star-Ledger.*"

"What about Sinatra?"

"Not a done deal yet. I'm gonna need a little help. But nothing you can do will get it done. I just got to have the right contact. I'll find a way to take care of it. You go out and get me Kiongosi's head on a platter."

"Not only will I do it, I'll serve it to you with an apple in his mouth."

"That's what I want to hear."

Sternburg stared at the blank paper in his typewriter for a moment. "How about this? 'Man of the people or user of the people?' Jackson Anderson asked reporters at his daily press conference at his headquarters yesterday. 'You have the power,' he continued. 'Go ask him why he won't debate me. He can label me an Uncle Tom all he wants. But let him come out of the shadows and prove it.'"

"Perfect! Keep it up! See you later. I've got a meeting with a banker over at First Fidelity." Anderson headed out the door. "If we get Francis Albert Sinatra, Bwana Kiongosi, you are yesterday's history."

~

Les Scarcella sat with his wife at a table in Don's 21, Newark's most famous Italian restaurant. He had come on this Saturday night knowing it would be the biggest night of the year at Don's 21, because Vic Damone would perform. The place was sold out. Don himself moved around the room, shaking hands, kissing housewives on the cheek, counting the house— not in that order.

Les watched Don while sipping chianti. The portly restaurant owner, genial without being patronizing, with a ready smile and black curly hair, could best be described as Southern Italian with his complexion. He was as close as 1968 Newark came to producing a Sherman Billingsley-type Manhattan Stork Club owner. On any Saturday night, even without entertainment, the room could feature the mayor, two or three congressmen, retired New York Yankees Phil Rizzuto and Yogi Berra, an active Met or Yankee, and a *Star-Ledger* gossip columnist.

Even in 1968, this was a Newark venue where race meant absolutely nothing.

Les was not surprised to see Richie "The Boot" Boiardo was at the head of the long table reserved for him, his family, and his retinue. In fact, Scarcella had counted on Boiardo coming to see Damone. Les knew he was stretching his neck across the chopping block, but if this worked, it would be worth the risk.

When Don reached Boiardo's table, Boiardo rose and embraced him so that their whispered conversation could not be overheard. Both men laughed louder than necessary. As they shook hands, Les knew Don was passing the note secreted in his hand without drawing attention.

When Boiardo glanced his way, Les gave a barely perceptible nod of his head and lifted his glass of chianti in a modest toast. Boiardo nodded back and looked away.

There was no spontaneous laughter at the table — the only levity was triggered when the Boot laughed. He was a short, squat man, with a round face and black hair. Unlike in his early days with the Mob, he was somewhat overweight. When he did laugh, his sports jacket opened wider, revealing a $10,000 diamond-studded belt.

So far, so good, Les thought. Five minutes later, he whispered to his wife that he needed to visit the men's room and left the table, noticing the Boot rise from his seat as well.

A few minutes later, as Les stood at the sink washing his hands, the restroom door opened, and one of Boiardo's largest men peered in and scanned around, before beckoning to his boss. The Boot entered, flanked by two of his entourage.

"You have interrupted my meal," the Boot said. "I want to finish it and hear Vic sing. I am here out of respect for the owner of this place, who is a friend of mine. You got five minutes and you are on the clock starting now. Whaddya want?"

"It's a matter that could be a favor to both of us."

"I doubt there is anything you can do for me right now."

"I promise you, I have a thought that could be very helpful." Les watched Boiardo's face closely. He could tell he had intrigued the man.

"Monday," the Boot said. "I am sure you don't want people to see me walking into your place, and I'd rather not have you in mine. Someone will call you promptly at eight thirty Monday morning. You will be told then where we can meet to discuss your offer. Now I have to piss. I do not like to piss in front of a crowd."

Les immediately gave a deep nod of his head. "Thank you, Mr. Boiardo."

~

Monday it rained, which suited Les just fine. If he was instructed to travel to meet the Boot, a large umbrella and rain gear properly handled could go a long way to disguise his identity when people weren't looking too closely.

At eight thirty, he received a telephone call, right on schedule. "The meeting is on for twelve thirty at the Vittorio Castle." The line went dead before he could respond.

Exactly at noon, Les drove up to the intersection of Summer and Eighth Avenue. In front of him loomed the towers and the Flemish brickwork of the castle Richie Boiardo built, an elaborate turret above the front entrance. The banquet hall inside the dining room could seat a few hundred people. Multicolored frescoes, gilded sconces, and mirrors adorned the walls, and gold-leaf chandeliers hung from a twenty-foot ceiling.

This was a joint frequented almost entirely by members of the Genovese crime family, the dominant crime family, and Les knew it, knew he was playing with fire. Richie "The Boot" Boiardo—so named because in his personal "enforcement" days, whether he used a gun or a knife or a crowbar, a ferocious kick to the head always put his signature on the episode—was its unchallenged godfather.

It was here that Boiardo entertained other Mafia pals, politicians, and his good friend Joe DiMaggio, to whom all of the North Ward continually paid homage. A non-uniformed gatekeeper took Les' car keys and parked the vehicle. Inside, another "assistant" took his umbrella and rain gear and frisked him in what seemed one singular motion.

The dining room was closed, the tables empty except for a booth in the back where the Boot sat alone, a half-empty espresso cup in front of him. The Boot rose, walked toward him, and said, "*Buon pomeriggio. Benvenuto nel mio ristorante.*"

Les shook his hand. "*Grazie per avermi invitato.*"

The Boot rubbed his hands together and said, "It's good to know you respect the old language. Now we talk in English. So what is this mutual favor you proposed the other night?"

"I will not waste your time. It's about the election. Do you plan to support any of the three candidates?"

"I do not answer questions like that. Once when I was a ward heeler, I needed everybody's vote. I no longer need such things. But since you brought it up, who do you support?"

"Nobody—unless you do."

"Then why this so-called proposal? But before you tell me, sit down and drink a glass with me and try the food. My menu is the best in all of Newark's Little Italy." He beckoned to the waiter, who knew what they would have without an order.

The waiter placed a bottle on the table and opened it. Boiardo sipped, swished it around his mouth, and nodded. The waiter poured for both of them.

Boiardo raised his glass. "*Salud.*"

Les raised his glass in return. He sat quietly, watching Boiardo carefully. He knew better than to push things too hard or too fast. He would wait for the right moment.

They drank and Boiardo laughed. "A long way from the shit I sold during Prohibition, but then how would you know at your young age?"

Les shrugged. No way would he disagree with the man. He smiled and sipped his wine again.

When the meal arrived, Boiardo said with some pride, "This is midday. I find when you have work to do it is best not to eat too much food. We will have a very nice *insalata frutti di mare*, and for the main course, *osso buco*, which I modestly say is the very best you will find anywhere. Let's eat and then I will hear your so-called proposition of mutual interest."

After a few bites, Les realized Boiardo had not exaggerated in his description of the meal. It was excellent. They ate in silence. When the table was cleared, the waiter brought two cups of espresso and a plate of *cioffe* (bowtie) cookies. Boiardo sipped his espresso, sighed, and put it down. He stared at Les and said, "So, what is this wonderful gift you bring me for our mutual benefit?"

Les replied, "I must first tell you that I believe the people need my center. We have many poor and struggling in the North Ward, no?"

"Agreed."

"That said, I will not insult a man of your knowledge and experience. I believe you understand what my center could do for the people of our ward. I understand what you already have done. For me, a receptive mayor could help us help our people. For you, well, if he wins with your help, what new mayor could not appreciate the expertise your organization could bring to so many City Hall departments in need of expertise, guidance, and contracted service? I am sure that Jackson Anderson, with your influence, knowledge, and organization, can be elected. I also am aware it is not worthy of your honor and dignity to present this offer to him. I am willing in such a matter to serve you, him, and most of all the people of our ward."

Boiardo sat quietly. Then he nodded once. "There are people to whom I must speak. If it's right, I will get back to you and tell you what we will authorize. Thank you for your time. Your car is out front."

Les closed the restaurant door behind him and headed for his car, whistling as he walked.

13

TRUE CONFESSIONS

Annie Mae lay in bed but far from sleep, not even aware of the voice and face of Johnny Carson commenting from her small TV set's screen. Charles hadn't been home or even called her in three weeks. T.C.'s report card went from a straight-A average to a mix of Cs and Ds. Three days ago, he tried to hide a bloody nose from his mother. He offered no explanations for any of these things.

Annie Mae knew her kids and she knew the city. She was convinced that his new problem wasn't gangs. It was race.

Was she wrong to move her family out of the projects and into the shadow of the Avenue to escape the lawlessness and the gangs and a growing drug epidemic? T.C. used to bring friends home. Now, in a ward where racial mixing was almost nil, he apparently had no friends. She agonized over whether she had made a crucial mistake. T.C.'s academics, his social life, and his safety were suddenly at risk. "Thank God for Mickey," she said out loud.

A knock on her bedroom door jolted her out of her self-examination. Mickey cracked the door open. She wore pajamas and a light bathrobe.

"Mama, can I come in?"

"Of course, baby. You should be asleep. What's wrong?"

Mickey sat on the edge of the bed and leaned forward. Annie Mae realized she was crying and reached up instinctively, taking her in her arms. She stroked her hair. "Whatever it is, baby, it can't be that bad. Take a deep breath and tell me about it."

Mickey swallowed hard and sat up. "Mama, I'm in love."

Relief flooded Annie Mae. She smiled. "Well, that's hardly a reason for all those tears. If he's the right man, it's a time for congratulations. Now tell me all about it. Who is he? Do I know him? Where did you meet him?"

"He's a fella I met at work down at the post office." Still sobbing, she wouldn't look at her mother. "He's smart and gentle and loving, and he goes to Montclair State. I never, ever knew anyone like him. He's everything you said to look for in a man when we had that talk."

"But you're still crying. So why don't you tell me what it is that you are trying not to tell me? Mickey, look at me and say it."

"I don't want you to be disappointed in me. You have worked so hard for this family. You're the one I want to make proud. You—"

"Say it, child." Annie Mae's heart beat hard as she wondered what could upset her daughter so badly.

"I know how hard this will be for so many people. But I love him. He's white and he's Italian and this damn city will never accept us."

Annie Mae let go of the breath she'd been holding, held her daughter tightly, and stroked her back. "I understand, Mickey, I understand. Oh, Lord, don't I understand. Haven't I been there? When you feel it and you really feel it, the last thing you need is outsiders trying to keep you apart. And there's nothing I or anyone else can tell you that would keep you two apart. But being sure is so hard at your age. It's August now and both of you will be back in school next month and maybe you will discover—"

"No. No, I want to live on campus with him . . . be where he is . . . show everyone how wrong they are about us. Don't you see? What you told me would happen for me really has. What never happened for you is happening for me, and I want it so much I ache all over. I don't wanna lose him, and I don't wanna hurt you. Help me, Mama, help me."

Annie Mae looked at her and silently weighed the possibilities. "Are you pregnant, Mickey?"

"No, Mama, he used protection."

"You sure?"

Mickey looked at her and actually smiled. "You know, Mama. You know a woman can feel the difference."

"Well, thank you, Jesus, for that. Has he told his parents?"

"I don't think so. He wants them to meet me when he does."

"Not a bad idea. What's his name?"

"Gerard Friscella Jr."

"All right. I understand, Mickey. Lord knows one woman in this family is entitled to luck in love. Maybe we can work it out. Tell him to meet me day after tomorrow at noon in Washington Park on his lunch hour. It's the worst time in this city ever for this, but if anyone can do it, maybe it's you guys. I don't know if you can. I don't even know if you should. I just want to look in his eyes. If I see what you deserve to be there is really there—if it is, then I don't give a damn about the city. You will find a way. If it's not, then, Mickey, I will do everything with every breath I have to see you don't get hurt. If it's not there, then I will not let this happen."

"You'll see it, Mama, you'll see it. I love him, and I love you. You guys are my shining stars."

"All right. Go back to sleep, baby. Lord knows, we are both going to need it."

～

Junior sat with Mickey in the break room eating lunch, their knees touching under the table. He knew something was on her mind. He could tell. They had never spent a full night together, but sex had become a regular and unpressured part of their relationship. It was almost as though the very act left in its wake the ability to feel the other's problems.

"I get the feeling there's something you want to tell me," he said.

"Baby, there's a lot I want to tell you, but most of it can wait. What can't wait is that I told my mother everything about us last night. She wants to meet you in Washington Park tomorrow without me being there."

"Well, don't worry. I'll be there. I want to meet her even more than she wants to meet me. How did she react?"

"She says she'll know after she sees you."

"I want so much to tell her how it is with us. I want to make her see the moon over our Staten Island Ferry, the red, white, and blue sky over the park when we gave ourselves to each other, the way we reflect in each other's eyes every time we meet. I love you, and she'll see that, too."

She pressed her knee tighter against his and reached under the table for his hand. "You know, when she gave me advice about men and told me the only qualities to accept when I thought the right one came along, she was really talking about you. She'll believe you. How could she look into your eyes and not?" She squeezed his hand even tighter.

Sometimes people in the break room saw them together and smiled. After June, July, and part of August, the relationship became apparent to so many—especially the women. Nobody had ever challenged them about it. That very fact had become a confidence-builder to Junior. When he mentioned that to Mickey, she had smiled and said, "In the United States Post Office break room is not the same thing as outside on Broad Street."

"Do you realize how far we have come since you wrote your phone number on the palm of my hand?" he asked.

"Of course I do. That's exactly the way I planned it." They laughed. Junior saw the heads that turned at the sound, the sound of a kind of oasis in a concrete desert, and the smiles on those faces.

∾

Washington Park spanned no more than six blocks. One side was flanked by a series of ornate office buildings, the Newark Museum, the historic public library, and a slice of the Rutgers-Newark campus. The weather-worn statue of George Washington standing next to his horse overlooked the narrow little park, not much more than a sitting park.

On a green bench a few feet from the statue, Annie Mae Washington sat in the sunshine, her telephone company building a few blocks away. The park was filled with noontime office workers and college kids. The former, mostly secretaries, opened brown-bag lunches. The latter were easily identified by the text-books on the ground around them, part of a decades-old ritual where the ground is more conducive for social interaction than the benches. Directly in front of her, two college kids sailed a Frisbee back and forth. She saw a young man crossing the park toward the statue and watched him approach. He saw her and waved. *Junior.* She waved back. He carried two brown bags in one hand.

"Junior?" she asked when he was a few feet away.

"The one and only," he replied, handing her a bag. "Lunch is on Mickey today. It's ham and cheese and an oatmeal raisin cookie. Tell Mickey you loved it, or she'll blame me. Pardon me a second. I'm gonna get us something to drink from the food truck on Washington. Is Coke all right?"

"It will be fine," she said.

Junior returned quickly. She took a bite of the sandwich as he sat down next to her. Nobody in the park appeared to pay them any attention.

"Gerry," she said, "I want to thank you for coming. I know this isn't easy for you."

"It's what I want, Mrs. Washington. I want to convince you how I feel about Mickey. I know I'm young, but I never felt this way about any woman before. It's not two young kids in puppy love, Mrs. Washington. She's the lady I want to share my life with forever."

"I know how she thinks she feels about you." Noticing the hurt expression when she used the word "thinks," she hastened to add, "And maybe she really does. At first I thought, like all mothers do, 'Well, she's only a baby to me and she has to think this through.' But that's not true either. Have you told your parents yet?"

"Not yet, but I will very soon."

"And how do you think they would have felt about this five years ago? Back then, who can say? Five years in the future, who can say? But now?"

"Mrs. Washington, my parents aren't like Paulie Tedesco. They are very nice people. They will love Mickey." He smiled. "Just as one day soon I hope you will love me. I have never heard my dad say anything negative about blacks or any other group in my life. You know Mickey better than anyone in this world. So I ask you, how could anyone not love her?"

"I'm sure you come from very good parents. I can tell it in the way you speak and in the respect you show. But, Gerry, that doesn't answer my question, does it?"

"Mrs. Washington, all I can tell you is the truth. I love Mickey and she loves me."

"Stand up," she said as she rose from the bench. She took his face in both hands and looked in his eyes. For a few seconds she remained silent. Then without breaking her gaze she spoke. "Gerry, I'm not saying I doubt you. I'm not saying this is impossible. All I'm saying is that you two sure picked a star-crossed time to fall in love. But I am also saying I don't want to see my baby hurt. You might not believe this, but I don't want to see you hurt either. Just don't be foolish. Maybe something will happen to make it better for the both of you, but Lord knows I can't imagine what. Just be careful and be patient. Gerry, don't let my child get hurt."

"Mrs. Washington, believe me. I would never hurt Mickey. I would never let anyone else hurt Mickey. You gotta believe that."

"I do, young man. I do. That's what makes all of this so hard. If I didn't believe you, this would be easy. Well, gracious. Look at the time. We better leave or we'll both get fired."

She started to leave, then suddenly turned back. "Gerry, do you have a sister? How old is she?"

"Yes, I do, Mrs. Washington. Her name is Angie and she's fifteen."

"Well, when I saw you coming toward me in the park, I thought, 'There is a really handsome young man.' I thought I could see where a young girl looking at you could get in a world of trouble. Then, when I looked in your eyes, well, those eyelashes. I know women who would kill for them. Maybe you should give them to Angie."

Then she laughed, turned, and walked away.

~

Annie Mae and her friend Elizabeth sat in the kitchen drinking coffee. Elizabeth, roughly the same age as she, has been her friend nearly her entire life. Now they even worked together. There were no secrets between them.

"Elizabeth, I mean, I just don't know what to do. He's a nice young man. And I guess they are in what at age twenty passes for love. But I just feel there ought to be some way to help them. Even if it's to end this thing."

"I know what you mean."

"She is a sensible girl. Mature beyond her years. She tells me she has found the love of her life. Imagine that at age twenty! I just don't know if she understands what that means. I have been talking to her night and day, and the only thing I can get out of her is that she loves the boy."

"Well, then, maybe she does. But you're her mother. I've known her since the day she was born. Sometimes, they listen better to an aunt in a situation like that. Maybe I can learn something you don't know. Maybe she would talk to me. If you approve."

Before Annie Mae could answer, the doorbell rang, long and hard, then continued until she covered her ears to block the incessant chiming. Annie Mae ran to answer it.

Talmadge. He stood framed in the doorway, scowling, and shoved his way past her, shouting, "Where the hell is that girl? I want to see her, and I mean now!" His gaze landed on Elizabeth, but he ignored her, whirled around, and demanded, "What the hell is going on here? Can't you control your own daughter?"

Annie Mae realized it was going to be one of those visits. She shouted back, "Just exactly what do you mean by that?"

"You know damn well what I mean. I seen Charles is what I mean, and he seen her with her white boy driving toward the park on July Fourth. Charles got more sense than this whole damn household put together. I'm gonna straighten her out, and if you get in the way, I'll straighten you out too."

"Don't you shout at me! Your time for straightening anyone out around here is long gone. You never were her father and you ain't gonna be now. Do I have to get the cops in here?"

Elizabeth sat frozen at the table. Annie Mae knew her best friend suspected what was about to happen. It was a rerun of an old scene she had witnessed many times before.

"She ain't here and won't be back anytime soon," Annie Mae said.

He got right in her face, obviously furious, but Annie Mae did not budge. Not one step.

"I'm not gonna have this shit! Understand me. She's turning out just like you. College girl, my ass! I never went to college and I turned out just fine."

"What I understand," Annie Mae said, "is that through no fault of your own you have a beautiful daughter with a beautiful soul. I understand that while you were still running the streets like an alley cat, she was in college trying to become everything you never could or will ever be."

"Shut up, bitch. Her college don't mean shit to me. I don't care if she never goes. What the hell does college mean in her life? I may be tomcattin', but I ain't tomcattin' with no white girl!"

"If you ain't," Elizabeth shouted from the table, "it's 'cause you ain't found one low enough and dumb enough to look at you."

"You shut up, bitch. You ain't got a nickel in this quarter! And you!" He turned to Annie Mae. "You so superior . . . so important." He affected a falsetto, mimicking her.

"'My baby is going to college.' This is all your doin'. You and her cloak-and-daggering me. I ain't gonna tolerate that bullshit. No daughter of mine is ever—"

"All right, now you listen to me. Who the hell do you think you are? What gives you the right to gorilla your way into the home you never paid for? You think you can come and go whenever you want and play daddy whenever the notion strikes you? This is *my* house, so understand *me*, Talmadge Washington, and understand me good. I will deal with Mickey's problems just like I deal with T.C.'s and try to deal with the ones Charles has. Now you just get on outta here before I call the—"

Talmadge lunged for her. Elizabeth ran to the sink, grabbed a frying pan, and started toward him. He turned. "You stay outta this, you pitiful, I-ain't-got-no-man bitch, or I'll be glad to bust your ugly face in half!" He whirled toward Annie Mae and fired a right hand to her mouth, splitting her lip. Blood poured from her mouth.

"I'll be back, and that little slut daughter of yours better be quits with that white boy the next time I see her. You understand what I'm sayin'?"

He stormed out, slamming the door behind him. Elizabeth raced to the refrigerator, grabbed a handful of ice from the freezer, and wrapped it in a towel. She moved to Annie Mae and held it against her broken lip.

"Are you hurt?" Elizabeth asked.

"Not anywhere that shows, Elizabeth. Not anywhere that shows."

14

STRANGE BEDFELLOWS

The mission statement of the St. Gerard Self-Help and Improvement Association left no doubt as to clarity. The organization was designed to help, improve, and abet the citizens of Newark's North Ward. In its twelve years, it had done just that. It was funded by government grants. But unlike its competitors, it had an impressive list of private donors.

It had a preschool with plans for a K-8 charter school. It delivered Meals on Wheels, ran secretarial classes, helped voters get to the polls, and invited the community to its headquarters to celebrate ethnic, religious, and civic holidays.

But Les Scarcella understood that there was always a struggle for extra funding. He had thought about that as well. Thought? Hell, it had become an obsession. Ever since his conversation with Gerard Friscella Sr. at the Friscella's Fourth of July cookout, he had played and replayed their talk over and over again.

Yes, the question he had asked was designed to sandbag the man, but his answer had provided another, larger question. Friscella, when pressed, had said he didn't care if the new mayor were black if he could end the tensions that tore at the soul of the city and restore some kind of civility to the situation. If the winner couldn't do that, knowing the original two candidates, Friscella worried for the future of his family and his city.

His answer hammered away at Scarcella's psyche with a question that could affect the very future of his organization. It was rooted in the fact that the two had known each other since childhood.

He did not take Friscella's opinion lightly. But how many others in the North Ward would think like him? How many would vote like him?

At his core, Les was still an astute politician. He knew instinctively that the answer to that last question was crucial because with two black candidates and one Italian American in the field, it would be the North Ward voters who would decide this election.

Twice, the intercom on his desk had buzzed and twice he had snapped at his secretary to hold all phone calls. His long friendship with Friscella was unquestioned. But were his friend's thoughts a legitimate barometer?

His eyes wandered to a large stack of papers on the right side of his desk. Each day he went to the public library and searched old newspaper clippings. He had collected hours of midnight data, so frustrated that he could not sleep. He drummed his fingers on the top of the pile.

Then he said the hell with it and began to run through them again, looking for something he had missed. And then he found it.

He held up a sheet, eyeing a very small picture. At its extreme left was the face of Paul Castellano, then the number-two man in the Gambino crime family. Mostly cropped out of the picture, but still perceptible if you really looked, was his boss, Carlo Gambino. The photo clearly had been taken in Las Vegas, the Desert Inn visible behind them. In the middle of the photo stood Frank Sinatra.

A month had passed since Les had met privately with Richie

Boiardo. The last thing Boiardo had told him was, "I will think about it. If I have interest, you will get a phone call."

But Les had heard nothing since.

He knew it was bad form to try to pressure the man with whom he would have to deal, but Les was a politician, and he reasoned that, with caution, he could handle it. One thing he could not do was remain silent. He reached for the phone and pushed the intercom button.

"Nancy," Les said, "please come in here."

His secretary held the door ajar and said, "You actually gonna talk to me this morning?"

"Don't be a smartass. I was wondering about your Uncle Pete. How's he doing? He's got to be seventy now. What's doing with him?"

"He's the same as always. It's still summer, so he takes the train to Monmouth Park each Saturday to bet the ponies. He sits outside the Liberty Club in the sun and drinks espresso with the old guys. He won't change. I try to invite him over for dinner, but he says I can't cook like his sister, so he goes to Biase's or Vesuvius and orders the same things each time and picks up his dessert at Calandra's Bakery. Every time I tell him we would like him to have a meal with us, he says everything he needs he can get on the Avenue. To answer your question, he's still a stubborn old man. Just ask the old geezers at the Branch Brook Park bocce court."

"So I take it you don't see much of him."

"He writes me letters. He says you never know who could be listening on the phone. The older he gets, the more he stays the same."

"But he's healthy?"

"Like a horse."

"Does he ever see . . . uh . . . his former . . . uh, colleagues?"

"I think so."

"Listen, give him a call and tell him I'd like to see him. There's something I would like to ask him to do for me."

"What?"

"Now that's more than *you* need to know."

She saluted and closed the door.

Three hours later she walked into his office and said, "Uncle Pete was here and didn't want to see you, but he said he had a message for you. I have no idea what it means. He said tomorrow . . . noon . . . the Castle. And come alone."

Les smiled. "Well, it means, as our esteemed ancestors used to say in old Rome, *carpe diem*."

~

The attendant who took his keys and parked his car last time wasn't there. Instead, after Les parked his car himself, he waited just inside the door. Unlike the last visit, he was instructed to face the wall, lift his arms, and spread his legs to be frisked.

This guy acts like he thinks I'm a hit man.

As though he'd read his mind, the man said, "Sorry, Mr. Scarcella, but orders are orders. You can go inside now."

The Boot, who was sitting alone in the back of the dining room, rose to meet him. "Lester, my friend, good to see you. Come sit down," he said, beckoning him forward and pulling out a chair from the table. He gestured to the waiter, who was standing nearby at a kind of military parade rest. A bottle of wine appeared. Boiardo took a sip, swished it around in his mouth, and nodded, giving the waiter permission to pour. Glass upraised, he tapped it against Les' glass and said a very hearty *"Salud."* It was step-by-step the same ritual that had preceded their first meeting.

Then he leaned forward and said, "It's good to see you again. I am interested to hear the first details of this plan of yours. But first we will eat. Midday, as I told you before, there is still work to be done, so we eat lightly. *Insalata de mare,* chicken *picatta.* And as before, you will have to admit that Castle Vittorio is the best the city has in Italian cuisine."

The waiter served. Les broke the silence with a remark designed to lighten the mood. "What was with the search at the door, Signore Boiardo? For a minute I thought you had me confused with the guy who shot Abe Lincoln."

The Boot threw back his head and laughed. "No, my civilian friend. You are not a threat. But you did mention someone who could be in your message. One cannot be too careful about things like that. Carlo and I are at best cautious friends. There is some less-than-good history between us. But neither of us is blind to a profitable deal."

"Well, then, I can see I have come to the right place." He thought, *I damn well better say that.*

For the rest of the meal they talked about the availability of the major Italian soccer league on television, the prospects for further success by Nino Benvenuti, the Italian boxer, who had won the middleweight title the year before, and the oppressive heat wave that was enveloping the city.

"You know, I was told," Boiardo said, "that some guy who opened a fire hydrant so the kids could play in the street was arrested. What do you think of that?" He leaned forward, awaiting an answer with a smile on his face.

"That depends," Les said.

"On what?"

"On whether he was Italian."

Boiardo's laugh echoed through the empty dining room.

The waiter was back, clearing dishes, placing espresso cups before them along with a plate of cannolis. He poured the thick black coffee.

They sipped. Boiardo picked up a cannoli, took a bite, and then spoke. "So, to business, my friend. Before we start, I will tell you that I was not pleased that your message included Carlo. We do not often agree. But we shall see about that. I also want to make something clear to you. I understand what your center does, and I approve. I never have, therefore, approached you on any matter or with any suggestion about what you should or shouldn't do. I have never attended any of your fundraisers. I know a certain kind of rumor would attach itself to your center if I did. I respect your business, as I hope you respect mine. But it was not helpful for you to include Carlo in whatever plans you have involving us. Now you will speak, and I will listen."

"As you surely recall," Les began, "I explained that Paulie Tedesco would be a liability to you as mayor because he incorporates all the stereotypical trappings that the people who don't like us attribute to all Italians, and, therefore, would impact us on anything he tried to do. And you, as well as I, believe that the man who calls himself Kiongosi would be even worse, for obvious reasons. It was my thought that the newcomer Jackson Anderson, college-educated, successful businessman with a heavy income of his own, could bring dignity to the job and represents everything his two rivals and the current mayor do not. He could put the new regime beyond criticism. But if he knew the identity of the man who made his election possible, he surely would be open to legitimately helping him in matters of patronage, appointments, and contracts. I also said, when we last met, that Anderson cannot win without the major inroads into the North Ward vote. He has rented the Mosque Theater for his first rally—several thousand seats. He has commitments from blockbuster black entertainers. The only way he can get North Ward voters into half of those seats would be if he gets Sinatra."

Boiardo showed no emotion as he listened. Then he spoke. "Like all Italians, I love the man and his music. But, my friend, I don't know how I can help. I do not know Sinatra."

"With all due respect, Carlo Gambino does. In nineteen sixty-four, he attended a Rat Pack concert involving Sinatra, Dean Martin, and Sammy Davis Jr., and gave each of them ten thousand dollars in cash. He, Paul Castellano, and other associates were photographed with Sinatra at Gambino's request. It was Gambino that requested the photo."

"And you think I should try to get Gambino to help?"

"Yes, if that becomes the only way."

"This requires meetings and concessions. But a deal makes sense. I will negotiate and we'll see what can happen. But I make no promise to you. I have a temper, as does Carlo." He paused, then said very slowly, "For your sake, I hope it goes well. Your car is ready out front. *Buona giornata.*"

This time Les did not exit whistling a happy tune. This time he wondered whether to celebrate or await the dropping of an unseen shoe.

~

L es was stunned two days later when Nancy tapped on his office door and said, "Hey, boss, you have a surprise visitor who insists on seeing you."

"What are you talking about?"

"I think you know my Uncle Pete." She turned and spoke to someone behind her. "Come in, sir."

She ushered him in. Les couldn't believe the man actually stood in his office. He stared, shocked that this Mafia legend had come to see him. God had burdened him with an active stenosis, but it had not altered his appearance. There he was with his double-breasted gray suit, his maroon tie, dark glasses, and fedora cocked ever so slightly to the right. The cane in his right hand was the perfect prop for a onetime Mafia enforcer and soldier.

And yet, the slight stoop of his shoulders, the white hair of his mustache, and the lines on his face belied his wardrobe, stamping him as a kind of time traveler. His days as a Mafia enforcer had long ago given way to espresso mornings at a table in the sun in front of the Liberty Club, watching the world go by on the Avenue. So what had brought him here? And was it good news or bad?

Nancy discreetly closed the door behind her.

"*Buongiorno*, Don Scarcella," Uncle Pete greeted him. "I have a message for you. The person we both know wants to know something. You have asked of him a favor that few or nobody outside our circle would dare ask. First, he wants to know what you risk in return. Second, he insists that I tell you he will not travel to see the man who must grant this favor. He has designated that you, with a letter from him, do that. Third, if this other person agrees in the matter of the singer, you will offer up the deal to your candidate for mayor. The man who sent me will work out such details that must be sworn between him and the man to whom you will deliver the letter. Finally, you will report all the results to him. *Capisci*?"

"But why should he speak to me?"

"The letter, Don Scarcella, the letter."

"But how will I find him?"

"He will find you, Don Scarcella. He will find you."

15

THE DEVIL IS IN THE DETAILS

The *Star-Ledger* newsroom had erupted into chaos. The usual discipline and decorum had broken down, replaced by the ear-splitting sound from a forbidden boom box, the unheard-of appearance of champagne and delicatessen sandwiches, and a long and noisy line of female reporters waiting to kiss sports columnist Jerry D'Amilio.

Earlier in the day, the Pulitzer Committee announced that D'Amilio had won the Pulitzer Prize for Commentary. He was only the second sports columnist to do that in the award's long history.

In 1968, a fierce professional loyalty served as a kind of unbreakable bond throughout the paper's newsroom. It had evolved from Newark's "other" newspaper into a renaissance that for years would make it one of the country's best.

Its outstanding coverage of the riot should have won a Pulitzer, but the importance of that coverage was dwarfed by the attitude of the committee that dictated coverage of anything on the east side of the Hudson was of far more importance.

But D'Amilio's Pulitzer was no consolation prize. His role as the eyes and ears of his readers was documented by his mastery of the language and his reportorial instincts. Some of his columns were even used as homework by Newark high school English teachers. Even his rivals in the big city across the river conceded it: He was the shining star of a newsroom filled with talent.

At the height of the celebration, the strait-laced managing editor stood on a chair in the middle of the room, raised a champagne glass, and shouted, "They got it right for a change. They got it right. Our guy is the best." Then he tripped and fell to the floor. The cheers that followed rocked the room.

In the midst of the laughter, a copy boy tapped D'Amilio on the shoulder and handed him a crumpled telephone message. It was just three words and an abbreviated signature:

Urgent you call—Les.

He crammed it in his shirt pocket and forgot it. Later that night when he was in the middle of a celebratory dinner with the publisher, he remembered, excused himself, and telephoned.

"How you been?" Les asked.

"Today was the best day of my life. I'm on cloud nine."

"Well, I need a favor. Drop by my house when you finish with your boss. You still drink amaretto in your after-dinner coffee?"

"Was Joe DiMaggio a Yankee?"

"Great. I got a bottle of amaretto with your name on it."

"See you in an hour."

Jerry D'Amilio's roots were in the North Ward, as they had been for his father and his father's father. He was a graduate of Barringer High School and the Newark branch of Rutgers University. A measure of his loyalty to his city was evident in the fact that while the university had gone to great lengths to call the school Rutgers-Newark, he always referred to it as Newark-Rutgers.

He was fully aware of Les' similar devotion to the city and the residents of the North Ward—not in that order. When Les had been a recreation director at the YMCA, D'Amilio had been the left fielder on his baseball team and the point guard on his basketball team. As the sportswriter grew older and became an influential force in journalism, their relationship had grown. The personalized autographed photos of Joe DiMaggio, Yogi Berra, and Nick Buoniconti that adorned the wall of Les' den were gifts from D'Amilio.

And when Nino Benvenuti, who was born in what was then the Italian possession of Isola d'Istria, won the middleweight title in a stunning upset win over Emile Griffith at Madison Square Garden, it was D'Amilio who provided ringside tickets for Les and his father.

Over the years, their mutual love of the city in which they were born, their shared pride in their Italian heritage, and whatever sport was in season kept their relationship alive.

Now the sports columnist was ringing the bell at Les' front door. Loretta Scarcella opened it and greeted him with a hug, then ushered him into her husband's den, where a carafe of coffee and a fancy-shape bottle of expensive amaretto sat on the low table that fronted the couch.

"Here comes our Pulitzer Prize winner," Les said as he rose. "You were a decent outfielder for me, and I thought maybe you'd make a pro one day, but this beats that by miles. You oughta be glad you never did learn to hit a curve." He gave his protégé a bear hug. "Sit down. Sit down." He turned to his wife. "Honey, we need a little privacy."

She closed the door behind her. Les poured coffee. "You can pour your own booze," he said. "It's good to see you, Ace. Remember? That's what I started to call you after we went up to Boston and you hit that game-winning homer and we took the tournament at Fenway Park. It seems like it was only yesterday."

"I read your note, Les. It didn't sound like you wanted to take a trip down memory lane. So why am I here?"

"That's why you won the Pulitzer, kid. You always cut past

the bullshit when a story breaks, and you go straight to the heart of it. So here it is. I need the kind of help I think only you can give me. Let me tell you why."

He told him everything . . . his thoughts on the election and what it meant to the city as well as what it could mean to his center . . . his two visits with Boiardo . . . and the letter he did not know how to deliver to Carlo Gambino. He held nothing back.

"And you are telling me this why?" D'Amilio asked.

"Before I answer that, I want you to take a minute to understand what this election means to our ward and our city. We can't afford to have Paulie Tedesco in City Hall as mayor. That would elevate racism to a new height and make every Italian look like they used to say we look. Kiongosi? It may be the black time in this city, but he is too inexperienced to make it work. Nobody in Trenton at the state legislature is going to pay any attention to him. He has an organization, but it is totally unsophisticated."

"So what you're telling me is that this is about Jackson Anderson?"

"Well, he's the only legitimate choice I see."

"And that justifies a deal with the Mafia?"

"Look, if they do what they have to do to get Anderson elected, and he does what he has to do when he is, what does the city lose? Mafia influence in contracts? Hello, this is Newark, remember? As long as the garbage gets picked up, nobody cares what it costs. Business as usual never hurt the city. But when business as usual means tension and racism, as usual, and even another riot, that's a different story."

"You're probably right. But why tell me?"

"The letter. It could heal the city if it helps the right guy get in. If we have the right end, then the means don't matter. But I can't deliver that letter without help. Boiardo is the only major contact I have with those people, and I'm not sure he even trusts me. When he told me how he wants to play this hand, he finished with what I correctly took to be a threat. To complicate it, Gambino actually hates him. But you know some people he might not hate. People who could get him to read the letter. People who can help. Come on, Ace, I saw who was at ringside when Benvenuti won the title. And from what I hear, a few of them even manage fighters."

"So you want me to get a guy to deliver the message, or at least pave the way for you to do it?"

"Yeah, I do. But don't forget why I want it done. Look, the United States Army used the Mafia to help us land at Sicily in World War Two. And Lucky Luciano, who controlled the New York docks, was released and deported for agreeing to use the Mob to prevent sabotage on the waterfront. Neither of those deals hurt this country. As a matter of fact, we won the war. Beyond that, do you recall the state YMCA basketball tournament when we were down twenty points at halftime? Do you remember what I told you guys?"

"Yeah, you said we can't get it all back at once, but we will get it all back before this game is history."

"And you won. We can't fix this city at once, but we can start to make it better until we can fix it. So?"

"Well, the first name that comes to mind is Tommy Eboli. I think he could do it. I got to know him pretty well when he was managing fighters under the name Tommy Ryan. He's pretty high up in the Genovese family. There's also Frankie Carbo, the Mafia guy tied closest to boxing. Hell, in some ways he just about owns it. But he's not too thrilled with some of the things I've written about him, so there's no help there. I'll talk to Eboli. But I can't guarantee anything." He paused before adding the obvious. "With those guys, nobody can."

~

E boli was an alumnus of the Lucky Luciano bootlegging fraternity during Prohibition. He graduated to serve as the bodyguard for Vito Genovese, who was Luciano's underboss. D'Amilio had heard that Eboli was involved in twenty murders for the family. That put him just slightly ahead of Carbo. But while Carbo mistrusted most newspaper guys, Eboli courted them during his days as a fight manager.

And his connections were just as good. When he started to train fighters, he had a young prospect named Vincent Gigante, who now was on the rise in the same Genovese Family. D'Amilio reasoned that if he could get anywhere on this bizarre mission, the road would have to go through Eboli. Gigante started out as a professional boxer and fought twenty-five bouts between 1944 and 1947, winning twenty-one of them, thirteen by knockout. Eboli, beyond managing him as a boxer, helped mentor him as Mafioso. He invited D'Amilio and Gigante to dinner before the local fights at the Robert Treat Hotel.

D'Amilio managed to arrange a meeting at the Vittorio Castle, where his two guests obviously knew the staff. He was surprised to learn that Richie the Boot was not there. But he was not surprised that the service and the food were top-of-the-line.

"There's a story here that you might not know," Eboli said over appetizers. "I know you are aware that Joe DiMaggio ate here often because he really loved the food and the privacy that Richie personally enforced for him. But I love this one because it shows that the Boot had a soft side that we almost never see." Eboli and Gigante laughed. "This was back in nineteen thirty-nine. They're sitting together here, and Joe kinda shyly admits he's gonna get married. 'Who's the lady?' the Boot asks. 'She's a genuine Hollywood starlet. Maybe you heard of her, Dorothy Arnold.' 'No, I haven't, but she must be special. Take a walk with me.' So they go in the back to his private office and there's this deep drawer in the bottom of his desk and he reached down and unlocked it. It's loaded with diamonds—maybe hundreds of them. And he reaches in and picks out one that's four and a half carats, and he hands it to Joe and says, 'For the little lady, with my blessing. Tell her we'll throw an engagement party for her.'"

Gigante laughed and said, "The Boot did that? Hey, you just never know about him."

Then Eboli turned to D'Amilio and said, "Not that I don't wanna see the fights tonight, and not that I don't like the way you write, but what the hell is this all about?"

D'Amilio took a deep breath and plunged forward. "Boxing, in a way. Remember, I was there when you trained Mr. Gigante here and I was there the night you were invited out of boxing."

"You remember that?"

"Just like it was yesterday. I've seen a lot of fights but I never saw anything like the night your guy Rocky Castellani got knocked on his ass twice by Ernie 'The Rock' Durando at the Garden."

Eboli laughed. "Son of a bitch. No wonder you won that fancy reporter prize. You never forget a damn thing, do you?"

"Well, it's sure as hell not something you could forget. The second time Rocky goes down, the joint went wild. Then Ray Miller, the referee, rushes in and stops the fight, and you jump into the ring and clock him with a pretty good right hand. So the cops get you out of the ring and you take a run at Al Weil, the promoter, and kick him where it really hurts because there was a deal for Castellani to win and he lost control. That's when they invited you out of boxing. You got sixty days in jail for assault— the only jail time you ever got, right up until this day. Am I right?"

"Well, that depends on how you look at it," Eboli said. "I mean, a deal is supposed to be a deal. A referee is not supposed to be intimidated by the crowd. Jersey loved Durando. That's why they called him the Rock. And half of Jersey was at the Garden that night. But what's this dinner have to do with that?"

"Well, we connected through boxing and now a really good

friend of mine has asked me, because of that connection, for a favor."

"Who is he?"

"Tommy, you should understand that I can't tell you that. It's personal, and he gets nothing out of it. I can't tell you that, but I can tell you why and who else is involved."

"I like that little bit of *omerta*," Eboli said. "So what's the deal?"

D'Amilio told them about the election and why it was important to the city and what he wanted him to do.

"Why should I give a flying fuck about that town?" Eboli said. "I got no finger in that pie, and I don't see a way to get any taste of what will come to the two guys who will if I do what you ask."

"Courtesy, Tommy, courtesy. I was born and raised here. I love this city, and those two guys could have difficulty doing their thing without a hole card, and for them it would only be business. That hole card would be Jackson Anderson."

"Look, I like you, kid. You treated me fairly when I had prospects like Gigante here. But why should I do a favor for Gambino and Boiardo? What are they to me?" He leaned forward, raising his voice. "They wouldn't do shit for me." He leaned even closer until his face was two inches from D'Amilio's, his eyes like a pair of lasers. "Are you stupid? *Are you stupid?*"

The sudden aggression stunned D'Amilio. Startled, he pulled away from Eboli's face, pressing into the back of the chair. He groped for words. "Well, well . . . I . . ."

Eboli threw his head back and laughed, as did Gigante. "Gotcha! Gotcha! Boy, you should see your face. You should have heard yourself talk about 'Oh, I love that city, help me. Help me.'" The two of them laughed so hard that Gigante pounded the table with his fist, making the wine glasses quiver.

"Give me the letter. No, that's not right. If I see it, I will have to read it. I don't want to see it. That way it's not my business. All I can ask him to do is read it. I'll talk to Carlo, and when I do

I'll tell him. As you said, that's a courtesy . . . Not for me . . . but for him and the Boot."

D'Amilio nodded and murmured his thanks, pulse still racing as he tried to calm down.

"Sorry about my little joke. I hope I didn't take away your appetite." Eboli slapped D'Amilio on the back. "*Mangiamo. Mangiamo.* Let's eat. So who do you like in the main event tonight?"

16

WHEN SUMMER ENDS

August seemed to pass in the blink of an eye. The end of summer meant the end of summer jobs, and for Junior and Mickey that was no small thing. It would be an end to Mickey waiting at the post office entrance with two Styrofoam cups of coffee, looking across the park, waiting for Junior to step off the bus as her heart noticeably beat faster. It would be an end to lunch in the break room with knees touching under the table and whispered plans they alone could hear.

With ten days left in August, Junior explained during lunch that football practice at Montclair State would begin the next week, he would have to move into his campus dorm room, and with two practices a day they wouldn't be seeing each other much for a while. The awkward silence that followed resonated through the break room.

"But I thought . . . I mean . . ." Mickey said. She paused and asked in an unusually soft voice, "Are you trying to tell me something else?"

"Maybe a week or two for practice. During the season there's ten games and that's ten more weeks of practice and schoolwork at the same time. But listen to me, that's all I'm saying and that's all I'm thinking—and I mean *all*."

144

He reached across the table and took her hand. "Look at me. Look into my eyes. Nothing bad is going to happen to us. I'll never let it. I'll always be there for you. Believe me." He lifted her hand to his lips and kissed it.

"I want to believe you," she said. "I need to believe you."

"You should. Football is part of my life. But, Mickey, you are *all* of my life. Don't you even think for a minute this is a summer romance. You know better. This job brought us together. That was a gift for us. Nothing, and I mean nothing, is gonna tear us apart."

Mickey smiled at him and pressed her knees against his.

Some of the older female employees at the post office had been watching them closely the past two months. Junior had taken note of the curious looks they attracted. And he could tell not all of them approved. So when two of them, Angie Paterno and Dorothy Johnson, approached their table, Junior watched them carefully in return. He knew these ladies were the kind of post-office lifers who would be there from high school graduation until retirement.

"We've been watching you two," Angie said. She added with a broad smile, "You just look like you belong together. Are we right?"

"Well . . . well . . ." Junior stumbled, and before he could put a sentence together Mickey jumped in.

Her face was a little flushed when she said, "Are we that obvious? Thank you for that. Look at us. We're a walking ad for Oreo cookies. You can see that we don't hear approval very much in this town. So thank you. It means a lot to us."

Junior, openly relieved at their attitude, added, "As my mother would tell you in Italian if she knew about us, 'From your mouth to God's ears.'"

Dorothy's eyes widened. "If she knew? For God's sake, boy, you both have got to tell her. And soon. You just might be surprised by what she says."

Angie added, "We didn't mean to interrupt anything. We just

wanted to wish you good luck. Things being what they are in Newark since the riot, I can imagine that it hasn't been easy for you. Aren't you a football player at Montclair State? And that's why you'll be leaving earlier than she is. Don't worry," she said, putting her arm around Mickey. "We'll take good care of her while you're gone. But please do us a favor. Score a touchdown this year for both of us and for both of you. And make sure to remember us when you get married and start having beautiful babies."

"The first time I score this fall it's for you two and I'll make sure you know about it," Junior said. "And, yes, ladies, we plan to have absolutely perfectly amazingly beautiful babies."

They both hugged the two older ladies.

That night after they made love, he held her tightly in the back seat of his father's car. They were parked in the South Mountain Reservation, and in the distance they could see the lights of Manhattan.

"Look at them. See the ones slowly going out?" he said. "That's the blue-collar people going to bed. And look there and there and there. See those other lights just turning on? Well, that's the night people starting their day. Maybe they clean offices or work factory night shifts, or maybe they're just burglars."

She punched him in the arm. "How can my hero be so sensitive and intelligent one minute and such a Jersey *cavone* the next?"

"Hey, where did you learn that word?"

"From you, idiot." She punched him in the arm again. Then she put her hands on his cheeks and gently kissed him. She nestled her head into the side of his neck, and he stroked her hair.

Remembering her panic attack that afternoon, he kissed her back and broke the silence, whispering in her ear, "Listen, girl. We talk around it and sometimes we even joke about it, but I want to tell you straight out. I love you. There it is right there on the table, baby, and it's really that simple."

"Yes," she said. "There it is for the both of us right there on the table—and it's really that complicated."

They stared at each other for a moment and then laughed and kissed again.

~

Jerry D'Amilio had to wait a whole week for an answer from Eboli. He was sitting at the desk in his den with a scotch neat in his hand. The letter was still in the inside pocket of the sports jacket he had worn that night. The last thing he wanted to hear from Les was that he had to deliver it himself.

He was waiting for a callback from Tommy Ryan. The sound of the phone caused him to jump. Ryan was Eboli's former "nom de boxing." D'Amilio grabbed the receiver, and when he heard the unmistakable voice, he looked toward the ceiling and said, "Thank you, Jesus."

"Hey, kid. I still can't get over the fact that you remember the night I sucker-punched that asshole referee."

"It's what I get paid to do, Tommy. And by the way, it was a hell of a right hand. It sure was a dramatic way to get yourself kicked out of boxing. Do you miss it?"

"Yeah, it's still in my blood. It occurred to me the other night when we were at the fights after our little talk. Never mind the fighters. Did you see those guys who called themselves managers standing behind the corner guys? Furriers and lawyers and Harvard guys with Phi Beta Kappa keys. They don't know shit about the game. They can't tell a right cross from a left hook, and they call themselves managers? And trainers? Maybe we got ten left who know that the jab is the key to all punches, or even how to stop a cut. Where's Ray Arcel and Whitey Bimstein and Eddie Futch? Yeah, maybe it's time to get back in."

"You got a lifetime ban. How you gonna do that?"

"Come on, Mr. Pulitzer Prize winner, you know better than that. This is boxing, ain't it? I'll leave it at that."

"Well, you didn't call me to announce your comeback, Tommy. So what's the news?"

"You know my business, kid. We got families and we got rules. There's some things I can do and some things I can't. This one I get to go halfway. Carlo says he'll listen. But he says you have to be the one he talks to—not the Boot and not the guy from the Center. He likes the way you write—especially the way you piss off Carbo. He really loves that. So that's the way it is. Personally, I don't trust either him or the Boot. So whaddya gonna do?"

"What do you think I should do?"

"Well, what about this Scarcella guy? Do you owe him?"

"Yeah, I guess I do. I was a snotty know-it-all kid headed for a lot of trouble until I walked into the YMCA and he made me a point guard and an outfielder, and he lobbied a lot of college coaches for me. That sent me to college and journalism. Yeah, I owe him big-time."

"Not really my business, kid. But a debt is a debt. I don't know about your business, but in mine it's a matter of honor. Ignore such a debt and you would be a hell of a lot better off in your business than you would be in mine. Think it over. You'll do the right thing. If you want to talk to Carlo and deliver the letter, I'll talk to him and he'll arrange it."

"I guess I have to do it."

"Okay, but one last thing. I like you, kid, so watch your ass."

～

Junior was scheduled to leave for football camp on Monday. On Saturday morning, he dressed early, finished packing, and opened the front door to retrieve the morning paper.

He was surprised to see Gerard Sr. in his tank-top undershirt, out front trimming the bushes.

"Hey, Dad, isn't it a little early for that? It's only six a.m."

"You might be thinking football, son, but it's still August and it's still hot and I figured I'd get this done before it gets even hotter. You got any plans for today?"

"No, just for tonight."

"Great. I haven't had my coffee yet." He put down the clippers and said, "How about we walk down to the diner and have some breakfast? I want to talk to you about a couple of things without your mother and sister around."

Artie's Diner was a kind of North Ward anachronism. The owner wasn't named Artie. Nobody named Artie had ever owned it. To compound that irony, the owner was the chef; his wife, Helen, was one of the waitresses; and nobody seemed to know their last names. The "diner" part of the name had to be taken on faith because in square footage the place was only the equal of an outsize luncheonette.

The waitress brought two coffees and took their order. Senior took a sip, leaned across the table, and said, "Remember when I used to bring you and Angie here for Saturday breakfast so we could let your mother sleep late?"

"Yeah, and I always wanted ice cream, and you always said, 'This is breakfast, boy. No ice cream before noon.'" They laughed. "So what is it you wanted to talk to me about, Dad?"

They paused while the waitress delivered their order. Then Senior forked up a bite of scrambled eggs and said, "Football."

"Please, you can't plan to give me a pep talk."

"Not about the game but about the schoolwork. We both love the game. Maybe a little too much. And I know we're both thinking about what Coach told you about how the Giants and the Eagles will be scouting you during the season. But it's not more important than that diploma. You're only two years away. It's somewhere nobody in this family ever got. I was lucky to finish Barringer. We had hard times then, and your grandfather was broke, and he and your grandmother needed me to bring in a third paycheck. So what I'm telling you is if the pros want you, that's terrific. But even then, bones break. Every pro football player pays a cost physically just to keep going. More times than not, they can't. I want you to do better than I'm doing. I want you to have a career instead of a job. Don't underestimate that piece of paper they call a diploma. Nobody in the family ever got one. Nobody. Not even your Uncle Tony. Two years at Rutgers . . . best linebacker to ever come out of the Avenue. First he knocks up a cheerleader and then he breaks a leg and then he quits school. So today he tends bar over in Union—and between the bookies and the shylocks he can't rub two quarters together."

His dad stopped and looked him square in the eye.

"Junior, you know there's no guarantees in football. Even if you're lucky, eventually there comes a time when the cheering stops. You got a good head on your shoulders. Westinghouse ain't for you. Don't neglect the books. The diploma is the only thing you can really depend on. Don't wind up like me. Don't wind up living from paycheck to paycheck."

"If I knew I could be like you, Dad, I would consider myself a success. You've always been there for Mom and Angie and me. You gave us the most important thing you could give—love. And that's a fact. Now what was the other thing you wanted to discuss?"

"Well, as a matter of fact, yes, there is something. You asked to borrow the car tonight, and since it's your last night before you leave, of course you can. But you've been borrowing it a lot this summer. I wasn't born yesterday. I don't exactly know what's going on"—he smiled—"but there's gotta be a young lady in all of this. Listen, whatever you're doing, I did it long before I met your mother. What I need to know is, is it serious?"

"Yeah, there is, Dad, and it is serious. It's someone I have strong feelings about."

"So why don't we know her? Why don't we have her over for dinner? What's her name?"

"Slow down, Dad. Her name is Mickey, and I've never felt like this before."

"But you *will* graduate?"

"I made that promise before and I'll make it again. If I'm lucky and get a pro contract, I'll go back in the off-season. If I don't get one, I'll graduate on time. Nothing is going to change that."

"And what does the young lady think?"

Junior laughed. "She's worse than you about this. We got a three-way deal here with her and you and Mom. She never met either of you. But she is tougher on me about that diploma than either of you guys."

"So when do we meet her?"

"Soon, Dad, soon."

"Take the car and drive carefully because you are probably driving the mother of my future grandchildren. Let's hope. You got a ride to campus?"

"Yeah, Allie is going to school to register. I'll call you Sunday night after I settle in."

"Love you, kid. You pick up the tab. I got a date with my hedge clippers."

~

That night, with a potential separation looming on the immediate horizon, Mickey and Junior tried to reaffirm what had been their night of mutual discovery by reaching back to the moment their relationship crossed the line from unexpected friendship to unashamed love.

"Where do you want to go?" Junior asked when he opened the car door for her. The library steps were a thing of the past. They were parked in front of her house. The pressure of a black/white relationship in a city that acted as though it never could accept them had eased on her with her mother's belief in

Junior's sincerity. Her idea about the wisdom of their love, however, was a very different matter.

"Let's go back to where it was safe and everything was right," she said. She smiled and moved closer to him on the front seat. "I want Chinese food and a ride on the Staten Island Ferry tonight, and, oh, yeah, include a full moon with that order."

"We'll see. I'm good but not that good."

"I'll be the judge of that."

He turned up the radio, and the voices of Marvin Gaye and Tammi Terrell filled the car. The timing was almost surreal. They were singing that no mountain was high enough and no valley low enough to keep the singer away from his girl.

"You knew that's what was playing," she said with a laugh. "You're impossible!"

"Just like I ordered," Junior replied.

He parked the car and they walked down Canal Street toward Mott when they passed the curio shop where he had purchased the two tiny Ho Tai idols, one black and one white.

"Let's go inside," she said, taking his arm. "I want to thank the clerk who sold them to you." She raised her arm, revealing for the first time that the twin gifts had become part of a charm bracelet.

The clerk stood behind the counter, a slightly plump women in her sixties who clearly had been an exotic beauty in her youth. "You're back," she squealed, clapping her hands. "And still together. Tell me the truth," she said, wrapping her arms around both their waists. "It was Ho Tai, wasn't it? Where are you kids from?"

"Newark," Junior answered.

"Ah, the place of the big riot." Her eyes softened at those words and she took Mickey's hand. "I'm sure that must be hard for a white boy and a black girl there right now. It's not like here in the city where there are more kids like you two than outsiders realize. But, oh, I'm so happy to see you again. I remember his sick-cow eyes each time he looked at you and the way you stared at him when he took your hand. You can laugh, but I know Ho Tai does his work well. I have a gift for you. Don't go away."

She disappeared into the back and returned with a small ring box in her hand. Inside was a silver ring with a little figurine sitting atop its circumference. "This is a boy riding a Chinese unicorn. It means much to Chinese women. Like generations of Chinese women before me, I myself wore one when I married. Chinese women wear it during the honeymoon time. Having a boy for your first child is much desired."

"Did it work?" Mickey asked.

"A month after I married, I was pregnant with my first son. I let my sisters borrow it when they married, and their first children were boys."

"The thought is so beautiful—I want it to pass on to our kids," Mickey told Junior, squeezing his hand. "But, you know, we don't want it to work too soon, do we?" The three of them laughed. Junior reached into his pocket, but the lady stopped him.

"No charge. I understand more about you than you think. When I was young, my father was enraged when I went to the prom with a white boy. I really cared for that guy. You two have the look that says you belong together. I want you to have this." She put the ring in his hand. "Don't thank me. I should have stayed with that white boy just to see where Ho Tai might have taken us. Now stop being nice to an old lady and take this girl to dinner. Leave here knowing I wish for you *Zhù nǐ men bǎi nián hǎo hé.*" She smiled and added, "Stop staring like a pair of ignorant *laowai.* I just said that I wish you all the best for the next one hundred years together—and I do."

They smiled all the way out of the store and onto the street.

"Wow," Mickey said. "Despite all the black-and-white nonsense in Newark, think of the number of strangers in New York who must see us exactly the way she does."

"I hadn't thought about it. But you're right. It might be tough in the neighborhood, but a lot of the rest of the world seems to know we belong together. I'll bet you didn't know about the Shrine of St. Gerard at St. Lucy's in the North Ward. He's the patron saint of childless women. Some come from around the world to pray for help from him. They keep coming and if it works, they come back to give thanks. Maybe that's why it seems like half the men in the ward are named Gerard."

She smiled. "Well, let's not push it. We both know there's a ceremony we have to take part in before that—something with a ring and a church. So cool it. Let's not talk about it now." She took a deep breath. "This is Mott Street and I'm starving. Feed me."

"Hang on. The Wu Hop is right over there." He took her hand. "For the record, you might take my breath away but not my appetite."

They seemed to fly down the ten steps to the basement-level restaurant, the same one where they had enjoyed their first dinner together. This night, like last time, they shared egg rolls and wanton soup and a main course of chow fun and pepper steak. The night had been everything they wanted, and the finish on the ferry was spectacular. A clear night, the lights of the city, and a surprising full moon on the water for which Junior tried to take credit. They stood at the rail, arms around each other the whole trip.

On the ride home, she never lifted her head from his shoulder until he parked in front of her house. He leaned across and kissed her. "Call you tomorrow night when I get settled."

She pulled away, looked at him intensely, and simply said, "Get out."

"What?"

"Get out of the car right now. You're coming upstairs with me."

"But your mother. We never—"

"My mother knows. I told her and she sent my brothers for an overnight with their uncle. Now give me your hand because you're not leaving here until very late tonight. Starting tomorrow a lot of coeds will be looking sideways at my football hero. So tonight, Miss Mickey Washington is going to mark her territory."

"In that case," Junior said, reaching for her hand, "why are we sitting here?"

THE MAN IN THE MIDDLE

T he Mets had an open date, so Jerry D'Amilio drove over to Brooklyn to meet up with Gil Hodges, their first-year manager. He had lived in Brooklyn ever since he played for the Dodgers. The two of them walked the streets together, Jerry listening as Gil shared his story.

"You have to love these people," Gil said. "I was a Hoosier hick when I came here to join the Dodgers. Playing here was like playing nowhere else. The park, the people, the intensity. These people knew the game. They called us Dem Bums, but they'd fight you if you used that name as a slur. You know, when I once went into a terrible batting slump, they actually held a prayer service on the steps of a Roman Catholic Church around the corner and prayed for me to get a hit that Sunday afternoon. Walter O'Malley never should have been allowed to move that team to L.A. He really hurt these people." He paused here to wave to a cop across the street. "They never forgot me."

This is a column, D'Amilio thought, *that almost writes itself—the profile of the Indiana farm boy who put down new but deep roots in the most legendary urban borough.*

By three o'clock, D'Amilio was back in the Newark office, where he wrote up the column and handed it to the slot man for editing. From there he drove up Route 21 to Don's 21 for dinner with Joe Buzas, an enterprising minor-league club owner who wanted to move a team to Newark if he could find a suitable stadium.

D'Amilio was the son of a ballplayer who never got out of the low minor leagues but even as an old man never stopped loving the game. His dad took him to his first baseball game to watch the AAA Bears, who were owned by the Yankees. As a kid, D'Amilio had seen Buzas when he played for Newark—and now here he sat having dinner and drinks with him. As the night wore on, they talked about the way the city was when Buzas played there and about what D'Amilio felt it had become. The beers were short but the conversation was long, and suddenly it was 1:00 a.m.

"I'll drive you back to your hotel," D'Amilio offered.

"No, it's late. I'll catch a cab. You go ahead, but be careful. We musta drank an ocean of Ballantine beer."

It had been a long day and a great evening but now, alone in his car, heading up Bloomfield Avenue toward Montclair, D'Amilio transitioned inwardly back to what had preoccupied him for days before he picked Hodges up at Shea Stadium.

"Goddamn it, Les!" he said out loud. "You got me in the middle of something way above my pay grade. But, hell, at least I'm not afraid for anyone but me. Brenda is out in Tinseltown trying to find herself since the divorce five years ago. We never did have the son I wanted. So, fuck it. I owe you, and I guess I owe the city, which has been pretty damn good to me. But I damn sure don't want to end up in debt to a pair of Mafiosi who hate each other."

No matter how he tried to relax, the concern remained in the back of his mind, gnawing away at him. The one consolation was that he'd heard nothing more since his last meeting.

His remote control raised the garage door. He parked and went inside. Dead tired, he kicked off his shoes and lay down on the bed fully clothed. He reclined for about ten minutes, then sat up, reached for the phone, and checked his messages, hoping the one he feared the most wasn't waiting for him.

There was a call from the pretty French teacher from Science High whom he had dated twice and never called back. "I probably should call her back, but . . ."

He skipped to the next message. "Jesus, Joseph, and Mary!" he shouted as the machine clicked ahead. This was the one—the one he didn't want to hear.

"This is Uncle Pete. My niece, she works for Mr. Scarcella, you know?" the voice said. "I was told you had a letter to deliver to a certain person. I have been asked to deliver you and that letter to that certain person. I'll pick you up at the paper tomorrow at noon. For both our sakes, please don't be late. The certain person is not a very patient man."

"Terrific! Just what I needed!" D'Amilio shouted. He threw the phone at the wall. His exhaustion from the long day evaporated, replaced by anxiety. No way would he get any sleep tonight.

∾

Junior was just finishing breakfast at seven thirty when he saw Allie pull up to the house.

"Come on in," his mom said, yelling through the open door. "You gotta eat. I got waffles."

"Love waffles," Allie said. "You musta planned this just for me, Mrs. F."

"Sit down and shut up," Junior said. "The more compliments you give her, the worse you make it for me. Hey, squirt!" he hollered over to Angie, who was staring at Allie in undisguised admiration. "Go get him the maple syrup and stop with the staring. He ain't worth it. His college grades are as bad as yours over at Barringer. The pain in the ass don't need you mooning over him."

Junior's mom pointed her finger at her son and sharply

cautioned, "Language, Junior. Language." Then she turned to face Allie, put a hand on his right shoulder, smiled, and got down to her real purpose. "So, Allie, what can you tell a mother about this mystery beauty queen who has hypnotized her son? I'm sure you've met her, which is more than I can say. You'd think a mother would be included in this. If she's so important to him, why hasn't he asked her to Sunday dinner to meet his family? What does she look like? Is she tall or short? Is she smart? Is she Italian? Beautiful or just cute?"

"Hey, Ma, enough. I told Dad you'd meet her soon."

"Excuse me, Junior, but I was raised to respect my elders," Allie said with mock solemnity. "Your mother asked me a few questions and I am in a position to answer them. Mrs. Friscella, believe me, and this is a promise, she is really something to see. Once you do, I promise you will never forget her looks. Her beauty is a kind I know you will remember. She's cute, she's smart, and he met her at Barringer. You might even say she's a neighborhood girl."

"Well, that's a relief. I couldn't ask for more."

Junior jumped up. "Uh, we gotta get going. Coach has called a ten a.m. team meeting, which is about the time Allie has to register for classes with the other non-athletic couch potatoes."

Once Allie turned the car up Bloomfield Avenue, Junior said, "I don't know whether to kick your ass or break out laughing or both. If the situation weren't so damn fucked up in this city, I would have laughed hard enough to piss my pants at that riff you just ran on my mom."

"Sorry, man, I couldn't help myself. But seriously, you know what I think about you guys and you know what I think about Mickey. You both are very special to me. I think watching the two of you helped me pull away from Chooch and Dominick. Thank God."

"No. Not really. That was bound to have happened," Junior said. "Listen. You and me, we just grew up like people do. Those two live in a time warp. They will always be stuck in high school. They will always be small because they will always think small. Allie, you're my best friend. You wouldn't be if you were anything like them. When everything seemed to be collapsing around me, you were the one I told about Mickey. All my life you've always been there for me. I could always count on you, and you never let me down. Believe me, you couldn't be like those two assholes if you tried."

"To tell you the truth," Allie said, "I'm an overweight slob. But the way you caught all those touchdown passes and the way you hit the ball over that short right field fence at Schools Stadium, you've always been a kind of hero to me. I never envied you. I guess what I wanted was to be your sidekick. I still do. Now, if you really think that highly of me, old friend, when are you gonna get Mickey to introduce me to Lois?"

"You serious?"

"I don't know. Yeah, I think I am, in a way, but not in the way you think. I mean, I'm not looking for a romance or anything resembling one. I just think the four of us could have some laughs, which is something I don't get much of these days. If she's Mickey's friend, then she sure as hell ain't no dope. That's a step in the right direction for me. I'm kinda sick of those gum-chewing, giggling manhunters I been dating."

Allie turned off Valley Road into the school's campus. On their left was Sprague Field, the brand-new football field they would dedicate in the home opener against Delaware State. That was a big leap forward for a Division III football program that had been forced to play its home games at a nearby high school field.

"Let me out here so I can tell Coach I'm back," Junior said. "You drive our stuff up to Bohn Hall since we'll be rooming together. And, Allie, since I am the brains of this alliance and you think you are the brawn, it wouldn't hurt for you to unload it." He grinned at his best friend and jumped out of the car before Allie could punch him in the arm.

∾

J erry D'Amilio was sick to his stomach. The high-pitched
sound of the alarm clock cut through his dream like a red-
hot spear. It jolted him out of a nightmare that had
immersed his entire body in a cold sweat. One minute he was in
the back of a butcher shop, his head squeezed in a vise, and
Carlo Gambino was about to swing a meat cleaver at his groin,
Uncle Pete was in the corner laughing, and Richie the Boot was
shouting, "No, no, no, Carlo. Let me kick him in the balls first."

He sat up in bed, still shaking. He took a deep breath and
hollered at himself as though he was trying to shut a door that
wouldn't close. "Idiot. This is nineteen sixty-eight. The Black
Hand days are long over. No Mafioso is going to kill a newspa-
perman. Get hold of yourself."

He showered and dressed and checked his schedule. Nothing
pressing there—no expense vouchers to turn in, no interviews
scheduled. Just five words: Uncle Pete—watch your ass. He had
written the last three right after Tommy Eboli spoke them over
the telephone.

"Well, fuck it and fuck them. I promised Les I'd do it, and I
will. After that, no more superhero. Just your everyday, ordinary
Pulitzer Prize winner."

He drove down to the *Star-Ledger*, parked in the garage, and
crossed the street. He stopped at the food truck and bought a
coffee with cream, no sugar. Then he rode the elevator to the
second floor to wait. The thought occurred to him that it couldn't
hurt to double back.

He had never covered an execution, but he thought this must
be how a guy headed for the electric chair would feel, hoping for
a call from the governor. He dialed Eboli's number.

"Tommy, just checking to see if you called Don Carlo,
because—"

"I don't know you," the voice answered. "Don't call this
number again."

The line went dead. He took a sip of his coffee, leaned over his wastebasket, and spit it out. "Been drinkin' that shit for three decades and it still tastes like shit."

He looked at the circular wall clock across the room. It was only eleven o'clock. The *Star-Ledger* was a morning paper and the newsroom was still fairly quiet. He reached over to the next desk and picked up that day's edition. His Joe Buzas column led the sports section.

"I wonder if Don Carlo ever heard of Joe. Hell, I wonder if Don Carlo ever saw a baseball game." He paused to study the picture of a young Buzas as a Newark Bear. Then the phone rang. "Christ on a crutch, what now?"

It was Evelyn, the lobby receptionist. "There's a guy here to see you. Dressed like he just got off a bus from nineteen thirty-six. Claims he's your uncle. Want me to call security?"

"Only if he starts shooting." He sighed and. "Send him up."

It was difficult at times to separate Mafia fact from North Ward fiction where Uncle Pete was concerned. Those who really knew would tell you that, yes, as a young man he was Gambino Mafia—the controller of the Gambino numbers runners. He was also a driver for Carlo, who, while yet to head his own family, was one of the most powerful mobsters in the country.

His fingerprints were said to be all over Gambino's inroads in loansharking, hijacking, extortion, and even murder. Again, the fiction was stronger than the fact, but D'Amilio knew this was not without some basis.

Now sixty-eight years old, Uncle Pete was rumored to be diabetic and walked with a pronounced stenosis. His exaggerated claims were tolerated throughout the North Ward, primarily because it was so difficult to tell where truth ended and Pete's imagination took over.

"If he's still Mafia," Eboli had told D'Amilio, "then his crimes are limited to the bocce courts at Branch Brook and several barber shops in walking distance of the Avenue. But age has screwed with his mind so much he can still be dangerous."

And now he walked into the newsroom. His blue single-breasted suit smelled faintly of mothballs. On his head he wore what had become his signature black fedora, tilted slightly to the left. He stared at D'Amilio and said simply, "You ready? Let's go."

"You first," D'Amilio said, gesturing toward the elevator. He fell in behind the aging Mafioso and noted the slight bulge at the rear of his belt.

A gun, he theorized. But with this guy who knows whether it's real or a water pistol.

Pete's car, a 1958 Lincoln, was parked just behind the food truck.

D'Amilio hesitated. "Where we going?"

"You'll know when we get there."

Uncle Pete drove down Broad Street and headed toward the North Ward.

Clearly, diabetes had affected Pete's vision, D'Amilio thought, his hand tight around the door handle. Twice the old man nearly sideswiped a car one lane over. The entrance to Branch Brook Park was on his left. Ahead loomed the still-impressive image of Schools Stadium. D'Amilio knew where they were headed.

"Yi Ki?" he asked.

"Whaddya know about the Yi Ki?"

"I was a kid in short pants eating chow mein there before I ever heard of Don Carlo Gambino."

"Watch your mouth, kid. You ain't there yet." Pete pulled to the curb. "You got the letter?"

"Of course."

"Then get out. I'll be back."

He stood on the street for a moment, running through opening lines that made no sense. *Jesus, I ain't picking up a girl.* He pushed the door and went inside.

A guy in a blue suit with a white shirt and a blue bow tie stepped from behind the reception desk with a menu in his right hand and asked, "Dinner for one?"

"I don't know. Someone is supposed to meet me here."

"Are you the man with the letter? I'll take it."

"No, you won't. Let's cut the cloak-and-dagger crap. You know who the letter is for, so take me to him or I'm outta here."

From just behind him a voice said, "Spoken like a true descendant of Garibaldi. Passion is an important ingredient in life. Come with me." It was Don Carlo Gambino. For somebody with such immense influence in his world, D'Amilio thought, the man was surprisingly short. But his hawk-like nose and rich head of gray hair radiated power, he clutched his trademark dark fedora in one hand, and his disarming smile was on full display. Gambino led the way past the bar, past another handful of tables, and stopped at a door. He opened it, revealing five or six men lounging around a large conference table.

"I suggest that you move your club meeting elsewhere," Gambino said. Amid mumbles of respect, the men left, and Gambino gestured to an empty seat at the highly polished table.

He sat, leaned across the table, and stared at D'Amilio. Then, with no visible sign that he had been summoned, a waiter appeared with a tray containing a bottle of Campari, a bottle of Italian carbonated water, and two glasses. He poured.

"Some people prefer this with citric water, but I find that too harsh," Gambino said. "So here we are, two men come together to study a business proposition from my occasional friend Richie Boiardo. He and I have had some difficulty in the past because, to quote an old Italian proverb, he sucks too much oxygen out of the room to let others breathe. English translation: He is an arrogant prick. But business is business. The letter, please."

D'Amilio reached into the inside pocket of his sports jacket and handed it to Gambino.

"You know, I do not much care for the American sports. Football is your name for a beautiful game that you have bastardized. But boxing, ah, boxing is one-on-one and honestly contested, always reveals the truth about the two participants.

Before we get to our business, I would like to express my admiration for the way you write. You tell the truth. When you criticize Frankie Carbo, the Lucchese soldier who runs boxing and calls himself Mr. Gray, I smile and say, 'Here is a journalist who knows the truth when he sees it and has the courage to tell it.' I enjoy the way you kick his ass because he affronts the sport. Like the Boot, his behavior is inclined to suck up too much oxygen in the room. Now I will read this letter and we will talk." He reached up to his neck, where a pair of reading glasses hung from a black ribbon and read. He said nothing as he digested the contents.

Eventually Gambino looked back up. "So if I am to believe my old enemy and occasional friend, he wants to form a partnership during this election to steal a city. Am I correct?"

"With all respect, Don Carlo, I am not here to interpret or judge. Just to see you get the letter. And by the way, I represent neither you nor Mr. Boiardo. I have no interest in this matter."

"I see. So why did you agree to deliver this?"

"I owe a debt to a man who is affiliated with neither of you but who does good work for the poor of our ward. I owe him, not you or Mr. Boiardo. He helped me when I was a kid headed for trouble, and none of what I have today as a writer and a person would ever have happened without him."

"Fair enough. A debt is a debt. No matter what you may have heard about us, we pay our debts. Now I want a favor from you, and if you can help, then consider me in *your* debt. Can this deal be done by two men who have trouble trusting each other?"

"I don't know. All I can say is that in the long run it would be better for a city torn apart by hate right now to come together about something."

Gambino laughed. "I am a businessman, not a social worker. But you have offered me something to think about. What helps the city that contributes to the income of my family would seem to be worth doing—maybe. Now, tell me, were you nervous when I demanded of Eboli that you be the messenger?"

"In response to your earlier Italian proverb, Don Carlo, I will offer you one from a second-generation American: Does a bear shit in the woods?"

Gambino laughed and pounded the table. "I like you, my young friend. So in parting I remind you that this conversation is not to be repeated—even to Boiardo. He and I will decide what we do—together or alone. Pete is at the bar waiting for you. Tell him nothing. Believe me, he will ask you everything. Oh, and by the way, congratulations on your Pulitzer. You think I didn't know? An Italian man of letters? What do you think? I only read the obituaries?"

Gambino laughed again and slapped him on the back.

18

THE DOUBLE DATE

Mickey and Lois sat on the edge of Mickey's bed, a pile of photos beside them. Mickey was sharing her life since Junior had entered it—a twilight view from the Staten Island Ferry, on a park bench outside the post office, Junior carrying her over a mud puddle in Branch Brook Park.

She held up an 8x10 color print of the two of them in front of a lifeguard stand on the beach at Coney Island. She was wearing an aqua bikini and he had on navy-blue swim trunks. They stood looking into each other's eyes, their faces just inches apart.

"You look like you were about to ravish him," Lois said, laughing and hitting the bed with her fist. "Poor baby, he never had a chance."

"Poor baby? Who was chasing whom? Listen, Miss 'I Don't Have a Date So I Guess I'll Wash My Hair Again Saturday Night,' it doesn't matter what you think. I've got him, I ain't turning him loose, and I haven't heard any complaints from him."

Lois suddenly leaned across her and almost dived into the pile of photos.

"Hey, girl, what are you trying to do?" Mickey said.

"What do you think I'm doing? I'm looking for a picture of

Allie Costa. If you don't have one, then start talking, girl. I need details."

"Well, I don't have one, but I already told you that he's a great guy or he wouldn't be Junior's best friend. He's about five foot ten, so that makes him six inches taller than you, so you can wear high heels. The rest is what you'd expect—dark hair, Italian features, a little overweight but not fat. And he's just looking for a friend. I really think you two could relate to each other. Not deep-breathing relate, but more like let's-share-an-ice-cream-cone relate."

"Well, I'll be the judge of that if and when it happens. Which, by the way, you have yet to tell me."

"I told you before, we'll do it as soon as Coach gives Junior a Sunday off and the four of us can have dinner."

As if on cue, the phone rang. "Bet that's lover boy checking in," Lois said. They both lunged for the phone at the same time. Lois won, assisted by a well-placed elbow.

"Well, hello, White Knight. Stormed any castles lately?"

"Not hardly," Junior said. "Coach is pushing us so hard I'll be lucky if I don't step on my tongue. Where's my African queen?"

"Not so fast, Buster. We got some business to discuss. When am I gonna meet Mr. Allie Costa? I have been given to understand he has asked you the same question more than once."

"That's why I called. Coach says no contact Sunday. Just a morning film session to break down last year's Delaware State game. We go down there for our opener. After that, we're off until Monday morning. You think we can make that work for us? I mean, as busy as your social calendar must be. If you do, then let me speak to Mickey. And if you don't, then let me speak to Mickey."

"Sunday is fine for me. If it's not for her, I'll go out with both of you. Hang on, she's right here and she's quivering in anticipation."

Mickey grabbed the phone, both girls giggling. "When am I going to see you?"

"Not at all, if you plan to keep on hiding out in Newark. I just told Lois, half-day session tomorrow. Does Lois have a car?"

"Of course. Why do you think I'm letting her tag along?"

"Pick us up in front of Bohn Hall at two thirty. I'll make Allie wear a clean shirt."

"You do the same. No tank top. I don't want you showing off those abs in front of Lois."

～

C hooch walked into the bowling alley and caught himself looking for his old friends, though he knew they wouldn't be there. First Junior and then Allie drifted away. He didn't get it, didn't understand why his best pals since forever had turned their backs on him. Clearly, the Bombers were no more. But old habits die slowly.

He and Dominick were still regulars at the bowling alley. So was Mary Theresa Gianetti, ostensibly the house waitress but in reality, Chooch could tell, a desperate lady in ferocious pursuit of a husband. Judging by her recent behavior, she had reluctantly put aside the torch she had carried for Junior since middle school. Now she was working hard to convince Dominick that she had eyes only for him. Or as Chooch overheard her tell one of her girlfriends, "Any port in a storm when you're fishing for a wedding ring. And I've got the right bait."

Chooch and Dominick were changing into their bowling shoes. As usual, the subject was the death of the Bombers.

"Never thought Mr. Football would go high-hat on us," Dominick said, launching into a familiar refrain. "No surprise about Allie. He'll never change. Wherever Junior leads, Allie will follow."

"College, that's what it is," Chooch replied. "They got too important to associate with us. Mr. Football believes his press clippings, and Allie probably reads them to him."

"Ha!" Mary T said, leaning forward, obviously to emphasize

her cleavage, and crossing her legs to show more thigh. She was on her break and took the opportunity to sit next to them. Chooch watched her to fawn all over Dominick. "You guys should have better things to think about than those two losers," she added, recrossing her legs and improving their view. "I'm going outside for a cigarette—just in case anyone cares." She smiled at Dominick, who immediately jumped up and accompanied her to the side exit.

Just as the door closed behind them, Chooch got a page from the front desk. It was a call from Paulie Tedesco. "Hey, boss. What's up?" Chooch said.

"I'm sittin' in the office wondering the same thing. Kiongosi must have lost his romance with the *Star-Ledger* since Anderson hit town. There hasn't been a line in the paper about him in a week. And Jackson Anderson has dropped off the map. It's almost like he's in the wind. It's too damn quiet. I don't like it."

"I'm about to bowl with Dominick, but I can cancel if you need me."

"No, there's nothing you can do right now. I had Anderson tailed this morning. He walked into the First Fidelity bank on Broad Street and got on the elevator that leads to the executive offices, and my guy couldn't follow because a bank guard barred the way. I'm thinking something is happening between him and bankers. But I don't have a clue. It makes no sense."

"Don't sweat it. We'll find out. All we gotta do is bank the North Ward votes and we win." Chooch hung up and glanced toward the side exit, where Dominick was trying to hold the door open for Mary T with one hand and zip up his fly with the other.

Chooch shook his head, knowing full well what had just happened between the two behind the building. "Mr. Football was right about one thing," he mumbled. "That skank has gone down more often and deeper than the Titanic."

"Say what?" the waitress said, straightening her skirt.

"I said, 'Let's bowl,'" he replied, walking ahead of them

toward their assigned lane. He was still mumbling and shaking his head when they got there.

～

Jackson Anderson and Fast Freddy Sternburg sat in Anderson's living room facing the wraparound picture window. A pile of newspaper clippings and polling data littered the coffee table in front of them. Freddy reached down and retrieved a sheet of paper, glanced at it, and remarked, "Damn, boss, this stuff is dynamite. Where did you get these? If they're on the money, then so are we."

"We're not supposed to have them. They come from a secret poll privately financed by the governor. He wants to run for re-election, win, and run for the U.S. Senate, but he's worried about the chain of events. He thinks that whoever wins the race for mayor here this fall just might be his next opponent—particularly if the margin of victory is big and the opponent is black."

"All I know is that according to this," Freddy said, waving the paper from which he was reading, "we are almost where we want to be."

"'Almost' doesn't feed the bulldog, Freddy," Anderson said. "Close means nothing. This ain't horseshoes. The next move has to make sure we *are* there. We need an incident. The kind of thing that will win over Italians who thought they never could vote for me."

"What kind of incident?" Freddy asked.

"Freddy, that's what I'm paying you for. Find one or make one."

"Well, while I got you, boss, what about Sinatra? Do we have him or not?"

"It's complicated, but I think we can do it. Let me worry about Sinatra. Just give me my incident."

～

Mickey and Lois stood at the sink doing the breakfast dishes. Annie Mae hovered in the doorway, eavesdropping.

When she'd heard enough, she interrupted. "Mickey said you guys were gonna check out the Montclair State campus this afternoon. You all know I'm a big booster of education, and far be it from me to interfere with yours, but Lois, it's only eight thirty in the morning. You rang the bell at six thirty a.m. Mickey said you all were going up there around two o'clock. So how come you've been here for two hours already?"

"You know how we are, Mrs. W. Girl talk is our life. You were young once."

"I was, and I'm still a girl, so let me in on the secret. What were you two discussing that needs all these hours between six thirty and one thirty?"

"Well, you know we both have dates, and it takes time to do our hair and—"

"Hold it, child. I'm pretty sure I know all about Mickey's date, but what does it have to do with you?"

"Well, he's Junior's friend, and—"

"Junior's *white* friend, I'm guessing."

"Well, yeah, but—"

"Listen, girl, you do know what happened in this city last summer. You do know what Mickey and Junior are going through, ducking and dodging to keep one step ahead of the bigots of both colors. Child, I told her, and I will tell you. They are perfectly fine young men, but nineteen sixty-eight isn't the time and this isn't the place for interracial dating. One more of his friends and one more of Mickey's and we might have to stand in front of City Hall and sing 'We Shall Overcome.' Don't get in water so deep, lady, that you can't swim to safety."

"No disrespect, Mrs. W., but I know Mickey is really in love. And I know there's nothing between Allie and me right now. Don't you think this is for us to decide?"

"It should be, child, but there's a lot of folks out there who are determined not to give you that chance."

"We know, Mama," Mickey said. "There's nothing between Allie and Lois, and there's everything between Junior and me. You raised me to be what I am and right now I'm a woman in love getting ready to meet her man." She kissed her mother. "I'm going to help Lois do her hair. It will be all right, you'll see."

"From your mouth to God's ears," Annie Mae said softly.

"That's strange, Mom. Junior told me that's what his mother says every time somebody in her family wishes for something. It's supposed to be an Italian saying, I think."

"Baby, it's something we all need to be saying twenty-four hours a day if we want to get this city through this nightmare."

~

I t was one of those Sundays that always seem to make up for the snow and the slush of winter and the nasty mosquito-breeding heat of summer in the city. The cycle of the changing landscape was what New Jersey in general and Newark in particular were all about each time the calendar was poised on the edge of another autumn. They were early, so Lois swung the car through Branch Brook Park.

The heat wave was over. Now it was a pleasant seventy-six degrees. The scorched grass of the park was slowly coming back to life. Rowboats glided across the lake. Families fired up portable grills. Over on the baseball diamond, two Essex County League amateur teams were already in the fifth inning,

"They can have Short Hills," Lois said. "Asbury Park and Belmar don't interest me. Look at the colors. The reds are redder. The greens are greener. We have our own master painter. Smell the smells. This is September in the city and we're going to meet our two hunks on a college campus. This damn city is so busy hating itself it doesn't even realize how lucky it could be if the bullshit stops."

"Maybe you should run for mayor," Mickey said. "You sure are starting to sound like you are."

"Look around you, girl. Open your eyes. This is what the city doesn't even know it has. In weather like this, in a situation like this, all I can tell you is this is what your mother was talkin' about when she said, 'Make sure you have protection in your purse.' She wasn't talkin' about a gun, girl. She was talking about hormones."

As Lois turned the corner onto Bloomfield Avenue and passed the ubiquitous longhaired dope-smoking teenagers across from the bank, one of them ran toward the curb, grabbed his crotch, and shouted, "Hey, pretty ladies, we got what you want."

"At least he didn't say 'niggers,'" Lois said, then adroitly gave him a single-digit salute with her middle finger. They left the city limits behind, crossing into Bloomfield with Glen Ridge and Montclair soon to come. In the span of just twenty-five minutes, traveling on one street without a single turn, the differences in housing bore witness to the differences in per-capita income.

Though they had crossed into a vastly different world, they were, in fact, only twelve miles from the very spot where the riot of 1967 had begun.

They turned onto Valley Road and were headed toward Upper Montclair, which was not a town at all but rather a mailing address designed to put its self-professed elite inhabitants into another postal zone.

The main entrance to the Montclair State campus was a few miles ahead, bracketed between the edge of the township and Route 46 east. When they made the turn through the entrance, they left traffic behind. They had eased into the world of a lazy-Sunday college campus. The roads were marked only by the foot traffic of college kids and the occasional bicyclist.

On their left sat Sprague Field, where scouts from the Giants and the Eagles would evaluate Junior as the season progressed. Ahead on their right was the main administration building.

"I don't have a clue where Bohn Hall is," Lois said. "But they do." She had stopped the car at an intersection where two coeds were waiting to cross. Both of them wore short-shorts and T-shirts that exaggerated the swell of their breasts. "Go ask your competition over there exactly where Bohn Hall is."

Once they got directions, they pulled in front of the building where Junior and Allie waited. As Lois drew to a stop. Mickey threw open the door and jumped into Junior's arms.

"Uh, that might take a little time," Lois said, holding out her hand to Allie, "so I'll introduce myself. I'm Lois and you're Allie, so show me around so we can get to know each other until someone dumps a bucket of cold water on them."

They walked ahead, Allie pointing out various buildings. Junior and Mickey were in no hurry to catch up, so as Allie and Lois walked, they talked about the only common experience they had shared: Barringer High School.

"To be honest, I really don't remember you," Allie said.

"How could you? Blacks and whites didn't exactly socialize back then. I mean, when we were both freshmen, I doubt if there were forty black kids in the school."

Allie threw both hands in the air. And stopped in his tracks. "You're black? You're *black*? Is that what you're saying? I'm stunned! Absolutely stunned. How could I tell?"

Lois turned two shades darker than Mickey. They both started to laugh. Lois punched him lightly in the arm and said, "I think I like you."

Junior and Mickey had caught up to them. Just ahead, three coeds wearing the obligatory short-shorts and Montclair State T-shirts were sprawled on the lawn sunning themselves. "Hey, Junior," a busty blonde yelled. "Come over here."

Mickey stiffened. Lois took a deep breath and stiffened as well. Allie said, "Football Annies. They don't even know him except through the school paper."

Junior hollered back, "Not a chance, ladies." He reached for Mickey's hand and kept walking.

"Well, now that you passed that test, Mr. White Knight," Lois said, "is it possible you guys can feed us? I'm starving."

~

That morning, at 4:30 a.m., state troopers Stanley Podolski and Harry Smith were parked in an unmarked car on the shoulder of the northbound lane two miles below exit 13A. Podolski held the radar gun as a low-flying white Cadillac rocketed into view. The gun flashed 87.6 mph.

"Let's go, Stash," Smith grunted, elbowing his dozing partner. "We're in the wrong business to get a good night's sleep." He flipped on the sirens and pursued the Cadillac.

The car they chased held two occupants. The driver, according to his license, was Charles Washington. The stop went smoothly until the troopers asked to search the trunk.

"You got no right to do that!" Charles shouted. "Where's your warrant? This is harassment. If I was white, we wouldn't even be conversatin' about this."

"Sir, you were traveling in excess of eighty-seven miles per hour. It is four thirty in the morning. So I'll ask you just one more time. Will you please open the trunk?"

"Hell, no," Charles said. "I don't even know what's in the damn trunk because it ain't my car. I picked it up in Philly from a guy who paid me a hundred bucks. I'm supposed to deliver it in East Orange and turn it over to a guy who will give me another hundred bucks. I swear to God, that's all I know."

"Harry," Podolski shouted to his partner, who had been questioning the other occupant of the car, "sit him down, go over to the car, and bring me the keys."

"This is false arrest," said Charles. "I'll sue your honky ass off. I know my rights."

"The only right you still have is to turn around and put your hands behind you. You are under arrest for resisting my lawful order and I think a lot more once we open that trunk."

Harry popped the trunk and Podolski shone his flashlight at the interior.

"My oh my," Podolski said. "Ain't this a pretty sight."

The guns were wrapped in plastic—three Glocks, a pair of .38-calibers, two AK-47s, and three Uzis. "Exactly what country have you declared war on?" Smith asked.

"I ain't sayin' nothin' except I want a lawyer."

"Well, I'll tell you this. You have the right to remain silent. Anything you say can and will be used against you in a court of law. If you cannot afford a lawyer, the court will appoint one for you."

"I'll cuff the other dummy," Podolski said.

~

Annie Mae Washington could barely breathe, the ferocious stress in her life squeezing to the point she knew she couldn't take any more. On one front, she was desperate to keep her daughter safe from the unchecked city-wide racial in-fighting that she knew could swallow both Mickey and Junior. On another, she had become a force in the PTA in an effort to keep the gangs out of her twelve-year-old son's schoolyard.

Her ex-husband, Talmadge, continued to harass her, ostensibly over rumors he'd heard about Mickey and a white boyfriend, but really over child support for T.C. To avoid payment, he'd moved from Essex County ten miles down Route ! to Union County, forcing her to start the legal process all over again.

She was well aware of the bureaucratic delays this would cause for her child-support checks. He had done it before.

And finally, she now had the added heartbreak surrounding her middle child, Charles, the one she kept foremost in her prayers every night. He was the only one of their children not angered by Talmadge's treatment of their mother.

A high school dropout whose only apparent income was as a street worker for Kiongosi's mayoral campaign, Charles worried her constantly. And in her heart, she knew the truth. On the few nights he slept at home, she had seen the bankroll on his nightstand. She had meant to confront him about it for months.

Now it didn't matter.

Charles had been arrested early that morning, but Annie Mae did not know until she and T.C. had returned from church early in the afternoon, when Charles finally got his one phone call. She let T.C. go to a friend's house, called Elizabeth, and then sat alone in the kitchen while she waited for her friend. She made no attempt to call Mickey, thinking, "Lord, she got enough trouble. Let her breathe happy while she has the chance."

Annie Mae had told Elizabeth everything she knew over the phone, but still she urgently wanted her friend by her side. An untouched cup of tea sat before her. In one hand she clutched a soggy tissue.

By the time Elizabeth arrived, Annie Mae could barely speak and was clearly in need of a lifeline. Her eyes were red. She had changed back into her night clothes. A faded green terrycloth robe was draped across her shoulders.

As a lifelong friend, Elizabeth knew what was required and immediately sprang into action. She poured the cold tea into the sink, put water on the stove to boil, and placed an arm around Annie Mae's shoulder.

"Lady, I've known you how many years? You are the strongest, most clearheaded woman I have ever known. I know it ain't gonna be easy, but I know you. Lord, honey, you trying to raise T.C. without a man in the house, Mickey got herself a white boy, and they fightin' the whole city. You got an ex-husband who uses you for target practice and won't pay a dime to help raise his own kids. And now this. You must feel like Pharaoh when Moses started throwing them plagues at him. But God gave you that strength. And now you are going to use it. Use it to deal with Talmadge and to help those two wonderful kids, and yes, do what you know is possible to help Charles. When is the arraignment?"

"Tomorrow morning."

She tightened her grip around Annie Mae's shoulder. "Does Talmadge know?"

"Not yet."

"Oh, Jesus. The worst plague is yet to come."

19

OUT OF THE CLOSET

The two-a-day practice sessions were over and the opener against Delaware State was just a week away. The campus had left summer behind and classes had begun. Junior and his quarterback, Johnny Jakes, headed to the cafeteria for lunch. Jakes was a highly recruited freshman, and the two had struck up a friendship their very first day in camp.

That was only natural between thrower and wide receiver, but there was more to it. Jakes was from Canastota, a small town in upstate New York. Montclair may have been suburban, but the heart of its student body was Essex County supplicated. Jakes' background stamped him to everyone as a shucks-and-gee-whiz guy, and because of the tension surrounding Junior's life, Jakes' openness attracted him.

They were exchanging ideas on how best to run a wide-receiver option pass play when Jakes caught sight of a coed. "So when you come around for the handoff, you . . . you . . . wow. Can't see her face or chest, but that sure is one attractive back porch swinging ahead of us."

"Can't argue with you about that. She is—" Junior followed Jakes' line of sight. He squinted. "Damn. She is *Mickey*." He ran ahead full speed to catch up to her.

She stopped and was laughing. "Hi, there, my football hero. What's up?"

"What's up, my ass. What are you doing here?"

"Well, actually, I just had a sociology class and I'm going to lunch. You, my friend, are speaking with a fully transferred and fully matriculated junior at Montclair State College."

"Lady, you are just too much. No, scratch that. You are just right, and I was too dumb to think of this. Does your mother know?"

"Oh, she knows. She wasn't happy, but she knows—she said if I'm going to be a teacher, this was the best school available to me. But the thing is, we sure won't be roommates. She said I could go but only if I was a commuting student. Don't look so glum. There is a beautiful surprise in all of this."

"Such as what?"

"I said it's a surprise. I'll tell when I think you should know."

Jakes had caught up with them but stood awkwardly silent until stammering out an attempt at conversation. "Uh . . . uh . . . I . . ."

"Calm down, Johnny," Junior broke in. She doesn't bite." He turned to Mickey. "You'll have to excuse him. This is Johnny Jakes, my quarterback. He comes from Canastota, New York, so excuse his shyness. The only introductions he gets where he comes from are to the guy next to him at a barn-raising or the girl in the sun bonnet at the church social. Johnny, this is my girl, Mickey Washington. Don't get fooled by her good looks. She's the one you have to answer to if you don't throw me the ball enough."

"I'm, uh, pleased to meet you," Jakes said, "and I do have to say he didn't exaggerate one bit when he told me how beautiful you are. I hope you plan to join us for lunch."

"Absolutely. I haven't seen this guy for ten days," she said, grabbing Junior's arm.

"So where's Lois?" he asked.

"Back where she belongs, at Newark State College in Union."

"Well, I'm glad she didn't talk you into going there instead of here."

"The whole thing was her idea. She pushed me and told me not to tell you, but she said if I wouldn't go to Montclair to join you, she would. I'm beginning to think I just might have to look out for that girl. You belong to me."

"Well, all right to Miss Lois."

"Uh, Miss Washington?" Jakes said.

"Mickey," she corrected him. They were close to the dining hall.

"Okay. Mickey. I know you have a lot to talk over, but do you think you could do it inside? I'm starving."

"Me too, Mr. Jakes. Race you to the entrance."

~

Later that afternoon, Junior told the coach he had some personal business he had to take care of, so he was excused from practice. At the end of the day he borrowed Allie's car and drove Mickey to Six Brothers Diner, at the edge of the campus facing Route 46.

Once the host seated them at a window booth, Mickey glanced at the menu and said, "I like this place."

"So does half the college. You should see it on a Saturday night."

The waitress took their orders. Mickey looked at him for a few seconds, then smiled and said with a softness in her eyes, "You know, except for Allie, today was the first time you ever introduced me to a friend. Does that mean we're out of the closet?"

"Out as we can be, lady. I'm too tired and you're too beautiful to keep on hiding like we have been. Friday night, we play Delaware State. Saturday morning, I tell my parents you are coming to meet the family for Sunday dinner. Saturday night, we are going to Greenwich Village for the Feast of San Gennaro—and the rest of the world can see us there."

"I was beginning to think you'd never ask. If this place weren't so crowded, I'd kiss you right here."

"Don't let that stop you."

She didn't.

When they broke apart, Junior told her, "By the way, Allie can pick you up Friday evening and take you and T.C. to the game. Bring Lois, and if your mom wants to go, bring her too. I'm playing this one for my family and friends."

"Well, Lois says her mother told my mother that you are going to be the first player from a Division III school to make All-American, so you better not let your fan club down."

"What are you? The president?"

"No. I'm the dictator."

Their food arrived. While they ate, Mickey talked about all the meals they had missed sharing and all the nights with stolen phone calls while Charles tried to eavesdrop.

The waitress brought a dessert menu. Junior started skimming it, then asked, "What's this big surprise I'm not supposed to ask about?"

Mickey smiled and prolonged his agony by humming.

"You're enjoying this, aren't you?"

"Not this. Just the look on your face. When I said I had a surprise, it was right after I told you my mom had insisted on me commuting to school. She also said she was young once too, and I might not believe this, but when she was my age there was a time or two when she didn't come home at night. And that she believed my first day here with you ought to end that way."

"Are you saying that . . ."

"Absolutely. Unless, of course, you have something better to do—"

"The hell with dessert. We're halfway out the door."

As they walked past the guard at Bohn Hall, he hollered after them, "You know the rules. No visitors after nine p.m. regardless of gender."

"We know. We know," Junior yelled back, and they kept going.

Just before they reached the elevator Mickey spotted the pay phone and said she'd only be a minute. He stood to the side, but he could hear her.

"Hey, Mom. I took your advice. I'll see you tomorrow after school. I guess since it will be a time or two that makes us even. I want you to know that you are the best role model any girl ever had."

She hung up, took his hand, and followed him into the elevator.

~

A nnie Mae got up early. She had been dead tired the night before and fell asleep with her clothes on. She hadn't been able to bring herself to tell Mickey about Charles. Let the young couple enjoy themselves another night as they started a life together. Mickey would find out soon enough.

Now she had to make up for lost time. She made T.C.'s lunch and awakened him. She dressed while he did and saw him off to wait for the school bus.

Mr. Jack, a former suitor and now a close friend, waited for her outside. He drove her to the city of Elizabeth and then to the Union County courthouse.

She didn't have to look for the legal-aid man. His name was William Flynn, and he was fresh out of Rutgers Law. He sat on a bench near the courtroom, a new leather briefcase at his feet. He was thumbing through some documents when she took a seat next to him.

Mr. Jack told her to call when she was ready.

"Mrs. Washington, this is complicated," Flynn began. "We're here in Union County Court because that county prosecutor gets first crack in this. The feds can take over if they feel the climate of opinion warrants it, but so far they indicate they don't want it. That's the good news. But there ain't much of it. He had ten guns in his possession. The serial numbers were filed off. Among the ten were two AK-47s and three Uzis. They are on the list that could push this to a class-C felony. That's the very bad news."

"Lord, help us," Annie Mae muttered.

"I searched and learned that he definitely is a first offender. I can argue that and ask for probation. They'll argue back with possession and intent to sell. Then I'll remind them that he is very small potatoes compared to the man who paid him to deliver and the man in East Orange who was the buyer. If he fingers them, we might get probation. I can't say either way, but the negotiating will start as soon as he is arraigned."

"When can I see him?"

"If we get bail, he'll go home today until either negotiations end or he goes to trial. If there's no bail, I will arrange for you to see him tomorrow. I wish I could guarantee something, but I can't."

Just then, the van from county jail pulled up outside the door, and prisoners, their ankles in chains, shuffled toward the courthouse.

"I have to go with him," Flynn said. "We'll talk after the arraignment."

Annie Mae followed him into the courtroom and took a seat for the proceedings.

They stood facing the judge, defense counsel, prisoner, and the assistant prosecutor. The charges were read, the judge asked for a plea, and Charles said in a very soft voice, "Not guilty."

The judge turned to the assistant prosecutor and asked, "What's your request on bail?"

"We ask for remand, Your Honor. Those guns could kill a lot of people."

Flynn argued for Charles. "Your Honor, Mr. Washington is a first offender. He is gainfully employed by a candidate for mayor of Newark. He has roots in the community, and he lives with his mother. We ask that he be released on O.R."

"Well," the judge said, pausing to wipe his glasses, "this is the way it's going to be. I do not belong to the NRA, Mr. Flynn. I believe if, as it claims, people kill people, they have a hell of a head start with a gun in their hand. I think Mr. Washington needs time for self-reflection. I remand him to Union County jail, with trial date to be set tomorrow."

He banged the gavel down, and the sound went straight to Annie Mae Washington's heart.

∾

The Kiongosi campaign had scheduled a rally for the front steps of City Hall. The current mayor was on the edge of having his indictment announced, so he raised no objection. But the candidate was not thinking about the rally. Instead, he was furious over the lead story in that morning's *Star-Ledger*.

Kiongosi Aide Arraigned on Gun Trafficking Charge

Kiongosi fumed. "What the hell are they doing over there? Kiongosi aide? He's a fuckin' coffee boy, a distributor of hand-bills. Who the fuck wrote this? Paulie Tedesco? Don't those motherfuckers even know who we really are? When I was a high school football coach, we started a little-brothers campaign to feed breakfast to my team's siblings. We started a literacy program for the team's parents who couldn't read. When a black cop shot an unarmed black kid, we didn't equivocate like the Uncle Toms did. We marched, and we demanded an inquest, and we got one. Freedom of the press, my ass!" He pointed his index finger at the assistant campaign manager, who was born and raised in Newark and who had been an assistant on Kiongosi's coaching staff. "You get down to the *Star-Ledger* and you straighten this out—and make them do it on page one. I want a retraction. I want the truth to be printed. We didn't know nothin' about no guns, and we know almost as little about

Charles Washington. He's a street kid with a street kid's mentality—we sure as hell didn't delegate any responsibility to him."

"I'm on it, boss. But I sure can't guarantee what their editorial board will do."

"If they give you some crap, then get a Newark minister to write an op-ed for them. Believe me, they won't turn that down."

~

T he rally began in a light drizzle, tamping down the enthusiasm level. A local drum-and-bugle corps did its best to raise the level of excitement, and two ministers who spoke of a new city and a new fairness and morality helped as well.

When Kiongosi stood silent at the microphone, the crowd got into it. He sensed that at least with this group he was back in business.

"This morning, the *Star-Ledger* printed a lie about my campaign on the first page." At the mention of the newspaper, the crowd booed and hooted. Kiongosi raised his hands to silence them. "Look at the numbers. We are now or soon will be a black city. Our brown brothers and sisters have slowly begun their own migration from Puerto Rico. Scattered Spanish-language signs already appear at the edge of the North Ward. I tell you this so that you will and must understand. For too long, the Uncle Toms on the city council talk big but defer to others. For too long, the current mayor plays us. For too long, they tell us to wait our turn. Now the waiting ends. My friends, our turn is now. Right now. And if we don't act, it will never come again. They made it about race. We didn't. They made it about votes, but you and you and you"—he pointed at the crowd—"you don't vote, and we lose, and that's why. So how will you vote this time—or will you vote at all? And who will you vote for?

Who? Who?" He cupped his ear and leaned toward the crowd. "*Who?*"

It was a question that demanded an answer. They knew it. They roared back, and from where they were gathered beneath the gold cupola that topped City Hall, the echoes resounded all the way down Broad Street:

"*Kiongosi! Kiongosi! Kiongosi!*"

He leaped off the steps and into the street, beckoning them to follow—and while they marched, a new chant arose.

"Our turn! Our turn! Our turn!"

They filled the streets, snarling traffic. They marched north until they hit Court Street, turned past the old neighborhood precinct house, and crossed Washington Street—jamming Court Street with chanting demonstrators. The street was bracketed by a high-rise apartment house and low-rent garden apartments. Just across the street from there stood another apartment house. Depending on which story one believed, that was a building from which sniper fire had erupted during the riot of the previous summer.

Their chants grew louder and then stopped. From the back of University Court, which much of the mob faced, a door opened, and a lone figure walked slowly toward them.

Kiongosi held up his hands. The crowd went silent.

The lone figure raised a bullhorn to address them. "For those who don't know me or can't put a face to what they see in the paper—my photo is god-awful, isn't it?—my name is Jerry D'Amilio. I am this paper's sports columnist. I covered your candidate when he coached high school football not far from this building. When the Board of Education had no money for tackling dummies or anything else football players need, I started a mailing campaign and raised the money. I ran a football game for twenty years that sent a lot of kids—probably yours—to college on academic scholarships. I was born here, ran the streets here, played ball here, and went to college at Rutgers-Newark down the street. So your concerns are my concerns. You delivered that message just now. I know all the candidates in this race. I don't take sides. I don't even know if I'll vote. But if you disperse now, I will talk with Kiongosi, sit him down with our editor-in-chief, and if he was treated unfairly, we'll rectify it."

Kiongosi took the bullhorn. "I believe him. He's honest. But before you go home, understand this. I believe in you. And we will win."

Slowly the crowd parted. The two walked into the *Star-Ledger* building.

The next morning, an op-ed piece written by the Rev. Theodore Manning, an influential Newark African American minister, appeared on the *Star-Ledger* editorial page. It scolded the paper for poor research on the Kiongosi article and lauded him as the right candidate.

Below it, a single paragraph appeared in italics:

Rev. Manning is a Newark resident and chairman of the Newark Ministerial Council. The opinions expressed above are his and are neither approved nor disapproved by the "Star-Ledger" editorial board.

20

MICKEY AT THE BAT

It was raining when Mr. Jack dropped Annie Mae off at the Carteret Hotel in Elizabeth. The rush-hour traffic had slowed to a crawl. They both had a lot on their minds, so they rode in silence. Annie Mae was preoccupied with self-condemnation.

Somehow, some way, I failed this child. Did I favor Mickey too much? Did I worry about T.C. too much? Did I blame Talmadge too much? Was I too quick to anger with him instead of listening?

She looked down, studied her hands, then closed her eyes. She did not trust herself to speak.

Mr. Jack glanced at her from the corner of his eye. "Annie, you're carrying too heavy a burden. Your eyes are so red, I can tell you've cried until there's no more tears left. If that boy were mine, I would have—damn. He should have been mine."

Annie Mae knew he meant well. "No sense wishing the past was different. Nothing gonna change the past. I gotta figure out what to do for him now."

Overpowering silence settled back across the car, broken only by the metronome thump-thump-thump of the windshield wipers. He braked and double-parked in front of the hotel, laid his right hand on top of her left, and said gently, "Want me to walk you inside?"

She sighed and reached for her purse. "No, I'm all right. I'll call you when we're done."

"I'll be a couple blocks away at the diner." Then, ignoring her protestations, he got out of the car, reached in the back for an umbrella, and escorted her to the revolving door at the entrance.

Flynn was on time. He walked with her to the hotel coffee shop. "How about some breakfast, Mrs. Washington? We can talk while you eat."

"No, just coffee," she told the waiter. "Am I going to see my boy today?"

"Just as soon as we leave here. But we need to talk. You heard the judge yesterday. He's no enemy of the Second Amendment. But I think he left us a pathway. Somebody handed Charles those guns in Georgia. Somebody prepaid to receive them in East Orange. That's two very important somebodies to the county prosecutor, Mrs. Washington. That's two keys to possible probation. That"—he leaned forward for emphasis—"is our possible escape hatch."

"He's got to do it, Mr. Flynn. He simply has got to do it. I am not going to let him throw his life away protecting two punks." Off that shred of hope, Annie Mae took a final sip of coffee, stood up, squared her shoulders, and stepped away from the table. Head held high, she was once again the Washington family matriarch on a mission.

～

The Union County jail, built in 1921, antiquated and overcrowded, loomed over Annie Mae. As a prisoner awaiting trial, her Charles was locked inside. She had no choice but to go in too, no matter how formidable the building seemed.

As they reached the front entrance, Flynn took Annie Mae's arm to steady her. "Don't take this personally, Mrs. Washington, but I can't afford to lose the mother of my best client at this point."

She appreciated his joke and smiled as he held the door open. "I predict a great future for you, young man."

Once inside, the humor died.

A desk sergeant kept a solitary vigil in the lobby. "Who have you come to see?" he asked.

Before Annie Mae could answer, Flynn stepped up. "Charles Washington."

"I'll see if he's still here," the desk sergeant replied, reaching for a thick ledger.

Annie Mae's breath caught in her throat. She grabbed Flynn's arm. "What does that mean? Why would they move him? Has something happened?"

He tightened his grip on her arm and whispered, "Just routine, that's all."

The desk sergeant looked up. "Fourth floor. I'll have him brought down."

He approached Annie Mae, but his eyes softened when he saw her flinch. "I'm sorry, ma'am, but I'm sure you understand that I have to do this."

He patted them down, Annie Mae and then Flynn, and told them that an officer would be there in a minute to escort them to the visitors' room.

Annie Mae froze, staring past the sergeant at the wall and the faint light that shone through a tiny window. *They have my baby. Charles, what have you done? What have you done?*

A second corrections officer led them through two locked doors to the visitors' room. The bare cinderblock walls were thinly whitewashed. Wooden chairs flanked a steel table. Annie Mae sat in one, back straight, hands clasped in her lap.

Flynn told her, "Relax, Mrs. Washington. He'll be along in a minute."

A door opposite her seat opened, and a guard beckoned Charles inside. He was slightly hunched over, head down, clad in a bright-orange jail jumpsuit. Though relief initially shot through her, she noticed he refused to make eye contact. He nodded at Flynn but said nothing.

Annie Mae said, "Speak to me, Charles."

After a long pause, he looked up. "You gonna yell at me? You gonna tell me what a disappointment I am? You gonna tell me I'm just like my father?"

"Charles, I didn't raise you to wind up here. Look at me. Don't look down. I'm speaking to you out of love—not anger. This isn't a lecture, and this isn't about how I feel. It's about what you feel and what we are going to do about this." She paused. "And there is something we can do."

She glanced at the guard who stood by the door, out of earshot to give them some privacy.

"Mama," he said. Her heart twisted—he hadn't called her that since he had moved out of the house. "Mama, I'm scared. I wanted money and I didn't know how to get it. I thought, well, maybe just this once. And now I'm here. I haven't seen Willie since I got locked up."

"Who is Willie, Charles?"

"He's the guy got busted with me. They separated us when they brought us here. I don't know why. I don't know what's happening."

"All right," Annie Mae said. "I don't know Willie, so I don't trust Willie. You got to listen very carefully to what I'm going to tell you. Do you trust Mr. Flynn here? Because I do."

Charles nodded, glancing at Flynn.

"He says it's your first time in a place like this and you can make it your last. Tell who gave you the guns in Georgia. Tell them who paid for them and was supposed to get them in East Orange. If you do, Mr. Flynn thinks you might get probation. But whatever happens, your conscience will be clear. Charles, I'm speaking to you as your mother. I carried you inside me for nine months. I fought to keep you when I sent your father packing. I told you once in the kitchen when we argued over this black-separatism thing that I would always love you. Now is the test.

Not for me, because I just gave you my answer. But for you, Charles, for you. Do you love and respect yourself enough to do what is the right thing for you and our family?"

The guard motioned to Flynn that the visit was over. Flynn looked hard at Charles. "I'll be here tomorrow morning and we'll talk," he said. "Your mother speaks from her heart. I speak from my knowledge of the law. You need to trust us both."

Charles slowly stood.

Annie Mae looked at the guard. "Can I touch him? Please, can I touch him?"

The guard nodded. She threw her arms around her son, hugged him as hard as she could, mixing that love with the ocean of pain and frustration deep within her. But she put her head just above his shoulder.

She didn't want him to see her tears.

～

That night after supper, she told Mickey. Supper itself had actually been a relief. T.C. talked about his visit to the Newark Boys Club on Littleton Avenue and his conversation with the director, a former middle-school football coach newly arrived from West Virginia.

"He's gonna start a Pop Warner football team, and I'm gonna be on it."

"That's great," Annie Mae said.

"You're not even gonna be the water boy," Mickey cut in, laughing, "unless you stop trading the lunches Mama makes for you to your classmates for their Ring Dings. You don't weigh enough to be a tackling dummy."

Both women started laughing and T.C tried to shout them down. "But I'm fast. Coach says I'm faster than a speeding bullet."

"T.C., that's just a line from the 'Superman' commercials," Annie Mae said, reaching over to rub his head.

"You're gonna see. Once they give me the ball it's Mr. Touchdown USA."

"It's Mr. Underweight USA," Mickey shot back, still laughing.

Annie Mae waved her off, figuring that enough teasing was enough teasing.

Then Mickey's face lit up. "You want to play football, T.C.? I mean, do you *really* want to play football? How would you like to meet a *real* football player and see a *real* football game?"

"Wow."

Annie Mae looked at her and said with a smile she tried to hide, "Well, who is this mystery man?"

"Oh, you know him. Lois and I call him the White Knight—and by the way, he says he would like you to come as well on Friday night. He says he's counting on it. His buddy Allie is going to pick us up."

T.C. jumped up, ran to his sister, and hugged her. "For real, is he a real person?"

"Oh, he's the realest person I know, T.C. You're going to love him."

"Homework, T.C., homework," Annie Mae said.

T.C. whistled as he headed for his room.

Mickey gathered the supper dishes and carried them to the sink.

"Let 'em wait, child," Annie Mae said. "Come sit down. We got another crisis." She poured them each a cup of coffee. Mickey sat quietly waiting.

Annie Mae joined her and took a deep breath. "It's about Charles. I know you two have had your differences, but—"

"He's a hardheaded racist, Mama—I told him so and I am not going to apologize to him for calling him that. He—"

"Child, just hush. This isn't about name-calling. Your brother is in Union County jail."

Mickey almost dropped her cup. "Oh, my God. What has he done?"

"He picked up ten guns from a man in Georgia and was paid a hundred dollars to deliver them to a man in East Orange for another hundred. He was going eighty-seven miles per hour when the police stopped him. The only thing he delivered was himself to county jail."

"What are we gonna do?"

"Well, we got this lawyer from Legal Aid named Mr. Flynn, and he thinks because Charles is a first offender that he can get probation if he gives them the names of the men at either end of his trip. But you know Charles."

"Mama, I can get him to do it. I know I can. Let me visit him alone. But let's not spoil T.C.'s excitement, and let's not spoil what Junior has planned. I'm going to meet his folks Saturday. But I promise you I can convince Charles. Let's just do this step by step."

"Promise me you will see Charles on Monday."

"I will."

"And Mickey, don't worry about meeting Junior's folks. Just remember the way they raised him is part of the reason you love him—and part of the reason I am beginning to love him too."

~

The house was quiet. Mickey and T.C. had gone to bed. Annie Mae was alone in the living room, a late-night talk show on the TV. But she was lost in thought. She had tried with Charles, Lord knows she had tried. But now she felt she was fresh out of alternatives. If only she had—

The blessed silence was gone in a heartbeat. Somebody rang the doorbell, then kicked the door and beat on it. Jolted from her thoughts, her stomach churned. Even before she heard the door break open, she knew. It was Talmadge, adding his signature to what had been a horrific day. Before she could react, he had splintered the front door and came charging at her.

She ran into the kitchen and shoved the table between them.

"Bitch!" he screamed. "You get that honky-lovin' daughter of yours out of bed and into this kitchen now! You let her run wild, and now I'm gonna take my belt to her."

She shoved the table at him. He pitched forward, enveloping her in a tidal wave of alcohol fumes.

"You get the hell out of here, now! You lay a hand on that girl, I will kill you and go to prison with a smile on my face." She ran to the cabinet and pulled out a carving knife. Turning to face him, she dropped her voice an octave, making sure her intent was clear. "I swear it and you better believe it. Talmadge, if you don't get out of here, I'll stick this squarely in your chest."

"Bitch!" he shouted. "If there's any killin' to be done here tonight, I'll do it and it'll be you and your slutty daughter."

~

In her room, Mickey sat straight up in bed, awakened by commotion in the house. Recognizing her father's voice, and the danger he could present, she slunk out of bed and down the hall to T.C.'s room.

"What's he yelling about?" T.C. asked her. "Is he gonna kill us?"

"Hush, baby, just get back into bed. Whatever you hear, you stay here. You don't come out. You understand?"

"Yes, but—"

"No buts about it, baby. I got something to do. We gotta protect Mama." She opened his closet door and rummaged around until she found what she was looking for. She put her index finger to her lips, reminding T.C. of the need for silence.

Barefoot in her nightgown, she snuck quietly down the hall. Just ahead she saw Talmadge swinging wildly at her mother, who still held the knife.

"That's enough!" Mickey shouted, freezing both parents where they stood. She gripped T.C.'s baseball bat in both hands and held it up for Talmadge to see.

Talmadge lurched forward.

"I warned you," Mickey said.

She swung from the heels. The bat slammed against Talmadge's skull. He crumpled near her mother's feet. Mama rushed over to him, but Mickey shouted again. "Don't help him! Don't touch him!"

"He's still your father, child."

"No, he's not. He's a bully and a drunk and he doesn't deserve to be in the same room with you."

Talmadge managed to rise to his feet, wavering and mumbling, "I got a concussion. Get me to a hospital."

"You take one step toward my mother, and the only place you're going is to the morgue."

"I'm your father. You have to help me."

"I'll help you out the front door, and that's all the help you'll ever get from me in this life. If you ever come here and threaten my mother again, you better have written your will."

The three stared one another down. Then Talmadge stumbled out through the damaged front door. Mother and daughter embraced and stood just clutching each other for five minutes.

"You should have seen yourself with that bat," her mama said.

"You should have seen yourself with that knife," Mickey said.

And then they laughed so hard they had to sit down.

21

FOR THE LOVE OF CHARLES

The day before state troopers busted him, virtually nobody knew Charles Washington's name. That was then. The morning after he was arrested, his picture was splashed across the front page of the *Star-Ledger*. He was also the main topic of conversation at Kiongosi's downtown headquarters, at Paulie Tedesco's White Citizens Council, and in Jackson Anderson's North Ward living room.

Rarely, if ever, had anyone achieved less and been talked about more in Newark since Robert Treat bought the land on which it still stands. Charles Washington had always wanted to be somebody. But locked away on the fourth floor of the Union County jail, he knew nothing about the local repercussions he'd caused.

Kiongosi had gotten his laudatory op-ed article, but it did not quell the noise around his alleged relationship with Washington, touched off by the original *Star-Ledger* story. Now, in a staff meeting, he pounded the desk and yelled, "This has got to stop! Somebody has to come up with an idea to disassociate myself from that street-level retard. Who in this room has any idea about how to handle this?"

"Well," his closest aide offered, "we got to find out who

bought those guns, and if he's white, we tie him to Paulie. Let's hope he is, because people in this town—even the whites —are pissed off about our crime rate and want somebody to blame."

"Do it," Kiongosi said. "Find a way and do it."

⌇

The topic was much the same at Paulie Tedesco's staff meeting at the White Citizens Council. "He's black—they can't deny that," Tedesco said, his voice tinged with new-found righteousness. "He was a street worker for Kiongosi—they can't deny that. What we got to do is find out who bought the guns and who sold them and who was at the other end."

"Well, we got a couple of correction officers and a couple of prisoners inside Union County jail," Chooch said. "Maybe they can get it out of the kid. He's the key—if he rats the guys out and their skin color works for us."

"Do it," Paulie said. "I don't care if they beat the shit out of him—as long as it doesn't show."

⌇

In the Anderson living room, in front of the picture window that looked out on a large, neatly manicured green lawn, Jackson Anderson and Fast Freddy Sternburg were wrestling with their own solution.

"It seems to me," Freddy said, "that it doesn't matter who bought the guns—white or black. We got one opponent from either persuasion. What we have to do is use it to ride the anger about crime in this city and turn it against one of them."

"So how do we do that?"

"We try to make contact with the kid somehow. That gives us a head start. We find out what he wants or needs and give it to him in order to get his information. Then, without knowing it, he's working for us. Whatever the facts, I won't let them get in the way."

～

Mickey waited for Lois. Both had decided to cut their morning classes after Lois had volunteered to drive her to the Union County jail. Mickey intended to keep her promise to her mother. She expected her meeting with Charles to be one of raw emotions and past anger renewed.

But she was ready to fight for her mother, for her younger brother, even for Charles himself. Somehow, subliminally, the baseball-bat confrontation with her father had punctuated her new family role.

When she opened the front door at the county jail, she was taken aback by the noise and the sight of two corrections officers struggling with a man in a torn T-shirt and a bandage caked with dried blood around the top of his head.

"Motherfuckers, I know my rights! I want your badge numbers. I want—" He hit the floor. One of the officers reached down and cuffed him from behind. "He's my fuckin' son!" the man shouted as he continued to struggle. As he turned over, Mickey saw his face and wanted to vomit. It was Talmadge Washington. Prone on the floor, he looked straight at her. "Tell these assholes who I am!"

"I told you," the angry desk sergeant, who had joined the struggle, yelled at him, "you ain't on his visitors list. But starting right now, you're gonna be on an inmates list all your own."

The two other officers had Talmadge on his feet, and the sergeant told them, "Get this piece of garbage out of my lobby— and do it now."

As they pulled him toward the elevator, Talmadge looked back at Mickey and shouted, "Get your rich faggot white boy to ask his mommy and daddy to get my bail! Don't forget who you are."

"I wish I could forget," she said to the desk sergeant. "I wish I could."

The desk sergeant looked at her and asked, "Do you know that idiot?"

"Yes. He's the father who shows up at my house once a month to beat up his ex-wife, who happens to be my mother. He's the father who never paid his child support. He's the father who never gave a damn about his kids. Yes, I know him, all right."

"Well, he's not gonna be around to beat on your mom for a while. I can guarantee that. So who are you, exactly?"

"My name is Mickey Washington and I'm here to see my brother Charles."

"Lady, do us both a favor and please tell me you're on the list."

"I think—"

Just then William Flynn, clutching his briefcase, came through the entrance door and shouted, "She is. She is. He put her on it after we consulted last night."

"At last," the desk sergeant mumbled and then sighed. "Law and order has been restored. Your name is right here, Miss Washington. Wait here with his attorney and somebody will be here shortly to pat you down and take you to the visitors' room." He motioned to a group of wooden chairs against a wall.

"Your mother," Flynn told her after they sat down, "is an extremely classy lady, and you sound like you're just like her. We need to talk before they come to get us. Your mom called me last night. She says you are strong—says you are family-strong. Well, here's what we need today. It's up to you to get him to give up those names directly to the county prosecutor. Guns are a big issue since the Newark riot. We had a small riot here in Plainfield. Nobody talks much about it, but we had a police officer killed. The prosecutor is very aware of public mood. Those names will feed right into his political ambitions. I can get

Charles probation if he flips for the county. But he has to cooperate. Can you get him to do it?"

"I don't know for sure, but I have the best chance in the
family. You saw that pitiful drunk being carted out when you
came in. That's my dad. Dear old Dad. The only mistake my
mom ever made." She paused. "I know the way Charles thinks. I
believe I can do this."

A corrections officer approached for the pat-down, and they
followed him to the elevator.

"Will I get a little privacy when I talk to him?" she asked.

"Miss, I can promise you I'll be a short distance away," the
guard said, "and I assure you I won't be listening. You can talk
about anything you want except a jailbreak." He saw the look on
her face and was quick to add, "Only joking, Miss, only joking."

The elevator stopped at the fourth floor and the guard led
them to the visitors' room. They found seats at the stainless-steel
table and waited.

Charles entered from the door behind their table, hands and
ankles shackled. His skin was ashy. He looked like he had
neither bathed nor slept much since his apprehension. His eyes
were red.

When she saw him, Mickey's heart skipped a beat. She rose
and started toward him, but Flynn interceded before the guard
could and took her back to her chair. "There will be a chance to
hug later," Flynn said. "Don't forget why you're here. Your mom
is counting on you."

Charles had yet to speak.

"Charles . . . Charles," she said, "why do you make it so hard
for us to love you?"

"Why are you here? Dad was supposed to—"

"You gotta learn that you can't count on him for anything.
Dad got busted. He made a scene when he found out you hadn't
put him on the visitors' list. He fought the guards and cursed
them. The only thing he learned this morning is that they are not
as easy to push around as our mother. They hit back."

"He okay?"

"He'll never be okay. He attacked Mom last night because you're in jail, and I'm dating a white boy whom I love."

"White boy, huh. The football player?"

"How did you know about him?"

Charles laughed, but it wasn't a happy sound. "Hey, girl, the street has eyes. More people than the two of you thought know about you guys. I heard it on the street."

"So you gonna start about Junior?"

"Junior? That's his name? Well, you get some time to think here. Is he good to you?"

"Better than anyone I ever knew, starting with our father. I love him—and you should be happy for me."

Charles smiled. "A white boy, huh? My big sister is finally in love, and she comes up with an albino who sure as hell ain't my idea of a brother-in-law. But if he respects you, I guess I have to lay off."

"Charles, I didn't come here to discuss my private life." She looked quickly over at Flynn, who nodded. "I came here for Mom and for T.C. and for you. Do you realize you are about to ruin your life? Look at me. I mean it—look at me."

"You gonna shout at me like everyone else? Is that what you here to do?"

"No, Charles, it's not. We've had our issues, but this is family. I'm here because I love you."

He stared at her as though he was trying to read her thoughts. The silence was intense. He lowered his voice and said in a half-snarl, "You wanna make me a rat. Is that what you want?"

Without waiting for confirmation from Flynn, she trudged on. "You and Willie, you both have what the prosecutor wants, Charles. You and Willie. You don't realize it, but it's you and Willie in a race and whoever talks first probably gets to walk. I want that to be you, Charles. All of us want that for you."

"I'll think about it."

"Charles, if you—"

"Damn it, I said I'd think about it!"

Flynn spoke for the first time. "Don't take too long. Your sister is dead right. Willie gets there first, you lose. It's that simple. I'll see you tomorrow morning."

The guard motioned that time was up. "You can hug him if you want," Flynn said.

She leaned across the table and put her arms out. As they embraced, she whispered in his ear, "Do it for Mama. Do it for T.C. Do it for me. And, Charles"—she tightened her grip—"do it for yourself."

The guard took his arm and he was gone.

~

By the time Lois picked her up at the jail, it was too late to head to Montclair State and Lois had already missed her classes at Kean. "How did it go in there?" she asked.

"Just another routine day in my life," Mickey said. "I walked in, and my father was on the lobby floor cursing at and fighting with two corrections officers. He was handcuffed, and then he saw me. And it got worse. He called me a slut. He said things about Junior I won't even repeat. Mr. Flynn was there, and we went upstairs to see Charles and I tried to convince him to give up the guys who paid him. The best I got was 'I'll think about it.'"

"And will he?"

"I don't know, Lois. It would mean so much to my mother and I guess me, too. I don't know. I . . . "

For the first time since she was a little girl, she started to cry —little sobs at first, and then the tears ran down her face in wide tributaries until there was nothing left, and she was reduced to sobs again.

Lois parked on the road shoulder, unbuckled her seat belt, opened the door, and walked around to Mickey's side.

She opened the door, pulled Mickey to her feet, and put her arms around her friend. "Let it all out, baby, and then hear me. You are tougher than this. You were tougher when you swung that bat at that drunken son of a bitch. You were tougher when you took Junior's hand and loved him and stood up, just the two of you, to fight this whole sick city. And you're going to meet Junior's parents. You are going to make T.C. very happy on Friday night. And you just might see me and Allie stand up for you when you get married."

"I swear, Lois, you are the bossiest, nosiest, crudest best friend a girl ever had in this world."

They sat there with their arms around each other, laughing and laughing. They didn't stop until Mickey's stomach started to rumble.

Lois stood up. "Get back in the car, girl. That's a Big Mac rumble if I ever heard one."

22

THE UGLY TRUTH SURFACES

Junior and Johnny Jakes knelt in the locker room with the rest of their team, after Coach Yablonski told them to take a knee. Junior thought he could almost see a smile on Coach's face and hoped he was pleased with what he'd seen during their final practice before the season opener on Friday. But Junior knew better than to expect high praise. He'd heard that Coach Yablonski threw around compliments as though they were manhole covers.

Still, Junior realized he and Jakes made a good combination. And the comments and attitudes of every player on the team told him they knew it too. A quiver of excitement shot through him at the notion that maybe, just maybe, with the pro scouts coming, he had a shot. Coach glanced his way and appeared to be trying to quell his own excitement. Maybe Coach Yablonski thought he had a shot too.

"All right," Coach said. "Not bad. Not bad, but don't let me smell a scintilla of overconfidence. Yes, last year we beat them by three touchdowns. What does that mean tomorrow night? Nothing, if you guys take them lightly. Everything, if they are motivated by revenge. Historically, my parents' ancestors used to say revenge is a dish best served cold. Just remember that the other guys have been chilling it for a whole year. Put that thought in the back of your head and bring it out three times tonight before you fall asleep. And Jakes, please note that we will be wearing red jerseys tomorrow night. Throw that ball to any other color shirt and I will not be happy—and you *will* want to keep me happy. Just ask the upperclassmen. All right, hit the shower, guys."

They had showered, changed, and were walking slowly toward the dorm when Junior told Jakes, "If Coach puts a curfew on us, I'm depending on you to cover for me. It might not be necessary, but if it is, tell him my dad's sick."

"I got your back, Junior."

"Great! And when you throw one of those nine-feet-too-high passes tomorrow night, don't worry, Johnny. I'll have yours."

Allie was already parked in front of Bohn Hall when Junior got there. "Got to go to the room and get something and then we'll go," Junior said. He was back five minutes later with a package in a Montclair State bookstore bag in his right hand. "Don't misread this. Mickey knows that you and Lois are platonic friends, but she invited her anyway."

"As long as the both of you know, because Lois and I agree on that," Allie said. "Does her mother know I'm coming?"

"Yes. I'm doing this because I don't want her going up to every white man in the neighborhood and asking if he's the one who is going to take her to the game. As ugly as you are, this will set the record straight."

It took them half an hour to get to Mickey's house. On the way, they talked about school and the game and where they would meet after. While Allie talked, Junior noticed that he kept sneaking looks at his rearview mirror.

When they crossed into the North Ward, Allie told him to hold on a minute. He cut off a red Ford and a kid on a bicycle and wound up in front of Ferrara's Bakery.

"What are you doing?" Junior said, annoyed at his friend's reckless driving.

"I'm covering your ass before your mother finds out how uncouth her son is. We are Mrs. Washington's dinner guests. Get your ass inside and get cannolis for dessert."

After Junior returned with a bakery box, Allie drove the remaining few blocks to Mickey's house in silence. When they pulled up to the curb, he turned to Junior and said, "Something is wrong."

"Is that why you kept checking the mirror?"

"Junior, don't go off the wall on me. But I think we were being followed."

"Wouldn't surprise me. Sometimes I get the feeling I'm living inside a soap opera, but this is a little too much. What are you studying in your film-appreciation class? James Bond's impact on the Italian community?"

"Just sayin'. Keep your eyes open."

❧

Mickey answered the doorbell. She kissed Junior and hugged Allie, then turned to her mother and T.C. and said, "These are my two best college friends. I think you already know Junior, Mom."

"You might say that, Mickey." She turned to Allie. "Are you the one that's supposed to keep those two out of trouble?"

"I do the best I can, Mrs. Washington, but sometimes it gets a little difficult."

"Been there and done that, Allie. Been there other times and tried to do that."

They sat in the living room. T.C. stared at the older boys but hadn't said a word.

Mickey said, "I told you you'd get to meet a football star—and here he is."

"For real?" T.C. asked.

"I don't know about me being a star. What about you? Here, catch!" Junior threw the Montclair State bag to him.

T.C. caught it, dropped it, then caught it again before it could hit the ground.

"Not bad," Junior said. "Open it. It's yours."

T.C. tore at the wrapping. Inside was a Montclair State Indians pennant, a Montclair State T-shirt, and a picture of Junior in full uniform, reaching up to catch a football. He had written in ink across the top:

For T.C., soon to be the Number One MSC Indians fan—Junior Friscella.

T.C. stared at Junior with wide eyes. "Is it all for me? Can I do what I want with it?"

"You heard the man, T.C.," Annie Mae said.

"Come on with me, Mr. Junior," T.C. said, stretching out a hand. He pulled Junior down the hall to his room. T.C. went straight to a picture of Matt Snell, the Jets running back, that T.C. had cut out of the *Star–Ledger*. He pulled it off the wall and tacked Junior's photo in its place.

"That's my spot of honor, Mr. Junior."

"Hey, let's get something straight. I'm not Mr. Junior. To you, I'm Junior. Just plain Junior. We're friends."

"Are you and Mickey friends?"

"Ask her. I think she'll tell you we are more than that."

Back in the living room, T.C. told everyone, "This is Junior. He's my friend and he said so. I asked if he was your friend, Mickey, and he said to ask you because he thinks you're more than that. He thinks—"

The doorbell rang. It was Lois.

"Thank God—saved by the bell," Mickey said. "Let's eat."

～

Annie Mae watched T.C. bouncing off the wall during supper. She knew he never could get Charles to spend time with him. Talmadge had never been there for him. Not once. All her children had grown up frightened of their father, frightened for her. T.C.'s older sister, not a brother or any other male, had protected her with his baseball bat. Annie Mae had long lamented the lack of male role models for her boys. But what could she do as a single mom? Keeping a roof over their heads and food on the table was a struggle.

But as she watched her son gazing at Junior with wide, bright eyes, she knew: Now her son had a male role model. All through the meal, he asked Junior questions. "How do you block a guy who's bigger than you?" "What's a post pattern?" "How many passes you gonna catch tomorrow night?" "Will you score a touchdown for me?"

"T.C.," Lois finally said, "if you don't let someone else talk, I'll show you how to tackle, and, trust me, you won't like that at all."

"Hey," Allie said, "lay off my old friend's new friend. I'll sit next to him tomorrow night and we can watch the game like men."

"I'm staying out of this," Mickey said. "I'm gonna do the dishes. T.C., you better get your narrow behind out of the kitchen and behind the desk in your room and start making a dent in your homework."

Junior put an arm over T.C.'s shoulder. "I'll get you started, kid. Maybe I can learn something from you."

Annie Mae watched Junior lead her son down the hall to help with homework. She felt the beginning of tears prick her eyes. Never in a million years would she have expected such a turn of events.

She looked at Lois. "Why don't you help Mickey so Allie and I can sit here and get to know each other better?"

Lois nodded, and scooped up her plate and silverware.

Annie Mae had always been a no-nonsense woman and saw no reason to start playing coy now. "So, Allie, what do you think about this black-white love affair, things being what they are in this city? Are they getting any pressure I don't know about? Can they handle it?"

"Mrs. W., I've known Junior all my life. Pressure never stopped him from doing what he wanted to do. When we were in grammar school and we played for the CYO basketball title, he was the one we wanted at the foul line when the game was up for grabs. When the homework was killing me at Barringer, he was the one who sat me down in my bedroom and taught me enough algebra to get by. I never had any black friends. Not because I didn't want any, but because there weren't any in my neighborhood. But when the North Ward went apeshit—uh, pardon me, Mrs. W., I meant when the adults went wild after the riot and blamed blacks for everything—he and Mickey taught me the biggest lesson of my life. They taught me how to cut through the crap and see the truth. Trust me, Junior and Mickey can handle anything the bigots throw at them. If Lois and I were more than friends, we could, too. I didn't mean to make a speech, but he was always my best friend, and now it's like she is his other half."

"Well, I thank you for that, Allie. And Lois—don't hurt her. Do you know she's my godchild?"

"I'll never hurt her. Lois and I are friends—in a very, very great way, close friends—but nothing more. That's all, but that means a lot to both of us."

"Young man, I want to tell you that this conversation has meant a lot to me. If you ever need another opinion on anything, I'm here for you. You are an unusual young man, and I think you and Lois have a genuine friendship. That's rare among young people. You both impress me."

They were all back at the kitchen table when the telephone rang. She excused herself. Mickey followed.

"It's Charles," she whispered to Mickey, receiver pinned to her chest. She raised it back to her face. "Charles, are you all right?"

"I'm scared, Mama. I'm scared. They cornered me and they—"

"Who cornered you, Charles? Tell me what happened."

"They jumped me and had me up against the wall. They wanted the names of the guy in Georgia and the guy in East Orange. They said if I told them I could get money and they would protect me."

"What did you do?"

"I hit one of them. A corrections officer heard us scuffling and separated us. He asked for my side of the story and I wouldn't tell him."

"What do you want me to do, Charles?"

"Call my lawyer, Mama. Tell him to come see me as soon as he can. He'll know what to do. I'm not a rat, but I'm not a fool. Tell him I said that. I gotta go. Goodbye."

Annie Mae didn't want to face the other children looking shaken up and teary. She went to the bathroom and washed her face, put on fresh lipstick, teased her hair. *Well, that's the best I can do.* She looked in the mirror. "Lord, I know you never give us more than we can handle, but isn't it time that boat finally sails?"

She walked back to the kitchen.

They were waiting for her to say their goodnights. She noticed Mickey had her coat on. *Well, if that's the way it's going to be, I have no right to complain.*

Just as they reached the door, the front window exploded.

Something fell to the floor as they all gasped and screamed. The boys moved to shield the women and T.C. Junior crept forward to investigate.

It was a decorative rock, the kind that marks the border of a homeowner's lawn. But it was coated with dog feces.

Junior and Allie raced out the door. A car was pulling away, horn blowing and verbal invective breaking the sound of silence that usually marked the neighborhood that time of evening.

"Get back in the house!" Junior shouted. "Don't come out. Call the cops."

Before ducking back inside her home, her sense of safety utterly violated, Annie Mae saw the car Junior and Allie had arrived in, where Allie had parked it under a streetlight. The faded green paint job on the old car wasn't much to look at. But there was no mistaking the huge letters splash-painted in white on the windshield: NIGGER LOVER.

"What kind of a sick mind would do this?" Allie said.

"I think you and I both know exactly who."

Shaking, Annie Mae went inside and called the police. She told them a half-truth, that they were finishing dinner when the rock crashed through the window. She did not mention her visitors or their car. The police reaction told her she had done the right thing. They showed no particular interest.

The kids' secret was out, whether they were ready to share it or not. And now they all had to deal with the consequences.

∿

Junior met Mickey at lunch the next day, as usual. Standing in line at the food counters, she put a hand on Junior's wrist and said in a very soft voice, "I'm scared. Before, I was just mad as hell at the bigots, at the city, at the situation. But last night I was scared for the first time. I'm scared for you, not us. Whoever did that knows who you are. They are cowards, and that makes them all the more to fear. They'll never face you. They could even be in this room."

Junior scooped a portion of green beans onto his plate and whispered, "Don't worry. They are garbage. You and I don't give in to garbage. They are not on my mind right now except to reassure you. Don't underestimate our love,. Right now, we are going to sit down and eat and tell each other great things, and then I'm going to kiss you and go back to the dorm to get ready for tonight. Allie has the tickets. He'll pick you guys up at five thirty. You be sure to tell T.C. the first touchdown we score is for him."

"I love you."

"In that case, the first touchdown is for you—but don't tell that to T.C."

23

T.C. GETS A ROLE MODEL

William Flynn was the hero of the day over at the Legal Aid office. In a world where Legal Aid lawyers spent day after day seeking plea bargains they couldn't get while defending clients who were no strangers to the system, he emerged as the man with a foolproof plan.

For once, Flynn was in a rare position in a "Legal Aid against the System" matchup, where he held the only cards that he knew could advance the politically aware county prosecutor's agenda.

He was dealt those cards that morning when his client Charles Washington, an alleged and about to be self-confessed gun smuggler, revealed them to Flynn during their hour-long consultation. Now Flynn was on his way to the prosecutor's office to propose a deal he believed the man could not refuse.

He was stunned when Annie Mae Washington called him late the night before to tell him that her son needed to see him as soon as possible. During his last visit, he had warned Charles that Willie Adams, who was arrested with him, was probably seeking a deal. The prosecutor had offered it to whoever gave up the information first. But Charles had shown no inclination to beat him to it.

The story he got from Washington that morning had all the earmarks of a game-changer.

"They came to me, two inmates, and offered me money to say a white guy paid me to do it," Charles said. "When I didn't answer, they jumped me. So we was fightin', and a CO broke it up and took me aside—and then he offered me money to say it was a black guy. I don't know what's going on, Mr. Flynn, but I'm sure it has to do with the election. What I know for sure is that I can't stay in this place without me gettin' hurt."

"I believe you," Flynn told him, "but we can't prove those accusations. Give me the names you dealt with at both ends of the gun deal and I think we can get you out of here with nothing more than probation. So who are they?"

"Don't take this personal, sir. But I ain't givin' them up until I find out what the deal is. You tell the prosecutor that. And one more thing. Is my father still in jail?"

"He is, and he will be arraigned later today for assaulting an officer. What else?"

"I want somethin' done to protect my mama. I been wrong about this, and it took my sister to prove it to me. Now I'm scared for my mama. As little as she is, he might have killed her the other night if my sister hadn't stopped him. Mama put my dad out, and then she raised all of us without him or any money from him. She put up with me and guided them. Is there some way we can keep him away from her?"

"Yes, there is. I'll talk to her and we'll fix up a peace bond for her. If he comes within two yards of her or her house, it's a crime. In return for that and hopefully probation, you got to give the prosecutor the names."

As he walked out of the jail, Flynn stopped to call Annie Mae Washington.

"Mr. Flynn, I'm working, so we can't talk long. Is Charles all right?"

"He's better than all right, Mrs. Washington. There's a chance I may have him home tonight, and I think it's important to know that he is concerned about his father hurting you. I suggested we go to court and request a peace bond. I told him if the judge agrees we'll get the bond, and it will be a crime for him to approach you."

"Charles did that? Lord, Mr. Flynn, you just touched a lady's heart. You tell him that, please. I have an unbreakable date with my daughter tonight. Can we do it tomorrow?"

"I'll talk to the judge this afternoon. You might be in for a nice surprise. When you and your daughter get home tonight, Charles might be there. I think no later than tomorrow."

"God bless you, Mr. Flynn."

"It's been a pleasure, Mrs. Washington," he said. He rubbed his hands together, thinking about the kudos waiting for him back at the office if he could persuade the prosecutor to give him what he wanted.

$$\sim$$

That same morning, the city was rocked by two announcements—the first by the Essex County Prosecutor, the second by the governor of New Jersey. The first one was no surprise. It had been a long time coming, but it was inevitable. The spur was garbage—something no city has a shortage of and something about which Newark politics had often raised suspicions. It was the mayor's granting of a no-bid contract to a private carter that was the straw that got a grand jury's attention and shattered the mayor's career.

The city always had its own sanitation department. But the mayor insisted it needed a backup. It was his most brazen move in a series of outrageous self-serving political maneuvers. He handed a contract to a suspect firm, and a year later, a grand jury indicted him. He announced he would not run for re-election.

When the governor, who was up for re-election in November, heard the news, he immediately acted to put as much political distance as possible between himself and the mayor. He didn't want the burden of an indicted mayor and political ally around his neck, so he employed an obscure loophole in the state Constitution to move the Newark municipal election up to late October, as was his right.

His decision only heightened the tension that was already rekindled and rebuilding in the racially torn city. All three mayoral candidates cried foul. They claimed the governor was trying to set up and fund a write-in candidate of his choice, who could well beat all three of them.

It was a thought brought front and center when the *Star-Ledger's* lead editorial writer commented in a front-page bylined article:

In a tense city still in the shadow of a horrific riot, this is about as beneficial an act as pouring gasoline on a cookout fire.

As every Newark schoolboy knows, Robert Treat and his Quakers built the first Newark with land purchased from the Lenni Lenape Indian tribe. Now 302 years later, the action of the state's self-serving governor threatens to tear it apart.

Don't let him get his wish. We offer this piece of advice to those who care about this city. Vote your conscience. That means, polarized as they may be, vote for one of the three existing legitimate candidates—no matter when the governor chooses to let us hold an election.

The reaction to the grand jury, the governor, and the editorial touched off a firestorm.

Kiongosi led a caravan of chartered buses to the State House in Trenton. It brought five hundred people to the front steps, and Kiongosi, bullhorn in hand, demanded to see the governor.

Paulie Tedesco, without a permit, blocked off part of Seventh Avenue and held a rally next to St. Lucy's School. He told the priest there that he was going to speak about the meaning of the neighborhood and unity. That was fine with the priest, but when Tedesco began to speak, he could not help himself. The subject switched from "us" to "us against them."

A lot of folks who understood what the neighborhood had meant to their fathers and mothers and grandparents were there. But like most, the city's populations were tired of being harangued by two apostles of twin folk myths. They had come for nostalgia and a reaffirmation of what their parents had built. Instead, they heard about a menace in which they were not sure they believed. The crowd broke up long before Tedesco finished.

Fast Freddy Sternburg, who undertook the mission behind "enemy lines," reported back to Jackson Anderson.

"You should have been there," Sternburg said. Then he immediately recanted. "Well, maybe not. But I'll tell you this. There were a lot of good people who were, and they left early. I think truth is making a dent. But, boss, Sinatra could make a bigger one."

〰

J unior made a special trip home after lunch to see his mom.

"So I am told that a mother is finally going to meet the first love of her son's life on Sunday," his mother said. "It's about time. Is she Italian?"

"No, Mom, she's not. That's why I came home after class. I have to get back to campus and the locker room. But I would like her to meet the family tomorrow morning. It's very important."

"Well, I don't see why, but if you think so, all right. Is there a problem?"

"I know you and Dad. I know how you raised me. I know how you respect family. Is there a problem? Based on everything you taught me . . . I'm sure there won't be." Then he hugged her and went back outside, where Allie was waiting to drive him back to school.

Both rode in silence until they crossed into Bloomfield. Allie asked, "Well, what happened?"

"Nothing. I trust them. I probably should have told them sooner, but I trust them. And I trust Mickey. She's probably the world's most charming ambassador. My folks are coming, so keep an eye out. I'd rather they not know until Mickey and I tell them together."

"Don't worry. They'll love her. Meanwhile I'm gonna sit next to T.C. and teach him football."

"Hey, man, you don't know a football from an egg."

"I know that. You know that. But T.C. doesn't know that. Don't go blowing my hole card. I like that kid."

They neared the campus. "I'm gonna drop you at the gym," Allie said. "You need anything?"

"Not unless you can teach Johnny Jakes how to recognize a post pattern before he throws."

Allie stopped in front of the gym. The players were already trickling in.

Junior opened the door but turned back. "You need money for Mickey and the family?"

"Hey, man, it's my family as well now. But you do owe me a hundred and fifty bucks for the paint job on the door. Actually, those jerkoffs did me a favor. It looked so bad I got the whole car painted."

"Okay. Gotta go."

"Don't worry even if you fumble—I'll make you look like a hero to T.C."

After taping up, the players sat around for about twenty minutes, then went out for warm-up. Junior looked up into the stands a couple of times, but the Washingtons hadn't arrived yet. He saw his folks sitting on the forty-yard line as he had instructed Allie and waved to them.

They left the field and jogged back to the locker room. Junior flopped down on a bench, anxious and eager, both about the game as well as his parents meeting Mickey. He wanted both events behind him and wanted both to result in a win. He knew he was the one who could make that happen. He squeezed his hand into a determined fist as Coach Yablonski walked out of his office. Then Junior did a double take. He couldn't believe his eyes. Walking beside Coach was a squat little man who was a familiar figure to every player in the room—and to everyone in New Jersey, for that matter. He was a resident Montclair celebrity.

Born in St. Louis, he played for the Newark Bears, then the Yankees, whom he later managed. He earned twenty-one World Series rings. When he played for Newark, he lived in Newark. When he played for the Yankees, he moved to Montclair. He was a local hero.

Junior clearly wasn't the only one stunned to see Yogi Berra in their locker room. The players jumped to their feet and applauded when they saw him. Coach Yablonski raised both arms for quiet. He walked to the rotating blackboard and flipped it over to reveal a single sentence: *Protect Johnny Jakes.*

Coach brushed chalk off his hands. "That's it. That's my speech. There's nothing more to say. You are ready to play and win this game. Last year we were sacked more than any other team on our schedule. That's last year. Memorize this sentence." He pointed to the chalkboard. "That shouldn't be too hard. Do it and we win. It's that simple. Don't, and you won't be happy, because I'll make sure you're not."

"And now, Mr. Berra is going to be our honorary captain for the coin toss. But first he has a few things to tell you."

Berra stood up on a bench. He looked at them for a few moments and then said, "I was there when them other guys got off their team bus. They look pretty big to me. But remember this. Even Napoleon got his ass kicked by the Duke of Ellington. I saw a fat lady in the crowd, and she's waiting to sing when you win. Go win it for her."

"You heard the man," Coach shouted. "Get out there and win it for the fat lady."

Laughter still ringing in their ears, the Montclair State Indians ran back onto the field.

⁓

The Washingtons were too late to see the warm-ups. They weren't ready when Allie came. Mickey kept running to change her outfit until her mother said, "You know, as pretty as you look, that boy's mind is on other things right now."

Allie was careful to sit the group on the home side of the field but twenty yards away from the Friscellas. When Montclair ran back on the field, the Washingtons, Lois, and Allie stood up and cheered. T.C. waved his banner, almost poking Lois in the eye, and shouted, "Which one is Junior?" He saw his mother's disapproving glance and amended it to, "Which one is Mr. Junior?"

"He's number eighty-two," Allie shouted over the crowd, which sent Lois into action.

She leaned over and said to Mickey, "Wow! That number eighty-two is really cute, even though you can't see his face hidden in all that armor."

Montclair got the ball first. Allie tried to follow the game, but T.C. kept asking things like, "What's number eighty-two gonna do now? Are they gonna throw him the ball?"

Junior lined up in the slot, and at the snap he shot downfield. The other players formed an iron cocoon around their quarterback.

Junior and a defender ran side by side, stride for stride, and then Junior pivoted and came back toward his quarterback, caught the ball, pivoted again, and won the footrace to the end zone.

The Montclair stands erupted into a roar. T.C. jumped and shouted and waved his banner—then asked Allie what had happened. By halftime, Junior had caught two more and won two more footraces to the end zone. Allie could see people pounding Senior Friscella on the back. At the half, Montclair had the game well in hand, 28-0.

During halftime, T.C. was fascinated by the two performing bands, while Annie Mae and Mickey talked as Lois listened. "So what are we going to do after the game?" Annie Mae asked.

"Well, T.C. wants to say hello to Junior."

"I need to get home as early as I can. Charles might be there." Then she told Mickey what Charles had said to his lawyer.

"He said that, Mom? That's not a change of heart or some of Charles' bullshit. That's an epiphany."

"I'd rather hear what you said without that language," Annie Mae said. "But I'm pleased you're impressed."

The second half was much like the first. Junior scored a fourth TD, and this time nobody had to tell T.C. what he had done. Allie pointed Junior's parents out at the finish. Mickey grabbed the pair of binoculars that Allie had thoughtfully brought and trained them on the Friscellas.

"Let me see them! Let me see them!" Lois demanded. She snatched them away from Mickey.

"Hey! Easy with those," Allie said. "That's the only pair I got."

"His mom kissed him, and his dad gave him a hug," Lois reported. "Nice. Very nice." Mickey reached for the binoculars, but Lois passed them to Annie Mae. "You'll see them soon enough, girl."

"Junior is leaving the field," Annie Mae said. "The parents look like they're heading to the exit."

Allie kept an eye on Junior. Halfway to the locker room, Junior turned and waved, then pointed furiously to the running track at ground level. "We'll have to wait a bit," Allie said, "but he wants to meet us there on the field as soon as he can."

They made their way down. Fifteen minutes later Junior met them. T.C., clutching his banner, said, "I'm never gonna take your picture down from my spot of honor."

"I've got something else for you," Junior said, bringing his hand from behind his back and showing off the game ball the coach had awarded him. "It's for you," he said and handed it to T.C.

"And what's for me?" Mickey asked, kissing his cheek. "I can't stay. If I'm going to meet your folks tomorrow, I need rest and preparation. And Charles seems to have made a monumental turnaround. He may only get probation. Might be home tonight. And he knows about you. He told me he can put up with a white brother-in-law if you can put up with a black one. He says he's eager to meet you."

"I don't want you guys to leave, but you're right," Junior said. "We have to be at our best tomorrow. Pick you up at nine thirty." He walked over to Annie Mae and kissed her.

Allie led the way back to his car. The only thing Annie Mae said on the ride home was just before they passed Bloomfield and reached Newark. "Who would have thought it at my age? Looks like I just got another son."

24

THE HAPPIEST DAY OF HER LIFE

Junior told Mickey he would pick her up at nine thirty, but he arrived an hour early. Since it was a Saturday, Annie Mae was home, as was Charles, who had received probation, and T.C., who ran to hug Junior as soon as he heard the doorbell.

At 10:00 a.m., Annie Mae was in the kitchen fixing breakfast, Mickey had trotted upstairs to change clothes for the third time, and T.C. appeared with last night's game ball, imploring Junior to go outside and play catch.

Charles sat in the living room across from Junior, staring him down. He sent T.C. outside and finally broke the silence.

"So you my sister's honky boyfriend," he said.

Junior refused to rise to the obvious bait. "And you're my girlfriend's racist brother."

"I don't want to hear that crap," Charles said.

"Don't stick your chin out when you're throwing bullshit and expect not to get hit back," Junior replied.

Charles narrowed his eyes but said nothing. They sat in silence until Annie Mae stood in the doorway, looked hard at both of them, and said, "If you all are going to have a staring contest, you might as well come into the kitchen and do it over breakfast. Otherwise you might be sitting here all day." She hollered down the hall, "Mickey, it don't matter how many times you change your outfit, you are still Mickey and beautiful. Get your narrow behind in here and eat your breakfast before Junior and your brother stare holes into each other's faces."

Mickey had changed into tan slacks and a black turtleneck sweater, accessorizing with a simple cross suspended from a tiny gold chain and a single gold bangle just above her left wrist.

She stood in the doorway and struck a theatrical pose until Annie Mae shook her head and said, "We all know what you look like, baby. Sit down and eat. This boyfriend of yours has been here since eight thirty and still hasn't eaten."

Mickey looked at Charles. "Thanks for listening to me. We need you at home. I assume you gave them the names we were talking about." She turned to Junior and said, "I see you and Charles have met."

Neither responded.

As they ate, Annie Mae tried unsuccessfully to move the conversation in a small-talk direction despite the clearly unsettled issues hanging over them. When Mickey went to clear the table, she paused to glare at Charles, who remained stone-faced. She motioned Junior into the kitchen.

They embraced and kissed. Arms around his neck, she pressed her body hard into his, holding tightly as though she was afraid to let go. Then she whispered, "I won't lie to you, baby. I'm scared."

He pulled her closer. "Don't be. I love you and you love me, and they are the same people that made me who I am. Trust me. I think we better go now."

They announced they were leaving, but the phone rang. Before they made it to the door, Annie Mae hollered, "Mickey, it's Lois."

Mickey took the phone. "Gotta go, girl. We're late—and before you ask, I am still scared to death. Say a little prayer for me. No, make it a big one."

"What are you wearing?"

Mickey told her.

"Smart choice. You look like the lady you are. But one more thing. Remember how we spied on them at the game through Allie's binoculars and the mom kissed Junior and the dad hugged him? They're good people, Mickey." She laughed and added, "Don't blow it. I want season tickets to the rest of his games."

~

"Tell me about your little sister," Mickey said as they drove down Bloomfield Avenue.

"Not much to say. Basically, she's a good kid but maybe a little airheaded at times. Just fifteen and not serious about school. A little boy-crazy, and that scares my folks. Make that more than a little. She actually shoves sweat socks in her bra and wears T-shirts a size too tight."

Mickey laughed. "Hate to give away all our girl secrets, but that's not a very small club, baby. And at fifteen we pretty much know what you're looking for. We just don't want to disappoint you guys."

Junior laughed. "You're talking about me at fifteen, and Allie and just about every other fifteen-year-old boy I ever knew." He turned and kissed her on the cheek.

She grinned and gave his arm a love tap. "Eyes on the road, Buster. Let's make sure we get where we're going."

Suddenly they were there. He pulled into the driveway, turned off the engine, and put an arm around her. "Listen to me. I love you now and I will still love you no matter what happens in the next thirty minutes. Count on it. That's it. This is not a test for you. This is just a formality for me. We will be the same an hour from now or a lifetime from now. Trust me. How could they not fall in love with the woman I fell in love with?"

When Junior turned his key in the front lock, the door almost hit Angie in the face. She knew Junior was bringing a girl and clearly couldn't wait to see her. If he'd taken another step forward, he would have knocked her over.

Junior laughed. Mickey smiled. Angie looked puzzled.

"Squirt," Junior said, "this is Mickey. She's my girl and she's my best friend. This is important. You ever know me to bring a girl home before?"

"Hi, Angie," Mickey said. She smiled and held out her hand.

Angie hesitated, unsure.

"You can shake it, squirt. Trust me. It doesn't rub off. I should know."

Angie shook hands. Then, she turned and hollered toward the kitchen, "Hey! Junior is here with his new girlfriend."

"It's about time," Gerard Sr. shouted back.

And then they saw her.

The silence that followed was perhaps twenty seconds, but it seemed like an hour.

Junior reached for Mickey's hand in an almost reflexive action and broke the silence. "Mom, Dad, this is Mickey. She's the girl I was telling you about, Dad, when we had breakfast at the diner. She's beautiful, she's smart, and she's a transfer student at Montclair State."

Mickey smiled. His mom and dad stood frozen.

Junior had no doubt what would follow. He knew the signs. He saw his dad clench and unclench his fists. Like always when he was struggling to control himself, a tiny vein began to throb on the right side of his forehead.

"Junior," he said. "You never told us she was black. Didn't you think we were entitled to know? All summer long, you two —and you never said a word, not one single word. Do you have any idea how impossible this is for me, your mother, you, and this girl?"

His father's raised voice sent his mother retreating into the kitchen, unsuccessfully trying to hold back tears. Great. Dad yelling and Mom in tears. Could this go any worse?

"She has a name, Dad. It's not 'this girl.' It's Mickey."

But his dad ignored him. "Did you even stop to think about what is still happening in this town? That more than twenty people died in the riot and that nobody can forget it because they don't want to forget it? That hatred isn't going to go away."

He got in Junior's face. Mickey stepped back. Angie had run to her room and closed the door.

His dad raised his voice even more. "This is not the time for heroics. There is never one person for any other person in this world. *Never*. Do you understand me?" He reached out and grabbed Junior's arm and pulled him down the hall to where he could see his mother sitting at the kitchen table, head buried in her arms. He could hear her crying. Mickey, not knowing what to do, followed them.

They stood there, the three of them, without a word. Senior suddenly turned toward Mickey and said, "I wish you didn't have to see this, Miss, but maybe you needed it as much as Junior does. Try to understand this isn't the time for it. Maybe five years in the future—maybe. But now? Impossible. We got a handful of lunatics running around the North Ward who say they are defending Bloomfield Avenue from invading blacks. We got a black candidate for mayor who talks like he's from Africa but has always lived in the Central Ward and who is trying to win an election shouting 'white oppression.' Do you want to have mixed children and throw them into that?"

Mickey and Junior said nothing.

"You're both young. You *think* you're in love. But how do you know? Give it some time. You'll each find someone else."

Junior stepped away from his father, put his arm around Mickey, and broke his silence. "How many times did you tell me, Dad, that you and Mom were soulmates? That she had to be the one you were destined to marry. That you couldn't have married anyone else because she was your other half. That you found the only woman in the world you understood and who understood you. How many times did you say that to me and Angie, Dad? How many times?"

Senior's rapid breathing slowed, and the tone of his voice softened just a little. He looked at both of them as though he were just now realizing how young they were. Then he spoke softly. "The city wasn't burning then. We weren't on the brink of a second riot. Don't you understand the people in this crazy town won't tolerate you?" And his voice rose again. "The blacks don't want you and the Italians don't want her, and nobody wants to see the two of you together. Nobody."

And then Mickey finally spoke. "No disrespect, Mr. Friscella. But you don't even know who I am. I'm the young woman who loves the son you love. How old were you when you and Mrs. Friscella married? I could never be disrespectful to either of you, so take it as a well-meant question."

"We were high school sweethearts and married at nineteen," Senior said. "But the world was so different then. People only married their own. We all kept to our own neighborhoods. And we weren't on our way to college."

"Mr. Friscella, we're not on our way to college. We're *in* college. We *will* graduate. So that's not relevant. I love him and he loves me, and we *will* graduate. We agreed about that from the time we started going together."

Behind his dad, Junior saw his mom lift her head from the kitchen table and look toward Mickey. His dad caught the exchange of glances and addressed Mickey.

"Young lady, you seem to be a very nice person, but in these times . . ." His voice trailed off.

Mickey took advantage of the pause to jump back in. "You don't know me. Please, let me tell you who I am and what shaped me—and why I understand what real love is."

Junior saw his mom had stopped crying and was looking past his dad, staring at him and Mickey.

"You don't have to do this," Senior said. "I can tell you were raised right, but—"

"I don't *have* to do it, Mr. Friscella, I *want* to do it. I want you to know who I really am. We lived in the Projects, my mother, two brothers, and me. My father is a bum and a liar. When he comes back on occasions, he hits my mother. I never knew a father's love. I'm happy that Junior does. My mother works at the phone company. Ever since my youngest brother—he's twelve now—was seven, my mother bought every stitch of clothes for everyone in the house until I started buying mine with my summer jobs. She puts the food on the table. I don't expect you to fully understand this, but where we lived, heroin was as common as candy bars. My mother sat us down and she asked us if we knew why they called it 'shit' and then she explained that they call it that because that's what it is. She told us we might live in the Projects, but she was never going to let the Projects live in us."

"Mickey," his dad said, using her name for the first time. "You don't have to . . . I mean, I'm sure your mother is a wonderful person—"

"Sometimes at night they broke the elevators, made them so they would be stuck on a higher floor. And then someone would come home, tired from working all day, but the elevator was stuck and so they would have to climb the stairs. Sometimes they were very old, and gang members would be waiting to rob them. It was horrible. My little brother, T.C., would talk about kids his age who died of an overdose the way kids your daughter's age would talk about a friend who broke a leg playing soccer. You could smell the garbage and sometimes even see it. Mr. Friscella, there's an army of people like her who had to raise their families under those conditions. Some of them are so worn out that they just give up. I had a friend. She was just fifteen. Her name was Marla Jackson. They—" Her voice caught, and she swallowed hard and struggled to speak. Junior reached for her. His dad finally looked at her with compassion. From the kitchen, so did his mom.

"Please," his dad said, looking at Junior, "she doesn't have to do this. The problem here has nothing to do with her or you separately. It's just that—"

Junior said in a soft but firm voice, "Let her finish, Dad. Let her finish."

He nodded to Mickey, now composed, and she continued. "They took her up to the roof, five of them, and they raped her in broad daylight, and when they were finished, they threw her over the side. That's when my mom knew she had to get us out of there. She was a woman alone with a deadbeat husband who would come home because he was in trouble—and then he'd beat her. But this wonderful woman, Mrs. Annie Mae Washington, cashed in her telephone-company pension, borrowed from her friends, and got us out. The thing is, she—"

Senior raised a hand. The strident tone of frustration returned to his voice. "Why can't you understand me? Don't you see this cannot work for either one of you? I know you have come through tough times, but I don't want to hear any more. I'm thinking of both of you when I say—"

And then something happened that caught Junior completely off-guard. He felt sure it had never before happened in this house—and probably never in this neighborhood, where Italian wives only criticized their husbands in the total privacy of the bedroom. Growing up, Junior had known his parents to disappear into the bedroom when they disagreed on something. But he had never, not once, seen his mother disagree with his father.

She stood up from the kitchen table and loudly, firmly interrupted her husband. "Enough, Gerard. That's enough."

Junior could have kissed her. He felt Mickey relax beside him as well.

He couldn't believe his eyes when she pushed past Senior and came over to them, fierce determination burning in her eyes. She put one arm around Mickey's shoulders and grabbed Junior with the other. And then she led them both past her husband and into her kitchen, her sanctuary, where her word was law.

"Yes, I can see why he loves you—and we will too." She kept

her eyes forward and her chin high. "Come into the kitchen, and the two of you sit down. I want to hear whatever else you have to say. I need to hear it."

They sat together for two hours, his mother listening and chatting, all smiles. His dad walked away—but within fifteen minutes he came and joined them at the kitchen table. He said nothing. He sat there and listened and looked at Mickey, his mixed feelings evident in his furrowed brow.

"Excuse me," he suddenly said. "But I would like Angie to hear the rest of this." Then he walked slowly out of the kitchen.

When he was out of earshot, Maria leaned over, took Mickey's hand, and whispered, her voice cracking as she struggled with her own emotions. "Junior, you just sit and listen and don't say a word. This is between Mickey and me. There's something she has to know. No matter what he said in the hall to both of you, Gerry Friscella Senior is a good man. You will see. We started with nothing. But he made this family happen. He made this home happen. And I say without fear of being wrong, Gerard Friscella Senior is going to be the proudest and the happiest grandfather you ever saw. Just give him a chance. But don't you repeat a word of this to him. And that goes for you, too, Junior."

"Not a word, Mom. Promise."

"Mickey, in all my married years I never corrected him in front of anyone. I think he's as stunned as I am. But this remains a secret between you and me. He will love you, I can promise you that. But right now, let's let him think this was all his idea."

When they finally sat down to lunch, Angie wouldn't stop talking to Mickey. "What's it like to be in college? Is it all studying and no fun? Can you get there with mediocre grades?"

Dad interrupted her. "Mediocre? Can you believe that, Maria? And all this time I thought her marks were simply lousy."

"*Daaaaddy,*" Angie said, rolling her eyes, "can't I talk to Mickey without you making fun of me?"

"Talk away," Mickey said. "I want to learn all there is I can about you, little sister."

"That's it," Junior interrupted. Rising from his chair, he said, "It's three o'clock and we have somewhere to go."

"Not that I know of," Mickey said. "I thought Angie would show me her room and we could share some girl talk."

"Well, be quiet for a minute, take a breath, and I'll tell you where we're going. We're going to leave my dad's car here, call Allie, and he and Lois are going to pick us up."

"So where are we going?"

"For a little first-hand Italian romance in the magical land of Little Italy. Girl, you are on the way to your first Feast of San Gennaro."

"The Feast of San Who?"

"San Gennaro. It's the biggest Italian-American festival in the country. It began in nineteen twenty-six. It honors an Italian saint. There is a Mass of celebration in the Church of the Precious Blood. The statue of the saint is carried out of the church and paraded through the streets of Little Italy. People pin money on the ribbons at the statue's base to be distributed by the church to help the poor. There's music everywhere, games of chance and skill, and food—Mickey, you never saw so much food in your life—and it's all Italian. It lasts eleven days, and more than a million people—white, black, Asian—take part. It's the biggest block party this side of Times Square on New Year's Eve. Many of the original settlers in the North Ward were from Naples. My Nonno, that means 'grandfather,' took me to the festival when I was ten. He used to say that he and my grandmother might have left Naples, but Naples never left them. He said that everyone who goes to the feast in Little Italy—and that includes you, my beautiful bambino—leaves it as an honorary Neapolitan."

"Bravo, *bravissimo*, Junior," his dad said, then reached over and thumped Junior on the back. "What a history lesson! After that speech, I'd even give you permission to escort Signorina Mickey to the Columbus Day parade next month."

They all laughed as they headed toward the front door. Angie was still talking to Mickey when Gerard Sr. got between them and pulled Mickey aside. Junior looked away and pretended not to listen, but he heard.

"Don't worry, young lady," his dad whispered. "Don't take what I said about you guys as a couple personally. It was the city talking, not me. You'll see. You and I together will figure this out." Then he turned away.

Junior opened the door and turned back to escort Mickey out. He caught his mom looking straight at Mickey. She stifled a smile and raised a finger to her closed lips in the traditional gesture of silence.

Then she winked at them both.

～

They drove into Manhattan, the men in the front and the girls in the back. It didn't take long for Lois to get to the point. "So what happened? Come on, speak, girl. Are you two still the outcasts of the North Ward?"

"I'm not sure. What do you think, Junior?"

"Mickey, you saw what happened. What do you think?"

"Well, at first his father was thunder and lightning. He said it was impossible. He said there was no chance for us to find happiness. He said the world was against us, that the people in the North Ward didn't want me and the people in the Central Ward didn't want him. And nobody anywhere wanted the two of us as a couple."

Lois reached over the seat and tapped Junior on the shoulder. "And what did you do, Buster? Did you come in like the White Knight on his charger and clean everything up?"

"No."

"No?"

"She never gave me the chance. Neither did my mother. Mickey launched into the story of her life and her mother's life, and then my mom took over. Long story short, the women won the game. By the time we left, the men were just spectators."

"Awright, girl," Lois said, hugging Mickey. "So everything is cool with the Friscellas?"

"Especially my sister," Junior said. "Next thing you know she'll be wearing an Afro."

"Don't you dare talk about my little sister. She's a sweetheart," Mickey said. "By the way, Junior, did you happen to see the wink your mom gave me after I said goodbye to your dad?"'

"I did. Like I said, the women won the day."

Allie meanwhile had turned off Eighth Avenue and into the Port Authority bus terminal parking lot. "Now that we have brought peace and harmony into the Friscella home, let's move. We still have to catch the number six subway to Spring Street and walk over to the festival. I don't want to miss the big-money battle of the egos."

"Can you bet on it?" Lois asked.

"I'd suggest you don't. It happens during the procession. The saint has ribbons pasted all around the base. People pin money for the poor on them. If it's a Mafioso or a community leader, the locals among the spectators are sure to count who puts up the most."

On Spring Street, they headed for Canal, then turned away from the Chinatown side of Canal. Within moments they were in the middle of a tradition that began a long time before any of them were born.

The festival stretched east to west from Grand to Hester between Mott and Baxter. The sight when they took in their surroundings was spectacular. They passed below a huge artificial floral sign bearing the colors of the Italian flag. By dark, the lights above the stage at the corner of Grand and Mulberry would be a blend of bright reds and bright greens, honoring the flag colors.

The army of human flesh shoehorned into the narrow streets was massive. The procession bearing the statue of the saint had just begun to leave the Church of the Precious Blood. Men from the community carried it on their shoulders, preceded by Red Mike's Festival Band, a fixture every year.

A little girl dressed in white ran from one side of the street to the other and toward the saint as fast as her little legs could carry her.

"Why is she in white?" Lois asked.

"She's supposed be an angel," Allie said.

The procession moved on, making their passage somewhat easier. On either side of the street stood colorful stalls. "

Wow," Mickey said. "Look at all that food. It looks interesting and it smells divine,"

"Wait until we get to the meatball-eating contest," Junior said.

"You got to be kidding."

"You think so? There's also a cannoli-eating contest and a pizza-eating contest."

"All this talk about food," Lois said. "I'm starving. This is supposed to be a feast. What's on the menu and the budget?"

"What isn't?" Junior shouted over the crowd. "Let's see. We got *mostaccioli*—chocolate cookie with fruit inside. We got stuffed pork with garlic, cheese, pepper, and oregano inside. We got pasta, pasta, and more pasta. We got honey-nugget candy. We got sausage and stuffed clams. We got—"

"So what are we waiting for?" Lois said.

They stopped to watch a street vendor opening clams with short, ferocious strokes of his knife. Mickey applauded, the guy gave a quick bow, and they bought some. The guys moved on to stuffed pork. Lois and Mickey had meatball sandwiches.

Allie bought the girls T-shirts that said, "Kiss Me, I'm Italian," then Mickey spotted a soda stand. "Too much spice in that meatball—I gotta put out the fire."

Junior ordered three sodas, saying he wasn't thirsty. When a vendor put them on the counter, Mickey opened hers, took a long sip, and handed it Junior, who said apologetically, "I guess the pork was a little hot too."

He drank. A female vendor who had been staring at the mixed couples stuck a finger in her mouth and pretended to vomit. "That's the most disgusting thing I have ever seen in my life," she said. "I hope you get all that nigger girl's germs."

Before Mickey or Junior could react, Allie leaned over the counter and said, "I guess you don't look in your mirror much. Now, *that* must be a disgusting sight." He stuck a finger in his mouth as though he were vomiting and then pulled the three away.

Both girls were angry.

Allie spoke before anyone else could. "If that's what you and Junior have to handle, I admire you. I couldn't do it. If she were a guy, I would have decked her. But she's just an idiot, and I knew I better *say* something before Junior *did* something. So that's that. And there's only one way to cool off. We're gonna find a gelato stand."

They found one. Mickey heard music coming from down the block, so they walked toward it with their cups. Red Mike's Festival Band, a fixture of the feast for years, was performing on the stage at the intersection of Grand and Mulberry, beating out "Sweet Caroline" while the crowd clapped along.

It was too good to ignore. Mickey and Lois did an impromptu dance step alongside the stage. They all forgot about the racist vendor, as they flashed smiles that could have been a billboard for the festival.

As they moved on, Junior exclaimed, "Hey! We forgot the best treat of all. We got to get the girls some *zeppole*."

"What kind of name is that?" Mickey asked.

"It's not in the name, it's in the taste," Allie said.

"Italian doughnuts," Junior explained. "Every black Italian girl should try them before she dies. It feeds the sex drive."

"Lead me to them, sir. I'm your candidate."

They quickly located a stand. Mickey and Lois declared the

zeppole to be as good as advertised. They strolled on, and soon found themselves standing in front of the famed Umberto's Clam House. The crowd swirling around them was predominantly white Italian. Occasionally they saw a black couple. Twice they saw mixed-race couples. Mickey and Lois nodded at them as if to say, "You show them. To hell with the racists. You guys know who you are and what you have."

Both couples nodded back in an unspoken message of assent. Mickey moved closer to Junior, put her arm around his waist, and whispered in his ear, "This is the happiest day of my life. I'm so happy I met your parents and your little sister. I'm so happy my mom has accepted you. I'm so happy we're here together. I love you, my White Knight."

Junior squeezed her against him, thrilled to see her so happy.

Then he looked up and spotted familiar faces turning a nearby corner. "Girls, it's better for you if we move on right now," he said.

Allie frowned, then saw what Junior had seen. He steered Lois away. "You don't want to meet these people."

It was too late.

25

SHOWDOWN ON SPRING STREET

J unior gritted his teeth, knowing they had no place to hide. Mary Theresa Gianetti pushed her way through the crowd with Chooch and Dominick close behind, shoving people aside in their haste. When a father holding the hand of a young kid protested, Dominick tried to kick him in the shin and then nearly fell down from the effort. Junior could tell that he was roaring drunk.

"What the hell are they doing here?" Junior said.

"I don't know," Allie responded, "but it ain't the kind of thing I want to stick around to find out."

"Who are they?" Mickey asked.

"You don't want to know," Allie said.

Junior nodded and lowered his voice. "We gotta get the girls out of here. If we get separated, take Lois down by the stage where we saw Red Mike. We'll meet you there."

Both girls protested mildly, but they went. They put distance between them and the trio they wanted to avoid, but the crush of the crowd separated Mickey and him from Allie and Lois.

"Can we slow down?" Mickey said. "What's the big hurry?"

"Listen. Don't worry, but you asked and I'll tell you. Those are the kind of people we've kept out of our lives and we're not going to let them back in—ever. We lost them, so, yes, we can slow down. You can browse a little, then we'll head back and hear some more Red Mike."

"But this time," Mickey said with a laugh, "I want you to dance with me. You can dance, can't you?"

"Lady, in some quarters I am known as the Dancing Wide Receiver."

"I'll be the judge of that."

Lois and Allie were standing at the edge of the crowd when they arrived at the stage. Red Mike's Festival Band was belting out one of their staples, "When the Saints Go Marching In." Lois bounced up and down in time with the music, trying to balance a slice of pizza on a paper plate.

"Allie says I'm now an honorary Italian."

"If you don't stop eating, you'll weigh more than the entire population of Naples," Allie cracked.

"Blame Junior. He's the one who told me if you don't keep eating at San Gennaro, you risk a lifetime ban from Mulberry Street."

Junior kept glancing behind them, keeping an eye out for the trio they had dodged. He knew he wouldn't be able to relax now that they were around. "Well, you definitely ate your quota. We all had a great time, but we gotta go."

He looked pointedly at Allie, who understood the concern and nodded in agreement. Junior felt a heavy weight lift from him once they left the festival and put some space between them. The girls joked and laughed, and his mood lightened considerably as they walked toward Spring Street and the subway station.

With barely a block to go, everything changed in a split second. What Junior had dreaded was there in front of him, a confrontation that he told himself he should have expected. With Mary T still in the lead, the three were about twenty yards ahead, stumbling drunkenly and talking much too loudly.

Mary T saw them first. She turned, presumably to say something to Chooch and Dominick, but her eyes caught Junior. "Well, well, look what I found! Two used-to-be friends and their nigger bitches. I'm surprised you guys still look white. Don't their shit rub off when you fuck?"

Junior grabbed Mickey's hand and felt her stiffen at the comment.

They all stopped and stood face to face. Allie spoke first. "Holy shit, if it ain't the queen of sexually transmitted diseases. Hey, Mary, give it a rest. You been stalking Junior since we all gang-banged you in the schoolyard."

"Fuck you," she shot back.

"Not with someone else's dick, asshole."

"Nobody talks like that to my woman," Dominick said, weaving on unsteady legs. "Especially not a nigger-lover who betrays his own race."

"Tell him, sweetheart," Mary T screeched. "Kick his ass, baby."

Junior shoved the girls behind him and out of harm's way. He turned to Chooch and said, "I suggest you put this baboon back where he belongs. Tedesco will be worried when he sees the cage is empty."

"You got some nerve talking like that after what you done to us!" Chooch shouted. "You turned your back on lifelong friends and everyone else in the North Ward—for what? Just because you wanted to change your luck by screwing a nigger."

Junior slammed a fist into Chooch's face. As right hands go, it wasn't a killer, but hard enough to put Chooch on his ass. Dominick leaped on Junior's back. While they grappled, Mary T swung at Mickey. Allie jumped in to try to break everybody up. Lois let out a scream that seemed to travel all the way from her feet through her mouth.

Mickey went down. Junior fought the urge to run to her as he fended off wild swings from Dominick, who was bleeding from the nose but kept flailing away. Mary T tried to claw Mickey's face with the long fingernail she was so proud of. Fury pulsed through Junior. He shoved Dominick backward hard and watched the drunk oaf land on his ass.

As Junior ran to Mickey, determined to get Mary T off her, he saw Chooch roll over, reach behind his belt, and draw a pistol—the pistol Junior knew he carried on his White Citizens Council patrols.

Allie dived at him, but too late. When he landed on Chooch, the gun went off. Junior felt a huge pain and fell to the pavement, his leg crumpled beneath him, screaming in agony.

Mickey shrieked and smacked Mary T, bringing a cry of pain. Dominick sagged to one knee and vomited. Chooch scrambled to his feet and shouted unintelligibly. The three of them staggered toward a corner as they tried to run.

Mickey raced to Junior's side, fell to her knees, and pulled his head into her lap. She looked up at Allie and Lois, who crouched over Junior. He knew everyone was asking questions, but he couldn't hear or think clearly. His left leg was bleeding a thick puddle on the ground.

"Lois, here!" Mickey said, pulling her friend down to take her place holding Junior's head. She stepped away and turned her back. She pulled her arms inside her sweater, contorted a bit, then yanked her bra into the open. She shoved her arms back through her sweater sleeves, turned, and nudged Lois aside so she could tie the bra above the leg wound as a tourniquet. She situated herself behind him again, holding his head off the concrete, gently stroking his hair and murmuring encouragement.

Lois sprinted to a nearby pay phone to call 911, but two cops patrolling the perimeter of the festival had heard the shot and ran toward them. The first one hit his walkie-talkie and shouted, "Man down. Gunshot wound. I need an ambulance outside the Spring Street Six station by Mulberry."

Allie tried to calm Mickey. The second cop, who was black, interviewed Lois. From the ground, Junior heard every word and was impressed with Lois' cool head. Despite her distress, she described the event perfectly.

"Are you saying they targeted him?" the cop asked.

"Absolutely. They knew who he was. I don't know them, but Allie here does, and he warned us."

The ambulance pulled up beside the curb. Mickey shouted to the paramedics to hurry, seeing that Junior had paled from loss of blood.

He reached for Mickey's hand and said, "Relax, baby. Bullets bounce off the White Knight."

"Please, can I ride with him?"

The paramedics allowed her to ride. Junior heard one of the cops tell her, "Come on. There's a cab around the corner. Tell your friends to grab it and meet us at St. Vincent's emergency ward. I know you've been through a lot, but tomorrow you come to the precinct and sign a complaint. I'll file your interview when I get back."

He helped Mickey climb into the ambulance. Still crying, she held his head, leaned over, and kissed him. Between sobs she said, "You're my strength, White Knight, so you stay strong. We'll beat this, baby. We'll beat them all—the bigots, the racists, the city. Stay strong. We have a lot of loving ahead of us."

∾

The Friscellas had just finished supper when the phone rang. Senior took the call and listened as Allie told him the story, ending with his son being shot. Senior said nothing, listening. When he ended the call, he relayed the news to Maria and Angie.

"We got to get to the hospital," Maria said, moving to gather her things.

"Is he gonna die?" Angie asked. "Is Mickey all right?"

"Nobody's gonna die. We are not gonna rush over there in the middle of the night." Senior put his arms around Maria and held her, adding gently, "It's a leg wound. And his friends and Mickey are with him. We'll go tomorrow. He'll be fine. They'll call us before we go to sleep tonight. Besides, visiting hours are over."

The call came later from Mickey, and the report was good. But Senior did not go to bed. Instead, he sat alone in the living room. He opened the double doors at the bottom of the armoire and withdrew the scrapbook he had secretly been keeping about Junior's football career.

He had started it when Junior was a freshman at Barringer, when Junior was twenty pounds lighter and still had acne. As Senior turned the pages, he felt as though he were reading his own life. He had been at the scene on which every clipping was based. He turned pages until he got to the year Barringer won the state title.

In the center of the left-hand page there was a large picture of Junior running at the end of a wide-receiver option play, and a big lineman, who happened to be black, was clearing the way. Junior had shared with Senior that the lineman was Mickey's cousin. In a second picture, Junior and the previously anonymous lineman were hugging in the end zone.

He studied the picture. It struck him that the yellowing photo in its way was a denial of all that was eroding the city and a promise of the way it ought to be. Too much bullshit and too many bullshitters had twisted logic for too long.

"Fuck this city. Somebody has to wake everyone up." He slammed the book shut, carefully replaced it in the armoire, and went to bed.

~

The Friscellas decided not to call off Sunday dinner when they learned that Junior would be home. Instead, they altered the guest list. They would invite Allie and Lois, and, at

Maria's insistence, Annie Mae and T.C. Washington. Maria made the calls early Sunday morning.

Annie Mae told her that Charles wouldn't be there, adding only that he still had some growing to think about. Mickey hadn't gotten home until 3:00 a.m. and was still sleeping. "We'll be there," Annie Mae said. "And, Mrs. Friscella, I have to tell you that you have one terrific son. I hope mine turn out like him."

"I know that, Annie Mae, and yesterday I found out that you have one terrific daughter." Then she called Allie who confirmed that Junior was coming home and offered to pick him up. She declined the offer with thanks and said that Senior preferred to do it by himself. She reminded him not to be late and to be sure to bring Lois.

At 9:00 a.m., Senior kissed his wife and daughter and started out the front door, then realized he'd forgotten something. He returned to the master bedroom, retrieved what he wanted, and left.

After conferring with Senior at breakfast, Maria made a major decision. For the first time in memory she made deletions on her Sunday-dinner guest list. She called the extended-family members who were usually there, told them Junior was in the hospital and was going to be released today. "The doctor wants him to rest, so you understand. Yes, he'll be fine. We'll see you next Sunday." Then she hollered down the hall to Angie, "Up and at 'em, kid. You and I have new guests coming and we have work to do right now."

~

Gerard Sr. did not go straight to the hospital. He stopped first at the local precinct in Greenwich Village, sought out the desk sergeant, and explained why Junior wasn't there to sign the complaint. "He'll be here tomorrow, and the son of a bitch that shot him will be here too."

"That may not be necessary—we've already issued an arrest warrant for the shooter," the desk sergeant told him.

Before Senior opened the car door, he patted his pants pocket and felt the object he had retrieved earlier. Reassured, he continued on.

At the hospital, a nurse gave him instructions the doctor had left and added that it was important that the family doctor check Junior's wound as soon as possible.

He found Junior in a wheelchair outside his room waiting along with an attendant, who helped him into the car. They rode in silence for a time. Then Junior said, "Allie can verify what happened if you doubt the story, Dad."

"Well, as I understand it, he shot you—that's all the verification I need. These people. Your grandfather would say about Chooch and Dominick and that bastard Tedesco, '*Ueste persone sono spazzatura.*' They are garbage. They are poisoning the city. I made a terrible mistake when I said you and Mickey could not happen now, when I said wait five or ten years. Your time is now. They are vultures, and we are not gonna let them take another bite out of us. This bullshit has got to stop."

"Dad, I'm alive. And Mickey wasn't hurt."

"Sorry, but understand you two have nothing to apologize for—and I mean nothing. Before we get home, I want you to know I owe you an apology. And there's a lot of self-serving shits who owe one to this city for what they've done to all of us." He reached over and squeezed Junior's arm. Twenty minutes later, they were home. A big hand-painted sign hung over the front door:

Welcome Home Our White Knight

"How do you like it?" Angie squealed. "T.C. and I made it."

"Magnificent. Spectacular," Junior said. "Now get out of the way—I'm not very good with these crutches." As he negotiated the steps, they took his arms and led him into the living room. Maria introduced Annie Mae, Lois, and T.C. to Senior. Allie shook their hands in greeting and smiled deeply at Lois.

Mickey stood away to one side, beckoned Junior over, and kissed him hard. Everyone applauded. Then T.C. said, "Can we eat now?"

∼

At six thirty that same morning, Les Scarcella's bedside phone refused to quit ringing. He reached across his sleeping wife, tried to grab the phone, and knocked it off the table and onto the floor. Angrily, he rolled out of bed, retrieved it, and shouted into the receiver, "Who the hell is this? The goddamn sun isn't even up."

"Signor Lester, this is Uncle Pete. I have a message for you. Sorry it's so early, but I have my instructions and the man said do it now. The man you first approached when he was eating dinner at Don's 21 several weeks ago will see you on Monday around noon. Go to work, I will pick you up. He wants your opinion on what happened last night."

The line went dead.

"Who was that?" his wife demanded, sitting up. "Somebody died? A car crash? One of the kids?" She picked up the clock. "Not even seven. Tell me what's wrong."

"Nothing. Go back to sleep. Just business, and the guy couldn't wait. I'll call you after I get to the center. I have my weekly staff meeting today."

He showered and shaved. As he wiped residue of shaving cream from his chin, he paused to look in the mirror. "What the hell have I gotten myself into? I don't know what's on this guy's mind. What would Machiavelli do?"

When he got to the center, Nancy, his secretary, had already arrived and was making a pot of coffee. "I'm only doing it because I want a cup," she said. "I'm a graduate of St. Elizabeth College. I also have a master's degree in education, which is one more master's degree than you have. New rule—whoever gets in first makes the coffee."

"New rule—we keep the old rule. Come in my office. And don't forget the coffee."

Ten minutes later, she handed him a cup and said, "That idiot who works for Paulie Tedesco shot and wounded Gerard Friscella Jr. at the feast yesterday. The word is all over the ward."

Scarcella shook his head. "That dumb piece of shit. Okay, we need to talk to Jerry D'Amilio right away. Also, see if you can find Gerard Friscella Sr."

"Why and why?" she asked.

"The first answer is, it's none of your business. The second answer is the same as the first. Let me know when everybody gets here for the meeting."

Twenty minutes later the staff was assembled in his office.

Scarcella sat on the edge of his desk. "I asked all of you," he said, pointing at his chief of staff, "to check out the old Mustache Pete clubs and the bars and the street to tell me what the ward's mood is now about this election. You give me nothing."

"Chief, everybody is so confused, they don't know what they think."

"Well, here's something to think about. Junior Friscella was shot last night. I'm talking about the kid who led Barringer to a state football title. I'm talking about the kid who is a superstar at Montclair State. I'm talking about the kid whose father and mother are pillars of the community. The guy who shot him was Chooch Castano, the chief of staff for Paulie Tedesco. If I have to tell you who Paulie is, you're fired. Nancy, how you coming on those phone calls?"

"D'Amilio is at Yankee Stadium but says he'll be home tonight. I'm still trying to find Gerard Sr. Nobody is answering the home phone."

"It's possible he's there, because his kid got shot last night. Where's Paulie tonight? Find him."

∼

Sunday dinner brought the first joy into the Friscella house since Allie's phone call on Saturday. Senior remained quiet, enjoying the sight of everyone chatting and getting along so well. Maria passed a plate of cannolis Annie Mae had brought from Ferrara's. Angie begged off, took Mickey and Lois by the hand, and led them down the hall to show off her bedroom. Senior smiled—it was as though they all had known each other for years.

Annie Mae shared how T.C. had attached himself to Junior after the football game. "You'd think he was his kid brother. It's the first time T.C. posted a picture of a white player in what he calls his special place. Maria, you know there's no father in our home. Whether Junior knows it or not, he's taken over that job for T.C."

Senior made up his mind and pushed his chair back from the table. "I'm afraid you'll have to excuse us. Allie and I have some unfinished business to take care of."

Allie looked confused. "Like what?"

"Like we're late, so let's go." He caught Allie by the arm and led him to the front door. He beckoned to the car in the driveway. Allie followed and got in.

"What's this about, Mr. F.?"

"The New York police have a warrant out for Chooch and Dominick. You and I are going to bring them in." He backed the car down the driveway before Allie could respond. He drove down the Avenue straight to the White Citizens Council headquarters. They walked in without knocking. Paulie was sitting behind his desk.

"Sorry about what Chooch did, Gerry, but it was an accident. You must know that. We need to talk about it."

"Where are they, the two of them, Paulie?"

"What are you gonna do, Friscella? Make a citizen's arrest?" He laughed.

The bastard. Senior reached into his pocket and pulled out a gun. Paulie stopped laughing. "You take us to them now," Senior said coldly.

Paulie held his hands up. "They're on patrol."

"I suggest you pick up your radio and find them—unless you want to take the blame for this."

Paulie reached for the radio. "Come in, Car One. Come in. Condition red. You're needed at headquarters. Repeat. Condition red."

Static from the other end. Then Chooch's voice. "Roger that. On the way now. ETA five minutes."

"Good," Senior said. "Now, sit down. No, not behind the desk. In that folding chair in the corner, where I can see your hands." He walked to Allie and whispered, "You're my backup. Put your right hand in your pocket like you have a gun and don't take it out." Senior and Paulie stared at each other as the minutes ticked by.

Car doors slammed in the street. Chooch and Dominick rushed in, saw the gun, and froze.

"What the fuck?" Chooch said.

Dominick was pale. "Yeah, what the fuck, Mr. F.?"

"I'll tell you what the fuck is. Allie, get those handcuffs these tinker-toy cops have in their back pockets and cuff them together. Now we'll sit a while."

"Listen, it was an accident, Mr. F.," Dominick said.

"You shot my son. This is the kid you two pieces of garbage looked up to since elementary school. The kid you cheered at football games. The kid whose pizza you shared at my house. You let that *puttana*, Mary T, drag you around by your dicks. Now that slut is going to be the most expensive piece of ass you'll ever have."

"But we—" Chooch started to say.

"You'll never get away with this. This is kidnapping!" Dominick screamed.

"Not if you went to school with the county sheriff, not if he's your daughter's godfather, and not"—he smiled—"if that sheriff deputized you this morning."

The New York cops came up Bloomfield Avenue with sirens and lights and everything that could spell a "we came for a bad guy" operation—at Senior's request. They were even louder as they started the return trip—much to Paulie's chagrin.

As Senior and Allie returned, Maria was moving their guests into the kitchen.

"Mrs. Friscella," Allie said, "your husband is a lunatic—and I love him. You should have been there. Let me tell you where we were and what he did." Allie told the story, and with each new sentence their jaws seemed to drop more while Senior sat and smiled.

"So I'm standing there with this tough-guy look on my face and my hand in my pocket holding this imaginary gun," Allie said. "The best part was when Dominick saw the cops, he pissed his pants."

The kitchen seemed to explode with laughter. Junior banged his crutch against the floor so hard that the bottom split.

Senior went to Junior and hugged him. "I was afraid I'd lose control and shoot them."

Annie Mae gazed at T.C. and said, "Now that's a father."

"Mr. Friscella," Mickey said, "you are terrific."

Senior went around to Mickey's side of the kitchen table and put both hands on her shoulders. "Nobody shoots my son. No slut hits his girl. Welcome to the family, young lady."

He had no idea why Maria winked at Mickey, but he felt too good to wonder about it.

⤳

Jerry D'Amilio returned Les Scarcella's call before he left the Yankee Stadium press box. By then, the story of Gerard Friscella Sr. the vigilante had spread all along the North Ward's underground telegraph. When Scarcella told D'Amilio what had happened, the sportswriter couldn't stop laughing. "My only regret, is that I couldn't see the look on that idiot Dominick's face when he pissed in his pants."

"So you're the Pulitzer Prize winner. How do we get the ink I need out of this?"

"Normally I'd say you can't—but it's funny enough that I could write a column." He broke up again. "Deputy Friscella and his one-man posse. I love it."

"But there's something else. And you're not gonna like it. I think the two guys you mediated with last time want you again."

"Les, gimme a break. They're out of my league. I'm only a foot soldier in the *Star-Ledger* army."

"Come on over tonight. We've still got that bottle of Amaretto to kill, and fresh coffee."

"Les, you're killing me. See you in half an hour."

26

THE ACCIDENTAL HERO

G erard Friscella Sr. finished his breakfast as Angie, two textbooks crooked below her left elbow, opened the front door on her way to school. An avalanche of shouted questions rumbled into the house. Angie immediately retreated from the cacophony and slammed the door.

"I'm not going to walk past that zoo to get to school. I'll stay home."

"No, you'll go to school," her father said. "I'll go outside and make the rules, and then you'll come out. You say nothing, keep walking, and I guarantee you nobody will interfere with you." He wiped his mouth and dropped the napkin on the table in disgust. He'd send these vultures on their way.

When he stepped outside, he realized he had underestimated the determination of the assembled reporters. They ran over from the curb and trampled his front lawn. Senior stepped forward and met them head-on.

Dozens of voices shouted a flood of questions all at once at an impossible volume, a convoluted barrage that sounded like a foreign language. He held his hands up to silence them. When they realized he wasn't going to respond, they quieted down.

"I know you have a job to do, but so do I. First, I'm going to get my little girl, and you are going back to the curb and leave the sidewalk clear for her so she can get on her way to school unimpeded. If you comply, I will stand here and talk to you for fifteen minutes. Then I will get in my car and drive to work. So let's do it my way, or we won't do it at all."

He opened the front door and she came out. He escorted her to the end of the block, and then she continued on her way.

When he returned, the first shouted question was, "Where is Junior and is he okay?"

"Junior is resting. And he's not coming out. He's mending. The doctor will check the wound today."

"Did you pull a gun on Paulie Tedesco?"

"Yes. He was harboring fugitives."

"Were you really deputized?"

"Ask the county prosecutor."

The competing questions grew so loud and garbled he threw his hands up. "Thanks for your courtesy," he said, "but I gotta go to work now." He turned to go back in the house, then noticed three cop cars turn the corner to clear the street. Good. He'd had as much of that crowd as he could handle.

Junior sat at the breakfast table with Mickey, who had stayed the night. Maria was at the stove scrambling eggs.

Senior said, "Nobody answers the door after I leave. I called Doc Grossman and he's on his way to check the wound. I know you wouldn't guess it, Mickey, but this usually is a quiet neighborhood. But this isn't a usual kind of day. Stay in the house until the doctor finishes."

He said goodbye and left. He got as far as the curb when a car pulled even with him. One of the occupants threw a rock toward him and shouted, "Nigger-lover!" The car sped away.

Trying to control his rage, he thought, "What's happening to my neighbors?" He climbed behind the wheel of his car, but before he could turn the key, he saw a flashing red light in his rearview mirror. He waited.

It was one of the county cars that had been assigned to move the reporters along. He recognized the officer as a classmate of Junior back at Barringer. The officer motioned him to roll down his window.

"I saw it all, Mr. Friscella. I got the plate number and in about five minutes we're gonna get those sons of bitches. But do yourself and your family a favor. Don't go to work today. Stay with your family."

Senior contemplated. He decided the suggestion was sound advice, and as much as he wanted to maintain his normal schedule, he needed to be home with his family today. He stepped out of the car, nodding his thanks.

Before he reached the porch, the officer called after him, "Between you and me, folks around here have had about enough of those assholes. Tell Junior we're all Montclair State fans now."

Senior smiled and waved.

Inside, Junior had shifted to the big living room chair, Mickey curled up on the floor at his feet. Maria was doing the dishes. Senior did not mention the rock-throwers.

"How you feeling, kid? The doc should be here any minute. Don't you have school today, Mickey?"

"I'm not going anywhere, Mr. F., until I hear what the doctor tells you." He saw she was holding Junior's hand.

I don't know where this is going, but I sure acted like an ass yesterday. The doorbell rang. Maria ran in from the kitchen insisting she would open it.

Dr. Grossman greeted the family when Maria let him in. He had been their family doctor since long before Junior was born. When he and Maria embraced, Senior heard him whisper, "No tears. He wasn't hit by a mortar, Maria, just a twenty-two-caliber."

He turned toward Junior, Senior, and Mickey. "Well, well, here I am in the land of the heroes. And I am pleased to note that Junior has his own Florence Nightingale at his feet." Mickey smiled, and the doctor took her hand. "So you're the Juliet our Romeo here tried to rescue."

Grossman knelt beside Mickey and examined the wound. As he moved his hands, he spoke. "I saw the X-ray—no broken bones. You were lucky it was a twenty-two. It didn't hit an artery or a major vein. Apparently, it even missed the muscle. Junior, from what I can see, you have what Wyatt Earp and Wild Bill Hickok would call a flesh wound. You might even play some football in a week or two."

Senior nearly crumpled with relief. He didn't realize how much anxiety he'd been carrying until heard the doctor's reassuring diagnosis.

"Tell me the truth," Junior said. "You're not just trying to cheer up your patient? Right?"

"Junior, I spanked your ass when you were born. I would not hesitate to spank it again. We'll have to test it to see when you can run and get hit on that leg. Because of the path of the slug, I'd say it will be sooner than you think. By the way, from what I was told, this young lady's tourniquet prevented you from bleeding out. Quick thinking, Miss. What did you use?"

Mickey blushed.

"She took off her bra," Junior said, laughing, "and tied off my wound. It was the most embarrassing moment of my life."

"Don't be a smartass, buster," Mickey said. "It wasn't the first time I took off my bra for you. But if you keep talking like that, it could be the last."

Everybody laughed.

The phone rang. Maria picked it up. Senior could hear a neighbor's voice shouting, "Turn on the TV! Turn on the TV! Channel Two!"

Maria ran to the set, flipped it on, and there was Les Scarcella in mid-interview.

"All the hatred, all the bigotry on both sides in this city, and along comes Gerard Friscella Sr. He's the damn hero this city has waited for. He cut through the crap, looked the bigots in the eye, and brought justice to his son. It's about time we all grew up. I think the mayor ought to give him a parade and the key to the city."

Everyone looked at Senior.

"Not a word out of any of you," he said. "I'm no hero. I've known Les Scarcella since high school. He's a friend. But I don't have a clue what he's trying to do here. Maybe he means well—but I'm not sure I like it."

~

L es Scarcella had a lot to think about. He sat alone, sipping an espresso at a table in the Liberty Club on Bloomfield Avenue. The club had been founded by immigrants from the province of Avellino, in Southern Italy. Alone in their new world they had a commonality acquired from a cluster of small towns east of Naples. Like all immigrants in Newark at that time, they were drawn together for social reasons.

Scarcella liked the club because, while he was respected for what his center had achieved, he was not necessarily a part of the Liberty Club's social life. That was the way he wanted it when he needed semi-isolation to think.

While he signaled the waiter for another espresso, Jerry D'Amilio walked in. As one of the lineal descendants of an Avellino family, he was greeted like a returning prodigal North Ward kid.

"Hey, Jerry, how come you don't write about our Squadra Azzurra?" the bartender shouted. "The Italian blues gonna win the World Cup this year. We already won the European Cup."

"Hey, Giuseppe, didn't your daddy ever tell you this place is called America—and your family's been here forty years? You need to be rooting for the New York Yankees. Ask your grandson who they are."

The whole room laughed. It was clear that while they loved Squadra Azzurra, they loved the success of the son of one of their own even more. D'Amilio threaded his way through the room, shaking hands and exchanging smiles, all the time working his way toward Scarcella.

"Hey, kid," Scarcella said. "Sit down, have an espresso." He signaled the waiter. "So how goes it in the world of balls, strikes, and touchdowns?"

"We got to talk now—and I mean in private. This situation is getting out of hand."

"Sure, we'll take a walk down the Avenue." He threw a bill on the table and guided him out the front door.

They walked in silence for a block. D'Amilio spoke first. "I'm supposed to set up a meeting between the two guys you touted me to. You got me playing with dynamite. Look, you know how I feel about you and Loretta. You know I'm more than aware that without the scholarship you got for me, I probably wouldn't be in my job. But this is too much. I can't get in any deeper with these two guys—and you know it. I'm for Anderson being the next mayor. You know how I feel. But goddamn it, you want this to happen, so it's time you did what you sent me to do."

"Well, think a minute," Scarcella said. "*They* want *you*—not me. So what do you think we should do?"

"To be honest, I don't know. But I know they trust me, and I don't need that kind of trust. You know as well as I that one day they'll blame me if this doesn't work. I had a life before this happened, Yes, you helped make that life possible. But now I think it's on you to straighten this mess out. I'd like to live long enough to receive my Pulitzer."

"Look, you're probably right in terms of ethics. But you either do this, or one of those imbeciles becomes mayor of the city both of us love. I'm asking you as a friend. Give it one more try."

"All right, one more try. But if you get me killed, I'll never speak to you again."

He turned and began the long walk to the *Star-Ledger*. When he arrived, Uncle Pete's car was idling at the back entrance.

He climbed in. The old man drove down to Washington

Street and headed toward the library. He turned onto Route 21 before he spoke.

"You got to understand, Mr. D'Amilio, that this meeting took a lot of maneuvering and trust. The first was not very hard. The second, well, I been around these people for a long time. I hear things and see things. And they stay with me. But when it comes to trust, with the history these two have, I just don't know."

"Well, that's reassuring. Particularly since I neither own nor carry a gun. What do they expect me to do for them?"

"I don't know for sure. But I think they won't ask something you can't do, because they dislike each other so much you are the one they have to depend upon. Use your head. Be careful what you say or promise. You have more of an edge than you think."

"I don't see it. Right now I trust you more than I trust either one of them."

Uncle Pete laughed. "That's a start, but I wouldn't count too much on that. I'll tell you this because it's news to you, but I knew your dad. I'll stand by what I said if you remember that we never had this conversation. So here it is. They will continue to respect you if you do one thing. Watch what you say but be your own man. That way they can't accuse you of siding with anyone. They'll be too busy trying to figure out how to win you over."

D'Amilio sat back and heaved a sigh. "My mother was right. I should have gone to law school."

27

ONCE AGAIN, JERRY IN THE MIDDLE

Annie Mae's house was atypically quiet. T.C. had stayed after school for a club meeting and Mickey was back at Montclair State, having found a dorm room to share for a few nights with a girl who'd been her classmate at Barringer. And Charles sat sullenly in the living room.

Annie Mae took advantage of their isolation to launch her latest plan. "Charles, it makes me happy to see you and Mickey finally talking again. She's your sister, and she came to your defense when you were jailed. You've got your father's hard heart, but you and Mickey have the same love in your souls. When it comes to you, I'm betting on that love."

"That's one bet I can guarantee you will win."

Encouraged by his positive response, she pressed on. "Even if she marries Junior? I've met his family. So has Mickey. So has T.C. Forget color. Give him a chance. Lord, I wish you could do that. Black skin and white skin doesn't think, doesn't hate, and doesn't even know. Charles, you got to look at Junior as a young man just like you. You got to look at Junior and the way he treats your sister. You got to look at the way he treats T.C. and the way he treats me. Open your eyes, son. There are few enough people anyone can trust without making color an extra burden."

Charles shifted his body and recrossed his legs. "I gave him a chance."

"You think saying that he's your sister's honky boyfriend is giving him a chance? Did he call you nigger? I don't think so. And when I see him look at your sister, all I see is love."

"Mama, it's still his people that enslaved ours. And his—"

"Charles, his people came from Naples, Italy. They never enslaved anyone, much less in our family. They came here and they did what we did. They created their own ghetto because nobody wanted to live next to them or hire them. If you found someone to marry who loves you the way Junior and Mickey love each other, I could ask nothing more for you."

"It's not what I was taught."

"By who, Charles? By Kiongosi, who never lifted a finger for you when you were in jail?"

Charles again shifted and recrossed his legs.

"Charles, you are smarter than that. Did you ever ask T.C. to come outside and throw a football around? Junior did. And that was the same football he was awarded as the MVP on the night T.C. went to see him play. You're his brother, but in that gesture Junior was more brother than you've ever been. Charles, Junior is a real person with real values. I know. T.C. knows. Mickey knows. Give him a chance. You are missing the opportunity to have a real older brother."

Charles was still silent. And then she said the most telling thing she could have said.

"Do you think a man like Junior, who loves your sister, could let your father abuse me? Read the newspaper. He already took a bullet for Mickey."

"I can't think when you say all that. Give me a chance. I came home, didn't I? I made peace with Mickey, didn't I? Give me a chance."

"Charles, it's time to give yourself a chance."

~

Pete turned off the highway and wound deeper and deeper into the drivable wild growth at the edge of Jersey Meadowlands. When Pete stopped the car, D'Amilio saw three black Lincolns.

"This is as far as it goes. Just get out and walk over there to those cars. I'm outta here now."

"What? Will I get home? How do I get home?"

"That will be up to you. Just be yourself. It will work out. Good luck. But I gotta go now. I got a date." He pulled away.

D'Amilio walked slowly toward the three cars. Most of the passengers had gotten out and faced him. Two of them came forward.

"You first?" one of them said.

"Entirely up to you."

D'Amilio stopped and at their instruction spread both arms wide. The one who'd spoken patted him down. The other said, "Sorry for the inconvenience, man, but you understand." They both gave a thumbs-up signal to the cars. One man emerged from each.

D'Amilio recognized the Boot and Don Carlo. With a sinking feeling, he thought, *This is either the beginning or the end of a beautiful friendship.* They beckoned him over and pointed to a car. He stepped forward and got in the back seat. A third man took the keys and backed away.

D'Amilio sat wedged between Gambino and the Boot. "I must admit," D'Amilio began, "I had been told you two do not like each other. So I did not like being chosen to meet with you. I must also tell you, I do this as a favor for an old friend. I have no side in this, no nickel in this quarter."

They both smiled. Gambino spoke. "So you wonder why with bad blood between us in the past we are together to meet you. Well, there is an old Italian proverb. 'When you finish the game, the king and the pawn end up in the same box.' In other words, we all meet the same end. We are not children, Mr.

D'Amilio. With mutual interest, there must be unity. You smile at this," he added. "Good—you have no reason to fear."

"Look, with all respect to both of you and my own father, I have had all the old-country proverbs I can handle. I'd like to get on with this so I can go back to the Yankees and the Giants."

"I understand," the Boot said. "So why are we here? With your indulgence, one last proverb: 'If you don't go, you won't see. If you don't see, you won't know. If you don't know, you'll take it in the ass every time.' We choose not to fall into that trap. So let's talk. You know that of course we trust you, but we both agree it is better for you not to repeat a single word spoken here."

"He knows," Gambino said. "He also knows what we want is an advantage with the new mayor. Which one do we back, and what do we have to give to get what we expect?"

"I am not a negotiator—I can only tell you what I know," D'Amilio said. "I know that two of the candidates are bad for the city and unreliable for you. Remember we have a mayor under indictment. I am told that the third one, Jackson Anderson, can win and attract more support for the city. I am told that he is supposed to have an open mind about municipal contracts. And I am also told that for him to win and favor you, what he needs is an appearance by Frank Sinatra—who could also bring Lena Horne and Aretha Franklin. He has booked the Mosque Theater. If he can divide the seats equally between blacks and Italians with proper undercover policing, he believes he can get one-third of the Italian votes and one-third of the black votes and win the thing. Now before you speak, understand this is what I am told. I have no basis to guarantee it."

They slipped into an exchange in Italian. Then Gambino said, "You are right. Frank is my friend. I do not know the two women, but Frank does. I will need—"

Boiardo interrupted. "*We* will need."

"Yes," Gambino continued, "we will need a guarantee from

Mr. Anderson. Now please step out of the car for a moment and wait."

Through the window he could see both men gesticulating. Then he heard a rap on the window. He re-entered.

"Mr. D'Amilio, you have shown respect and done a good job, but we need one more thing."

"What?" He heard the hint of anger in his voice but couldn't help himself.

"Well, of course, we need Mr. Anderson. Get him to see us in private. And then we not only are finished asking for your help, but down the line, perhaps you, yourself, will need a favor. You have only to call either of us. Until then, *addio e buona fortuna*."

One of the underlings drove him back to the *Star-Ledger*. At his desk, he picked up the phone and called Scarcella. "Okay. This is your big chance. You get Anderson to see him. I love you, I love Loretta, but I am out of this forever. Let me know how you make out."

28

SENIOR TAKES A STAND

J unior Friscella, walking slowly, limping but without crutches, a cast boot on his left leg, moved from the locker room to the base of the bleachers. He hadn't been on the field or at practice since he took a bullet to the leg. But he'd been given the okay, cleared by his doctor to return to practice. He was late, but he was here, and hoped to speak with his coach unobtrusively, without disrupting practice. He stepped to the sidelines.

Everyone in the stadium froze.

A single voice broke the silence, chanting, "Junior . . . Junior . . . Junior." It grew from an uncertain squeak to a crescendo of hope until the whole team, scattered across Sprague Field, chanted in unison.

So much for a quiet return.

Teammates surrounded him and slapped him on the back. He was at the epicenter of an island of dirty practice jerseys. Raftery, the assistant coach, pushed his way through. "So you're celebrating what? He ain't caught a pass this week and you don't even know if he's gonna play on Saturday. Now get back where you belong and work!"

Coach Yablonski stood at the top of the bleachers, bullhorn in hand. Junior limped his way toward his coach, who continued shouting as practice resumed.

"No, no, hell no, Johnny Jakes!" his amplified voice boomed. "For Christ's sake, Johnny. You aren't throwing the ball to fuckin' Wilt Chamberlain. That receiver is five foot ten. Open your fuckin' eyes. You ain't gonna have Junior Friscella to bail you out Saturday. Run it again and again until you get the damn thing right!" To an assistant next to him who was scribbling on a clipboard, the coach said, "We don't have Junior. We do have Trenton State on Saturday, and for the past three years they've had our number. If Jakes doesn't settle down, it's gonna be beyond embarrassing. Those guys are just—"

Junior pointed to his booted foot.

Coach draped an arm around Junior's shoulders and steered him to the edge of the bleachers. "So how do you feel, kid?"

"Sore, but they say I can play."

"And exactly who are *they*? Is one of them a doctor, by any chance, or are they just your adoring fans?"

"Coach, my family doctor says I got what Wild Bill Hickok would call a flesh wound. He says it'll be sore, but I can go. He's known me since the day I was born."

Coach crossed his arms and frowned. "Listen to me, kid. I'm sure he's capable, but you don't set one foot on this field until whoever our medical staff sends you to clears you."

Junior had expected a little more enthusiasm. And expected to return to the field no questions asked. "But, Coach—"

"Listen, kid, you have the talent and the instincts to be a Sunday-afternoon player one day. If you didn't, you wouldn't be on both the Eagles' and Giants' scouting lists. I'm not about to let you risk that to win a couple more games for me. You'll see the team doctor no later than tomorrow morning. Come by the office after practice, and we'll get you the appointment. If he clears you, then I want to see you run some patterns. After that, you won't decide. I will."

The next day, the boot came off. Then Junior passed the

wind-sprint tests, and the doctor cleared him to play—but he took some time to warn Junior that he would also have to beat himself. "You can run. You can stop. You can pivot. But don't be tentative. Can you re-injure the area? Yes. But the odds are you won't unless . . ."

"Unless what?" Junior asked.

"Unless it starts to hurt. If that happens, understand that your body is trying to tell you something. Listen to it. You were a hero once. Don't try for a repeat. Now relax and catch some passes."

Coach held him out of contact drills all week, but Junior continued practicing. Between football and schoolwork, he hadn't seen Mickey since the night she stayed at his house. Maria had invited Allie and Lois to join Mickey and Junior for Thursday dinner. But the family dynamic had changed.

Gerard Friscella Sr. had become a hero with a hero's obligations. Les Scarcella reached out and arranged for his appearance on several TV shows. CBS's *60 Minutes* had come to the house to interview him. When the show's reps found out that Mickey and Junior would be there, it suddenly became a package deal.

"Maybe they should stay for dinner," Senior told Maria.

"Maybe they shouldn't," Maria said. "Look, I am proud of you. I am proud of Junior. But I am also proud of my lasagna. I don't serve it cold or reheated, Mr. Hero. You tell them they got one hour to tape and fifteen minutes to pack and leave."

The director put Senior, Junior, and Mickey on the couch. They rolled cameras and began to tape. The host began, "So you know the men who attacked you guys?"

"Of course," Junior said. "We grew up together."

"And you are sure it was racial?"

Junior said, "What do you think, after the way they threw the word 'nigger' around? Yeah, I threw the first punch. Who wouldn't after the things he said about Mickey?" He reached for her hand.

The host turned to her. "And what do you think, Mickey?"

"I think everybody is missing one thing. It was the girl. I don't even know her name. She wasn't arrested. She's hiding. But it was the girl who started the name-calling, who urged them on, and whose challenge to their manhood made it happen. Believe me, we were trying to walk away."

The host nodded thoughtfully. "This one is for Senior. Do you think this attack was connected to the White Citizens Council? Didn't these guys work for Paulie Tedesco?"

"They do, and he hasn't said that they don't work for him anymore. But I think it was more personal between them and my son. Although it was clearly and totally racial."

"But one way or another, the election is part of this, isn't it?"

Senior leaned forward. "Listen to me and let me be clear. I was born in this town and in this ward. So were these two thugs. My son was born in this town and in this ward. Mickey here was born in this town but not in this ward. The difference here stands out. She's black. My son is white. They are in love. Some people in this town don't like that. Hell, they hate it. I'm going to have something to say about this election later this week. The hatred is killing what was once a beautiful city."

"You want to elaborate on that?"

"Not now. See that woman over there? She warned me not to let her lasagna get cold. I sleep with her, not you. Thanks for interviewing us."

The host didn't take the hint. "One year after this city was torn apart by a riot, you can almost see the acrimony as you walk its streets. This clearly isn't over. We will keep the CBS eye on this tension as it continues to grow."

Junior saw his mother glare at his father. Five minutes later, the news crew was out the door.

The table was already set. Before anyone else spoke, Angie had muscled her way into a seat next to Mickey. "Did you really take off your bra to make a tourniquet for Junior?" she asked eagerly.

"Angie," Maria almost shouted, "that's more than enough!"

"I'd say it was true love," Senior interrupted.

"Can we just eat dinner?" Junior pleaded.

∾

"So what are we gonna do?" Jerry D'Amilio asked.
"I was gonna ask you the same question," Les Scarcella said.

They sat at a table in the rear of the Liberty Club. Out of respect for the sports columnist, and out of a little bit of fear of the center's director, the other patrons were careful not to acknowledge them. But as it had for the rest of the city, the coming election had split their ranks as well.

"Well, somebody has to get the word to Anderson," D'Amilio said. "Neither of us knows him. And you don't just walk up to a politician who says he will clean up the city and say a couple of Mafia guys want to make a deal with him."

"You're right. I can't. But you can. You have a reputation as a stand-up guy. The Pulitzer makes it even better. These two Mafiosi trust you. They don't trust many people. It has to be you."

"Les, I'm getting a little tired of this. I love you, but you're gonna get me killed."

"Nobody is gonna die here. This ain't the movies. It's more politics than Mob. If it was just politics, I could handle it. We're out of ideas. Why don't you call Ryan or Eboli or whatever the hell his name is? He should know what our next move is."

"You may recall the last time I spoke to him, he said he didn't know me and hung up."

"You got a better idea?" Scarcella asked.

"Yeah, I walk outta here and we forget the whole thing." He sighed. "All right. I'll make the call."

Eboli picked up on the second ring. When he heard D'Amilio's voice, he blurted, "Oh, shit." Then he added, "I told you, I don't know you."

"Don't hang up, Tommy. I got a problem."

"And you think I should make it my problem?"

"No. I need advice. I'll forget who gave it to me. That's a promise. But I'm in over my head. I need an expert for this, and I'm not one." He brought him up to date.

"So what's the problem?"

"I need to know how to approach Anderson and keep the two Mafia guys happy."

"You know, for a big-shot newspaper guy who has lunch with the governor, you amaze me with the way you freeze up when a member of La Famiglia looks sideways at you. You might know every batting average on the Mets, but you don't know shit about Cosa Nostra. Relax, kid. Nobody is going to kill you. These guys try *not* to kill civilians unless it's personal. Think of it like you were a real-estate agent showing a house. They don't kill the agent because the seller won't deal. I'm not telling you to do this because the two guys you are in the middle of ain't exactly the brightest bulbs on Broadway. Me? I never trusted either of them motherfuckers. But I had, let's say, a different business relationship with them. The last thing they want is to hurt a civilian who is a kind of celebrity. Go do your thing, if that's what you want. But maybe you should tell that coat-holder it's his turn."

"Coat-holder?"

"Yeah, a guy who starts the fight and never has the *coglioni* to get into it. Instead, he holds the coats. Get it? Sorry, kid, don't have the time to give you a language lesson. Do what you choose to do, don't worry, and for Christ's sake, please, please lose my phone number and forget my name."

The line went dead.

~

For the first time, Charles was seeing who and what his mother was. Since the day Annie Mae had told Talmadge to leave, Charles had always believed his mother had deprived him of a hero, the masculine oracle who could answer everything he believed his mother could not—from the first sprouts of hair around his genitals to wet dreams, from how to field a ground ball to how to shoot a free throw.

His mother nagged him about his grades—he dropped out of school. His mother gave him a nightly curfew—he made a point of violating it. The more his mother demanded to know about his friends and his private life, the more he sneaked out to visit his father—when he could find him.

It led to Charles' recruitment by Kiongosi, his determination to be valued by that new force in his life, and his hatred of everything and everybody white to prove that he was more his father than his mother. His very involvement in the gun-running act was akin to an act of revocation of everything his mother expected of him.

But now every value he had formed was in disrepair. He weighed the evidence: Mickey protecting her mother with a baseball bat . . . his father of no help to him, well, really, ever . . . and now being asked to sanction his sister's love affair with a guy who was white and, beyond that, who seemed to be everything he was not.

Ironically, the answer to his unasked questions that weighed the most with him came from his little brother.

"Why is it you can't wait to hang out with him?" Charles asked after what seemed like the twentieth time T.C. had recounted Junior's role in beating Delaware State. "There's more to life than football."

"Maybe. But he treats me like I'm his brother. Ask Mickey. She'll tell you."

It was that reference to Mickey that hurt the most. It stayed with him for days. He and his mom had begun to spend a lot of time together at night. She didn't preach, she reacted. He listened, and when Charles asked her why she thought so highly of Junior, she didn't hedge.

"He proved himself. He took a bullet for your sister. He acts like a brother with T.C. but isn't acting. I know his mom and dad —they raised him right. I can't tell you what to do. But you best think about it."

Charles felt a surge of emotions rolling around inside him— and he wasn't sure what to do with them.

~

M ickey and Allie sat together alone at the top of the bleacher risers, watching the usual Thursday late-night practice under the lights. Junior had told Mickey the coaching staff scheduled practice so late to accommodate the evening classes of four starters. About two dozen other students had gathered to watch.

"I know he can run," Mickey said. She laughed and added, "To prove it, he made me chase him halfway across campus. When he doesn't let me catch him, you know he can run."

"I read in the *Star-Ledger* yesterday that Yablonski told the writer he didn't know yet if Junior could go. He said he wouldn't know until game time."

"That's exactly why I like him. He protects his players, especially the one I care about."

Raftery called them in, and the entire team took a knee to listen. They broke into their units, and Mickey and Allie moved along the bleachers for a better view of where the offense was running the game plan against the defense. Raftery was still holding Junior out. He stood behind them with an assistant coach, watching.

Just as they moved, Mickey hesitated.

"What's wrong?" Allie asked.

"I don't know. I thought I recognized somebody I never

expected to see here. He was in the bleachers on the other side of the field. But I guess I'm wrong. It couldn't be him."

"Are you sure you're okay? It wasn't Chooch or Dominick. The only guy over at that end is black."

"Oh, boy. I was right. It's Charles, the brother you never met. That's all I need right now."

"Is it trouble?"

"I don't know. Let's just wait and keep an eye on him. I have no idea what this is about."

Practice ended an hour and a half later. Mickey and Allie were climbing down to the field. She saw Junior and Johnny Jakes walking toward the locker room. Then she saw Charles come onto the field on the other side, running toward Junior.

Allie saw it too. "Oh, shit."

They started to run, but they were too late. Mickey saw Charles tap Junior on the shoulder. "What is he doing?" she wondered.

The two talked briefly. Then Junior led him back toward the bleachers.

Allie laid a cautionary hand on Mickey's arm. "We ought to wait here and see what's going on."

"I need to hear what that brother of mine is saying." Mickey crept closer to listen. She heard Junior's voice first.

"So you came all the way up from Newark to see me. Well, here I am. So talk."

"Don't rush me. This ain't easy. I know I said some terrible things to you, and you came back pretty good at me. What I want to talk about is T.C."

"Not Mickey?"

"Well, that, too. But mostly T.C. He got me thinking. He don't see you as white. He sees you as his potential brother. And that hurts me."

"Whose fault is that?"

Charles paused. He bit his lip and stared at Junior. "Mine."

Mickey sucked in a breath. She couldn't believe what she was hearing.

"I see the way he acts with you, and I'm jealous. But I know I never earned that. So"—Charles took a deep breath—"what do you say we start over? No more 'honky' stuff." He stuck out his hand. "My name is Charles. Pleased to meet you, Junior. I guess Mickey knows what she's doing. Don't hurt her, or I'll hurt you."

Junior smiled. "I doubt you could, but then, I could never hurt her. Nice to meet you, Charles. See that guy waiting for me over there? He's my quarterback. His name is Johnny Jakes and I want you to meet him."

Mickey and Allie heard every word, but Junior and Charles never saw them.

"Go say something," Allie said, pushing her to follow them.

"No," Mickey said, "let's go." Then she offered up a radiant smile. "This moment is best left in their hands."

2 9

THE ART OF THE DEAL

Jackson Anderson held a rolled-up *Star-Ledger* in his right
hand, beating time against the dashboard to the "Toreador
Song" aria from *Carmen*.

Fast Freddy Sternburg, behind the steering wheel, glanced at
him. "Boss, you certainly ain't no stereotype. You're the only
black guy I know with tickets to the Metropolitan Opera. Who
did you date in college? The first violinist in the Rutgers
Symphony Orchestra?"

"You are closer to the truth than you think. I played the cello.
That's how I learned to fight in an all-white town—carrying it to
and from school. The dates, well, I did all right there. Don't
forget I played football."

"Then maybe we ought to discuss the playbook for this
morning's meeting. These guys ain't exactly advocates of honest
government. They will want something big in return."

"Freddy, there was a poet named Edgar A. Guest—a real
Pollyanna of a rhymer. He got a lot of attention for writing 'a
promise made is a debt unpaid.' I see it differently. I subscribe to
what a very smart Jewish professor of business tactics once told
my class. 'Promise a deal, but don't be a schlemiel.'"

"All right, boss. So what's the plan? We've got to go in there with more than a smile."

"We let them think they control the deal. Hell, it's America, ain't it? They have that right. So they can think what they want. After we get Frank, Gambino's role diminishes. As for the Boot, we can get what he promises us if we open the old wound Gambino left in their relationship. They won't let you tape this, or take notes, so don't even try. We have to be above suspicion. Listen closely to every word—we'll need the ammunition later. Listen. Don't speak. I know what I need to do. If they ask you something, follow my lead."

They pulled into the lot next to the town cars at six thirty. The building shielded them from the rush-hour traffic of the morning. They walked quickly to the back door as they had been instructed, knocked twice, paused, then knocked three times. The owner immediately opened the door.

"Right on time," he said. "Before we go further, I want to make sure you understand you're using my place as a service to a mutual friend. That would be the newspaper columnist Jerry D'Amilio. Neither he nor I have any interest in what is discussed here. Please remember that. And honor it with your silence. Understood?"

Both men nodded assent. They were led down a hall and ushered into a room. Both Mafiosi rose to greet their guests. Don Carlo "supervised" the introductions. Boiardo wore a frozen smile.

"You spoke with the sports columnist?" Gambino asked.

"I did," Anderson replied. "Before you ask, he did not name either of you. As I recall, he used the phrase 'tough guys' and said he thought you would contact me."

Both Gambino and Boiardo laughed.

"Tough guys, huh?" Gambino said. "I think we scared the shit out of him. Sorry, I didn't mean to laugh. Actually he appears to be a nice young man and, we're told, quite competent at what he does. Do you know him well?"

"We have never met. He called one day to tell me I would be hearing from you."

Gambino and the Boot turned away and conferred in Italian. Then Gambino spoke. *"Parli Italiano?"*

Sternburg and Anderson looked blankly at him.

"Please excuse my, uh, my friend here," Gambino said. "We just needed to know if you speak Italian. You apparently don't, so we can keep our little secrets. Now tell us why and how we should throw our support to your candidacy."

The Boot interrupted. "Now we tell it like it is. Why do you bring us such a very difficult task? You are an outsider in this city. It's my business to know that. The other black man tells his people you are unreal, rich, and not what they are. I believe he uses the term 'Uncle Tom.' So with your own people you are starting the race from twenty yards behind. With our people in the North Ward you are worse than an outsider. Their candidate calls you a monkey. We are not without resources. You want Frank. We—I mean he—can produce him. You need street workers—I can produce them. If you need money, which they say you don't, we both can produce it. As I said before, let's tell it like it is. What do we get in return after you win?" He leaned back in his chair and fixed Anderson with an icy stare.

Anderson surprised himself with a slightly aggressive tone. These guys scared him, but he managed to keep his voice even, with no hint of the jitters in his stomach. "You know what I want. My requests are simple. I do not ask for a stuffed ballot box. I do not ask for pressure on another candidate. What I ask for are easily done favors. All I ask for is the support of an entertainer and the ground force, which you would have to get from someone else. In no case do I want or expect you to break a single law. There is absolutely nothing in what you'll do that would require you to hire a lawyer or spend a single day in court. Of course, there are favors and contracts that you should and would obtain. That would be fair and should be expected by you. But I cannot spell them out in detail until if and when I am elected. I have nothing to gain by not honoring this trust at that time—and much more to lose. So that, as you like to say, is telling it like it is."

He reached out and poured himself and Sternburg each a glass of Campari, sat back, and fixed his potential partners with his own frigid stare. The silence hung heavily over all of them. Then Anderson poured Campari for the two Mafiosi, leaving just the right amount of space for club soda if they so desired.

The two nodded in thanks. Anderson smiled broadly. "So shall we say *salud*?"

The Boot laughed, turned to Don Carlo, and slapped him on the back. "Incredible. He turned into a regular *consigliere*. I swear, this black son of a bitch has Italian *coglioni*. So, Don Carlo?"

In unison the two shouted, "*Salud!*"

~

Paulie Tedesco was in a full-blown rage. Overnight, his chief of staff was out on bail awaiting trial for aggravated assault with a deadly weapon. His muscle guy got off with a fine, but it was clear that he and an unidentified woman set in motion the events that led to Chooch's arrest.

The duo sat against the wall in folding chairs while Tedesco paced back and forth in front of them. Each stride was punctuated with a curse.

"You ignorant cocksuckers . . . stupid bastards . . . fuckin' morons! Did you hear what Friscella Senior said about me on *60 Minutes*? Do you realize that Les Scarcella has organized a rally to honor him as a ward-raised Italian American hero? Do you understand that you've taken this campaign from the penthouse all the way down to the shithouse? And all because you think with your little heads instead of the big ones. You let some *puttana* put at risk every single thing we have worked for since the riot. Assholes! Now I have to try to find a way to undo the damage you motherfuckers have caused us. Do me a favor. Take a week off and then come back right here and I'll have figured out something we can do to set things right. One week. Be here, jerkoffs—and keep your dicks in your pants and your mouths absolutely shut tight."

~

Almost as if by magic, the handbills appeared in every ward—on lampposts, empty buildings, and even the sides of overpasses, inviting all to come to the rally honoring Senior Friscella's defense of Newark's family values on the lawn of the St. Gerard Self-Help and Improvement Community Center, rain or shine.

"I don't want to do this," Senior told Maria one night. "I *have* to do this. Nobody in this family is going to be pushed into being a guinea or a wop again, and that's exactly where we all will be headed if this little North Ward jerkoff wins this election. Nobody is ever going to threaten or attack anyone in this family again."

"And if it breaks that way, will that include Mickey as well?" Maria asked.

"It will definitely include Mickey and anyone else she brings into this family."

~

At the same time in the Scarcella home, Loretta poured coffee and Amaretto, and then she, her husband, and Jerry D'Amilio raised their cups in salute as Les shouted, "New day a-coming!"

30

A FATHER SPEAKS

A t 5:30 a.m., in the half light of the false dawn, fifty workmen swarmed over a large patch of ground directly in front of the St. Gerard Center. In the midst of them, Les Scarcella shouted instructions through a bullhorn.

Jerry D'Amilio had parked his car behind the building and walked slowly toward Scarcella, shaking his head with every step.

"Les, who the hell are these people? They don't work for you. There's not a center employee in the bunch."

"We got a deadline, Jerry. I can't use amateurs for this. They are union people sent over by our two new friends to help the cause."

"Look, I delivered a couple of messages for you, out of respect and to keep you out of the glare of publicity. But you're walking a very fine line. You could lose the respect of your constituency."

"In the end, we're helping the North Ward, and that's what counts. We let Paulie win this thing and we are set back decades. Your father and my father would understand. It's not about being Italian. We had a mayor who forgot who we are. It's about the sons and grandsons of this ward who brought us progress with their own sweat and their own two hands. We just finished with an indicted mayor who did nothing for any of us in this city —white or black. We don't need—" He lifted his bullhorn and yelled, "The flags—where the hell are the flags? No, not Italian. The American flags. You got to drape them over the platform railings. No, no, not like that. I told you before, all the way around. This ain't an award ceremony for the Italian American merchant of the year. It's a save-our-city rally."

He stood back and inspected their handiwork.

D'Amilio again shook his head. "Les, take this the way it's meant. Save the city, but don't sell it to the devil. I know who sent this work crew over for you. I know the Friscella kid's father. Most people in this city agree with what he did. That took guts. But for Christ's sake, don't let him become a political pawn."

"Jerry, we built the center when politicians didn't want it. Now it's a force for good for the poor people it serves. Friscella knows that. He's nobody's pawn."

"I hope not," D'Amilio said.

At 9:00 a.m., the members of the center's middle-school fife-drum-bugle corps drifted toward their roped-off assembly site. Their warm-up efforts mingled along the empty street with the harsh sounds of hammers and saws.

"So how are you going to do this?" D'Amilio said.

"Well, I'll be the emcee. I want you to say—"

"No, Les, no. I did what I did because I owe you and because I think it might be the best thing for this city. But I'm done. I want this rally to work. But don't do anything to jeopardize our friendship. I mean it. Don't introduce me to the crowd. Don't ask me to speak. I agree with what you've done, but now it's your ballgame. I'm going to watch from inside the center at that window, second from the left, first floor."

At ten thirty, the television crews arrived.

Les Scarcella hadn't seen Gerard Senior yet. He ensured that the stage had been readied to his satisfaction, then went looking for his main attraction. The fife-drum-bugle corps had played two songs already for the early arrivals, and he noted that with more than an hour before the scheduled start of his rally, the crowd had filled the lawn and the street in front and was still growing.

He went inside the center and found Gerard Senior and his family hunkered at tables in the cafeteria. He couldn't have his city hero hiding out and looking glum. Somehow they'd managed to quietly sneak in without anyone noticing. Les was certain the crowd would have reacted if anyone had spotted Senior, Junior, or Mickey.

"Nervous?" Scarcella asked, placing a hand on Senior's shoulder. "I got a speech I wrote last night for you if you want it."

"I'm okay," Senior said. "I don't need a speech. These people could have killed my son. By the way, this beautiful young lady is my son's girlfriend—she made the tourniquet that saved his life. This is Mickey Washington, her mother, Annie Mae, and her brother, T.C."

"It's a pleasure, ladies, and you too, young man," Scarcella said. It was the first he knew that the son had a black girlfriend. He silently categorized it as a political plus for his own agenda. "Where is Junior?" he asked.

"He and his buddy Allie will be here. I need a favor, Les. Please don't introduce him."

"It's your show, Gerry. You call the shots. But I want to make something clear. For me, this isn't politics. For me, it's the ward and the city and a guy I went to Barringer with, and his son—of whom all of us can be proud."

All heads in the cafeteria turned toward the doorway as Junior, Allie, and Jerry D'Amilio walked in. Applause broke out. Mickey and T.C. jumped up and joined the clapping.

Les saw D'Amilio pull up a chair and strike up a conversation with Junior. Meanwhile, Annie Mae approached. "I like what I've heard about the center, Mr. Scarcella. Do you have any programs T.C. could fit into?"

"He told me about the Pop Warner team at the Boys Club," Scarcella said. "He's in the right place with the right coach. But if he has any academic problem, you send him here and I'll make sure he gets what he needs."

His chief of staff came over and whispered in Scarcella's ear. The director jumped up. "It's time, folks. You're on, Gerry. Make us proud."

As Scarcella and Senior came into view, the music grew louder. The drums took over when the two ascended to the stage.

The local precinct captain stepped up and murmured to Scarcella, "You got about a thousand people out here, Les. Keep it calm. I mean it. I don't need to handle another riot. Get it? I cannot believe that you guys have split the Italians."

Scarcella just smiled at him and stepped to the microphone. He raised his arms and quieted the gathering. He knew how to work a crowd, whether in a room or at a parade. "Good morning. We are here to honor one of our own, Gerry Friscella. For me, it's personal. I've known him since we were ten. We grew up together on Mama's spaghetti and Ting-a -Ling's lemon ice. We went to Barringer together. I can't remember a moment when we didn't know each other. His son was injured by two local thugs who happened to work for the president of the ward's White Citizens Council—who has to disavow them as his employees. So to them, to their boss, I say this morning, when you attack Gerry Friscella's family, you attack me. You all know what his response was to them. We are here to put a punctuation mark to that response."

The cheering drowned him out. He knew enough to let it go for about three minutes. Then he raised his arms, cut it off, and continued. "We are not surprised at what he did to protect his family. There is nobody, and I mean nobody, in this huge crowd who wouldn't have done the same. Ladies and gentlemen, let your applause confirm that. I introduce Gerry Friscella Sr."

The band struck up its version of a tarantella. The crowd noise shattered the humid air. Gerard Friscella stepped to the microphone. He was handed a plaque from Scarcella and the center. Then he spoke.

"I'm a machinist at Westinghouse—not a politician. I am a father—not a politician. I've been a blue-collar worker all my life. I pay my taxes and I always vote. But now I am heartsick over the bigotry and hatred that hang over my hometown. That was the formula that could have cost my son his life but for the quick thinking of his girlfriend, who is standing next to me and who just happens to be an attractive black woman."

Mickey was flustered by the unexpected burst of applause led by center employees scattered among the crowd. She turned her head toward Maria, who put her finger to her lips and winked at her. Les smiled. *Beautiful.* He couldn't have scripted this better himself.

"I am not a politician," Senior repeated as the noise faded, "but I cannot stand by while others who preach hate run for the highest office this city has. Until this morning, I had never met Jackson Anderson. We talked. So it comes down to this. I cannot watch Paulie Tedesco steal this election by appealing to your ethnicity. I cannot watch the man who calls himself Kiongosi win by default. In so many ways, he preaches the same gospel of hate and distrust that Paulie does. I love my family, I love my ward, and I love my city. All three have made my life better. I don't say that Mr. Anderson has all the answers. I say that of the three, he is the one candidate with the education, the intention, and the ability to heal this city. I have never voted for a black man, but I will vote for him. I ask you to do the same."

A moment of total silence fell over the rally. Then the crowd found its voice, reacting with a thunderous ovation. Scarcella shook Senior's hand and then watched the man make his way through the noise and the tumult, seeming to melt away.

～

Thursday night, the night before the game, Maria Friscella and Mickey Washington sat in the bleachers of Sprague Field while the Montclair State Indians went through practice under the bright lights. Maria and Mickey stared downfield, where Junior stood in a corner of the end zone while the team doctor and Coach Yablonski evaluated his leg. Occasionally, the doctor gestured toward his own leg to make a point.

Mickey had seen the other players steal an occasional glance that way. She knew they, like Maria and herself, were all wondering about the doctor's decision.

The school newspaper's sports section that day headlined the message: *Does Friscella Have a Leg Up? We'll Know Tonight.*

Besides the team on the field, perhaps a hundred students were scattered throughout the bleachers, watching and presumably also hoping for the news.

"He wasn't limping at lunch," Mickey said to Maria. "But he's so stubborn I don't know whether it's improved or he's just disguising it. What do you think?"

"I think he is his father's son, so I don't have a clue. If he doesn't tell you, all I can do is hope he tells the doctor. He'll never tell the coach."

The conference down below broke up and Junior headed for the locker room. Yablonski resumed his position in the bleachers and shouted comments at the offense and defense.

After a sweep to the right blew itself apart, the coach was livid. "Open your eyes, damn it! This ain't last week—it's this week. We've been playing Trenton State for a gazillion years. They don't like us. We don't like them. Now get with the damn program. They won't give you a thing on Saturday. Run it again."

"There he is!" Mickey shouted. Junior had re-emerged from the locker room. He paused to tie his shoes. Then he headed for the bleachers as the coach came down to meet him. The doctor joined them.

Yablonski raised the megaphone and hollered. "All right, all right! Offense versus defense. And don't treat Junior as though he were made out of china. If you have to hit him, hit him."

Mickey, on her feet, clenched her fists. "Come on," she muttered, terrified at the thought of seeing Junior suffer more injury.

The huddle broke, and the offense lined up with Junior in the slot. Johnny Jakes, possibly even more nervous than Junior, launched a pass that sailed high. Junior had to stretch up, but he pulled it in. Off balance, he fell.

Mickey gasped. "No, no!"

As if to silence criticism before it began, Junior jumped to his feet quicker than necessary.

They ran an off-tackle dive to keep the defense honest—then threw to him again. This time he ran a square-out where he ran down the left side, stopped, pivoted, caught the ball, and stepped out of bounds.

Two plays later, Jakes threw long. It was a stop-and-go pattern for Junior. Stride for stride, the defender stayed with him, and then Junior juked left, cut right, never broke stride, made the grab, and scored untouched.

After the play, he huddled with the doctor and the coach one last time.

"Come on, let's go," Maria said to Mickey.

Mickey followed her out of the stands. As they got closer to the huddled trio, she strained her ears, eager for news. But they were out of earshot. The doctor gesticulated as he had last time, pointing to his leg, and then walked away.

The women cornered Coach Yablonski as he was leaving the field.

"I understand it's your decision," Maria said, "but I'm his mother and I'd like to know."

"I'd tell you if I could, Mrs. Friscella. But we're not sure yet. The doc wants him to test it again tomorrow. Vince Lombardi used to say football is not a contact sport, it's a hitting sport. I'm not going to jeopardize him if the doc says no."

"Does he know this yet?"

"No, and I'd rather we wait until we see how he does tomorrow before somebody tells him."

"I just hope," Mickey said, "that the someone doesn't have to be me."

But it was.

∾

Junior sat across the table from Mickey having lunch in the cafeteria. "I saw you and Mom with the coach at practice last night," he said. "But you both left before I came out of the locker room. Kinda seemed like you were avoiding me."

Mickey shook her head and took another bite. But she wouldn't meet his eyes. Her innocent act wasn't flying with him.

"What do you know that I don't know? I know there's something, Mickey, because you won't look at me."

"Don't yell at me," she said.

That indicated to him that she did, in fact, know something she was keeping from him. He banged the table with his fist. "I want to know right now."

"It's nothing," she said. "He just said the doctor isn't sure. They plan to test you again tonight."

"Why didn't you tell me last night?"

"Because I knew you'd act like this. Lower your voice. People are looking at us."

"I should be able to count on you."

Mickey frowned. "You can."

"I just don't know."

"What do you mean, you don't know?"

"I thought you understood how much this means to me."

He stood abruptly, scowled at her, and stormed out.

~

M ickey's last class was at 2:00 p.m., but she knew Allie was in a nearby building taking a history test. She needed to talk to him, so she waited outside for him to emerge. She hadn't been able to focus during class at all. Worry about Junior gnawed at her stomach. He had never raised his voice to her before, never looked so angry. And she didn't even understand what she'd done that so upset him.

Allie smiled when he saw her. "Where's the White Knight?" he asked. Then he saw she had been crying. He put his arm around her and walked her to a bench.

She let him lead her. This was exactly what she needed. Surely Junior's best friend could explain his bizarre reaction at lunch. She'd been honest with him. What in the world had set him off?

"What happened?" he asked.

"I don't know. He saw his mom and me at practice last night. He saw us with the coach. Today at lunch I told him they were going to test him again tonight—and he just blew up. He demanded to know why I hadn't come and told him. It made no sense. He never spoke to me like that, ever. It was so unfair."

She began to cry again.

Allie put a hand under her chin. "Look at me. He's wrong and we both know it. But let me explain this. There are some things he won't tell you, because he believes they would make him look like less in your eyes."

"How could he even think that?"

"It's the way we were raised in our neighborhood. The man shoulders all the responsibility. You didn't see the look in his eyes when that girl insulted the two of you at the soda stand at San Gennaro."

"But you were the one who got in that girl's face."

"Only because I knew if I didn't, he was going right across the counter to slap the crap out of her. He worries that the leg might prevent him from ever playing the game he loves. Now his father is under enormous pressure about endorsing a black mayoral candidate. He worries about that. Do you have any idea how many people in our ward might hate his old man for that? And all the time he worries about you. He worries someone will insult you over this racial crap, and in a crazy way he blames himself for putting you in that position. But I know how much he loves you. And he feels guilty as hell that it took so long to introduce you to his family because he didn't trust them to accept a black-white relationship. I know him. He's always been like this—captain of the team, the best grades, the perfect son. He's a leader, and he tries to make everything perfect. He worries he can't live up to it. He overthinks everything. That's what makes him such a great football player—because he can tell you where every other receiver should be on any play and what each one will have to do to beat the coverage. But off the field, he wants everything perfect. He's scared it won't be. If it isn't, he blames himself. He wants to be the one who makes everything right for everybody. And I'll tell you something else of which I am positive. He worries he is not good enough for you."

Allie stopped and took a deep breath. Mickey stared at him wide-eyed. "But that's ridiculous. I worry I might not be good enough for *him*."

"Listen to me. I know the man. He'd never walk away from you. He'd die first. But he's scared to death you might quit him."

"I don't know what to think. None of this ever entered my mind."

"He would deny it if you ever told him. So don't."

"But I have to make this right."

"No, you don't. Let me do it. All our lives we've been

straightening each other out. He just needs to know this macho bullshit is not something to put on a sweet lady like you."

"Alphonse Costa, if I didn't love Junior so much, I'd kiss you. So right now, in front of all these students, I'm going to put my arms around you and hug you as hard as I can."

"I'll handle it just as he would if it were the other way around. But, lady, I'm begging you. Cool it with the Alphonse stuff. Somebody might hear you."

31

DOING BUSINESS IN VEGAS

Don Carlo Gambino and his second-in-command, Frank Costello, flew to Vegas with Richie "The Boot" Boiardo, who brought his son, Tony Boy. Gambino felt it was only fair that each of them meet Frank Sinatra in person, and that each of them bring a second. This way, they would be evenly represented, and no one would feel slighted.

Vegas proved to be a refreshing change, a relaxing neutral location for the men accustomed to watching their backs and constantly on edge, concerned about being whacked by a rival. Gambino felt his normal state of anxiety melt away in the desert heat. He could breathe easily for the first time in as long as he could remember.

Showered and dressed to the nines, the four shared a table in the Sands Copa Show Room, waiting for their hero's dinner show. Gambino sipped his drink. He should get away more often. This was a business trip, but the change of surroundings was good for him.

The house lights darkened. A voice so demanding it seemed to be on steroids filled the room with high-intensity audio:

"Ladies and gentlemen, Mr. Francis . . . Albert . . . Sinatra."

The room exploded in a tsunami of applause as Sinatra

entered stage-left. He wore a midnight-blue tuxedo and bow tie on a light-blue shirt. As the spotlight followed him across the dark stage, he moved toward a lone folding chair turned backward and a small table that held two glasses of water.

Sinatra hesitated in front of the chair, then sat, leaning on the chair's back and crossing his arms over it. He yanked at his tie, hung it loosely around his neck, and finally spoke as he unbuttoned his shirt collar. "Now that's more like it. Good evening, ladies and gentlemen, and welcome to Lost Wages, Nevada. Are you enjoying your trip?"

More applause.

"Well, make the most of it—because the only thing that happens in Las Vegas and stays in Las Vegas, according to the wise guys, is your money. But they're not as smart as they think they are, because after you leave here you will always have something no wise guy can ever take from you—the memories of this magic city."

Then he rose. In the same warm voice and with the same broad smile that had conquered thousands of audiences on thousands of stages, he said, "So whaddya say? Let's make a few more right now. Let's rock this joint. If Mr. Music over there with the baton under his arm will release all those musicians behind him, I'm set. I'm ready. So let's go."

He pointed once again, and the room seemed to explode with the sound of a typical Sinatra opening—heavy on the brass and heavier on the beat. Even before he sang the first lyric, the feet under all those showroom tables began to beat time, and the four Mafiosi fixated on what was erupting. Francis Albert Sinatra had the whole joint in the palm of his hand.

"The Lady Is a Tramp" was followed by many of the usual standards, which the four thugs recognized as bookmarks to their own lives and times.

Just like all the squares of their generation in the same audience, they could identify a memory with each song . . . their high school dances . . . cruising along in their first cars, windows open to make it seem to the girls at their sides that they were going even faster than they were . . . and, most of all, getting laid in the back seat.

Alone with their own thoughts, Gambino and Boiardo were temporarily distracted from their mutual hatred by memories of their youth. Near the show's end, Sinatra broke into "High Hopes," and with each verse the ladies screamed and the men cheered. The house lights came up. Sinatra took three curtain calls before the crowd began to shuffle toward the exit.

At that point, a security guard approached Gambino's table. "I have a message for you from Mr. Sinatra. He says he would be honored to see you in his dressing room. If you gentlemen will follow me, I'll get you through all these tourists."

At the exit, where the crowd turned right, the guard turned left. The foursome followed the guard to a dressing room door. He knocked, then opened it a crack. "Mr. Sinatra, they're here."

"Well, all right, let them in," Sinatra's booming voice replied.

Gambino led the group inside. Sinatra sat on a love seat dressed in a white terry-cloth robe with a drink in his hand. "Charlie," he said to the casino host who had been assigned to him, "see what my guys want to drink."

At a table, Charlie poured. All eyes moved to Sinatra. "So, they treating you right? You need anything—booze, broads, or credit—just ask Charlie here, right, Charlie?"

"Like for you, Mr. Sinatra, their wish is my command."

Sinatra laughed. "What's happening back in the Garden State? Anybody shoot anybody over a parking spot in Hoboken?"

"No," Gambino replied, "but I wouldn't mind finding a way to sell them."

They all laughed. Gambino noticed Boiardo remained silent, which made sense, considering he was the one with the relationship to Sinatra. Boiardo was along for the ride and to keep things fair.

"Well, you know, both Ricardo and I have interests in

Newark," Gambino said. "He more than I, but if you grant us a favor, he will be happy, and I will have more of an interest. Isn't that correct, my friend?" Gambino opened the door for Boiardo to join in.

"Yes," the Boot responded. "Up to a point, yes. It's about the election, Frank. You can help us. We will benefit. The city will be better off. And both of us shall be forever in your debt. As you know, Francesco—do you mind if I use the Italian out of friendship?" Sinatra smiled and nodded. "Well, of course we would benefit. But, my friend, this is a bitter political battle. There are two black candidates and one white. The white boy is named Paulie Tedesco."

"Italian?" Sinatra asked.

"Yes, much to our shame," Gambino answered. "He is not Italian like you and Ricardo and me. It might surprise you, but we do not want this *figlio d'un cane* to win. He is a disgrace to us. He is the head of the White Citizens Council. We know how you fought discrimination on the Strip here in Las Vegas. We know how you fought and threatened just to get Sammy Davis and Lena Horne the right to live in the hotel where they performed. We have a ward in Newark made up primarily of Italians. They have worked hard to rise from Mustache Petes to respected blue-collar workers. This guy whose name is Paulie Tedesco would set them back thirty years. Yes, we will make money if you help us, but we also need to stop him to help our fellow Italians."

"So what are the other options?" Sinatra asked, addressing Gambino. "I don't quite understand."

"I would prefer that Mr. Costello answer that," Gambino said, nodding toward his second-in-command. "He is much closer to this situation."

"The other candidates are both black," Costello began. "The first wants to turn the city into a kind of transplanted Africa. The second has money, education, and no prejudice whatsoever—and, yes, I admit, would be very favorable to us. His name is Jackson Anderson."

"Well, what can I do about it?" Sinatra asked.

"Come to Newark. Bring Lena Horne and Aretha Franklin, if you know her. Perform at our rally for Anderson in front of thirty-six hundred people—white and black. And endorse him. Such an endorsement by the greatest Italian singer of them all, a man from our own Hoboken whose mother was politically active there, delivering six hundred votes a year as a ward leader, a man who has fought for the rights of blacks and Italians and is without prejudice, doing that in a city wracked with suspicion and hate and racial division . . . such a man could save this city, help the blacks, help the Italians, and, we admit, help us. And as Ricardo earlier said, it would put all of us—the mayor, the city, Ricardo, and Don Carlo—in your debt."

Sinatra lifted his glass and drank deeply.

Costello continued. "Frank, it's a win-win situation. And we guarantee that the audience at the Mosque Theater that night will be half Italian and half black. People who bought your records and heard you on the radio but have never seen you perform in person. They won't forget you. The city won't forget you. The new mayor won't forget us. And we don't forget. We are all Italians in this room and, therefore, descendants of Ancient Rome. I do not mean to preach, but as Cicero said in Roman times, 'Gratitude is not only the greatest of virtues but parent of all others.' I repeat, the men in this room will not forget."

The silence that followed was total. Gambino slapped Costello on the shoulder and told Sinatra, "Now you know why I love this man. Now you know why my families and, yes, other families call this man the Prime Minister."

Sinatra jumped to his feet. He turned to Charlie. "Get a photographer in here right now. I'm going to launch a one-night stand."

∾

G erard Sr. rode the bus to work with three fat manila envelopes in his lap. His memory bank was working overtime. His entire life had changed from the moment he stood on the platform in front of Les Scarcella's center, took the microphone, and began to speak.

He had never faced a crowd that big in his life. Mostly, they were Scarcella partisans, and so they were friendly. But he couldn't miss the undercurrent of muttered anger among those who weren't. Some of them he had gone to high school with. Some of them were fellow workers down at Westinghouse.

All his life, he believed in three things, like most of his friends and co-workers and everyone else in his ward: family, neighbors, and the Barringer football team. In his heart, he knew he was not like Junior. He was lucky to get through high school and had never been a leader. He'd never wanted to be one, and he wondered how many of his friends and neighbors were about to turn against him. And all because his son fell in love with a black girl. But he knew that when he met her, he was like them— they didn't know her but would admire and adore her if they did know her. They didn't know that her mother would sacrifice everything for her family, just like he and his neighbors would. He'd always trusted his neighbors. Could he take this stand without creating more of the anger that was tearing his city apart?

Right before he'd held the microphone at the rally, he had thought, *But that was my son they shot. That was my son bleeding on the ground in New York. And that was his black girlfriend who treated that wound and kept him alive. Well, fuck it and fuck those who don't like it—I am going to say what's in my heart.*

And of course he did, and a firestorm ensued when he endorsed the one candidate for mayor who was a total outsider to all of them. Who was black, and who came from an economic and social background completely unlike any of theirs. Hell, his folks never even had to worry about making a mortgage payment.

That same night, at his home, two teenagers jumped out of a late-model Ford and used sledgehammers to break his car's windshield as the family slept. Two days later, the postman delivered so much hate mail to his door that he had to ring the doorbell because it couldn't fit in the mailbox.

And that morning, as he opened the front door to get the newspaper before he left for work, he discovered a huge pile of dog feces spread across the welcome mat. He ducked back inside and picked up all the hate mail and stuffed it into manila envelopes. He knew how some of his colleagues would feel about this.

They wanted a confrontation? He'd give them a confrontation. *Don't fuck with my family.* His own anger dominated his thoughts as he stepped off the bus at Westinghouse. As usual, a line had formed at the food truck out front.

It had always been a pre-work gathering spot. He had always looked forward to the conversations: what the Yankees did last night, Barringer's chances to make the state football playoffs. Just a few years ago, they talked regularly about his son, the *Star-Ledger* All-State wide receiver.

When Senior joined the line, he felt the icy vibrations radiating from some of the men. It began with the man who had made his anti-black feelings known during lunch on the day the *Star-Ledger* endorsed Jackson Anderson.

"Hey, Gerard. They got a ceremony when you turn black? Something like the Jews do when they cut off a slice of your prick?"

Friscella grabbed the envelopes he had placed on the ground and began throwing the contents one by one in the loudmouth's face.

A third man retrieved a couple of them and read one out loud. "'Dear nigger lover . . .' No signature, just 'a U.S. war veteran' at the bottom."

The tension grew along the line. The loudmouth was cursing in an attempt at sotto voce. Senior tried to ignore it. He hollered over to a young machinist getting coffee from the Greek guy who owned the truck. "Vito, you watch the Series last night? How about them Tigers? They win it in seven."

"Yeah," the loudmouth interrupted, moving to face Senior from a foot away. "Yeah, musta hurt you when that nigger pitcher Gibson give up those runs."

"Not as much as it's gonna hurt you when you grow up and learn you ain't living in an all-white world. Maybe you should move to Norway."

The loudmouth turned away. Senior lowered his guard. But suddenly the man spun around and unloaded a sucker punch to Senior's face. All of his building rage and frustration hit a boiling point. He pounced and tackled the loudmouth. Senior felt many hands on him as co-workers pulled them apart.

Both men were bleeding. The attacker, his arms gripped by two workers, hollered, "Remember, guys! Remember I warned him the day he first spoke about voting for a nigger! I said, 'Wait until your kid shows up with a nigger grandchild. Then you'll see.' That's exactly what I said."

The guys hauled him aside. Then Vito, the young machinist, led Senior in the opposite direction. "Gerard, try to calm down," he said. "He's a jerk, but I ain't taking sides in this. Personally, I don't give a shit who the mayor is. None of them ever did a thing for me. But watch your back. This is only the beginning."

❧

Junior walked out the front door of Bohn Hall, head down, filled with guilt over how he'd treated his girl. He was determined to make it right. He looked up, and there was Mickey standing in front of a bench twenty yards away holding two Styrofoam coffee cups.

When she caught sight of him, she smiled and almost shouted, "Mickey's takeout service—coffee, cream, no sugar."

Memories of their summer together, learning how to know each other, growing to love her, filled his mind. He put his arms around her and held her face in both hands. Then, almost as though it were scripted, they said in unison, "I'm sorry, baby. I am so sorry. I love you."

"Okay," Mickey added, "I'll admit it. My best friend is white."

"And I thought that first day at the post office, after we argued, 'I think the woman I will love is gonna be black.' And now I know it."

Arms entwined around each other, they kissed. Students heading for class stopped in their tracks and applauded.

"I'm gonna play tonight," he told her. "Will you be there?"

"I know. Your mom told me. Me and my mom and T.C. and even Charles and Lois are gonna meet your folks for a tailgate up near the football field. We're gonna be the loudest, nastiest Montclair fans in the place. We can't lose. T.C. is wearing your Montclair State hat. Allie is holding seats for us on the fifty-yard line."

"Speaking of Allie," Junior said, "why did you sic him on me? He was really pissed. He was tougher on me than my old man. How did he get into this? What do you know that I don't know?"

"That's between me and Allie, buster. Now go out tonight and kick Trenton State's ass."

"Your wish, lady, is my command."

∼

A little after noon, Don Carlo Gambino and "The Prime Minister," Frank Costello, sat down with Richie "The Boot" at the Vittorio Castle for lunch. The Boot had invited them, saying, "Since we both are going to own a piece of Newark, I think we should have a business lunch."

The waiter brought drinks and appetizers. Gambino proposed a toast. As he was forming a loud "*salud,*" a waiter hurried over and whispered in Boiardo's ear.

"Of course," the Boot answered. "Bring the phone here. It's for you, Carlo."

"Nobody knows I'm here—Ricardo, I don't like this."

Gambino reached for the receiver. "Who is this?"

"It's Jerry D'Amilio, sir. I hope your trip to Vegas was successful."

"I am having lunch with another acquaintance of yours. He calls himself the Boot."

"Give him my regards. "

"So why do you interrupt our lunch?"

"You may recall we made a deal. If I told you how scared I was, you said that you would be indebted to me for some small favor. You must remember that I said something about a bear shitting in the woods."

Gambino placed his hand over the receiver and shared the story with the Boot in Italian. They laughed. He returned to D'Amilio. "So what is it you require? What small favor?"

"The son of the man who made that courageous endorsement of our candidate in defiance of the North Ward Citizens Council, that boy is in a big football game tonight. I was hoping you and your new friend could help."

"Consider it done, my friend. Consider it done. And by the way, from where did you say your people came to America from?"

"I am told Scopello, in Sicily. Do you know it?"

"Does a bear shit in the woods?"

3 2

THE OLD-SCHOOL TIES

The posters went up all over Newark within hours. Paulie saw a kid attaching one to a streetlight on the Avenue in front of Biase's Restaurant, across from Schools Stadium. The left half of the placard was printed in the colors of the Italian flag, the right in the colors of the black-liberation flag. Just above them was an American flag.

Sinatra's picture smiled out from the left. Photos of Lena Horne and Aretha Franklin were on the right. Across the top, large letters trumpeted, "FRANK, ARETHA, AND LENA RALLY FOR JACKSON ANDERSON, THE NEXT MAYOR"

Across the bottom, one sentence proclaimed the new campaign slogan: "One City, One People, One Newark."

"Goddamn that fuckin' Friscella!" Paulie shouted as he swung the wheel to keep his car from jumping the curb after the distraction. "That motherfucker. His kid screws a nigger and he can't keep his mouth shut. It isn't like the fuckin' kid died." Furious, he parked, hopped out of the car, tore the poster down, and shoved the kid into the gutter. He slammed the car door and drove away.

Back at the White Citizens Council headquarters, he sent all of the volunteers out to the streets with orders to tear down every poster in the North Ward. Then he glared across his desk at Chooch and Dominick.

"We had the fuckin' election won!" he shouted. "The two niggers would split the vote and we would walk in. *Walk in!*" He slammed both fists down on the desk. "Then you two jerkoffs shot the wrong guy's kid! And for what? Because that *puttana* Maria Gianetti has the hots for him and can't get him, so she spreads her legs for assholes like you? Because of that manipulating bitch, you shoot that kid! That kid has been a North Ward hero since he took Barringer to the state title. And now you two imbeciles make an even bigger hero out of his old man?"

"It was an accident, Paulie," Chooch said. "He—"

"You dumb shits! I shoulda left the two of you in jail. So what do you think we can do now, geniuses?"

"Well, I say we find a way to smear the kid and the old man," Chooch replied.

"Wonderful. We got a North Ward football hero who won for Barringer and who the whole ward loves, and his father, who made a citizen's arrest out of love for his son—and we're going to *smear* them? How? Jeez, if your combined IQs were ten points higher, you'd be a head of cabbage."

"I say we go up there and scare his kid sister," Dominick suggested. "Grab her off the street and tell her what we do to her if her brother don't shut up. Scare the mother, too."

"Dominick, shut the fuck up. You might occasionally be useful muscle, but you are significantly retarded. We don't have to scare anybody. What we do is make them hate Anderson. That's the target. When he declared he was gonna run, they were already halfway to where we want them. I heard there was a fight over at Westinghouse involving the father. Turn it into something we can use. Spread the word. Blame him and Anderson for the tension in our ward. And while you're at it, tell that fuck Les Scarcella to mind his own business. Tell him we're looking into his government grants. Find a broad to say the Friscella kid raped her and find someone who can turn his black angel into a nymphomaniac. We got more than enough nigger-haters in the ward to pull this off—and it's a nigger girl that was the reason behind all this. Use it. Use the father's fight. Make shit up but stoke their anger. Do it right and we got a chance. Now get the fuck out of here."

~

Meanwhile, at Kiongosi's downtown headquarters, all hell was breaking loose. The audio car with Aretha Franklin's recorded voice circled his headquarter's block. At record-decibel levels, the message was the same over and over. "R-E-S-P-E-C-T . . . R-E-S-P-E-C-T!"

The music died under the recorded voice of Jackson Anderson repeating, "Join Frank, Lena, and Aretha at the Mosque Theater in two weeks. Apply for concert tickets to P.O. Box 2626 at the Newark main post office. 'One people, one city, one Newark.'"

Kiongosi was in mid-meltdown. "So Paulie Tedesco and his goons shoot a white kid for banging a black girl, and we have to pay the price? We got to apologize for a white kid who got shot by two white men? All right—we can turn this against Paulie, but what about Anderson? The black voters say he's an Uncle Tom, the white ones say he's just another nigger hiding in a three-piece suit. Hell, even he don't know what he is. But, damn it, we got to do something in one hell of a hurry."

A volunteer opened the door to the street. Aretha's voice once again filled the room. "R-E-S-P-E-C-T . . . R-E-S-P-E-C-T. . . ."

"Can't somebody please shoot that motherfuckin' driver?" Kiongosi yelled.

"Boss," his chief of staff said, "we ain't gonna get any votes up in the North Ward anyway. I say fuck Paulie. We got to put the heat on right here in the North and Central Wards. We got to sabotage Anderson. We got to fuck up his rally and put the blame on him. We got to discredit the girl and the football kid. If we do it right, we just might win City Hall."

"I want a plan by tomorrow morning," Kiongosi said. "I mean, I want *all of it* laid out. How we deal with the football kid and the girl . . . how we get people hating the father as just another honky gasbag who never raised his voice in our defense. And you got to paint Jackson Anderson as a traitor to his race, a guy who takes the white man's money. How come he's so cozy with those racists at the Newark banks? Then we—"

Somebody in the next room opened the door again—another dose of "R-E-S-P-E-C-T! Sock it to me, sock it to me, sock—"

"Somebody go out there and shoot that motherfucker! Kill his ass dead!" Kiongosi shouted.

∽

"You're late," Jackson Anderson said as Fast Freddy Sternburg walked into his living room. "Usually I can set my watch by you. So whatever it is, I hope it's good news."

"Your chief of staff says your schedule is wide open tonight."

"So?"

"Well, it ain't anymore." He reached into a pocket of his jacket and pulled out a business-size envelope. "Dust off your old raccoon coat. I'll buy the hot dogs. Tonight you are going back to the gridiron."

"What the hell are you talking about?"

"Football, boss, football. Remember? You played it at Rutgers. Tonight you are going to pay your respects to the wide receiver on the Montclair State football team who got shot by Paulie's goons, and to his father, who will be in the crowd with his family and his son's black girlfriend and her family—you know, these are the folks who are going to win this election for us. You'll sit near them. You'll cheer for their son. You'll shake hands. If they bring babies, you'll kiss babies. The *Star-Ledger* will be there. That guy D'Amilio will write about the kid, and if we play our cards right, he'll write about you. This guy is a Pulitzer Prize winner. When he writes this story, papers all around the country will pick it up, and then the father will have to give them interviews. Right now he says he's done enough talking, but, trust me, after D'Amilio writes this story, it will grow legs."

"And?"

"It will work. Our new friends will keep the whispers running through the ward on the Italian underground wire, and we'll get the slice of Italian votes we need. Trust me on this. That's why they call me Fast Freddy."

Anderson stood and walked across the room to Sternburg's chair. He smiled as he punched him on the arm, filled the room with laughter, and hollered, "You bet your Jewish ass it will work! Freddy, you're the best nonstop ballbuster I ever hired. Now get on up to the Montclair State bookstore and buy me the loudest red-and-white school sweater they have. Check the weather report—if the temperature is going to drop, then also buy me a red-and-white windbreaker."

"Boss," Sternburg said, his expression sheer admiration, "you just might be a bigger hustler than I am."

∿

"T.C.," Annie Mae said firmly, "you are not taking that football to the game. The hat's okay, the pennant's okay. But put that football back in your closet where it belongs. Charles, help me carry the food out to the car. Mickey will meet us at the tailgate site. This is the first time you'll meet the Friscellas. Remember how loving they have been to your sister. Do not embarrass our family."

"That shit—uh, stuff—is behind me. Mickey and I made up. I went to Montclair State to apologize to Junior. So how about trusting me?"

Two hours later, they met the Friscellas. T.C. ran to Angie, who called him "my kid brother," and showed her his Montclair State banner. Charles seemed to get along fine with Senior. The two women hugged, and Mickey waved to the families of other students she knew.

Allie ran over to Mickey. "I got to get to the stadium and save bleacher seats. Something I don't understand is going on. The line at the box office is huge. We didn't even come close to selling out when they dedicated the stadium. It only seats about six thousand—it looks to me that this crowd could double that."

"I saw a guy holding a sign that said 'Barringer Grads Love Junior and His Dad,'" Mickey said, "and another one said 'Gerard Friscella Sr. Is a North Ward Hero.'"

"It's crazy. Here are your tickets, but nothing is reserved, so I gotta get my rear end back to the stadium and defend your seats. Counting me, that's seven seats." He took off running.

～

When Allie reached the entrance to the field, he saw Chooch and a group of North Ward Citizens Council people huddled together. They were obviously there to start trouble, Allie saw. Dominick held a sign that said "Stick With Our Own. Paulie for Newark Mayor."

Allie cursed under his breath, turned away, and moved toward the seats. Inside, he passed the editor of the school newspaper. "Where did all these people come from? Who are they?" Allie asked him.

"I don't know, but it's one hell of a crowd for us. I spoke to one of the box-office guys, and he can't explain it either. Look, they just shut the ticket window, an hour and a half before the game. Maybe Junior has made new fans for us."

Fans or enemies? Allie thought.

The gates opened, and Dominick led the Citizens group in as he waved his sign. Just inside the gates, two heavily muscled guys approached him. Allie noticed they each wore a blue-and-white button on their sweaters that read "Local 560 Teamsters—We Move What America Needs."

"Hi, Dominick—let me carry that sign for you," one of them said. He reached for it.

Dominick pulled away. "Hey, I never saw you before in my life. Who are you?"

"Just a messenger." He put his arm around him. "We need to talk."

Allie watched the men steer Dominick to a secluded spot under the bleachers past the end zone. Allie knew he needed to get up to the seats, but he had to see what would happen.

"What the hell are you talking about?" he heard Dominick ask. "What message?"

"This one," the second guy said. An overhand right crashed against Dominick's jaw, followed by a left hook to the solar plexus. Dominick dropped like a stone. Both guys kicked him over and over. Blood ran down Dominick's face. He vomited.

"Maybe we should shove the sign up his ass," the first guy said.

"No—rip it up. We're done. I want to get to my seat and see if this Junior Friscella can really play this game."

Allie had seen as much as he could stomach. He wasn't Dominick's friend anymore, but he didn't enjoy seeing him take a beating. He hurried off to the bleachers.

Soon, Junior's family, accompanied by Mickey and her family, joined him. Allie was relieved he could stop holding on to seats. He had spotted several small melees nearby and across the field, and at first he thought it was people fighting over seats. But after witnessing what had happened to Dominick and realizing that many people in the scuffles wore green-and-white buttons that read Local 1 ILA, he watched more intently. The button-wearers inevitably went after people Allie knew were involved with the White Citizens Council, like Dominick. Allie knew something was definitely up. But he couldn't say what, and he couldn't explain it.

When the Montclair State players ran out to the field to warm up, a flood of noise greeted them. Allie forgot about the men wearing the buttons and Dominick getting roughed up. He and the Washington and Friscella families jumped to their feet and joined in the cheering.

"I see him, I see him!" T.C. shouted, grabbing Angie's arm and pointing toward the end zone, where Junior was running short patterns as Johnny Jakes fired passes at him.

Junior pulled up and faced the home-side fans. He waved to where Allie had told him the families would be sitting. Mickey turned and hugged Maria. "There he is, your beautiful son!"

While everyone else kept cheering, Allie noticed a small group of African Americans wearing Kiongosi T-shirts and heading toward where the Friscellas and the Washingtons were sitting. *What was happening? White Citizens Council and now Kiongosi supporters?* He'd never seen anything like this at a football game before. He looked at Junior's dad, wondering if he'd noticed. But he and the rest of the group were focused on Junior. What would they do if these guys started something?

They never got there.

A pack of men wearing blue-and-orange buttons that identified them as members of a local laborers' union cut them off. Before the cops could even show up, the scuffle was over, and the Kiongosi supporters had left the field. Few seemed to notice —the band was playing, the cheerleaders were cartwheeling, and an orchard of signs supporting Junior and his dad waved from the crowd in time with the music.

Up in the stands at the fifty-yard line, the three parents chatted, Mickey and Lois were talking to a couple of students in the next row, and, wonder of wonders, Allie struck up a conversation with Charles. Much to his surprise, he found common ground.

Just before the teams returned from their pregame locker room talks, Jackson Anderson and a photographer, led by Freddy Sternburg, threaded their way through the crowd.

Anderson, resplendent in his new Montclair State sweater and cap, reached out from the aisle and shook Senior's hand.

"Gerard," Anderson said, "it took guts to make that speech. It crossed the forbidden color line that is strangling this town. I won't let you down." He extended his arm past Senior to shake Maria's hand, then smiled broadly as his hand stretched toward Mickey. "Young lady, you and your boyfriend are teaching this town a lesson it will never forget."

An avalanche of noise rocked the stadium. In addition to the fans of both teams, the three unions were there because their locals had bought the tickets—4,000 of them. They were the loudest fans in the crowd as the team captains met at midfield for the coin toss.

Senior suddenly leaned over and took Mickey's hand. "What do you think? Is his leg really all right? He never really told us."

"I wish I knew. He never said a word about it." Then she laughed. "North Ward macho. Know what I mean?"

"Touché," Senior said with a laugh. "Touché."

It was time for the kickoff.

Trenton won the coin toss and elected to defer, giving the ball to Montclair. From the moment the Montclair safety caught the kickoff, it was clear why Trenton had chosen to give it up at the start. The Trenton kickoff team was faster than Montclair's. The Trenton defensive line outweighed Montclair's by twenty pounds per man. Montclair's return was smothered on the eighteen-yard line.

On the first play from scrimmage, Trenton blitzed two linebackers. Both of them got to the backfield and slammed Jakes to the ground for a seven-yard loss. They double-teamed Junior on the next two plays. Montclair punted.

It was not an easy first period for Montclair. The heavier, stronger Trenton offensive line moved the ball. The defensive line harried Jakes. The defensive backs were all over Junior. Yablonski, who called their plays from the sideline, began to use Junior as a decoy.

Away from the action, he was roughed up three times. The first time, the refs called a "hands to the face" penalty. The second, officials missed a holding call, and the roar from the union section of the stands let him know about it. The third time, Junior went down underneath the full weights of the safety and the cornerback.

When Junior lay still and didn't get up, a heavy silence pressed down on the field. Two trainers tended to him. With just over four minutes left in the first half, Junior limped off between them. He did not return in the half.

As the teams left the field, Allie spoke to Junior's mother but put an arm around both ladies. "He'll be all right. I saw him take worse than that in high school. I'm going down there. I know the student manager. I'll see what I can find out."

"Don't worry," Senior told the women. "He's a tough kid. I'm not worried."

Maria draped an arm around Mickey and said softly, "I hope the doctor made the right decision. Maybe he shouldn't have played."

"If the doctor said no, he would have played anyway. He's that stubborn, and I think both of us know it."

As the teams returned for the second half, Lois scanned them through her binoculars. "He's not there," she said. Then Allie fought his way up the aisle through the crowd and returned.

"He's okay. He's okay. They're icing the leg. I don't know if he'll play. That's all I could get out of the student manager."

Early in the half, Trenton scored on a thirty-six-yard field goal that wobbled like a wounded duck as it barely cleared the crossbar. Other than that, the first-half pattern continued. The defense hounded Jakes. Montclair stopped Trenton. It was 3-0 when the fourth quarter began.

A sudden roar came from the union section. Allie, the Washingtons, and the Friscellas craned their necks to see what was happening.

Junior Friscella was limping his way out of the tunnel to the sidelines.

"There he is!" Allie shouted, pointing to the sidelines.

The two families, led by Mickey, rose to their feet and joined the noise.

T.C. yelled to Angie, "Touch my lucky hat! Junior gave it to me. We ain't gonna lose."

With three minutes and twelve seconds left to play, Junior Friscella jogged onto the field. He could not totally disguise the limp. Montclair had the ball on its own thirty-five-yard line.

On the first play, Junior again was a decoy. Jakes threw to the tight end for twelve yards. The next play, Junior ran a slant, cut in front of a linebacker, veered left, made a catch, and picked up fourteen yards and another first down. Now it was first down on the Trenton thirty-nine. The clock was down to two minutes and twelve seconds.

Jakes took the snap, took three steps to his left, and handed off to Junior, who came the opposite way from his receiver spot. He ran toward the line of scrimmage, then pulled up and threw downfield to Jakes, who had sneaked down the left side undetected. He caught the ball and stepped out of bounds on the twelve.

A fullback dive picked up three. With under a minute left, Jakes called signals, took the snap, faked a pass, brought his arm down, and again slipped it to Junior coming around. Allie heard shouts of "Pass! Pass!" from the assistant coaches on the sidelines.

Junior did not pass. He was running for daylight. A pulling guard made the opening a little wider, and Junior was in the clear. At the five, a safety came up to meet him. Junior caught him with a violent stiff-arm. He staggered back. Junior hit the end zone.

When the gun went off, the union guys rushed the field along with the students. They carried Junior around on a forest of upraised arms. The political signs about him and his father sprouted new life. People rushed to congratulate the Friscellas and the Washingtons. Lois and Mickey, arms around each other, jumped up and down.

Allie, Senior, and Charles fought their way through the massive crush of people, until they made it to the locker room to join Junior. They arrived just as the coach finished his speech and presented Junior with another game ball and the entire team shouted in approval.

Jerry D'Amilio came by to interview Junior. Just as they shook hands and D'Amilio left, the scout from the New York Giants appeared.

"Great game, kid. You know, as a junior you can declare for the NFL draft."

"I don't know," Junior said. "I sorta promised some people I'd stick around and graduate."

"Well, you could always go back in the off-season. Think it over. You could wind up with us and play where your family could see you. Think about it."

Allie did not envy Junior the decision he now faced.

Mickey and the rest of the family waited outside. She kissed and hugged him. "We have to talk," he said. "I've got to tell you what the Giants scout said."

"What about your promise to me? What about our promise to your parents?"

"We'll have to talk about that. It's complicated."

"It shouldn't be," she said. "We can't hurt them. We owe them better."

33

SINATRA SINGS FOR THE CAUSE

The Mosque Theater was one of the few architectural reminders of a time when Newark was a cultural beacon for all that was exciting about New Jersey. Built by the Shriners, a Masonic order, in 1925, it had stood the test of time for decades, but like the city itself, it ultimately changed to the point where classical-music giants like Arturo Rubenstein and Jascha Heifetz and world-class troupes like the Ballet Russe de Monte Carlo no longer drew a Newark audience.

For a long time, the venue drew well with big bands and pop vocalists. In 1961, it set an all-time attendance record when Judy Garland drew a standing-room crowd of well over 3,000. In less-gaudy circumstances, it changed the course of American pop music with a skinny kid from Hoboken named Frank Sinatra.

As the stretch limo brought him and his fellow passengers from Manhattan through the Lincoln Tunnel and into the outskirts of Newark, Sinatra shared his history with the others in the car. A quarter of a century earlier, he'd played the Mosque. "The joint was half empty," he recalled. "I had just left Tommy Dorsey and his orchestra to go solo. Nobody cared. Bookings for me were scarce. I was lucky to get the Mosque."

"That's hard to believe," said Freddy Sternburg, who was on one of the jump seats.

"Believe it, kid, believe it. But all of a sudden, for some reason, teenage girls went crazy over me. All I had to do was walk out and they started screaming. After one performance, a couple of them threw their panties on the stage. The guy who owned the New York Paramount was there looking for talent. He called me that night and booked me. That's when half the young broads in New York went Sinatra-crazy."

"I never knew that," Jackson Anderson, who was sitting on the other jump, said. "To me, you were always just here. Always. My parents loved your music. You sang the songs that marked their lives. On our radio, you were always there. I can't picture you in a situation where you weren't America's singer. You were always the man."

"Thanks. But not exactly. Sometimes when I look at my career's ups and downs, and the marriages, I feel like I had four lives."

"Well, I can promise you," Sternburg said, "they still love you here in the North Ward—and after tonight, particularly with you ladies at center stage"—he turned toward Lena Horne and Aretha Franklin—"Mr. Sinatra will have new fans in the black neighborhoods."

"Except for one guy," Anderson said, and then told the story of Aretha's recorded voice, the sound car, and Kiongosi's rage. The whole group erupted in laughter.

The limo arrived at the theater, and they stepped out. Sinatra paused to look up at the building's massive Ionic columns. "Not the same," he said, noting the new lettering above the front doors: Newark Symphony Hall.

As they moved through the halls of the empty building, Sinatra shook his head. "They could use a little paint on the walls."

The performers disappeared into their dressing rooms.

～

A nderson's people and their "new friends" had printed more tickets than seats. They wanted to shatter Judy Garland's record and leave no doubts about their candidate's popularity.

As Anderson wanted, half the seats went to North Ward Italians, the other half mainly to blacks and a smaller group of Puerto Ricans. Scarcella's center handled the Italians, and two former football giants handled the distribution to blacks from one of Anderson's headquarters.

Someone knocked three times on a rear door of the theater. Freddy Sternburg, who had been awaiting the arrival there alongside Anderson, knocked twice in response and opened the door.

"Good evening, guys," he said.

"You're the man they call the 'fast one'?" Carlo Gambino replied.

"You got it, Mr. Gambino."

Richie Boiardo interrupted. "Never mind the bullshit. Is the security in place?"

"The Italian side is crawling with your guys. A Nation of Islam security firm is handling the other half. But when Frank sings, you watch, they'll forget about color and dance the tarantella together in the aisles."

"You better be right," the Boot said. "Take us to Frank and the ladies."

He led them down a dark hall toward the dressing rooms.

"Be kind enough to ask the ladies to come to Frank's room," Gambino said.

When they were all gathered there, Sinatra poured drinks for the men and lemonade for the women. Frank Costello and the Boot's son, who were on hand as the Mafiosi's security guard, remained in front of the door until Gambino said, "Please, gentlemen, join us."

His request was meant mainly for Costello, who, taking a cue from Gambino, raised a glass and offered a toast.

"Ladies," the Prime Minister said, "we are here on more than business. Yes, my two friends will profit from the end result, but we are here because the pure beauty of your voices combined with that of our Francesco here are going to change history. Generally, what my friend and I do is for our organization, but tonight, remember this. Tonight, you sing for the future of all blacks and Italians in this city. You bring a message of love and harmony, and we thank you profusely."

The women looked at each other as if trying to solve a puzzle, but Sinatra applauded and said to them, "Music has no politics. We three are going to sing for all the people tonight. Ladies"—he raised his glass toward them—"I love you and I salute you. Now you bums get outta here. We got a show to do."

They left laughing.

∾

Jackson Anderson rubbed his hands together. He couldn't believe this was happening. He'd made some promises, sure, but these men were upholding their end of the bargain. Sinatra had flown from Vegas to Newark to support his mayoral bid. Nothing could go wrong now.

Except maybe the opening-act comic. He had been allotted ten minutes to do some stand-up bits to warm up the audience— and Anderson, standing in the wings, suddenly realized the guy had been out there hamming it up for at least twenty-five minutes. Scarcella realized it too—he moved to the edge of the stage and whispered hoarsely down to the conductor in the orchestra pit, "Get that fuckin' *stronzo* off before Frank comes out and does it himself!"

The conductor jumped into action with his baton—his musicians broke into a tune and played the comic off the stage.

Moments later, the lights dimmed, the kettle drum

resounded, and an announcer voice said, "Ladies and gentlemen! Mr. Francis . . . Albert . . . Sinatra . . . and the soulful voices of Miss Aretha Franklin and Miss Lena Horne."

Both sides of the room unleashed thunderous applause. And then the trio was there in the spotlight, holding hands. The conductor picked up the beat, heavy on the brass, and Aretha's magnificent voice broke into what had become known as Jackson Anderson's theme song. "*Respect . . . Respect . . .*" The building went wild. Then came Lena Horne and "The Eagle and Me."

Both vocalists took a step back, and Sinatra took two steps forward. "I played this joint twenty-five years ago when Newark was this state's emotional capital," he said. "I see and hear there have been a few changes since then. Except for a successful gig with a man I knew as John F. Kennedy, this is new territory for me. But here I am to help as a guy who can bring it all back . . . who can bring us back to a day when in this town you could say 'Good morning' to a guy on the street and not get back, 'What the hell do you mean by that?' This is what we all want, deep down."

The orchestra, softly at first, grew louder with an intro, and Ol' Blue Eyes began to sing.

It took more than a few beats, but the audience finally got it. As he continued, they stomped and whistled and cheered. Without a pause, the orchestra upped the beat. So did Sinatra, who broke into an oldie called "Shake a Hand."

As if on cue, Scarcella's plants in the audience reached out from the Italian side to the blacks across the aisles and began to shake hands. As Sinatra sang, more and more on both sides joined them.

And then Jackson Anderson walked to center stage and shouted, "One city, one people."

The timing was perfect. The old walls of the theater seemed to shake.

The rest of the concert went off as planned and without a

hitch. Anderson spoke about an end to hatred. He spoke about whether white or black or Latino, there would be no favoritism in City Hall. He spoke about the blue-collar struggles in every ward. At the end, he had them on their feet cheering with his closer. "Don't vote with your color. Vote with your heart. Vote for nothing more or less than the future of your children." Then he pointed to the Washington and Friscella families in the audience, identified them, and just as Sternburg in the wings made a "cut" sign across his throat, the candidate added, "So let's hear the music of these three again—and when we vote, bring the music of a new Newark to a crescendo."

~

The next day, the *Star-Ledger* politics guy wrote, "A musical and political triumph."

Gambino put down his paper and said to Boiardo, who had agreed to meet with him for breakfast, "Time for Plan B of the plan."

Boiardo put down his cup and nodded. "Definitely. Definitely."

~

On Saturday, Gerard Sr. watched the Johnny Jakes-Gerard Friscella Jr. combination lead undefeated Montclair State to an easy 35-10 victory over Glassboro State. Both families were back on the fifty-yard line, and most of the spectators waved to them whenever they went to the refreshment stand and again as they returned to their seats.

Senior nodded at them, pride in his son rising with each wave.

The next day, the mood in the Friscella household was euphoric. Senior spoke with Maria, who agreed that it was time the rest of the family met Mickey. Maria suggested the traditional Sunday dinner as the way to do it. She hadn't hosted one in more than a month.

But when Senior overheard her inviting her sister and ex-boyfriend Tony, who'd been a football legend at Barringer and played two years at Rutgers until he hit hard times, he argued against it.

"He and Junior have a lot in common with football," she said.

"He's a bum," Senior answered. "A certified loser who screwed over your sister, gambled away what they had, and makes book on the side when he tends bar. I don't want him in my house."

"Give him a chance," Maria said. "The way Junior is playing and the attention he's getting, I think it might help Tony to get to know him."

"It's your dinner, Maria. But I don't like it." He walked away shaking his head, knowing in his gut this would not turn out well. But the man was part of Maria's family. What could he do?

On Sunday, Annie Mae and Mickey came early to help with the preparations. Senior opened the door for them, beaming. Annie Mae carried something in her hands.

"What you got there, Annie Mae?" he asked.

"I know it may be a bit unusual for an Italian dinner," she said, holding up a pie plate, "but I brought my own personal specialty—homemade sweet-potato pie."

"It smells amazing! I can't wait to try a slice." He took the pie and carried it to the kitchen for her.

Charles and T.C. arrived later. Senior let them in, and Mickey stuck her head out of the kitchen, wiping her hands on her apron. "Mr. Friscella and Junior are surfing the TV set in the living room," she told her brothers. "Go on in there and see if you can help them find a football game. Stay there—do not come in this kitchen and get in our way. In the meantime, Charles, you and T.C. need to get to know the family members who'll be here soon."

Each time the bell rang, Senior hoisted himself out of his

chair to open the door to them—the blood relatives and the in-laws, the lifetime friends and even their children, much to the delight of T.C., who organized an after-dinner football game.

Senior introduced them all. They knew Mickey was related to Charles and T.C. They had yet to meet her, but none of them was hesitant to first shake Charles' hand and then smile at T.C.

Except for Maria's former flame, Tony, the man the family knew as the best running back to ever grow up on the Avenue. He declined Charles' outstretched hand, and his grunted hello bordered on aggressively rude. Senior narrowed his eyes but held his tongue.

Mickey worked on setting the table with Angie. Fourteen people would squeeze into the dining room. The children were at a separate table in the kitchen with Angie in charge and T.C. as her designated lieutenant. Senior took it all in, basking in this gathering of people he loved.

Maria asked Senior to bless the table. He asked everyone to join hands. "We are lucky to have friends and relatives like this. I'm so happy to have the opportunity to introduce you all to Mickey, who, I hope, will soon join this family." He blessed the meal, and the room seemed to explode into happy, hungry conversation.

Senior glanced occasionally into the kitchen to check on the kids' table. T.C. was the only African American kid there, but Senior was delighted to see it was no problem for T.C., who dominated the conversation. "You know," Senior heard T.C. tell them, "my future brother, Junior, is the best wide receiver in all of America."

"What makes you so sure?" one of them asked.

"Oh, I know. Believe me. I know. I'm the best wide receiver on the Boys Club Little Giants football team. So I know."

"Don't talk with food in your mouth, T.C.," Angie ordered.

The kids all laughed, and Senior hid his smile—it was clear T.C. had made some new friends. And Senior couldn't be happier with how well the dinner was going.

His niece Michelle, a schoolteacher for fifteen years at Ridge Street Elementary, paused between bites to ask her uncle, "What's that Anderson guy like? I know you support him, but I don't know much about him."

"I was gonna vote for Paulie," Senior's sister, Anne Marie, put in.

"Anne," Senior said, pausing for emphasis. "Paulie's goons shot your nephew. You want to reward him?"

"Well, my mind is made up," their mother interjected. "Frank wouldn't have come here if he didn't believe in the guy. I ain't goin' against Frank. I like what this guy says. I'm sick and tired of 'us against them' and 'them against us.' How long are we gonna be about black and white?"

Tony jumped to his feet, glaring at all of them, and shook his head. "Listen to you phony freakin' liberals. I'm not gonna buy this bullshit." He imitated the women in a high-pitched falsetto. "'Frank wants this. Frank wants that. Oh, those bad guys shot my son, who betrayed everything his grandfather believed in.'" He smirked. "This is what you want? Charles there is gonna go to college, and everyone says, 'Oh, how marvelous.' So tell me, other than his black skin, why does he get a free ride?"

Senior stood up, shooting a warning look at Tony.

"And, young lady"—Tony pointed at Mickey—"I ain't never gonna welcome no nigger baby into this family. Never. Paulie Tedesco is just fine with me. Is this a case of white and black? You bet your ass it is, and always will be. And it's white that counts."

Senior saw that Mickey was physically shaken. The other guests were frozen in shock. Junior jumped to his feet, but Senior got to Tony first.

"Listen, you fuckin' racist," he seethed in his face, "don't ever set foot in this house again. You blew your marriage. You abandoned your kids. You insulted this young woman who saved your nephew's life." He grabbed Tony's arm and pushed him toward the door.

Tony twisted free and punched Senior in the stomach. Senior grabbed Tony by the throat, banged his head against the wall, spun him around, and pushed him out onto the porch. Then he kicked him down the stairs and slammed the door.

He took several deep breaths before returning to the dining room. He was determined that the meal would continue. "Please, please, sit down. Please don't insult my wife's cooking by not eating."

They attempted to settle back into the pleasant atmosphere they'd enjoyed before Tony shattered it. But all were clearly shaken.

Annie Mae looked at Senior—and then took matters into her own hands. "I know I'm an outsider, but I'd like to share something. I was totally against it when my daughter told me she was in love with a white boy. Lord, how would they make it in a city that would not tolerate it? But then I got to know this young man. I saw the way he treated my daughter and the way she treated him. It made me young again. It reminded me about the way love is supposed to be. And the Friscellas, from Maria and Senior on down to young Angie here, all went through the same thing. I ask you to give them the same chance."

The guests smiled and nodded. Senior nearly hugged Annie Mae for managing to break the tension and save the dinner party.

She went on. "Now, before T.C. and his new friends have their football game, I have another favor to ask. I know that this was a traditional Italian Sunday dinner, and I loved every bite of it. You can cook, girl, you can cook! But I can bake, and I want you to try something new—my sweet-potato pie."

Mickey and Angie brought the pies in. As the guests were finishing dessert, Anne Marie looked across the table. "Mrs. Washington, I just have to have the recipe for this."

Senior took a deep breath and relaxed, forking another bite of pie. The family—those who mattered, anyway—accepted Mickey and her family. The road ahead of them wouldn't always be smooth, but the important people in his life would always accept and love his son and Mickey.

~

Invitations were delivered by a Newark messenger service. Printed on exclusive bond paper with no letterhead, they read simply:

"Some influential people with your interest at heart invite you to attend a small dinner party at Thomm's Restaurant, corner of Park and Mount Prospect Avenue, tomorrow at 7:30 p.m. Attire casual."

Each recipient had also received an anonymous phone call confirming the invitations. The caller said the dinner party was, as stated, important to their interests, but perhaps even more important to their health.

At seven o'clock the next night, they began to arrive. Paulie Tedesco and his entourage first, then Jackson Anderson, and finally Kiongosi. They eyed one another with hostility until four newcomers joined the group—Richie "The Boot" Boiardo and his son, Tony Boy, plus Carlo Gambino and Frank Costello.

Waiters took drink orders. Tedesco asked, "What the hell is going on here?"

Costello, with a tone that belied the broad smile on his face, answered first. "When you are invited into the lion's den, you do not question the lion. My friends have invited you here because they have a proposition that will benefit the city, benefit themselves, and directly benefit the three of you. But first we ask that all but the three recipients of personal invitations should enjoy your drinks, say your good-nights, and leave. If you don't do so, this meeting is over. If you do, my friends have an interesting proposition for you."

Fifteen minutes later, the excess people were gone, and Gambino arose to speak.

"Gentlemen, first I want you to know that I speak on behalf

of both my friend Mr. Boiardo and myself. We have many contacts here and in the governor's office that can be of use to you. We are not greedy. If you cooperate, we would share some of them—up to a point. I now yield the floor to my Prime Minister, Mr. Frank Costello."

"Gentlemen, we have a dilemma," said Costello, likewise on his feet. "A city in crisis, and each of us with our own needs at stake. We also have a conclusion and a compromise. Mr. Tedesco and Mr. Kiongosi, I must tell you that you cannot—I repeat, cannot—win this election. Of that there is no doubt. But you can save face and further your ambitions if you will cooperate. We have in place a radical but foolproof mechanism to satisfy those needs. We have already secured the cooperation of the candidates for North Ward and Central Ward councilmen. Now it is up to you. We have the army of volunteers in place to execute our plan. You each can withdraw from the race for mayor and run virtually unopposed to represent your wards on the City Council. You will become write-in candidates with no organized opposition from those on the ballot. Our people will knock on every door, and you will be a powerful majority when the write-in votes are counted. And I am sure that our next mayor will treat you with the same respect we expect you to treat him with. I can guarantee you your council seats if you cooperate. I can, as well, positively guarantee both of you a definite finish to your political careers if you don't. Stay for dinner or leave as you choose. But we expect an answer from you tomorrow. Simply call Mr. Scarcella at his center with a two-word message—'I agree'—if you want those City Council seats. I guarantee that without this consent from you tomorrow, you will have nothing."

And then the Mafiosi were gone in a New Jersey heartbeat.

34

CITYWIDE SECRETS

L es Scarcella sat alone outside at a table in front of the Liberty Club. He was reading the *Star-Ledger*, and he didn't have to go past page one to read a leaked story that Paulie and Kiongosi had met secretly, negotiated with council candidates in their wards to withdraw, and had agreed they would abandon the race for mayor and challenge for councilman in their own wards.

He scanned the continuation three pages inside and was relieved to see that neither his name nor those of the Mafiosi appeared anywhere. "Lucky for us," he muttered. He motioned to the waiter for a second cup of coffee.

He nodded to the guy at the next table, recognizing him. The man was a county parks worker whom Scarcella had helped get the job. The guy leaned over and said, "How come Friscella used your place to make his speech?"

"You didn't agree with him?" Scarcella asked. "A guy shoots his kid, and you don't agree with him?"

"I didn't say that. I just wondered how come he made that speech in your front yard with your kiddie band on your stage."

"Because he asked me. So tell me why you ask."

"Look, Les, I ain't got nothing against Friscella and the old man. What Paulie's guys did to the kid was wrong. But on the other hand, maybe he shoulda found himself a nice white girl . . . Yeah, one of them Montclair State coeds. I don't hold much for race-mixing—especially in these times. I don't have anything against the coloreds, but you know, I'm just sayin'."

"She *is* a nice coed, Ray—a really sweet black coed. I think you're just sayin' what you think, Ray. I'm thinkin' you're about twenty years behind where the rest of us are headed. Now, excuse me. I have an appointment with that fellow walking this way. And the next time you want to say hello, do us both a favor —don't."

He raised the newspaper in greeting as Jerry D'Amilio walked toward him.

"I saw it, Les," he said. "I didn't like it, because I don't think it's honest journalism. We both know who really negotiated that deal. I don't know who leaked it to us, but my guess is that it was that hotshot Fast Freddy Sternburg. I don't like my paper being used that way. On the other hand, I have to agree that those sons of bitches did come up with the right solutions." He smiled. "If they're not careful, they're gonna give the Mafia a good name."

"Well, it ain't over yet. But I got three hundred street workers handing out samples of write-in ballots and telling the North Ward why they should get the real thing and write in a vote for our guy. I've been thinkin' that after it's over, Anderson won't stick around long. He'll try to run for the New Jersey Senate as soon as he can—and we got a shot to make Gerald Friscella Sr. our next Italian mayor." Then he laughed. "Just like in the old days. Sit down. I'm buying."

D'Amilio looked at his old mentor as though seeing him for the first time. "Sorry, Les, but I'm done with this. I think the city will be better off this way—for now. But, Les, the day Friscella spoke on the lawn at your place, his son did a strange thing. He asked me, 'Mr. D'Amilio, do you think Mr. Scarcella is using my old man?' And I looked him in the eye and lied to him. I said that would never happen. But now I know better. I did the dirty work as a go-between because I owe you so much. And I admire a lot of the things your center does for the ward. But lately I'm seeing things I don't like. Les, if you have any feelings for this city, then prove me wrong. Don't bust into the life Gerry Senior has and push him into a new one that is way over his head. And, for God's sake, leave those two kids alone. They have been through enough, and, knowing this city, there's a lot more to come. Now I gotta go. Do us both a favor. Don't take that Machiavelli crap you hide behind too seriously. The guy who helped raise me was a good man. Don't change his image."

~

"So what do you think of my new handbills?" Kiongosi asked his chief of staff. He had one spread out on the desk in front of him. Printed in the black, red, and green color scheme of the black-liberation flag, a single line across the top read: "Black Is Beautiful. Keep the Central Ward That Way."

Below it was a picture of Kiongosi in a colorful dashiki surrounded by a children's dance group to whom he was giving a trophy. On the other side, a photo featured him looking through the mesh openings of a backstop at a Central Ward Little League game. At the bottom was a line: "He's Running to Be Your Councilman in Our Ward. Vote for the Man Who Has Walked in Your Shoes."

"Boss, that's great," his chief of staff said. "It's a hell of a lot easier than trying to get votes out of the Italians."

"And a hell of a lot more quiet," Kiongosi interjected. "We got that damn sound truck removed as part of the deal."

"It's a nice change."

"No, you don't get it. It's *no change* at all. We go after Paulie as soon as the new mayor does what he will surely do—run for the U.S. Senate. Then, with the Puerto Ricans only adding to the number of voters of color, we will kick his ass and take control of

328

the city. So in the long run, it's worth a couple more years of waiting."

He put his finger to his lips and smiled. "Listen to the silence. We can finally open the front door without Aretha busting inside."

~

Chooch hesitated before he opened the front door to the North Ward Citizens Council. He hadn't been back since the day Tedesco had ripped into him and Dominick and kicked them out of the office.

"Come in. Come in. I missed you," Tedesco said. "Life has gotten a lot easier since the day we had our little disagreement. We don't need to chase nigger votes. Now we can talk the language of our own people. We can solidify our appeal to every Italian American in the North Ward and then, you know, that rich nigger ain't gonna be satisfied just by running a city that used to belong to us. The arrogant shit wants the U.S. Senate and then the presidency. So, Chooch, think of this. He wins City Hall. We can't stop that, but it's only halftime in this game. He'll be gone before the third quarter. But we'll still be here. And we will take back the city. Our Italian mayor fucked up? Okay. We paid. But we're smarter than them. We vote more than they do. We know how to run a city. They don't. So here's where we have the edge. We'll turn out all our people to vote for me to lead this ward. That's where you and Dominick and the guys you control get out in the street and get it done. We steamroll this ward—and Anderson and Kiongosi are chopped liver the minute Anderson shows what he is by jumping ship after a year to run for the Senate."

He paused, nodding his head slowly. "And, Chooch, let me be clear on this. I want everyone in our ward to get amnesia when either of the Friscella names come up. From this moment on they are traitors to their own people. Get out there and sell that idea. I don't want Gerry Sr. even in the picture when we make our move. And Gerry Jr. and his nigger girlfriend are beneath contempt. I want the girl turned into a whore and her boyfriend into the inevitable symbol of turning on his own race. Get to the social clubs and the church groups and the old folks who go to Scarcella's center. I want it to get so hot for Friscella Sr. that he won't even be welcome at the Branch Brook Park bocce courts." Tedesco stood up again. "And tell Dominick to come out of hiding. You—I mean, *we* are gonna need his muscle to counter Scarcella's street workers."

"What kind of muscle? "

"I shouldn't even have to explain that."

"Sorry, boss. I'll pick up Dominick and we're on it."

J ackson Anderson and Freddy Sternburg were campaigning on foot along the Avenue. The candidate shook hands, a big smile on his face. "A pleasure," he said, vigorously pumping the outstretched hand of the proprietor of an Ace Hardware store. He posed for a picture with the man's wife.

They moved on. Anderson noticed a number of the locals turned their backs on him. "These people don't fool me," he said, lowering his voice and turning to Sternburg. "Our anonymous friends have wrapped this up for me, but don't get fooled. They hate each other even more than they did when this thing started. 'The Prime Minister' didn't negotiate a peace treaty—he simply scared the shit out of them. And once I go, watch them explode. And I am going. Are the rumors true? You can bet your ass that I'll be out of here as soon as the old man retires from his Senate seat. Then let the two sides kill each other for all I care. I'll be long gone and telling the newspapers how sad I feel about what will follow. Now you know why my family lives in Mountain Lakes."

"Boss, I wouldn't say that too loudly around here. Don't blow the good will Sinatra has built for us."

"Freddy, you listen to me. I don't give a shit about these people and their city. The Senate is the target, and the presidency is the long-term goal. I like you. I love the job you've done for me. But if you want to keep on moving up with me, then it's time to smell the coffee. Once we've won this thing, we don't need this place anymore."

Sternburg moved on in silence. He spotted a couple with a baby in a carriage and ran over to them. "Say hello to Mr. and Mrs. Fratello, boss," he said to Anderson. "They want to know if you will have any Italians in your administration."

The candidate reached out and grasped their hands. "I mean what I say, and I say what I mean. My campaign is for all the people of this city. My aides will earn their jobs on merit, not on race. That means I need everyone in this city to help us heal."

The couple looked at each other. Mrs. Fratello grabbed the candidate's hand again and said, "I believe you, Mr. Anderson. Go to it. Heal this city, and if you do, God bless you."

They strolled away. Anderson turned to his man. "Mother Teresa couldn't heal this dung heap. Count on it—they'll get what they deserve." He glanced at the diamond-studded Rolex on his right wrist. "Christ, I got to meet some people and I'm running late. That's enough for now. The election is won. Nobody is going to cross our new friends. That includes me. For as long as I need them, I'll give them what they want. Bring the car around, Freddy, before one of these families invites me to spaghetti dinner. I got to get out of here."

~

The Montclair State football team had run its unbeaten streak to seven. Next on the schedule was Jersey City State. Everyone assumed the game would be an easy win, but Coach Yablonski was worried. A victory here meant a Division

III post-season playoff spot. He studied his team on Monday, Tuesday, and Wednesday. They were loose—too loose. He sensed that they thought all they had to do Friday night was show up.

He paced the sidelines as he always did half an hour before practice started. He watched his kids drift onto the playing surface in small groups. He saw T.C. lining up footballs on the other sideline and smiled. Annie Mae had been driving T.C. to evening practices for a couple of weeks now, ever since Yablonski had named him the official game-day ball boy of Montclair State.

Yablonski waved to him and smiled. The kid had started out as a pain in the ass with all that hero worship for Junior, but the whole team had fallen in love with him. Yablonski motioned for him to come over. T.C. turned his Montclair State baseball cap around backward and loped over to him.

"We gonna kick ass Saturday night, Coach. I feel it."

"Well, we haven't lost a game since you started working for us, so maybe you're right. But I need a favor."

"I'm your man, Coach."

"Why do you think we're going to win this game?"

"Easy. First off, we got the better team. Second—or maybe I should have said first—we got my man Junior Friscella, and he *is* the best."

"You think so? I don't know."

"I do know, so don't worry, Coach Y. I'll give him my special pep talk when he comes over to pick up my sister tomorrow."

"I got a better idea," Yablonski said, a smile playing at the corners of his mouth. "How about you give that talk to the whole team? Before the game?"

"If I do, can I borrow your whistle?"

"Tell you what. If you do a good job, you don't have to borrow it. You can keep it."

"Wow! I don't have time to talk now—I got to go and help wheel out the Gatorade for tonight. But you got a deal, Coach, and T.C. Washington don't go back on his word."

Yablonski watched him disappear into '
the locker room. *Hey, I've had crazier ideas*
what he says. Then he walked toward where his
bled in a large semicircle and blew his whistle.

"I know you ladies are too important to get your ₁
but what say you roll around in the grass a little bu
tonight? And Junior, nobody in a Jersey City jersey is gonna
for your autograph Saturday night. But if you score a pair,
might just run into the end zone to get it."

❧

T he next night, Junior rang the doorbell at Mickey's house.
Charles answered. "Hey, All-American, what's up?" he
intoned. Junior was glad the two of them had forgotten their
early shadowboxing, and he knew what bonded them was their
mutual love for Mickey and for football. Charles never had the
chance to play, because of his high school grades and his even-
tual dropout status. But Junior could tell he loved the game.

A week before, when Charles pinch-hit for Annie Mae as
T.C.'s driver to Montclair State, Junior had thrown the ball at
him as he stood on the sidelines. Charles fired it back. "Wow,"
Junior said, flapping his hand in mock pain, "you got a wing
there, buddy. You ever get back in school, maybe you'll wind up
one day on this field."

It was the broadest of exaggerations, but Charles clearly
appreciated it. They were not exactly friends yet, but their love
for Mickey was moving them in that direction.

"You wanna hit the fast foods around the corner and get
something to eat?" Charles asked.

"Well, I sorta promised Mickey I'd try her cooking tonight."

"Forget it, buddy—she came home early from school, and she
keeps running to the bathroom to throw up. Started all of a
sudden. Must be one of those viruses going around. You got it
up at Montclair?"

I wondered why I missed her at lunch. You think it's
ious?"

"Not as serious as her *luuuv* bug. You console her, man. She's
your problem." He punched Junior on the arm and hollered,
"I'm hungry and I'm gone. See ya later."

Junior waited on the couch outside her bathroom. She
emerged, saw him there, and turned away. "Don't look at me.
I'm a mess."

Junior sauntered over in his best John Wayne imitation and
drawled, "You're beautiful, Pilgrim," and kissed her.

"Oh, oh, oh! Sit down, I'll be right back!" She bolted back to
the bathroom.

Junior furrowed his brow and paced. He hated seeing her
sick. No way would she try to cook tonight. When she re-
emerged, he sat on the couch and pulled her to his side, holding
her close, wishing he could make her better. "Just rest, baby," he
said. "Don't worry about me."

Eventually, though, she lifted her head and sent him back to
campus. "Don't know what I got, baby. But you got a game
coming up—you cannot get sick. Go back to school and get some
rest. And do me a favor. Forget you ever saw me looking like
this. I don't want you checking out those blond cheerleaders."

"You know that's never happening," he assured her.

When she insisted, he reluctantly headed for the door.

He threw a glance over his shoulder on the way out, in time
to see her dash for the bathroom again. He hoped she'd be well
enough to watch him play. He needed his girl in the stands.

35

IT AIN'T OVER UNTIL IT'S OVER

Annie Mae and Elizabeth were drinking coffee in the kitchen. Annie Mae moved toward the counter to pour a second cup for her friend. "I might be crazy, but I get the feeling that things are just going too darn well." She laughed and added, "My daughter has a young man who loves her. Charles is back home and studying for his GED. T.C. is finally a happy child thanks to his football hero, my future son-in-law. Girl, I have to tell you that I'm just not used to this. It almost scares me."

"I think you've had to put up with so much crap for so long, you don't realize that right now there is no crap to put up with. And you deserve it. You haven't heard from that bum Talmadge in how long?"

"Not since Mickey hit a bases-loaded home run upside his head with T.C.'s favorite bat." They laughed. "Girl, you should have seen her and heard the things she yelled at him. Big, bad macho man—she knocked him right on his ass."

"Well, if she hit him in the head, that was a waste of time— there ain't never been nothin' in there. But right now, tell me about that big Sunday dinner with your potential in-laws."

"It was beautiful. Just beautiful. Except for some guy named

Tony, who went off on Junior's dad and on Mickey—and for a moment I was reminded we were still in the city of Newark. But, child, you should have seen that father. He hit that racist son of a bitch in the belly, knocked his ass on the floor, grabbed him, opened the front door, and kicked him down the stairs."

"Really?"

"Absolutely! And then I got up and spoke about giving the kids a chance. And they all really listened. Then I played my ace card."

"Which was what?"

"Sweet-potato pie, straight from Annie Mae's oven and into their hearts. We had a real Italian meal—his mother is some cook. But I said, 'I had dinner in your world, now you have dessert in mine. Try that down-home pie.'"

"And?"

"Girl, they loved it. They are beautiful people. We been to a couple of football games with them. Junior is the big star up there, and the team made T.C. its honorary game-day ball boy. He's so proud, walks around with that Montclair hat Junior gave him. It's like he knows he has people who care for him."

"Well, I feel like—"

The doorbell rang.

Annie Mae got up, frowning. She wasn't expecting anyone.

Talmadge.

Head still bandaged, cap in hand, eyes riveted downward, he seemed to have trouble getting words out. "I . . . I got a problem, Annie. I'm sick and I got nowhere to go, and I was hopin' you—"

"Well, you can just un-hope right now. You had enough 'one more chances.' You ain't gonna bring your self-righteous poison into this house ever again."

"But the docs say it's cancer. And the VA hospital says I ain't getting in there, not with my bad-conduct discharge. I don't know what to do."

"Well, I do. Wait right where you are." She went down the

hall, opened her purse, took out some bills. She pressed them into his hand. "There's enough money here to get you a bus ticket to Clifton Forge, Virginia, which as I recollect is where your brother lives. Nobody in this house wants or needs to see you again. And if you think you can raise your fist to me, well, see those pots in the sink? Elizabeth and I will slam them right to the same spot Mickey started on."

He fixed his face in the glummest expression he could manage. "Well, could you give me a little more money? I gotta eat until I get there."

His dejected expression tugged at her heart. But Elizabeth, who'd walked over to stand shoulder to shoulder with her, spoke next. "You best get your narrow ass outta here—now. Before I make this woman forget that a child of God you ain't." Elizabeth slammed the door in his face.

Relief washed over Annie Mae. She'd done it. She'd stood up to him and sent him away. She clapped her hands and went to the refrigerator. "This calls for ice cream and cake. It's an old-fashioned goodbye and a don't-let-the-door-hit-you-in-the-ass celebration."

As she and Elizabeth laughed and dug into huge dishes of ice cream, she sincerely hoped it was the last time any of them would ever see Talmadge Washington.

~

On Thursday, Mickey returned to class and met Junior at lunch. Junior was sitting with Johnny Jakes when she arrived. He jumped to his feet and said, "I hope you feel better, Miss Mickey. I was worried."

She touched his cheek. "Johnny Jakes, stay as sweet as you are. And don't date any of these brazen coeds until you clear them with me."

Jakes said he was going back for dessert, but they both knew he had an uncanny sense of understanding when they needed to be alone.

She slid into a seat next to Junior and reached under the table for his hand. "I never want you to see me like that again."

"What was wrong?"

"I don't know for sure. An upset stomach. I love this school, but the food in the dining hall is not exactly the reason people enroll here. I'm okay now. I'm beautiful again. Tell me you think I'm beautiful."

"Okay. 'You think I'm beautiful.' Did I say it right?"

She grabbed his spoon and took a bite of his bread pudding. "You're lucky we like the same things."

"How's T.C. doing?"

"He's driving the whole family nuts. He goes in the bathroom and locks the door, and it gets real quiet. Just as we start to think he's doing something he shouldn't be doing, he clears his throat and practices some speech we never heard before."

Jakes had rejoined them in time to hear the bit about T.C. He laughed and pounded the table. "I knew it. I knew it."

Junior laughed with him.

"What's so funny?" Mickey asked. "Or is it secret macho talk?"

"No, no," Junior said. "Coach is trying to motivate us—he thinks we're taking this game too lightly. He has delegated a special guest to make the pregame talk."

"You can't mean . . ."

"We do," they chorused. "Mr. T.C. Washington is going to address us before the game Saturday night. We can't wait to hear what he says."

"Don't embarrass him," Mickey insisted. "You know he's very sensitive."

"Oh, yeah, like when he told Angie he's a great football player with his underweight self and that one day she'll be paying to see him play," Junior said.

"It won't be like that, Miss Mickey," Jakes assured her. "All the guys love him. They plan to give him a standing ovation and dedicate the game to him."

"That's beautiful," Mickey said, "but Johnny Jakes, if you don't stop calling me Miss Mickey I'm gonna sack you harder than anybody on the Jersey City State team could."

~

T.C. practiced his speech all the way from the North Ward to Sprague Field, much to Charles' irritation. He knew how important this game was, how important a win was. He could not mess this up.

"Look, kid. I love you," Charles said. "You're my brother. But if you don't knock it off, I'm gonna shove you into the Jersey City State locker room instead. Give your speech there and they'll eat you alive. Now, please—until we get there."

Charles parked and accompanied T.C. to the Montclair State locker room.

November was knocking on the calendar, but the night was clear and about sixty-five degrees. "Okay, T.C.," Charles said at the door. "It's a great night for football and perfect for pep talks. Give 'em hell."

T.C. went in and changed into a black Montclair State sweatshirt with matching sweatpants. At seven thirty, following the pregame warm-ups, the team sat in the locker room and waited for Coach. T.C. turned his baseball cap backward, took a deep breath, and blew his whistle. The room went silent.

Just as he and the coach had practiced, he jumped up on a bench and faced them. Yablonski had moved to the back of the room and sat next to Charles.

Before he could speak, T.C. was taken aback by a chain of rhythmic applause, accompanied by fifty teammates shouting, "Speech, T.C.! Speech! Speech, T.C.!" Each time he began, they repeated the chant. The boy began to tear up.

Yablonski stood. "All right, ladies, stop the shit. I chose him to speak because unlike me, he believes in you. Go ahead, T.C. Give 'em hell."

"Guys, I'm twelve years old, and this is the greatest team I have ever seen in my whole entire life. And I know something about that because I'm a starter on the Boys and Girls Club Little Giants."

More applause.

"I want everyone to play hard tonight. This will be the most important game I have ever witnessed in my whole entire life. So you must win it—"

"Because," the team shouted back, "this is the most important game in your whole entire life!" They stood up and stomped and whistled and cheered. "T.C.! T.C.! T.C.!"

T.C. gave them a fist in the air and yelled, "Let's go!"

Yablonski put an arm around T.C. "One more thing, coach-for-the-night." He handed him a Montclair jersey with the number "1/2" on the back where the player's name would usually go. "Okay, squirt. You lead them out."

Shocked, T.C. did just that, throwing both arms over his head. When the crowd saw him up front, it roared approval. At the team bench, Junior draped an arm over his shoulders. "You're not finished. You and I will call the coin toss. If we win, say you defer and give them the ball first."

Shaking, but trying to appear calm for Junior, T.C. walked with him to the middle of the field. They won the toss and headed back to the bench amid more applause. He looked up into the stands. On the fifty-yard line, the Washingtons and the Friscellas accounted for a high percentage of the noise.

Montclair kicked off. They were so relaxed, they played a fantastic game. On the opening kickoff the Jersey City returner was hit so hard he fumbled. Montclair took over on the eleven and scored in two plays. T.C. pumped a fist, sure his speech had propelled them to a great start.

At halftime, the score was 35-0. By the end, T.C. had cheered his throat raw. Junior had scored three times and Johnny Jakes set a school record for completions. The score ended 66-0. They celebrated the playoff bid.

In the locker room, the team threw T.C. in the shower while he laughed and yelled, "I told you guys, I told you guys!"

Junior showered, and they walked back together toward the refreshment stand to meet the families. T.C. could not stop smiling. Everyone said T.C. was terrific during the coin toss.

Coach Yablonski joined them briefly to tell Annie Mae, "We couldn't have done it without your son."

T.C. remembered he had left his Montclair State Jersey in the locker room and yelled over his shoulder, "Wait for me, I'll be right back!"

～

When he was gone for more than thirty minutes, Mickey and Annie Mae were worried. Junior tried to reassure them, then went back to the locker room to check. As he neared it, he saw a small figure sitting on the floor just outside the door. Alarmed, he picked up his pace. It was T.C., and he was crying. He wouldn't look at Junior.

"Look at me," Junior said, grabbing him by the shoulders. "Look at me. Whatever it is, tell me. I'll understand. I'm gonna marry your sister and give you lots of baby cousins who'll look up to you. You gotta trust me. Now look at me and tell me what's wrong."

"They twisted my arm. They hurt me. They said—"

"Who did this? Who?"

"I don't know. They said if your father got involved in this election, they'd hurt him and your mom and you. They said they'd hurt Mickey. They called her a whore. Then they twisted my arm again and said to make sure I told you and Mickey. I don't know who they are. I never saw them before."

"Describe them to me."

"I can't. I was too scared. One guy called the other one Chick."

"Are you sure it wasn't 'Chooch'?"

"I don't know, Junior. I'm not sure."

"All right, T.C. I'm sure, and it ain't ever gonna happen again. Now wipe your eyes. We don't want to tell Mickey about this. I'll take care of it."

He helped T.C. to his feet, wrapped an arm around his shoulders, and started back with him toward the families. As they passed the bleachers, two black men confronted them.

"Mr. Friscella, do you know who I am?"

"We never met, but I've seen your picture in the *Star-Ledger*. You're Kiongosi."

"That's right. Now listen to me. I have nothing against you. I have nothing against your father, your mother, or your girlfriend. But I suggest you pay attention. Election Day ain't gonna be the end of this. That Uncle Tom might be mayor, but he ain't gonna stay, and we all know that. So you got to keep your old man and this boy's sister out of the news. We have too much at stake. This ain't a threat. It's a promise. Somebody will get hurt. It's between Paulie and me, and we don't want your dad, your girl, or you, taking sides. What I'm telling you is not a warning. As your dad would say in Italian, it's a *momento della verità*—a moment of truth. Just play football. Keep your nose clean. And screw your girl for me—we were probably cousins back in Africa."

Kiongosi never saw the punch coming. Junior hit him with a straight right hand to the jaw and knocked him down. His chief of staff pulled out a pistol, but Kiongosi waved him off.

"We don't need that. He got the message, or he wouldn't have hit me. He knows. So let's go."

The overhead stadium lights were out, so they ducked back into the shadows. Junior put his arm back around T.C.'s shoulders and walked him toward the refreshment stand and the families.

Just as they came into view, Junior said softly in T.C.'s ear, "Not a word. I'll handle everything. Don't scare your mom or Mickey, and especially Charles. I'll tell your sister after I take care of a few things."

When they got there, Annie Mae put her hands on her hips and said, "T.C., where have you been? You know better than to scare us like this."

"I went back for my jersey."

"So where is it?"

"We started to look for it in the dark," Junior interrupted, "but we couldn't find it. I'll get him a new one from Coach tomorrow. Can't have our visiting coach without his uniform."

NATURE SEALS THE DEAL

R ichie Boiardo believed he was finished with meetings regarding the candidates for mayor. He and his associates had taken care of the election. As far as he was concerned, there would be one more meeting, and only one—the one that would determine which family got what when their candidate became mayor under the terms they had negotiated. But as a result of the Prime Minister's diplomacy, the Boot agreed to meet yet again before what would be the scheduled final meeting.

At the Boot's insistence, the meeting was held in the private basement room at Don's 21. "It has to be neutral ground," he told the Prime Minister. Carlo Gambino agreed. They met a week before the election.

The Boot entered through the back door with his son, Tony Boy, passed through the kitchen, and took the ten stairs down to the meeting room. Gambino and Costello were already there. Boiardo and Costello shook hands, then sent their bodyguards upstairs to the bar. The restaurant was closed, with a sign on the door: "Private Party Tonight. Reopening Tomorrow for Lunch."

Don took their drink orders himself.

"Whatever you choose is fine for the meal," Costello said. "I don't think we want a heavy dinner at this hour."

"So why the hurry, Carlo?" the Boot asked. "I was led to believe everything was settled. Is our candidate about to double-cross us—or are you?"

Costello's right arm reached out with surprising speed to prevent Gambino, who was already halfway out of his seat, from rising. "Richie, this is a business deal," the negotiator said. "We cannot negotiate by innuendo."

Both nodded, and Costello continued. "This is the news that has come to my attention—not rumor, not gossip, but fact. I bring it to you to see how you may want to act. Impeccable sources have informed me that our candidate is not entirely honorable. He is truthful about leaving to run for the Senate when the old man who holds the seat retires."

The Boot looked at Gambino.

"But he tells our North Ward Italian that when he leaves, he will support him in the election for a new mayor," Costello added. "Then he tells Kiongosi the same story. Now what do you think?"

The Boot laughed. "If I were him, I would do the same fuckin' thing."

Gambino laughed as well, then shrugged. "Me too."

"So, thinking ahead," Costello put in, "what do you agree on when it happens?"

"Fuck both of them," Gambino said.

"I agree," the Boot added. "It's my understanding that both men have already threatened Friscella's son, and the black family as well. Both of them, I was told, threatened the son and the little boy. And I am told that the Italians physically hurt the child."

"*Bastardi, Animali.*" The Boot mimed spitting on the floor. "We don't touch families. These animals have no class—none. Okay, I go with our candidate. I salute him for pissing on these guys. And, Carlo, my friend, in the end they will have nothing, but you and I will have a United States senator—and perhaps also, my friend, the president of the United States."

The three raised their glasses in salute.

~

J unior didn't like keeping anything from Mickey. But he also didn't want to worry her. He had a plan, but she didn't need to know it. He would take care of this himself. But he needed one thing from her.

Mickey eyed him suspiciously when he asked for her cousin's phone number.

Junior squirmed under her scrutiny. "Well, I knew him from football at Barringer, and you said he had some nice things to say about me. I'll be new to his family. I understand he's going to transfer to Rutgers, so he could be home now. I thought . . ."

When he trailed off, she prompted him. "You thought what?"

"Well, I mean . . ." *Damn.* Why hadn't he thought of a better excuse for needing this phone number? He couldn't think straight with her giving him that look.

"I don't know what you mean, but it's not what you're saying. Eventually, you'll tell me. So, yes, I'll get it for you. But for the record, I know that look on your face. You are not telling me the truth, but I'll let it pass this time."

"Are you that good at telling when I lie?"

"You bet I am. So you better watch what you lie about."

With the hardest part of his plan behind him, Junior called Chuck Washington. As he'd heard, Chuck had left Grambling and announced his plans to transfer to Rutgers in the fall. He was more than happy to do what Junior asked of him.

"You know," he said on the phone, "I understood how things were at Barringer with forty black kids coming into an all-Italian school at once. But you weren't part of that as far as I was concerned. So, yeah, give me some phone numbers, and I'll take care of business for you and for my cousin."

Two days later, Junior and seven other Montclair State players charged through the front door of the North Ward White

Citizens Council. Three of them held baseball bats. As frightened as he was confused, Paulie Tedesco jumped out of his desk chair.

"Hey, Junior, what the hell is going on here?"

"What's it look like to you? We are here to set you straight or kick your ass. Your two dummies threatened my girlfriend's baby brother. Then they put their hands on him."

"I don't know nothin' about that. If you ain't lying, then maybe they were just high on pot. Hey, you know Dominick ain't the sharpest tool in the shed. Relax—maybe the little nigger kid was lying."

Junior grabbed him by the collar and banged his head against the wall. Still holding his shirt, he leaned in until their heads nearly touched. "Paulie, your guys scared the shit of that little boy. He's twelve years old. You got that? Twelve years old. Okay, hero, I'm a little older. So is everyone else here. Pick one of us to threaten, tough guy, or say you understand you'll never go near that child or anyone else in his family ever again in this lifetime. If you don't get it, then I won't bring these guys next time—I'll just personally kick the shit out of you and both of your errand boys. *Capisci?*"

He gave Paulie's head one more bounce off the wall before he and his teammates marched out. A block later, at a pay phone on the Avenue, he called Chuck Washington, who had assembled a dozen black Montclair State players. "It's a go, Chuck. Bring Mr. Kiongosi the facts of life."

The same scene was repeated at Kiongosi's headquarters. When Kiongosi denied the story, Washington dropped him with a left hook. "That little boy is my baby cousin," he announced. "That fine-lookin' girl is my ace boon coon. And her boyfriend was my high school football captain. I assume you got the message. Now get up off the damn floor. And don't make us pay a return visit."

Washington and his newly introduced friends walked out onto Broad Street and slapped palms.

~

Jackson Anderson, the soon-to-be mayor of Newark, New Jersey, as he now thought of himself, turned down Richie the Boot's offer to use the Vittorio Castle for his post-election victory rally. The Boot voiced his displeasure. "This is hardly in the spirit of cooperation I expected, Mr. Anderson."

"No," Anderson responded, "but it's in your best interest. I don't know your business, but I know mine, and I know the publicity you'd get would not be helpful to our private business interest." He laughed, tapped the Boot on the shoulder, and said, "*Capisci?*"

Boiardo paused and appeared to weigh his response carefully. He broke into a broad smile. "Spoken like a son of Sicily, my African friend. But permit me to fund it wherever it is held."

Anderson hid the relief he felt. He knew angering this man would not end well for him. "I've already reserved the ballroom of the Robert Treat Hotel. But if you care to donate, well, I am an equal-opportunity candidate. But it's not necessary. Several bankers have graciously helped with the costs of the victory rally. Meanwhile, my friend, with the election secure, I believe we should meet at my home three days after it's official. Does it suit you?"

"Of course. But I would prefer not to have to tell Gambino. He is an ally, not a friend. And alliances often are no stronger than the web of a very small spider. I must personally think of my family's future. But you go ahead and schedule the meeting. I'll be there."

Later that day, after approving the schedule for the victory rally, Anderson confided a major fear to Freddy Sternburg. "Our new friends are making disturbing comments about each other. I'm not ready for this alliance to fall apart. Yet."

"There's only one way to handle this, boss. You can't take sides, but you can make each of them think he is the one you're backing."

"That's what I thought you'd say. And I'm glad to hear you say it, because you are going to get it done."

"How the hell am I supposed to do that?"

"I know them. Sometime before we all meet, both of them are going to come at you to find out what I'm thinking. So you will lie to them with a wink and a smile. Convince each he's the one. And they need to know is that we already have the bankers we need." He paused. "Can you do this?"

"Boss, when I came into this business, I worked for a high-powered agency that had more senators as clients than all the others put together. I wanted to show the head man how enthusiastic I was, so I'd get to work before him. No matter how early he got there, I was half an hour ahead of him. He demanded I put six sharpened pencils on his desk each day before he arrived. They were always waiting for him—no matter what time he got there, I was always a half hour ahead of him. Well, after a week of this, he'd come in, sit down, break all the pencil points, and demand to know why he didn't have sharpened pencils."

"How is this relevant?"

"I threw away all his pencils before he arrived the next morning, and I replaced them with automatic lead pencils. He never harassed me again. So this will be easy. These guys' egos are my biggest edge—they each want that wink and that nod. Want? Hell, they expect it. Consider it done."

"I discussed another matter with you the other day," Anderson pointed out, "and you didn't respond. We talked about my next move. Are you with me, or do I need someone else for the senatorial campaign? You owe me an answer."

"Ask me after the election," Sternburg said. "Right now, I gotta check on Scarcella's army. I'll be back later."

L es Scarcella couldn't be happier. His man had all but won the election at the expense of the two he hated. He had made two powerful allies—both of them feared and respected, in that order—who made up in power and influence for what they lacked in ethics.

Now, his workers were moving block by block through the North Ward to ensure a healthy turnout of write-in votes for Paulie Tedesco's bid for the job he didn't want but was forced to take. And Scarcella was about to tackle his most ambitious plan.

He needed his own mayor—not a transient stranger who would soon be gone. The answer was simple, but the implementation might just be beyond him. For that, he needed one last favor from his protégé, the newspaper columnist.

Jerry D'Amilio was not going to be an easy sell. Scarcella had already pushed the debt D'Amilio felt he owed his old mentor beyond its logical limits. But the columnist had the confidence of the Friscella family—and Gerard Friscella Sr. was the one guy who could win that job once Jackson Anderson left it.

Scarcella's road to getting Friscella Senior came through his son. D'Amilio could help with that.

He was finishing his first cup of coffee when he pressed the intercom button and hollered, "Nancy. Get Jerry D. on the phone for me. Now, please."

"Before your second cup of coffee? This must be really important. You must have inside information on the Montclair State playoff game."

"If I wanted a smartass for a secretary, I could have hired half the girls in the North Ward. Just get him. And, Nancy, this time please don't listen in."

She buzzed back twenty minutes later. "It took a little effort to locate him. He was up at the Giants' training facility at Fairfield University. I'll transfer him to you."

"Good morning, Jerry!" Scarcella greeted him.

D'Amilio's voice crackled through the line. "Hey, I thought

AFTER THE FIRE

we agreed to disagree, so I hope this isn't about any of the Friscellas."

"No, I just called to see if you had any tickets for the playoff game up at Montclair State this weekend. You know Junior played in a couple of our rec leagues. The center kinda has a rooting interest. Just to ease your overburdened ethical mind, it's the son, not the father, I want to see play."

"All right. The athletic director owes me his lungs for the columns I did. I'll have two at the will-call window. If they win this and then their bowl game, you might consider honoring him with a day at the center. If you can keep politics out of it, you might be doing a good thing."

"Politics?" Scarcella said. "He's a North Ward kid. Don't insult me, Jerry."

Scarcella hung up and smiled. *Perfect.*

◇

Annie Mae woke to knocking on her bedroom door. She glanced at her clock. *After midnight.* She sat up. "Come in."

One look at Mickey's tear-stained face told her something was very wrong. But she kept her face neutral. Overreacting would not help anything. "Sit here, baby," she said, motioning her to the bed.

She put her arms around her daughter, who burst into tears. Mickey leaned her head against her mother's chest, her body shaking with the force of her sobs.

She rubbed Mickey's back, rocking her gently, until Mickey seemed to have calmed down a bit. When she remained silent, Annie Mae held her at arm's length and wiped away her tears.

"Tell me," she said. "Tell me. Whatever it is."

"I'm pregnant."

Not entirely surprised, she smiled. "So?" She stroked Mickey's hair. "Why all these tears? He loves you, and it shows. You love him—and you're going to start to show." She shifted on the bed. "Did you tell him?"

"He's under so much pressure because of me. His family is under so much pressure because of me. I'm scared. I don't know what to do."

"Well, I do. Are you afraid he'll leave you?"

"Maybe. I don't know."

"I think you do know. I think you are letting fear control your brain. Baby, he has proven over and over how much he loves you. Trust him. Trust yourself. Trust your family, and his."

~

As always, Mickey and Junior had agreed that he should sleep in the dorm the night before a game. They met for dinner at the diner just off campus. Mickey insisted that they take a booth in the back where the lighting was less garish and the tables near them were empty.

"What's going on?" Junior asked. "Did T.C. say something to you?"

She took a deep breath, gearing up to break the news. But she did a double take. "I don't know what you mean. I don't know what T.C. could have said that would upset me. But never mind that now. We have something else to talk about."

"Okay. What is it?"

"For openers, are you going to declare for the draft or finish school?"

"Whoa, there. I don't know. But it's something we—you and I—have to decide."

"Wrong. The 'we' also includes your mom and dad. They have, as you would say, more than a nickel in this quarter. We have to include them in this decision. You know it, and I mean it, Junior. So talk to me."

"Okay, you're right. We will. But you said 'to start with.' What else?"

She reached across the table and took his hand. Her voice dropped an octave as a defense against prying ears. "Baby, I'm pregnant."

"Are you sure we are?"

The words she'd rehearsed in her head over and over flew out the window. "Did you say *we*? Did you really mean *we*?"

"Baby, each of us stopped being 'I' that night in Branch Brook Park. Whether it's a problem or a blessing, it will always be 'we.' Now it's dark enough in this corner—you can kiss me. And tomorrow night I play for the three of us." He grinned broadly. "Now let's eat. I'm starving."

Tears filling her eyes, she leaned across the table, grabbed the back of his head, and pulled him into the deepest, tenderest kiss they'd shared yet. In that moment, she couldn't remember what she'd been so upset about. This man was the one she wanted to spend the rest of her life with.

∽

Junior and Mickey shared the news with his father and mother. After the two left, Gerry Sr. sat quietly at the kitchen table. He'd kept a smile on his face for the kids, but now he sorted through his feelings. The news didn't shock him, exactly. But it did come as one hell of a surprise. The timing didn't seem great.

"I don't know," Senior said to Maria.

"I do," she responded, a gentle smile on her face.

"Look. I like this girl—a lot. She makes Junior happy. But marriage is a huge step for them both. Bad as it's been, it'll get nastier and meaner for them."

She placed a hand over his. "Tell me something, Gerry. Did you not, at your age, get into a fistfight at work defending this girl our son loves?"

"Yes. But . . ." He'd known this was inevitable. Hell, he wanted the girl in their family. But they hadn't finished college.

Junior had a football career in front of him. Everything was happening too quickly, changing too quickly.

"Yes, but what?"

"Well, there's family to consider."

"We are the family—you and me and Annie Mae."

"That's true. But marriage now, in this city, at this time—"

"What should these kids do? Run away? Raise my grandbaby somewhere else, away from us? No, I won't have it. They should find a church, and we should make plans."

"What if it's not a Catholic church?"

"We'll figure it out."

"I just wish that—"

"Don't worry about what you wish. Worry about what you ought to remember."

"What's that mean?"

"It means, dummy"—she flashed a huge smile at him —"you have a very short memory. You ought to remember that I walked down the aisle at St. Lucy's with our families in the pews and a two-month-old baby bump walking ahead of me. And I'd say things turned out pretty darn good."

～

They were the strangest victory parties ever held for any election. At the Robert Treat Hotel, more than fifteen hundred people turned out to see results that were already preordained.

In the North Ward, Paulie Tedesco stepped to the microphone in front of an audience of hard-liners at School Stadium. He pledged no peace agreement with the new mayor—and a nonstop campaign against him.

And in the auditorium at Central High School, Kiongosi addressed a standing-room-only crowd. "The fight for equality does not end simply because a black man has been elected, when that particular black man is a carpetbagging outsider who was overfriendly with a cartel of bankers."

All of the above was how peace came to the city. Tenuous and brief, perhaps, but peace.

Three days later, two Mafiosi with separate retinues sat down in the living room of the mayor-elect and discussed sanitation, grants to allegedly nonprofit organizations, municipal construction projects, and subcontracting of city contracts.

When the talks ended, the visitors, smiling profusely, saluted the new mayor with upraised glasses. The Prime Minister toasted, "Here's to a successful and enduring tenure as mayor of this great city."

The mayor-elect looked over at Fast Freddy Sternburg and winked.

~

Montclair State moved on undefeated to the Stagg Bowl in Pasadena, California. Johnny Jakes set a completion record, and Junior caught three touchdown passes, but St. John's of Minnesota won a 42-38 shootout.

Two nights earlier, at dinner, Mickey had told the Friscellas that Junior was not going to declare for the draft. He would graduate on time the next year. Then Annie Mae told her that if she went to summer school, she could graduate with him— because the parents would split babysitting duties. Mickey could see everything coming together for them.

A week later, with football behind him, and college plans in place, they began to plan the wedding. "We have to find a church," Junior said.

"What's the matter with St. Lucy's?"

"Well, that's a problem, since you're not Catholic."

"But I am."

Junior blinked. "You never told me."'

"You never asked."

"I'm confused."

"Don't be. My mom always thought about my education. She didn't like our neighborhood school, so she took me up to Queen of Angels and registered me in the third grade. Then, so I wouldn't feel left out, she had me baptized."

"St. Lucy's it is."

～

On February 8th, 1969, Junior stood at the altar beside the priest, Allie at his side as best man. T.C. and Johnny Jakes were their ushers. With huge smiles, they had seated family and friends. Angie came down the aisle beaming, delighted, Junior knew, to be asked to be a bridesmaid. Lois, the maid of honor, walked down the aisle last.

Junior bounced on his toes a bit, excitement getting the better of him. He looked at his parents in the front pew. His mom dabbed at her eyes with a hankie but couldn't stop smiling. His dad nodded at him, that one small gesture communicating his full support.

Then, the music changed, the doors reopened, and there stood Mickey, his other half, the most beautiful woman he'd ever seen, more radiant and breathtaking than ever before. Her white taffeta gown with its bouffant skirt deftly disguised her developing baby bump, if anyone could take their eyes off her glowing face. Their friends and family rose and applauded. Junior saw Charles drape an arm around Annie Mae's shoulders. Like his mother, Annie Mae held a hankie to her eyes, but she was smiling through the happy tears. He heard Charles whisper, "That's our girl."

Junior locked gazes with Mickey, and he saw no one else. She carried a large bouquet of pink roses, white carnations, and baby's breath in front of her. Nobody noticed how close to her stomach she carried it as she walked down the aisle toward him, ready to take on the world together.

The Lovebirds

Author Jerry Izenberg with wife, Aileen

ABOUT THE AUTHOR

Jerry Izenberg, columnist emeritus at the New Jersey *Star-Ledger*, is a five-time winner of the New Jersey Sportswriter of the Year Award, and a winner of the coveted Red Smith Award—the highest honor given by the Associated Press Sports Editors. He and his wife Aileen live in Henderson, NV and have four children, nine grandchildren, and one great grandchild. Writing this novel at age 90 was on the top of his bucket list.

ALSO BY JERRY IZENBERG

Once There Were Giants: The Golden Age of Heavyweight Boxing

Rozelle: A Biography

No Medals For Trying

Through My Eyes

The Jerry Izenberg Collection

How Many Miles to Camelot: The All-American Sports Myth?

New York Giants: Seventy Five Years

The Greatest Game Ever Played

The Proud People

The Rivals

At Large With Jerry Izenberg

Championship: The NFL Title Story